Jessica Adams is an [...] *Cosmopolitan* astrologer. S[...] the *Girls' Night In* series [...] the author of *The New A*[...] co-author of *21st Century* [...] *White E-Mail, Tom, Dick and Debbie Harry, I'm A Believer, Cool for Cats* and *The Summer Psychic*, are all published by Black Swan. Visit her website on jessicaadams.com.

Acclaim for *Single White E-Mail*:

'Sexy, funny, smart, For any woman who has ever been single'
Cosmopolitan

'A blissfully refreshing treat. I found it very, very funny and quirky enough to be really original. It was *Muriel's Wedding, sex, lies and videotape*, and *Ally McBeal* all rolled into one, and I defy any woman of my age not to relate to Victoria'
Fiona Walker

'She gives Nick Hornby and Helen Fielding a damn good run for their money . . . thoroughly enjoyable'
Daily Telegraph

'Extremely funny' *Ms London*

'Fresh, frenetic and fun' *Elle*

'A Very funny novel - read it and recognise yourself'
New Weekly

'Appealing' *Prima*

'A very funny, insightful novel about dating'
Cosmopolitan Australia

'The search for the next Bridget Jones goes on . . . the best so far is *Single White E-Mail*'
Newcastle Sunday Sun

'A modern classic' *19*

'Smart 'n'sexy' *B*

'Recommended . . . the e-mail of the species is deadlier than the mail' *Marie Claire*

www.booksattransworld.co.uk

Also by Jessica Adams

TOM, DICK AND DEBBIE HARRY
I'M A BELIEVER
COOL FOR CATS
THE SUMMER PSYCHIC

and published by Black Swan

THE NEW ASTROLOGY FOR WOMEN
21st CENTURY GODDESS (with Jelena Glisic and Anthea Paul)

and published by Corgi Books

SINGLE WHITE
E-MAIL

Jessica Adams

BLACK SWAN

SINGLE WHITE E-MAIL
A BLACK SWAN BOOK : 9780552772785

First publication in Great Britain

PRINTING HISTORY
Black Swan edition published 1999
Black Swan edition reissued 2006

1 3 5 7 9 10 8 6 4 2

Set in 11pt Melior by
County Typesetters, Margate, Kent.

Black Swan Books are published by Transworld Publishers,
61–63 Uxbridge Road, London W5 5SA,
a division of The Random House Group Ltd.

Addresses for Random House Group Ltd companies outside the UK
can be found at: www.randomhouse.co.uk
The Random House Group Ltd Reg. No. 954009.

Printed and bound in Great Britain by
Cox & Wyman Ltd, Reading, Berkshire.

The Random House Group Limited supports The Forest Stewardship
Council (FSC), the leading international forest certification organisation.
All our titles that are printed on Greenpeace approved FSC certified paper
carry the FSC logo. Our paper procurement policy can be found at:
www.rbooks.co.uk/environment.

This edition published 2008 for Index Books Ltd

For Ben, because a promise is a promise

Acknowledgements

This book wouldn't have happened at all if Cate Paterson hadn't come to lunch and said, 'Why don't you try fiction?' I would like to thank her for taking a gamble, and being so passionate about the end result. The perfect publisher.

Elvis Presley said you always need someone responsible for TCB — Taking Care of Business. I count myself lucky to have found Sophie Lance at Hickson Associates. An Aries with the Moon in Gemini, she was so good at TCB that I actually managed to finish this book.

Jessica Adams
http://www.jessicaadams.com.au/SingleWhiteEmail

One

Another man, another haircut. It's funny how we always do the same things, every single time, whenever we break up with people. I'm not stupid, I know there's a pattern. I only have to look at my photo albums:

Year: 1985
The Man: Greg Daly, bushwalker.
The Problem: Annalise Someone, a German exchange student, also a bushwalker.
Two Months Later: The shaggy Bananarama.

Year: 1987
The Man: Phillip Zebruscki, who liked to have sex two to three times a day.
The Problem: He called me clingy.
Four Days Later: The Princess Diana Flicked Fringe.

Year: 1990
The Man: Jamie Streeton, baseball-mad American.
The Problem: I was too cold for him.
Four Days Later: The unfortunate home perm.

Year: 1993
The Man: Leon Mercer, mature-age student radical.
The Problem: Huge fight over me borrowing cash from Socialist Workers Party raffle tin to buy Toblerone.
One Month Later: The kitchen scissors DIY job.

Year: 1994
The Man: Anthony Anderson, de facto 'partner', potential husband of the future.
The Problem: He fiddled with the TV remote control, spent more time in front of the mirror than I did, always asked me how he looked before we went out, never remembered the names of any of my friends, and used to wash his puffy out-doorsy jackets with tennis balls in the machine to keep them puffy. Also spent his whole time scuba diving, talking about scuba diving and pinning up scuba-diving calendars. Also had sticker on his car saying 'Scuba Divers Do It With Depth.' A total lie, as well as a bad sticker.
One Week Later: The Linda Evangelista bob.

If I'm being totally honest with myself I can't say that any of these new-look hair tactics have ever worked. When I had the Princess Diana fringe after Phillip Zebruscki left me, I just became more depressed. I stank of hair mousse. Nobody came near me for months.

When I had the Linda Evangelista bob after I walked out on Anthony Anderson the Bastard Scuba Diver and our little semi, I didn't go out with anyone for two whole years. However. I need a haircut now. I need to feel new again. And like all women who have crashed in love, I need all my little familiar rituals around me. A new haircut, a new life, you know how it works.

I think I need a new colour too. I want it very short, and very red this time. In fact, whatever I wasn't last time. It might even make me look tough for a change, and I'm going to need that kind of defence if I ever run into Dan in the street. Or Dan and a new woman. Oh God. The thought of running into Dan and a new woman . . .

That must be the worst part of splitting up. The stunning ease with which you can imagine someone, who a few weeks before was attached to your arm, now sticking his tongue inside your replacement's mouth. And I have to say, the only reason I find it so easy to imagine is that it's actually happened. It's always happening. To me, to my friends. It's just a dismal fact of single life.

Someone, after all, had caught Anthony the Bastard Scuba Diver with a corporate-looking woman just a few months after I'd moved out of our flat. And it took about five minutes to lose that pseudo-happy single air I'd been cultivating so carefully.

I'd had it all sorted out up until that moment. I was going out more, and trying harder, and spending more time putting my foundation on in the mornings, because you can when you're single. Then someone saw him out with the corporate-looking woman one night, and the jealousy nearly ate me from the inside. At the time I even thought it would give me cancer.

Even though I knew Anthony and I weren't good for each other, even though I'd spent God knows how many phone conversations moaning about him to my friends, even though I hated him so much when I left I chucked his snorkel from one end of the bedroom to the other . . . when he started holding hands on the street with the corporate-looking woman, I don't think I ever wanted Anthony the Bastard Scuba Diver more in my whole life.

I did the whole thing. Ringing up, then slamming the phone down. Finding the most boring and impersonal things, like Anthony's credit card bills, and taking them to work with me so I could sigh over them in my lunch hour. And you know what? I'm in for this all over again. Because if I know one thing about Dan, my love, my only love, it's this: he's not capable of spending more than a few weeks doing any kind of emotional processing. Now I'm out, someone else will be in. It's really just a matter of time before someone sees them out together and rings me up to tell me. Or – worst case scenario – I see him myself.

The hairdresser's is packed this morning, and there's even a bride having her hair done behind me. It's amazing how the entire staff of the salon seem to have migrated over there. Part of me wants to go over there and ask her how the hell she managed to pull the whole thing off anyway, and part of me – I'm ashamed to admit – wants to leap up from my chair and projectile vomit all over her white suede shoes.

I wonder if Dan really was my last chance? Statistically I know he won't be. Given the current divorce rate (and Hilary, who is single like me, spent hours working it out for me last night) every single female now aged thirty to thirty-eight will stand a one in three chance of grabbing a desperate divorced male now approaching his mid forties.

Perhaps I should get up in my socks on the black swivel chair and tell all the single women in the hairdresser's the good news. And that includes the streaky blonde with foils in her hair who was obviously lying

12

when she told the hairdresser she was going out tonight, and also the bridesmaid who has come along with the bride in the corner for moral support. And I know what the bridesmaid is thinking too: Will this ever happen to me? Ever? Even in the year 2040? Is there a pair of white suede shoes for me?

I know Hilary's right about there being a male, divorced, fortysomething out there somewhere. Being a librarian, she's usually right on statistics. What worries me is, I won't be able to fall in love with him when we finally meet. Or any of them. Whereas, I was most definitely in love with Dan. And I still am. How old do you have to be before you learn how to cut down on your recovery time?

Hilary wants me to call him the Loathsome Lawyer from Leichhardt, because a nickname you can spit out like that always takes the sting away. But it's not working. Or maybe I need her around so I can practise. Right now, here in the salon, he's just Dan to me. And just as it was at the start, like a love-sick fourteen year old I want to write his name in big loopy biro capitals on bits of paper with hearts around it.

I haven't actually cried yet, which must be a first. I was so pissed at my birthday party that I thought I might have done, but no. Perhaps it was the fact that everyone expected me to. People were practically doing a pre-emptive strike, squeezing my hand, muttering things about how bad Dan's timing was, and how (yes, we know, boring, boring) all men were bastards and how a good cry would make me feel better. Meanwhile I remember eating nachos, very calmly, and swigging vodka and tonic. Feeling nothing at all, for the record.

I do remember sweating a lot though, despite the lack of weeping. Perhaps the huge amounts of alcohol

I consumed were actually making the tears leak out of my armpits.

Something else I remember drunkenly debating with Hilary after Dan had ended it, after he'd left the party, after he'd driven off, is the stupidity of Nature. Why does love linger when it's of no earthly help to the human race? I can be of no use at all to the advancement of the species at the moment. I am not using my reproductive organs. And because I am still in love with Dan, and not in the least in love with any of the available males in the Divorced Fortysomething army, it doesn't look as if I'll be using said organs for quite a while. I've got nature's great bonding emotion with nobody to bond with, in fact. So what's the bloody point?

I know it's only been forty-eight hours since Dan walked out, but the symptoms are still there. Leaping up when the phone rings, even streaking naked from the shower like some seventies cricket fan to take Dan's calls, only to find out it's not him on the other end, and never will be. Because it never is. Those are the rules of breaking up, aren't they? For every heart palpitation you register when the telephone starts up, you can register one minute of total unconcern from him, wherever he is. You pant and race to the phone, he stirs another sugar into his coffee, very slowly, somewhere on the other side of town.

You're doodling his name on the back of pizza home delivery menus, you're discussing him endlessly with people who've only met him twice and start to twitch when they see you're about to start on him again. He's . . . doing nothing. Doing the same things, in fact. Just not thinking about you much, that's all.

I've also been picturing Dan taking off some other lawyer's bra. Very slowly and lovingly. God help me, I can even see the bra. It's tartan, with white frills around the edges. The lawyer is more intelligent than me. She's been a size ten since the age of sixteen. She owns her own house. She belongs to a gym.

I must control myself, I know, or I will definitely end up like Hilary during Mad Month. She did Mad Month in August last year when one of the other librarians at her work (it was an Adult Library-Children's Library cross-romance) called it off.

Actually, he was too nice to call it off. He led her on some midnight ramble around the zoo and said he really hoped they could keep talking on the inter-library phone every day because he enjoyed it so much, and that he really wanted to be her friend too, because he really, really cared about her and she was such a great person. Then he let her run off in floods of tears to find a cab, nearly getting run over in the process.

The result of all this was Hilary's Mad Month. The Chief Children's Librarian actually had to send a note round by courier because he couldn't get through on the phone. It turned out Hilary had used up all her sick days in one hit, staying in bed ringing up every tele-phone psychic she could find advertised in the back of women's magazines (which she had stolen from the library, it turned out). She showed me the credit card bill later. Three hundred and eighty dollars to find out from ten different psychics that the adult librarian wasn't coming back.

I even remember going round there one day and dis-covering that she had been wearing her pink terry-towelling dressing gown for so long that it had started to turn brown on the collar. The poor girl had also been picking the tops off those little round biscuits with the chocolate on them, sucking the marshmallow off and throwing away the crust.

So that was Mad Month. With me, haircuts. With Hilary, telephone psychics. My other friends do everything from talking about stuffing prawns into his curtain rods, to flying to America to attend *Men Are From Mars, Women Are From Venus* seminars. I don't know what Jodie does when she breaks up with people. Maybe they've got some gay support network for it, they seem to have a network for everything else.

One thing I do remember from the party is dragging Jodie into a corner and asking her, in all seriousness, if she thought I could ever go over to The Other Side.

A lot of gay women might have punched me at that point, but all I seem to remember Jodie doing is blinking at me with those slightly fish-faced eyes of hers, then wandering off to get me another drink and plate of corn chips.

Even though I was drunk, and I was joking, some part of me probably meant that question too. Jodie does have the perfect life. She is always going to dance parties. She has a sultry-looking girlfriend who makes amazing vegetarian pasta. When Jodie needs a lawyer, she gets one from the lesbian mafia. When she wants to move house, she can use their women-only share accommodation register. They even found her a job as a naturopath at a women's health centre. It's incredible. It's like joining the navy or something, being gay. Your whole life is taken care of.

Even when she was single, Jodie never had a lonely Saturday night at home. All she had to do was volunteer for something like the nude netball team, or Dykes On Bikes, and her entire social life was mapped out for a month.

Unfortunately, my parents did all the wrong things

with me. Despite the fact that they divorced, thus paving the way for a bit of confusion in the old sexual role-model stakes, I am still a boring hetero.

I think you know these things when you have your hair done too. Some instinct that tells you not to point at the picture of k.d. lang when the hairdresser asks you what you want. I should have realized years ago that I was never going to make it as a lesbian. Yes, it would solve all my problems. No, I can't do it. What do they do in bed, anyway, that doesn't involve a truck-load of very expensive equipment?

It's funny, actually. Jodie and Hilary both said they'd drop into the hairdresser's this morning to say hello — i.e., to make sure I wasn't having a post break-up nervous breakdown in the sink. Neither of them has appeared yet, which I suppose means they've been sidetracked in a coffee shop and are talking about me. It's OK. I don't mind. That's what friends are for really, behind-your-back therapy. The only thing both of them have in common is me, so they may as well get a bit of mileage out of it.

I can see it now. Hilary will be in her librarian-off-duty outfit, which means the same navy blue jumper she's worn all week plus tracksuit bottoms and big dangly earrings. And Jodie will have her eyeliner drawn on all wrong, as she usually does when she has a hangover, and her John Travolta T-shirt. Hilary will be drinking cappuccino and eating raisin toast and Jodie will be drinking peppermint tea and eating nothing. And Hilary will be saying, 'I didn't trust Dan from the moment I saw him' and Jodie will be saying, 'Poor Victoria, she always goes for the commitment phobics.'

Despite this, Jodie actually quite liked Dan. Not that she's going to admit it to Hilary at this crucial stage in the girl-talk proceedings, but I dragged Jodie off to watch him playing footy one Saturday afternoon, and she even said he had balls. Quite a compliment coming from her.

I have to say, there is – sorry, was – nothing sexier than Dan straight after football. He was always wet-haired from the shower, and pink, and scrubbed, and smelling of lemon gel, and healthy. After a game, he was so tired and bruised he used to just fall straight into me. It was the most amazing feeling.

Evil coupley thoughts begone! I've really got to stop this. It's just that there's nothing else to think about except him. The bloody bride has nicked all the decent magazines, and I've been left with an Ikea catalogue with bits of chopped hair all over it.

I'm beginning to worry about my head, too. It's starting to itch, and there's red dye on my ear which may become a permanent stain if someone doesn't come to rub it off soon.

Hairdressers really should have a distress flare that you can send off when things like this happen. At least in a cafeteria you can bang your tray on the counter, or hit the little round bell near the cash register. Perhaps if I swing my head around wildly from side to side? Perhaps if I start to cry?

I really should drag myself into work after all this, too. I was useless on Friday. Hungover, heartbroken, everything at once. We've got a new account to work on as well, for the Breakfast Grits cereal people. They want to give away a free frisbee, shaped like a Breakfast Grit, inside the packet. It's the sort of stupid little job that should take me ten minutes. On Friday, though, writing a blurb for Breakfast Grit Frisbees was like asking me to write *War and Peace*.

Sometimes life is just so stupidly cruel. I cannot

believe that I am going to have to spend Saturday afternoon sitting over a computer at work, thinking of things which rhyme with Grit while the cleaners vacuum around me. And my answering machine is broken too. Just when I need it most. Even if Dan was going to have a 48-hour turnaround (and I've got to stop counting on this) he wouldn't be able to get hold of me.

I think everybody who has been dropped should have an answering machine. The agony you go through without one is just too much. I remember Hilary sat by the phone for weeks once waiting for some Indian man to ring her, after they'd done a curry master-class course and had a fling.

Whenever the phone rang, it was never ever him. So she gave up eventually and started another evening class, yoga or something. Then, one night when she was out, he rang. Not just once, but three times. And then he decided that it was a sign, an omen, a portent to avoid her, and gave up on the relationship forever.

She found out about the three phone calls a year later, when she bumped into him at a party. He had become engaged. And she was still single. After that, I found a secondhand answering machine on a market stall and gave it to her for Christmas.

The other stupid thing about breaking up with men is that you suddenly realize there is nobody to fix things for you. And I know Jodie thinks this is heinous talk, but I don't care. I can't do car repairs, I can't tune the TV, I can't understand oven fans, and I don't know how to hook up a stereo.

My only hope now that Dan has gone is probably Bill, the computer boffin who's just moved into the flat upstairs. He did mutter something about having a look at my food processor, which was lying face-up on the kitchen table with half a Mars Bar stuck in it when he dropped in.

I think Bill might be answering machine capable too. He's got that look about him. But I'll have to pace Bill the Boffin very carefully. I can only give him one broken thing a month, or this chummy new neighbour thing could disintegrate.

I'm sure he'll want to lend assistance with my new computer though. Dad, rather predictably, forgot to send the instruction manuals with the box. It just arrived from some hi-tech department store in Los Angeles with the usual vague birthday card message from him, about how he thought I should go global and hook up to the Internet and become a woman of the nineties, and that was it.

That's another thing I've inherited from my parents apart from boring heterosexuality. Total uselessness with technology. I'm not complaining about the laptop. Everybody at the party was jealous enough when I unwrapped it. For a brief moment, Dan probably even thought it would be worth staying on with me for an extra month or two.

It's just that computers scare me. We have this technobimbo streak in our family which means nobody can do anything – even putting in torch batteries the right way up. When the agency gave me my first computer, I used to yank the plug out at the mains to turn it off, then wonder why nothing I ever wrote on it was there the next time.

Fortunately, my mother – the main technobimbo in the family – is now rich enough to pay a handyman to take care of everything. Even the lightbulbs, which she just used to let die and hang there. But Dad can't even operate his girlfriend's jetski. He sent me this other

20

birthday present from LA once – a kind of furry green ball with an alarm clock inside it. It sat under my bed for two years, still in its wrapping, until Dan drop-kicked it out of the window one day.

I suppose my new computer will be a diversion, if nothing else. A way of taking my mind off things (if I didn't know better I'd say Dad had planned the whole thing from LA). Jodie was dying to use the Internet anyway, so she could look up the Ellen de Generes home page. And it means I can e-mail Hilary all day as well (much better than phone calls, no more black looks from the Chief Librarian).

Judging by their non-appearance, both Jodie and Hilary must have got lost by now. Either that or they have both decided to go off to Dan's footy match and take him on personally. I do vaguely remember some other drunken party, right at the beginning of the Dan thing, and Hilary vowing that if anything went wrong this time, she'd personally disembowel him. I even remember her saying something really pathetic, like, 'Victoria. You've been hurt enough!'

It's sweet. We tell each other this kind of thing all the time. But we've all been hurt enough by the age of thirty. Realistically, Dan stood no more chance of becoming The One with me than any of the others. Look at the odds. I'm a professional single white female. I'm one of the never married. It's like throwing a dice at the beginning of Cluedo and hoping for a double six, for God's sake.

I love the way my father rings up from LA with relationship advice, too. 'Victoria, you can't be looking for perfection all the time. It doesn't exist. Just find a nice guy you can be happy with and blah blah blah.' This is quite brilliant coming from a man who couldn't even keep his marriage together long enough to wait until the kids had grown up. Or, the kid I should say. Me.

What Dad doesn't realize is the pressure. I'm sure it's far worse than it was in the fifties or the late fourteenth century or whenever it was he and Mum did the evil deed. From the time I was four years old, it's all been about living happily ever after. Not by yourself. Never by yourself. With him. With The One.

I don't ever recall being handed a Ladybird book with a lovely fairy story about a beautiful advertising copywriter who breaks up with loads of men then decides to spend the rest of her life in serial monogamy punctuated by celibacy and sporadic masturbation.

Nothing's changed, either. Every other month we get some bank campaign at the agency. And I have to put up with the Marketing Director (in adultery) and the Art Director (recovering from his second divorce) showing me photographs of smiling couples. We get these male models and female models, cast them, tell them to pretend they're married, then stand them on the front doorstep of a house with a SOLD sign out the front, take a photograph and stick it in a bank leaflet about interest rates.

It's got to be love. And it's got to be marriage. Nothing else will do in this world, apparently. The only time we cast single women at the agency is when we're doing a laxatives ad, and we always get someone who looks depressed.

If I'm being honest, I'll admit that I've been sucked in just as successfully as everybody else. When Mrs Goble used to read us stories in Grade Two at Littlewood Primary, I used to cross my legs tightly and risk weeing all over the carpet rather than miss the handsome prince arriving at the end of Cinderella.

In high school if you didn't have a boy you were

nothing. I remember Eva the Maths Genius. She used to get twenty-five out of twenty-five for everything, and the only boy in the whole class who seemed to like her (a Science Genius, naturally enough) never went near her because every other male in the class would have ostracized him. Eva was quite nice, really. The only thing wrong with her, from memory, is that her cheeks were permanently red.

She was the only person in the whole school who qualified to get into Medicine. She was the only girl to ever win anything at swimming carnivals (the rest of us were smokers.) But I still remember her weeping quietly in her tent on the annual school camping trip. We'd all been playing Spin The Bottle late at night and someone had pointed it at her and asked if she was ever going to actually kiss anyone. It makes me shudder now. But it's just the same at thirty, now, as it was at thirteen. No Boy, No Nothing.

I know my only married friend from school, Helena Chettle, has never been quite as boring as she is now, in her fifth year of wedded babied bliss. I know one in three people get divorced and it's a total disaster. I know all this, I know. But from Ladybird books to bank leaflets, I appear to have been sucked in. Nothing less than a white veil and a child in a kilt will do for me now.

Maybe I should send the hairdresser over to the bride in the corner with a hidden microphone and a series of questions. Someone has to tell me how it's done. God knows my parents couldn't.

Question One: Tell me, Oh Bride, how did you know he was The One?
Question Two: Or are you pretending he is, for the sake of the mortgage?

23

Question Three: How can you possibly know that you will want to have sex with each other until you die (statistics: Hilary) at the median age of eighty?

Question Four: If he has an affair, will you leave him, or can you put up with it?

Question Five: Why do brides always have white shoes anyway? If you wear Doc Martens, does that automatically mean divorce?

The other question I really want to ask, but The Bride could never in a million years tell me, is: What do you do if you think you've found The One and he doesn't love you? Because, with Dan, this time I basically have. It scares me, but it's true. It's not like Anthony the Bastard Scuba Diver at all this time. And I think I sorted all of that out when I looked after Dan's mother's dog.

It sounds stupid. But really, it's normally exactly the kind of thing that would pave the way to disaster. Eventually the dog episode would have become part of a litany of reasons for leaving Dan. I could see myself telling Hilary and Jodie all about it: 'He was just so selfish, getting me to take all his family responsibilities, blah blah blah.' The fact that Dan asked me to look after his mother's dog when they all trooped off to Bali for a family holiday would have become the centre-piece for a full-scale psychoanalysis of his Oedipus complex. Or something.

But instead I was flattered. I couldn't say yes quickly enough. To be offered responsibility for — I can hardly say the word — Pistachio — was like being asked into the family. And I really wanted to be in there. I wanted to have my photo up on the piano along with all the other wives who seemed to end up hitched to Dan's multitude of brothers. When the dog arrived (and I

can't stand yappy white poodles with brown bottoms)
I even looked forward to walking it because it was
almost like being with Dan. When he rang up from Bali
with his mother hanging over his shoulder, I even
picked the dog up and made it snuffle into the phone,
so they could all hear it saying hello. I suppose I'll
know I'm truly over Dan when I can remember this and
feel sick. At the moment, though, it still rings true.
Embarrassingly true.

And there were all the other things, too. There were
his old school friends who I actually trained myself to
like, despite the fact that they were mostly wankers
to a man. And then there was his food stealing in
restaurants – basically, he just used to mindlessly help
himself to whatever was on my plate – which Hilary
used to roll her eyes at but I learned to love. And his
terrible taste in footwear (fluorescent masseur sandals!
Nooooo!) which I forced myself to pretend didn't
matter. And what's weird is, eventually none of these
things mattered any more. I just loved all of him –
mother's dog, terrible friends, restaurant theft, masseur
sandals, the whole thing.

I suppose I did with Dan what I could never do with
any of the rest, which is let every flaw, every pore,
every irritation and every sad and unavoidable reality
seep under my skin. I knew Dan was never going to
make it into big-time law. It didn't bother me. I knew
he was never going to get over his hang-up about his
boofhead father. No problem. For the first time in my
life, I heard that Billy Joel song on the radio – I love
you just the way you are, or something – and instead of
wanting to wrench the radio antenna out of its socket
and jump up and down on it, I could actually understand what he was going on about. I related to a Billy
Joel song!

25

And for all that, nothing. Dan couldn't even wait until my thirtieth birthday party was officially over to walk out. In fact, he seemed to have planned the whole thing. A card with a whole lot of rubbish about respect and fondness scrawled all over it, and how I'd make a magnificent old lady, and how he still wanted to know me in thirty years, and an antique bracelet he knew I wanted.

It was one of those birthday cards where you read between the lines. And I did.

Twenty minutes before he handed my birthday card over, he was Mr Possible, the one I could actually squint into the future with, the one I could imagine lacing his son's rugby boots, or letting his daughter bash him around the head. Basically, I thought he was The One. Twenty minutes after the card, I just had a sinking feeling. He might have been The One for me, but I clearly meant something very different to him. I wonder what. A shag? A friend? Someone to cover the entertainment questions in Trivial Pursuit while he did all the sports ones?

'Thanks, Dan. It's not very passionate, is it?'

'Well. What do you want?'

The answer to that one would have taken all night. But it's funny how I've never been able to say these things. In my head though, I can have the whole conversation.

'I want something more from you than this crap on the card about me turning into a magnificent old lady, that's what I want.'

Or

'I want you to take this further. We've been together for six months – haven't we – and we're both in our bloody thirties.'

Or (honest but feeble reply)

'I want you to tell me you love me.'

I must force myself to think of Dan as The Loathsome Lawyer from Leichhardt, I must. But what if he bumps into me walking out of the hairdresser's with my new red hair, and drags me into an alley and kisses the life out of me? And says it's all been a terrible mistake and he can't eat, can't sleep?

I don't know the statistical chances of that, but they must be there somewhere. There must be a chance. And what if he rings up drunk one night when I'm out? Telling me he's been an idiot and he can't stop thinking about me?

I can't help imagining that all this energy I'm trying to put into hating him will have gone to waste. There always seems to be this danger that you can talk yourself into loathing someone so successfully that when they finally come crawling back, you've killed everything off. And what if Dan really has been my last chance, what then?

It's enough to give me a headache, even if clouds of hairspray from the bride's end of the room weren't wafting up my nose and doing the job already.

At least my new hair can't be too far away now. We have progressed to hairdrier stage, although my head still looks like the cat's fur after it's had a stomach operation. Sticky, spiky, strange.

Jodie once taught me this positive visualization exercise, where you put yourself in a pink bubble. Then you imagine yourself inside the bubble, living a fabulous new life.

I can see myself now, with these amazingly tight black leather pants on. I've been going to the gym or something, and I've even got gaps between my thighs. I'm at a party, it's Christmas in the year 2010, and out of the corner of my eye I see Dan. He's by himself. He looks older, fatter, tired, a little sad. There are bags under his eyes.

I have a little crowd of people around me. I'm being fabulously entertaining and witty. A man pushes through the crowd. He has sexy, spiky hair like me. Except his is blond. Dan has a gut like Winston Churchill. He's lost half his hair. The spiky blond man and I disappear into a corner together for a quiet moment. We laugh together, then we kiss each other, enjoying a private joke.

Without making a sound, Dan turns and leaves the room. I don't even notice. As he gets into his car in the street outside, he can hear me and the blond man laughing through the open window. In anguish, he sinks his head onto the steering wheel and moans. Then he goes home and puts on an old Smith's record and hangs himself.

I wonder if it's wrong to imagine bad things for other people inside the pink bubble? Then again, Starsky and Hutch, who cares?

Jodie and Didi actually asked me to join their all-female discussion group, Women's Circle, where apparently they sit around and do the pink bubble exercise all the time. I know Hilary said she would go along, but I don't think I can face it. I went to one of Jodie's things a few years ago. We had to come up with a new name for our secret women's business bits. Apparently men had given them too many vile names in the past, so the idea was to reclaim your bits by thinking up some poetic new title for them. Jodie thought she might call hers The Posy of Passionate Possibilities. I don't know. I just couldn't do it. Breakfast Grits campaign, yes. New name for my labia, no.

They do other activities in Women's Circle now,

Jodie tells me. They write down the names of people who have hurt them on post-it notes and then they all hire a boat and go out on the sea (her women's group is full of people with nifty skills, like navigation) and shred them, and toss them into the waves. I could try that with you, Dan, but it wouldn't change anything. I could shred you over Bass Strait, or even into the hairdresser's sink. But I know – just as I knew with all the rest – it's going to take years to get over you.

That's what I hate about serial monogamy. It's all so predictable. You know that if you're the dumper, you're in for guilt plus lonely tea-drinking. And if you're the dumped, you're in for rage, denial and fear plus lonely tea-drinking.

I can count all my ex boyfriends, Dumpers and Dumped on the fingers of both hands. But I wonder if my left hand – let's face it, the wedding ring hand – should be allocated to Those I Dumped or Those Who Dumped Me? It's interesting that God hasn't provided us with a third hand, so we can finger-count Those Participating in Mutual Dumping. Perhaps that's because it never happens. Ha.

I like to think it pans out pretty evenly. On the fingers of my left hand, the hand designated for Those I Dumped, I can tick off Leon Mercer and Anthony Anderson. On my right hand, designated for Those Who Dumped Me, I can count Greg Daly, Phillip Zebruscki, Jamie Streeton and Daniel Hawker. If I waggle the Greg and Jamie fingers, I feel nothing of course. But if I waggle the Daniel finger, I almost feel like crying all over the hairdresser's.

I have to say that one of the other things that always, always, happens when I break up with people is that any reference to the man-woman thing – in music, in films, on TV – suddenly leaps out at you and becomes unbelievably significant. There's another crapulous song on the radio now (why do hairdressers always have the same station on, the one with ads for car mufflers?) It sounds like it could be Billy Joel's younger sister singing. And it's the kind of bland meaningless ballad that I normally wouldn't even notice. It sounds like white chocolate being glooped into a bucket. But now every line of the song is full of a heartfelt kind of philosophy. It actually has something to say to me. God help me, I'm straining to hear every word.

I should have called Jodie and asked her to bring some herbal potion for my aching back. That's another thing I've noticed after fourteen years of break-ups. Your body aches all over for the first couple of days, as if you've just crawled out of a massive car accident.

They should really set up a hospital wing for it. Just some quiet place you can go where they tuck you in and give you painkillers, then attach electrodes to whichever part of your brain is still carrying all the data on him. If I ever get rich I'll bequeath all my money to a fund for setting one of these up. They can call it the Victoria Shepworth Total Bloody Relationship Disaster Wing.

All you would have to do after he's walked out is ring an emergency number and a kind of love ambulance would turn up at your door with stretcher men ready to collect you. They'd knock you out with a gigantic injection, then . . . nothing. When you'd wake up, you'd forget you ever knew the man. You wouldn't even be able to remember what his bottom looked like. Perfect.

Really, I do feel as if I'm going mad. I can see one of Hilary's Mad Months coming on already. I wonder if this red hair dye is affecting my brain? Apparently it can seep in through the pores of your skin and cause lasting damage. Along with everything else in the world, like the Mars Bar milkshake I was trying to make last night, and the cup of coffee the hairdresser was going to give me, but hasn't yet.

The bride is beginning to look bride-like. The bridesmaid is handing sprigs of baby's breath to the junior hairdresser, who is then clipping each flower with a pair of manicure scissors and handing them to the senior hairdresser. Who is my allocated hairdresser too.

I wonder if I should just stomp over there leaving a trail of blood-red dye all over the floor? And where the hell are Jodie and Hilary?

Breathe. Think pink bubble. Breathe. Perhaps I should join Hilary and go along to Jodie's Women's Circle after all. There are lots of Friday and Saturday nights stretching ahead of me now, and I'm going to need something to fill them in. What else is there? Hilary always has reams of brochures on different classes and courses. Stone Age Man And What We Can Learn From Him (absolutely nothing). Cooking For A Happy Healthy Heart (does that include Mars Bars milkshakes?). Jazz Appreciation Nights (Oh my god, the divorced fortysomething male army).

Saturday night is a nightmare when you're single. If you stay at home with a $4 overnight video of *When Harry Met Sally*, you always feel slightly stupid. As if you're having yourself on, and having a date with yourself at the same time. Which, in fact, you are. If you go out, it's always with women friends, and you look like some desperate roaming female pack.

Saturday night is couples night, and everybody knows it. Like special fares to Bali, electric blankets with dual controls and home mortgages, Saturday nights are designed for couples. And what am I doing

31

tonight? Absolutely nothing. The friends who were at the party on Thursday and went through the Dan departure with me have been too scared to call. There's nothing on television except a bloody Marlene Dietrich special. Hilary will have Outer Mongolian Macrame Weaving or something, and Jodie will have her girl-friend and vegetarian pasta.

So, Saturday night. Welcome to the world of the Suddenly Single.

Two

Dan rings up last thing on Sunday night, just before I've put out the recycling bin with all the gift wrapping left over from the party, just after I've spilled all the little polystyrene balls from the computer box all over the street. I try not to cry when I hear his voice again, but I lose it in the first five seconds.

'Are you OK?'

'Don't say that! Of course I'm not OK.'

'I'm sorry it had to finish right then.'

'Well, you said it all in your birthday card, didn't you. Might as well get it all out in the open now. You don't care do you?'

'I never said that.'

'Well, you can just piss off then.'

Oh brilliant, Victoria, well done. I reach for the next tissue to blow my nose, and bang, he's gone. A gentle click just as I pick the receiver up for the next round.

When I call back, he's engaged. Which means he might be trying to ring me back, and God I hope he is. But . . . fifteen minutes later everybody else in the flats is putting their recycling bin out too, and the phone's still silent. He must be talking to one of his multitude of brothers about me. Or maybe he's just flicked through his address book and found a woman to talk to who won't snuffle in his ear or tell him to piss off in the first five minutes.

I'm sorry to say that this stupid, jabbing little argument is enough to keep me occupied for the rest of the night. Until around 3 a.m. in fact, when I finally do what Hilary has been telling me to do for days ('Just call. Any time.') only to find her half-asleep, irritable, dazed and confused.

'I blew it, Hil.'

'How?'

'I caused another argument. You know. I was upset.'

She can't offer me much, and it's not surprising. I've shared hotel rooms with Hilary, and she sleeps like a buffalo in a coma. The vague hope I might have had that a quick chat would make me feel better disappears as soon as I hear her yawning. I'm becoming boring. Four days after the end of it all, and I'm already becoming boring.

The sheets are too hot. Then my feet are tucked in too tightly at the end of the bed. Then I almost doze off to discover one of them is hanging off the edge of the mattress and going numb. I think pink bubble, and get into the leather pants and spiky blond-haired man and Dan's Winston Churchill gut fantasy. It works for a while, then it is replaced by a vision of something much more realistic – Dan breathing in the scent from a woman lawyer's neck. Dan removing the tartan bra with the white frills.

After this, it's the Breakfast Grits Frisbees campaign. That occupies me from around 3 a.m. to 6 a.m., when I hear Bill the Boffin lurching down the stairs to do his jogging, or whatever it is he does at this ungodly hour of the morning. It's funny when someone new moves

34

into the flat above you. There's a whole new range of sounds and little daily patterns that you have to get used to. Before Bill, it was a Japanese couple who used to make thumping sounds when they rolled up their futon – among other things. With Bill, it's just the occasional shower, the odd blast of Elvis Costello, and the faithful sounds of hearty morning exercise.

Breakfast Grits, Breakfast Grits. Maybe if I lie on my back it will come to me more easily. Throw yourself into Breakfast Grits! (No, too obvious.) Come back to Breakfast Grits and their frisbee will come back to you! (Oh for God's sake, Victoria.)

The stupid thing is, when I wake up, all I want is a big bowl of them. Nasty, big, brown, sugary flakes. I look at my eyes in the mirror. I need the same amount of foundation that they used on Eva Peron's corpse. On the way to work, I hardly notice that I've been standing up for the entire train journey while old men have been making spaces for me. In short, I'm well and truly out of it.

My office is one of those floating 'people areas' which they box in with screens and pretend is actually a room. Kylie, the junior copywriter they dragged down from Queensland, sits next to me. She has various furry things with suckers on their feet plastered all over the tiny bit of glass that separates us, which means whenever I turn my head to yell at her over the partition, all I see is strange bits of blue and green furry monster feet, and round plastic blobs. All I have on my side is a photo of Dan, which I deliberately left up all the way through Friday just in case he came back to me in time for Monday.

Kylie was at the party. She knows.

'You OK then, Vicki? Hey I like your new haircut.'

God I wish she wouldn't call me Vicki.

'Yeah, I'm OK. I'm just wondering if I should take his picture down.'

'Paper shredder over there.'

It turns out she has been put onto the Breakfast Grits Frisbee campaign as well. There is to be what Kylie calls a three-pronged attack. First the radio ads. Then special little coupons (she has to write the miserable ten sentences on the front of each coupon) then the back of the cereal packet (mine, all mine.)

'Is bitchwoman working on this too?'

She's the graphic designer we all love to hate.

'Nah, got someone else coming in.'

'Well, that's something. Cappuccino?'

'Yes please, Vicki,' she says brightly and politely.

The silly thing about the partitions is that when we want to talk to each other for, you know, professional reasons, they don't seem to be there. And yet when we're on the phone (as Kylie was to the abortion clinic one memorable day) they're supposed to matter. Like some force field around Batman, they flick on and off. We see, we don't see. We hear, we don't hear.

I know bloody well that if Jodie calls me now for a little therapeutic chat about Dan, Kylie will be modestly working away on her Breakfast Grits coupons on the computer, separated by a wall of small furry animal feet and plastic blobs, while she listens to every word. So I cheat. I take the copywriter's collective mobile phone ('It must never leave this office, people. Are we all straight on that? Never!') and piss off to the coffee shop with it, talking while I wait for the two standard Monday morning cappuccinos in polystyrene cups.

'Jodie. It's me.'

'Oh hi. I'm really sorry about Saturday morning, I tried to call you Sunday but your phone was off the hook. What happened?'

'I was out so I took it off.'

'Oh, you took it off the hook, then?'

'My answering machine's stuffed. I didn't want Dan calling me on Sunday without a machine there.'

'Oh. So he didn't call. You OK?'

'Yeah. No. He did call. I got Hilary out of bed at 3 a.m.'

'Wow. Sounds like you had a bad night.'

'Yup. Oh hell. I've got to go. The coffee's here.'

'How did your hair go?'

'Oh, all right. You know. Like an Annie Lennox red thing. It's short. See you.'

Unfortunately Jodie did one of these women's group counselling courses a few years ago, the kind where they train you to parrot everything back to people. I forget, usually, until I find myself in some kind of trouble and realize I'm being counselled.

She means well, it's just that she always slips back into it without thinking. You could roll up to Jodie's place one night, get her and Didi out of bed, and tell them you had chopped off one of your own arms with a meat cleaver, and Jodie would say:

'So, you chopped off your own arm with a meat cleaver, how do you feel about that?'

It gets to me sometimes, that's all. At the moment, I suppose I just want someone to cry with me, rant and rave with me, or direct general streams of abuse at Dan with me.

Although everything could predictably get to me today. And it's really nothing to do with Jodie. The fact that they've filled the cappuccino cups up to the brim, for instance, is enough to get to me. The fact that all the fluffy white stuff is dribbling out of the slot in the top. The fact that when I nip into the loo on the way back to the third floor, the secret women's business box (that blue thing that looks like no other object on earth) is full up again with other people's monthly ghastliness.

Also, too, the fact that when I get back to the office, Kylie has some freelance guy squeezed into the partition with her, keeping her back to me for a few extra crucial seconds, just so that I understand there's a man with her, and there's something interesting going on, and she's really rather special and important in the scheme of things. The others are supposed to get it too. Kylie's little giggles floating over the partition walls are all there for a purpose.

It's pathetic what relentless, daily boredom can do. To me, as well as to her. But anyway, she finally pretends to notice I'm there with the coffee, and swings her chair around just tightly enough to make sure the freelance guy has contact with the top half of her velvet mini-skirt.

'Oh thanks, Vicki. This is Liam. He's going to be working with us for a few weeks.'

Liam has the bags under his eyes that all the freelance art guys have. But he's sexy. A very dark, intense look. A lovely smile. Shorter than me, just by a fraction. But he's got something.

'Have you worked out what rhymes with Grit yet?' he says.

'That's funny. Actually I was thinking about that last night.'

'Kylie was saying you're part of the three-pronged attack.'

(Good, he knows how to take the piss.)

'Yes. It's true. I am one of the prongs.'

A little laugh. Kylie's arm shoots forward to grab the coffee, in a back-to-your-partition-woman gesture. But there's something about Liam. He's interesting, or something. Enough to take my mind off the photo of Dan for a few minutes.

When he's gone I flip the photo back up again, just to see if anything's changed. Nope. Nothing has. Dan still looks alive (how silly, Victoria, he's just gone, not dead) and there's a stupid ache from about the bottom of my throat to the end of my ribs that means I still need him. The sort of physical ache that in my dreams would mean the love ambulance was about to call and throw me on a stretcher.

'Liam's kind of cute, don't you think?'

'Yeah, yeah.'

Kylie swings around in her chair again, back to the computer. I can see what she's doing as well. Writing a letter to her mother in Brisbane.

Something awful has come up on my screen while Liam's been hovering. It's a copy of yet another mortgage brochure I'd forgotten about. They want me to write more copy because they can't blow up the pretend wife's face enough to fill the space. (Probably got too many wrinkles under her eyes or something, and they don't want to airbrush it in case she won't look real.)

I mean, my job. Good grief. Trying to write more words to fill up an empty space because a hired model, pretending to be a fake wife, has to have a real-looking face, but not too real. I notice the husband they've hired this time is wearing a red shirt. This is rather adventurous. It's usually blue gingham. But anyway, here we go. Think married. Think happily married. Think 'Oh, how we love the bank for giving us a 25-year mortgage.' Think security, think couples, think polished floorboards.

It takes me about ten slurps of cappuccino to realize it's not going to happen. Part of the reason it's not going to happen is the husband on the front of the brochure. He came to our Christmas thing last year wearing a peacock feather party mask, and was, as my mother likes to say, 'A bit of a bloke-lady.' They do use gay models here, mostly to grab what the MD is always dismally calling The Pink Dollar. But this guy looks too butch apparently. So they use him for the chunky, smiling husband-ish ads. He's got one of those big, strong arms that always seems to look at home plonked around a woman's shoulder.

Something moves in one of the partitions to the left of me, and my peripheral vision tells me it might be Liam's head. Worth another look. So I slide my eyes across, beyond the furry green monster feet and plastic suckers, only to find Kylie looking the same way. Very depressing. Liam appears to be charming the accounts people on the other side of the floor. Smart move for a freelancer. I've just realized Liam is wearing the same kind of suede jacket that Dan wanted a few months ago.

'Come home to the bank that wants to come home to you.' Nope. Unfortunately this is too much like coming back to the Breakfast Grit that comes back to you. Always, every time I try to write any kind of copy at the moment, it's about people coming back. Funny about that.

Dan's at work now. Probably still in with the nasty insurance firm he's been trying to represent in a case where nobody believes him. I haven't helped his sleep quota this weekend, either. I owe him an apology. Poor Dan. Can't we leave it feeling OK between us.

Ring, ring. Slam. I get out of the call just in time to hear the strange, muffled sound of his work answering machine clicking on. In a minute, there'll be the familiar sound of him (never sounding quite like him) saying 'Thank you for calling the offices of Daniel Hawker. Unfortunately . . .' I know this is utterly pathetic, but four days into a break-up, that message alone is enough to sound like an exotic love poem, a Shakespearean sonnet. The kind of thing I'd kill to hear over and over again, in fact.

Something whizzes over the partition. It is half a Kit Kat. That's Kylie's way of saying she's heard the whole thing, knows exactly what's going on, but is too cool to talk about it. Also her way of saving a few calories off her daily snack quota, but she means well.

Back to the bank brochure. 'More than a bank. A friend for both of you.' Perhaps married people with no friends will like that one. 'The security of knowing we're there for you always.' Yeah. And don't we all need someone there for us always, especially when we're thirty, loveless and female. I can see myself at thirty-eight. I'll be doing Summer Basket-making Seminars with Hilary and we'll both be wearing our work jumpers with our tracksuit pants on the weekends, competing for the one available divorced fortysomething male in the class.

The phone rings.

My hand snaps onto the receiver so fast I'm in danger of breaking off my own call. And my own wrist.

Dan. Dan. Yes. Yes.

'Oh hi, is that Vicky?'

'Victoria.'

Damn. Not Dan.

'This is Liam. I'm just on the way out actually, in the car park. I didn't think of it before, but you might be on e-mail?'

'What? Oh yes. I am.'

A total lie. But whatever.

'Kylie told me you'd just got the whole package for your birthday.'

'Yes, I did. I am.'

'What's your address?'

Bugger.

'Er. I've forgotten it.'

'Oh well. Send me something and I'll bookmark you in. I'm Liam at Ozemail.'

Of course you are. Why do I understand nothing this man is saying to me?

'OK then.'

If Kylie's ear rotates much further to the left she'll be picking up CNN on satellite.

E-mail. Liam. Yes. I must get Bill the Boffin onto it. And I must get him a present for helping with the computer. But what do you get a man with almost no personality? I mean, he *looks* OK. Big, chunky country shoulders. Honest eyes the colour of China Black tea bags. It's just that there's nothing going on inside.

Three

I come home to find my answering machine wrapped inside a plastic bag on my front doorstep, with a note from Bill. It's amazing. I threw it at him on my way to work, and it's now back at 6 p.m. and he's even cleaned off all the old cigarette scorch marks from the days when I used to smoke, before Dan made me give it up. I wonder why he's left it on the doormat, then remember him mumbling something about being from Dorrigo. It must be nice to grow up in the sort of trusting country town where you can leave things like answering machines and washing machines around in the street without eighteen-year-olds in gigantic shorts nicking them.

Dan hasn't left flowers or anything. Funny about that. He did actually do it once, when we had a huge fight over the fact that I had laughed at his mother for continually buying ornaments from Franklin Mint ('Send no payment now, Mrs Hawker, for your Tutankhamen Boy King statuette.') Dan has always been sniffy about his family. Anyway, he took a low punch, saying at least his parents were still together, and I howled in front of him for about an hour, and then we had the usual 'You're dysfunctional because of your family' – 'No, excuse me *you're* dysfunctional because of your family' argument. We were both pissed. And the next day he sent me a huge bunch of white tulips carefully timed to arrive at work – Kylie was most impressed – and a card which is still tucked away in my bra drawer. I want to go and look at the card now. Part of me even wants to smell it, just to see if there's any identifying Dan smell left in the ink. But I'm not going to. No. Absolutely not, Victoria.

The trouble with something like flowers happening once is that you can't help but hope it's going to happen again. White tulips six months ago, why not white tulips now? I make myself some calming chamomile tea – a present, from Jodie last Christmas, which I've never used – and wait for the florist to knock on the door with Dan's tulips and note. I feel like that woman in *The English Patient*, stuck in a cave waiting for Ralph (why does he pronounce it Rafe, it's so irritating) Fiennes (why does it have to be Fines, that's even worse) to come back.

One of the other things they didn't tell you in the Ladybird fairytale books at Littlewood Primary is that having a love life involves so much waiting around. You wait for him to make the first move, you wait for him to call you after the first time you've had sex, you wait for him to come round after a fight, you wait for him to come back to you, you wait for him to say 'I love you', you wait to find out if you're pregnant, and I suppose ultimately you wait for him to die. Comparatively speaking, Snow White in her coffin had an instant result.

Taking any of my exes at random – Greg Daly, for example – I'm sure I could find whole chunks of my life have been wasted in various waiting games. Really, I could count days, months and years. To begin with,

Greg was one of those rather earnest, bushwalking types who only have eyes for trees. I basically had to unzip him at the fly before he realized, hey, she actually likes me. So that wasted a lot of time, right from the start.

When I was in love with Greg, I spent eight entire months walking around with him, and all the rest of them, in his Wilderness Walks group, carrying dried apricots and freeze-dried soup in a rucksack. Nothing happened. Absolutely nothing happened. I pretended I had a leech up my leg once in the hopes that he would help roll my trouser leg up. I think I said, 'Oh Greg, something's on my leg, it might be a leech' and he said 'Put freeze-dried soup on it until it drops off.'

Added to the eight months of boring bushwalking, I could also add the endless nights I spent listening to King Crimson records, trying to like them – or at least trying to understand the song titles – just hoping for the day when Greg would play his King Crimson tape in the car and I could say casually, 'Oh, isn't that from their first album?'

When he started disappearing up mountains with Annalise the German exchange student, there was more waiting. There may have even been as much as six more months of it, six months I could have spent learning the Alexander Technique, or learning to cast the I Ching or something useful.

Love. It's basically like standing in a queue at a baggage terminal while your eyes glaze over. And here I am again, however many years later (Greg's in Tibet, still going up mountains with that bitch, Annalise) and I'm still hanging around waiting for phone calls, waiting for white tulips that aren't going to turn up, waiting for miracles, waiting for things to happen.

Playing around with my answering machine

message now takes the best part of the night. Free entertainment for singles, and better than TV too. It's amazing the number of different messages and different voices you can use when you know there's a three per cent chance your ex boyfriend is going to call when you're not there.

You can do a bright, chirpy, busy version (My life is a social whirl and I'm just out for ten minutes being handcuffed to a bed by three guys I met in a nightclub.) You can do calm, relaxed and centred (I'm very zen since you left me, Dan. Relationships are just karmic, cleansing processes.) You can do brave and holding back the tears (just a hint of noble suffering, though, nothing too obvious.) In the end I do the usual boring thing, because you never can tell if your next call is going to be a very serious woman in a suit from Breakfast Grits.

When the phone rings, I leap about three metres in the air.

'It's Bill. Is everything working? Have you plugged it in?'

'Actually, Bill, could you do me another favour?'

Five seconds later, he rings back and does his test message, as requested, into the machine. He sounds very boffin-like and embarrassed. I can hear the ABC on in the background. He's watching the same boring program on robots I switched off five minutes ago.

'Er, hello Victoria. This is your test message. From Bill. Thanks. Bye.'

Not for the first time, I find myself wondering if Bill would be right for Hilary. He's not as exotic as the Indian Cookery Class Man, but he's got that basic Dorrigo niceness which she likes. And she's always been a sucker for men who wear Blundstones. It certainly wouldn't be hard to organize an introduction. I could just send another Mars Bar through my food processor, get it stuck, and send her upstairs to get it fixed again.

Mars Bar, Mars Bar. No, camomile tea, camomile tea. Then the phone rings again. I hope it's not Bill letting me know he just, er, left a message. I couldn't stand it. As it happens, it's Mum.

'Your father tells me you split up with your boyfriend again.'

What does she mean, again?

'When were you talking to him?'

'I rang him up to say how nice it was that he'd sent you a computer. Very nice present.'

'Well, it would be if I knew how to use it.'

'Any more information on the boyfriend then?'

'Nope.'

'It's like that then, is it?'

'Yup.'

'You're not crying are you, Victoria, oh dear.'

My head feels like a greyhound track at the moment. All my ideas about life, about Dan, about love, about the breakup, are racing ahead of each other. The winning dog at the moment happens to be the one called Divorced Parents. It goes something like this. If she'd actually managed to stay married to Dad, I might have learned something about how to keep a relationship together.

'Go and have a nice bath in that oil I sent you.'

'I haven't got a bath.'

'Oh, you've got that shallow thing, haven't you. Well, come and have a bath here.'

'It's ten o'clock at night. I'm not going over there just so I can have a bath.'

'Did you thank your father for the computer?'

'Yes.'

47

'Well then, that's all right. I'll say good night now. How is Mrs Whatsername taking it, do you know?'

'I've got no idea.'

'She was funny with that poodle, wasn't she. Oh well. Bye now.'

I have thought about the Hawker family's reaction to it all. It was part of the 2 a.m.–3 a.m. worry shift in bed last night. I expect little Pistachio will be dancing around the garden, clapping his paws in the air and speaking in tongues. Likewise Dan's brothers, who found me about as interesting as one of Mrs Hawker's Franklin Mint ornaments.

When the phone rings again, it's Hilary.

'Hil, do me a favour. Ring back and listen to this message and tell me if it sounds wanky. Then ring back again, could you?'

'Don't you know how to switch the machine—'

'No I don't. Can you just ring?'

She does. Then she rings me back and tells me I sound like an idiot child.

'Why are you speaking so slow-ly on it? Do it again. Anyway, I've got a favour to ask you. Have you set up the computer yet?'

'I'm waiting for Bill the Boffin to do it, and I can only give him one thing at a time, as you know.'

'Oh. Hmm. Bill. Interesting.'

'I was just thinking about that.'

'Although now I've joined the Women's Circle I don't have much time for dates.'

I love the way she calls it dates. It's like *Happy Days* never ended. I'm surprised she's joined Jodie's women's thing though. She must be getting really desperate.

'So what's Bill like?' she asks, trying to sound interested. 'I can always stop Women's Circle.'

'He's not bad looking! He's got interesting eyes. But he's from Dorrigo. And he's always got this big Elastoplast over his jaw.'

'Ooh. That's a bit weird. Has he got a strong jaw?'

'Yes. And he's got, you know, shoulders.'

'What's his flat like?'

'Boring. There's nothing in it except for mousepads.'

'Would he like me?'

'I reckon.'

'Would it last?'

'Oh, for God's sake, Hilary, I'm not Mystic Bloody Meg!'

I tell her my mother rang and nearly had me crying.

'Well, that's all in Women's Circle in week four. The silent mother-daughter conspiracy.'

'So then your life becomes perfect, does it, once you've worked that out? Anyway it's not a silent conspiracy. She never stops talking. She's pissed off that she only bought me some bath oil for my birthday and Dad got me a computer.'

'But that's been going on for years.'

'Has it?'

'Don't you remember, at school, when they were splitting up, he'd give you something like a Wurlitzer organ, and she'd get you a pair of clogs. God, we were so jealous. We all wanted divorced parents.'

'Did you?'

'Look, my parents are still together, and what do I get for my birthday? Bloody tickets to *Lord of the Dance*. Bloody Michael Flatley.'

'He has to have sex after every performance you know.'

'Of course he does! THAT IS WHY THE MOTHERS CANNOT RESIST!'

When I go to bed I'm feeling almost relaxed. A

definite achievement. I'm not sure if it's the vague possibility of Bill and Hilary being set up that's giving me something else to think about, or Liam's phone call this afternoon or . . . terrifying thought, maybe my mother does have a good effect on me after all.

Four

I'm in the middle of nothing much at work, basically trying to make things rhyme with Grit, when Liam appears. Kylie's taken an early lunch so she can go to step aerobics, thank God. Liam stands behind me with his arms folded, looking on. He's wearing the same suede jacket, again.

'So have you ever tasted a Breakfast Grit, this world famous Breakfast Grit that we're all meant to be working on?'

'No. Although I did wake up craving them the other morning.'

'You must be working too hard.'

'No, I haven't been. Actually.'

Why am I flirting? It's a weird feeling, to be doing this kind of thing again. Especially when I've been locked off with Dan for so many months.

'My e-mail address. I meant to tell you. I haven't actually got one yet. In fact, I haven't even got the thing working.'

'I knew you were faking it.'

'But can I write yours down again?'

'Hand me one of Miss Kylie's lovely writing implements and I will.'

Liam's hands are typical artsy hands. Long fingers. Quite smooth. Paper-cut scars, and nothing much else.

'There you go. And there's my phone number.'

From a distance of twenty metres this might look like a freelance graphic designer handing his business card to a senior copywriter. But here, right now, it's definitely a man-woman moment. A pheromone exchange, you might say. Well, at least from my armpits anyway.

Then one of the Accounts girls starts bearing down on us, waving something. Liam's first cheque, by the look of it. Of course, she didn't have to bring it all the way down here to hand deliver it. But there's something about Liam that makes people want to do things for him.

'Anyway, I'll see you. Or maybe I'll get your e-mail.'

'When I work out how to plug it in, ha ha ha.'

I think I'm actually laughing like that, too. Ha ha ha. How embarrassing. My flirting skills seem to have regressed since I've broken up with Dan. I'm behaving like an Avon Lady trying to sell men an aftershave they don't want.

When he goes, there's a kind of gap for a while. It happened last time as well. It's enough to bother me while I'm juggling Breakfast Grits copy around on the computer. And it's enough to make me vow to knock on Bill's door when I get home, even though the interval between answering machine favour and computer favour will be less than a week.

When Kylie gets back, she finds Liam's design mock-ups on her desk.

'Vicki. Did you see Liam?'

'Yes.'

'Did he say anything?'

'No. He just came and went.'

'There was a cheque I was going to pass onto him. From Accounts.'

'I think he got it.'

'I actually had a few things to talk about with him.'

A pause. She's pissed off. Really pissed off. Then, a few minutes later:

'Heard from Dan yet?'

And I'm not even going to answer that one. But part of me feels sorry for her too. She doesn't stand a chance with Liam. Not a chance. And neither does the girl from Accounts with the clunky platform shoes and the clunky daisy necklace who stomped down with his money. To be quite honest, though, I'm not sure if any of us have a chance. I mean, as if I were interested anyway. Ha.

When I get home, I run into Bill parking his car out the front of the block. He's a very bad parker, perhaps because he's used to navigating around cows, or grapevines, or combine harvesters – or whatever it is they have in Dorrigo. He winds the window down.

'I meant to say to you the other day, any time you want me to look at that computer . . .'

'Well, it is still sitting there, actually.'

'You busy now?'

'No, come round.'

Which he does, just as I'm about to get in the shower. I answer the door in my old grey cotton dressing gown, let him in, then zoom up the corridor before the blush creeping up his neck can get any further up his face and work its way around his Elastoplast. Country manners, I suppose. Then I glance at myself in the bathroom mirror and realize it's the dressing gown which shows my nipples. Whoops.

Is Hilary really a Bill option? She could at least help rip off his Elastoplast for him. I'm sure he's dying to ask someone else to do it. And as a fellow single person, I know the agony of having nobody to even do the surprise Elastoplast rip for you. Poor Bill.

When I emerge dried off, dressed, deodorized, lip-glossed and brushed, he's staring at a picture of Bart Simpson which has mysteriously appeared on my computer screen.

'Is it happening?'

'It's happening.'

He types in something else, then a few minutes later, there's a picture of Elvis Costello.

'Anything you want to look at?'

'Brad Pitt naked. Oh, my God, this is so exciting. I must call Hilary and Jodie so they can come and try it out.'

'Er, you can't. Well, you can. But you'll have to go off-line.'

'Switch the Internet off?'

'Yes. Look. I'll show you how to do it yourself then I'll go. I've got squash tonight.'

'Oh, Hilary used to play squash.' (Edge her in, Victoria, you can do it.)

'Do you play?'

Is he mad? Surely he saw enough of my body in the revealing grey cotton dressing gown to realize that sport and I are indifferent strangers. But anyway.

'Hilary would love a game, you know.'

'Well, any time.'

And then he's gone. What a strange man he is. His ears stick out slightly, just like those old pictures of Aussie blokes from the 1940s that you see hanging up in RSL clubs or Anzac Memorial Halls. And he's so polite. Yes, the more I think about Bill the Boffin, the more I can imagine Hilary squealing. It has to happen. It must happen.

When I call her she doesn't seem interested, though.

'As we say in Women's Circle, men are like food processors. We all want one, but we're not sure why.'

'I thought you wanted to be introduced!'

'Oh, I don't know. I think I've gone off him.'

'But you never even met him!'

'What if he's gay? You know I've been down that road before in this town.'

'Anyway, are you coming over?'

'Yes. As long as you're not going to set me up with Bill.'

'As if. Anyway, he's at squash.'

Then I call Jodie and Didi, who sound as if they are rolling around on the futon smoking dope, which of course they are, but the prospect of sending e-mail to Camille Paglia and looking at the Ellen de Generes home page is too much for them.

'Come over,' I say, sounding like a schoolgirl asking her friends round so she can show off her new Barbie caravan.

'Can we?' says Jodie. Then Didi grabs the phone.

'We can use it for research!' she says, sounding squeaky and excited. 'For our doco!'

Jodie and Didi's 'doco', which is wank speak for documentary, only exists on a piece of paper at the moment, but after God knows how many failed funding applications over the years, Jodie has taken to talking about it as if it's actually happening, probably because a white witch in Byron Bay told her if you talk about things as if they're actually real, then they'll become real. Or something.

The subjects of Jodie and Didi's documentary proposals have changed over the years. How could Hilary and I ever forget Women and their Moustaches – a Historical Perspective. Or indeed My Grandmother's

Feet? The theme hardly ever changes though. Basically it can't involve men, and it has to involve at least one female body part. This time round, though, they're waiting to hear about (working title) Love and the Female Experience. I helped them with the application, doing endless photocopying at the agency after everyone else had gone home. So I suppose I should be a bit more enthusiastic. But really, Jodie's documentaries are like my boyfriends – serial non-events.

'See you in a while then, chicks,' I say. I love calling them chicks. It taunts them.

'Yeah, right.'

When everyone finally turns up to my flat and we crowd around the computer together, it really is like schoolgirls oohing and aahing over some Barbie accessory. Didi, who seems to be good at things like ovens and computers ('Left brain lover,' says Jodie), gets me into e-mail.

'Did he do all this for you?' she asks.

'Do what? Who?'

'Well,' she says, pointing to a scrawled piece of paper, 'That guy upstairs. He's got you the service provider sorted out, and the password, and the whole bit. Must like you, Victoria,' she snorts.

'Oh, he just likes computers.'

My password, according to Jodie, is lotsotroxo.

'Can you remember that?'

'But everyone's heard it now. No, I don't think I will remember that somehow.'

'Get it tattooed on your butt,' says Jodie, and swans off into the kitchen to see if there's anything non-meaty to eat.

Everyone is quite amazed when I tell them I've already got two people to send e-mail to.

'Well, Bill. I've got his address. And I should thank

him for helping me, shouldn't I. And this guy from work I know.'

And Bill's easy enough. I just write something about how eternally grateful I am for his boffin-like genius, and how I must have him round for dinner one night. I mean it too. I can have him, Hilary, and some other people who won't mind about the Elastoplast.

When it's time to write to Liam, though, I find I can't think of anything to say at all. You use computers to compose Breakfast Grit slogans on, for God's sake, not to come up with cunningly flirty messages.

'Who is this Liam anyway?' Hilary asks, on her second glass of wine.

'Oh, just another Eligible.'

Jodie and Didi open another bottle of wine at this early sign of boring boy talk, and disappear into my kitchen to try to make eggplant risotto with all my usual politically incorrect ingredients.

'And why is Liam an Eligible?' Hilary persists, waving her glass around.

'I don't know. Maybe it's because of Dan going. I just suddenly like him.'

'What are you going to say then?'

'Oh . . . I don't know. Something about Breakfast Grits.'

In the end, I send this:

From: shep@mpx.com.au
To: liam@ozemail.com.au
Subject: Test Message

Dear Liam, I have finally got my e-mail connected, so you are the proud recipient of my second ever message. I hope this gets through. I'll see you at work, Victoria.

Hilary's left eyebrow is raised so high she looks like a drag queen.

'Welllll . . . that was very *interesting*.'

'Oh, shut up. I don't know what to say.'

'Let me type something then.'

'No!'

Basically because Hilary's bigger than me, I let her. When she's finished, I read:

From: shep@mpx.com.au
To: liam@ozemail.com.au
Subject: Your Underpants

Dear Liam, Just wanted to know if you've got anything in leopardskin. We're doing a survey. Love, Victoria Shepworth.

'Great.'

'Well at least it's more interesting than "You are the proud recipient of my second ever message." Anyway, I've deleted it.'

'Good.'

And that would have all been fine, except for the fact that Hilary's computer skills are even worse than mine, especially under the influence of Margaret River chardonnay. And a few minutes later, as the eggplant risotto is being doled out, this arrives.

From: liam@ozemail.com.au
To: shep@mpx.com.au
Subject: Real Men Don't Wear Leopardskin

Dear Victoria, Luckily I happen to be doing a bit of late night e-mailing in my red boxers, so I can prove

**to you that real men don't wear anything else.
Yours, Liam.**

'Classic,' Hilary laughs, pronouncing it with that slight swishing sound which means she's already gone on three glasses.

Didi says nothing and starts pouring more wine for everyone.

Jodie massages my shoulders.

Then I drop boiling hot eggplant on my knees, and swear at Hilary when she tries to fuss around me with a soggy teatowel.

'Get a sense of humour,' Hilary tells the floor, drunkenly.

'What sort of dickhead thing was that to write, anyway?' I yell at her.

I take my wine glass, go into the bathroom, cry for a bit and think about Dan, then put on a lot of purple eye pencil and come out again, stop, go back in a second time and howl this time – really howl. In a funny way, it's the first time I've cried – properly cried – since he left. I've had lots of those little chicken sobs, but none of those great, hearty, wrenching yowls that are supposed to do you good.

When I come back into the room they've eaten all the food and are ignoring me, playing with the computer and looking at a Spice Girls Worship site.

'It is my computer you know.'

'Sorry,' Hilary says, pretending to chew risotto so it actually sounds like she's saying 'Swy' instead. She's always swallowed her apologies, even at school when she once borrowed my lipgloss without asking and ended up giving me her herpes.

'Liam now has totally the wrong impression of me, that's all.'

'But look how much faster things have progressed!'

'Sure.'

At this point in proceedings, Didi starts massaging Jodie's shoulders. It's a toss-up if she's going to get the Ylang Ylang out of her backpack, but in the end she does, and proceeds to oil Jodie's shoulders like she's basting the wings on a rotisserie chicken. Perhaps it's a vegetarian fantasy or something.

'Didn't you want to check out the Ellen de Generes page?' Hilary asks casually, as if it's the most normal thing in the world to address two women who are on the verge of drunken, stoned, rabbity excitement.

Jodie makes the kind of noise you'd expect to hear from someone who is trying to be polite while their girlfriend is pushing their face into the floor.

'Maybe not,' says Hilary who, while she appears to be good at Women's Circle, is not so good at being cool about mushy gay couple behaviour.

'Hey, what about this, Vic,' she says carefully. 'The Secret Piners' page. If you secretly pine after someone, leave your message at www.secret piner.com.au and watch your dreams come true anonymously.'

'Tch. Americans . . .'

'How do you know it's American?'

'It's exactly the kind of wanky idea they'd come up with.'

'It's Australian, darl.'

'Oh well.'

'Anyway, we could leave a message for Li-am,' she says in a cutesy-putesy voice and starts waving her wine glass around in circles again.

'Don't push it.'

'Don't worry about it, Vic. Look, he'll have the first message from you, and realize that someone else pushed in and obviously and naturally wrote that other stupid message. As you would, if the first person had put something very boring.'

'But he'll still know!'

'Know what?'

'Oh, I don't know.'

We try out a few more web pages – pictures of Pop Tarts exploding, evidence of UFO landings in shopping centres, that kind of thing. Then we get onto the Anagrams page, which Hilary says all the librarians in the world are addicted to, and put in my name, her name, Jodie's name, Saddam Hussein's name, and – I can't help myself – Dan's name.

The results are interesting. From my name you get herpes, which is probably about the borrowed lipgloss episode at school. From Daniel Hawker you get denial, which I think is deeply meaningful but Hilary doesn't. From her name, Hilary Grove, you get groovy. Which puts paid to any credibility the Anagram Theory has about people's personalities. Saddam Hussein, of course, spells this: madman mashes USA.

By the time we get around to doing Jodie and Didi, we realize they've quietly fallen asleep on the floor. It occurs to me that Bill might drop in to see how things are going, in which case I am going to have to clear them into the broom cupboard, or hide them under the bed, like something out of an old *Fawlty Towers* episode.

'Can I send Bill an e-mail?' says Hilary a little later, when she thinks I've forgiven her.

'No, you cannot. You're dangerous. Anyway I thought he was like a food processor.'

She ignores me, in that drunken, wildly staring way that only a woman on half a bottle of chardonnay can.

'Just to say hi, I'm Victoria's friend, my name's Hilary, and I'm using this computer. All right?'

'No.'

We then do what we always do, which is wonder aloud why we are not gay and having a happy love life, while Didi and Jodie snore all over each other like a couple of hippos. Then we turn on the TV for yet another bloody war film with Michael Redgrave in it, which does nothing to take my mind off Dan, or that embarrassing message to Liam, at all.

'Stop thinking about it,' says Hilary in the ad break.

'You don't have to work with him! You don't have to front up on Monday!'

'I wish I did. Front up and work with him. Red boxer shorts. Mmmm. Do you realize I've never seen a man wearing boxer shorts except in a catalogue?'

We then launch into another old favourite – the Build Your Perfect Man discussion. It's always interesting to see what Hilary's changed since the last time. For example – whenever we got drunk and did this a few months ago, her Perfect Man had the ability to laugh silently. ('You can tell he's laughing, but you don't hear anything. Very sexy.') Now, she's moved on.

'I'd like a bit of noise to come out when he laughs. Not too much, just a bit.'

'Yeah?'

'But I still want the glasses, definitely still got to have the glasses.'

One of the things about Build Your Perfect Man is that you can't wait for the other person to shut up so you can get on with your bit. We both know this, so we stretch it out and make each other wait.

'And another thing I thought of . . .'

'Isn't it my turn?'

'Oh all right.'

So I hold the wine glass seriously in both my hands,

twiddling the stem, and make her wait. Then I make my decision.

'He's English.'

'Wasn't it Argentinian last time?'

'English. They know how to behave.'

'Aah, I know what you're up to. That's Earl thingie. Diana's brother. I saw you watching the funeral, everybody else was taking it seriously and crying and you were just thinking, "Phwaah, that Earl Spencer . . ."'

'NO. Nothing to do with that. What do you mean Earl Spencer anyway, I thought we'd gone off him after his divorce? Anyway, I'd like that, and . . .'

'What's wrong with Australian men, your own kith and kin?'

'Look. You know what's wrong with Australian men. You're an Australian woman, aren't you? Has it ever worked out? With any of them?'

'I just don't think we should be nationally biased about this.'

'That's good coming from you, Hilary, you're the one who came back from Italy and said ALL Italian men were comfortable in their masculinity, if I remember. You know, ALL Italian men are sexy, ALL Italian men are relaxed about their nudity, blah blah.'

And she really has no comeback here, because it's true.

'Anyway,' she says finally. 'Go on. Your perfect man is an English man.'

'Yes, but an English man who's travelled.'

'Benny Hill was English. I'm sure he travelled. Why don't you go off and marry him?'

'He's dead. Don't be stupid. And my tits aren't big enough.'

Hilary laughs her pissed laugh, which consists of a duck-like quack. I'm not sure why. I'm not being very funny, but then perhaps she's not being very sober either.

'You know,' she slurs, wine glass circling, 'every woman thinks the men in her own country are the worst in the world. It's not just us.'

'No, Australian men are stuffed.'

'How?'

'We have a smaller population. Smaller population is limited choice.'

'Maybe.'

Because I'm less drunk, I find myself talking more.

'What have we got after all? Ferals, *Footy Show* men, inner city boys with Triple J promotional condoms, criminals, paedophiles, people from Bondi who wear sunglasses that make them look like blowflies, and men who wear their baseball caps backwards.'

'You forgot lawyers.'

'Yeah, lawyers. And doctors.'

'I like inner city boys with Triple J promotional condoms,' Hilary protests.

'Well, I don't. Not when they've gone past their use-by date.'

'Who, the men or the condoms?'

I make a noise to show her I think this is the worst joke I've ever heard.

'I don't care if I have to get married before I'm thirty-nine and eleven months,' I say, 'I'm having none of them.'

Jodie's head suddenly sticks up from Didi's chest, where it's been serenely planted for the past half an hour.

'I think inner city boys, with Triple J promotional condoms keep you going,' Hilary keeps saying, 'they do things like getting their ears pierced on the spur of the moment. And trying out all the latest designer drugs, and putting up Winona Ryder stickers on the fridge.'

'My friend slept with one of those,' Didi interrupts, suddenly awake. 'Plus he was forty-two years old. Can you believe it? I mean he was *forty-two*!'

'That still passes for boyhood in the inner city,' I say.

'Why don't you like ferals?' Didi asks nobody in particular. 'They can be really gentle.'

'And they'll plait your armpit hair for nothing,' Jodie adds.

'Oh, my God, I think Jodie made a joke,' Hilary says. Then everyone goes quiet.

Funny about that.

Then there's a crashing sound outside the front door and we all wake up again.

'Someone's trying to break in, Vic,' yawns Hilary.

But when I go outside to look, there's nobody there except Bill the Boffin, clambering up the stairs to his flat.

'Sorry,' he yells down. 'I dropped my racket.'

'That's all right,' I slur back.

Honestly, I've never seen anyone go red in the face so often, for so little reason. Bill could blush for Australia at the next Olympics.

Finally I boot everyone out. I suppose it's a single kind of evening really. And it's not so bad. Until I go to bed, and realize the following depressing facts:

a) Daniel Hawker spells denial and wanker.
b) None of the bitches washed up before they left.
c) I'm going to have a hangover tomorrow.
d) I've managed to talk myself into believing that every man in Australia is stuffed.
e) Liam now thinks I'm out for it. Even before I've decided that I might be.

Five

The hangover makes itself felt at 5 a.m. and my head is so bad I can't even manage the tap. So I drink from the kettle instead and cut my lip on the plastic spout.

I'm in the afternoon stages of it now, getting to that bizarre point where you feel like an egg and bacon sandwich at half past three in the afternoon. Kylie keeps saying, 'Go on, have one' and I keep saying, 'No, I can't.'

Liam, thank God, isn't in today. The Breakfast Grit Frisbee campaign is undergoing a 'rethink,' according to Kylie, who hears these things before I do. Apparently it has to be redesigned in another shade of brown, owing to its similarity to one of those joke plastic vomit things that fifteen-year-old boys buy from wacky party shops. Actually, I think if they do this, it will sell thousands more packets of cereal, but nobody listens to me around here.

Finally, after my bank brochure has been accepted ('Come to the bank that feels as good as a roaring fire at home on a cold winter's night,' Aaaagh!) I'm let off the lead. And when I use the work computer to log in and check my e-mail at home (nifty Bill the Boffin trick) I find this.

To: shep@mpx.com.au
From: liam@ozemail.com.au
Subject: If you're not doing anything . . .

Hi Victoria.
If you're not doing anything on Friday night, I'm playing in a band called A Word From Our Sponsors (AWFOS, for short, you might have heard of us, but then again, probably not. Most people try to forget). We do covers of ad jingles. Please don't tell me you're washing your hair. We need all the crowd we can get. Liam. PS: If you are interested, it's 8 p.m. at The Crow.

'I'm going too,' Kylie says smugly.

'What does he do in the band?'

'Keyboard player. My other boyfriend in Brisbane was a keyboard player.'

What does she mean, her other boyfriend?

'Are you going to take anyone with you?' Kylie pesters me.

'Oh, I'll see.'

'You haven't heard from Dan?' she asks for the ninety-ninth, totally unecessary, time.

'Not speaking. No.'

All of which poses a classic Suddenly Single problem. At short notice, who am I going to find on a Friday night who can go with me to the Crow so I don't look like a loser?

The mobile phone we all share is lying tantalizingly on top of the photocopier.

'Back in a sec,' I tell Kylie.

But when I take the phone into the office kitchen (God, I wish someone would take that Who's Been Stealing My Strawberry Yoghurt, Exclamation Mark,

Exclamation Mark notice off the fridge), Hilary's already planned to see a film with someone. When I call Jodie, she tells me she and Didi have a big dinner on. Running right down the list, even as low as boring old Helena Chettle, who can never do anything because she always has a baby called Olga glued to her nipple, I finally settle on my mother. The only untried number in my address book, in fact. Sad though it is, this is what my life has come to.

There is only one option which remains and that is grovelling and begging.

'Please Hilary, I can't go on my own, I'll look like a groupie.'

'Put it off then.'

'But I've got nothing to do on Friday night!'

'What about Jodie and Didi?'

'Dinner party. Fundraiser for Pakistani women's legal service. $100 a ticket.'

Finally, she gives in. Which is the nice thing about Hilary, because she always does. Despite her eight-week Assertiveness Training Course last year, which was all women anyway ('A total joke, not an Eligible in sight'), she can always be counted on to buckle in the name of loyalty.

So, in the end, the two of us wind up in my flat getting ready for a night of high culture and the possibility of seeing Liam making a complete dick of himself. Hilary arrives wearing a black dress and black opaque tights and black shoes. I am wearing black pants and a black leather jacket and black boots. And when I'm pouring a glass of wine in the kitchen, she goes into the bathroom and sprays my Eternity all over herself. So now we smell the same and look the same.

'I'm getting changed.'

'Oh, it doesn't matter.'

'We look like a couple of prostitutes!'

When we finally get there (jeans, blue T-shirt, black leather jacket, lipstick over my cut lip) there's a cattle dog with a very thin string tied to its collar, hanging around in front of the women's toilets.

'Very classy,' says Hilary, doing her drag-queen eyebrow raise. 'God, this takes me back.'

'How long since you saw a band then?'

'1885.'

I get her to tell me how old she thinks Liam is when AWFOS come on stage, just in case he's in danger of revealing himself as an inner city boy with Triple J promotional condoms.

Kylie and the girl from Accounts with the daisy necklace are here. They are both wearing micro-mini kilts and knee-high boots and pretending not to see me, because it's not cool to wave at people you know from work. Then they realize they don't know anybody else, so they come over.

'By the way,' says Kylie, 'I just saw Dan.'

'Dead on the road?' Hilary asks loyally.

'He was with someone. Having dinner. Oh, they're on. I'll tell you later, Vicki.' And the lights go down, and guitars start thundering out of the PA, and she wanders off.

Hilary offers me a cigarette. It's been months since I gave up. It's menthol. I hate menthol, it's like inhaling toothpaste. I take it, light it, and love every minute of it.

'Don't worry about it,' she yells sympathetically.

'BASTARD!' I yell back.

The great thing about cigarette smoking, which I have completely forgotten, is that you can't cry and inhale at the same time.

I can't believe Dan. I can't. I suppose it was really

easy for him, too. Couple of drinks after work, she's the lawyer on the opposite team, simple.

Hilary shoves me again and yells into my ear, 'It might not be anything.'

But I know it is, that's the problem. Dan doesn't have platonic female friends. He's not capable of it.

'I have to go,' I yell back. 'You stay.'

I can barely see Liam at the side of the stage anyway, the lighting guy's one of those demented people who keep everything black except the drummer and the singer, both looking pink and purple by turns. And AWFOS are awful. They play heavy metal versions of old TV ad themes – Vegemite, Milo, Decore – in the hopes that the extreme irony involved will leave everyone sobbing helplessly with laughter and slapping their thighs, I suppose. Well, I'm not. Even if I was feeling fabulous right now, which I'm not, I don't think I could ever like AWFOS.

Stumbling to the bar, I pick Kylie out at the front of the stage. Where else?

I elbow her.

'Where did you see him?' I bellow in her ear, over the sound of the Aeroplane Jelly song.

'I'll tell you later,' she moos back.

And she swings around to face the stage again.

So. Dan. Something one of his wanker footy friends used to say about him comes back to me now. 'Dan the Man.' It was that side of him that I always hated, the bit that pretended to be one of the boys, when he wasn't really. I'm guessing – and I think I'm guessing correctly – that if he isn't out with a lawyer tonight, he's out with one of the footy girls. They all wear little blue and pink angora jumpers. And you're never quite sure who's going out with who, but they're always there. With the guys. At the pub. Hanging around.

The dog is still hanging around, too, in front of the toilets. They have those cheap fluorescent strip lights above the mirrors, and I look like shit. It's worse than looking at yourself in an aeroplane toilet. The red hair is still too red, the bits above the ears are still too short. I look about eighty, not thirty. And suddenly, I can't cry any more. I just don't have the energy.

So I crawl home, via the 7-11, where I pick up a tub of Homer Hudson ice cream and a video of *When Harry Met Sally*. Yes, I know. And I watch it all the way through, crying all the way through, and eating all the way through.

When Hilary rings from a phone box at midnight, just to check that I'm still alive, I say yes I am, and I'm going to bed.

But going to bed is the worst idea in the world at the moment. Think about it. Trying to go to sleep on an object where you used to have sex with the man who is now having sex with someone else. How can it possibly work? Why did I ever think it would?

Actually, as I toss and turn, it occurs to me that it's not the sex that's killing me. It's the intimacy. I'm sure Dan is doing his usual routine, pages two hundred to two hundred and five of *The Joy of Sex*, trying everything out with someone new, enjoying the buzz of being with a different body. Let's face it, a better body. Every woman who came before you, or comes after you, always has a better body. Fact.

But that stuff's just porn. It's like a cheap video. Any idiot can do it, and it's not what tortures me most. The thing that is keeping me awake, apart from the fact that I'm lying on the most unsuitable object in the world to sleep on, is this: the kissing. And the joking around. Kissing and joking around are me and Dan things, and the knowledge that he's now doing this with an angora jumper woman is enough to kill sleep for good.

At 2 a.m. I give up, get up, make a cup of tea and pad around the flat in my pyjamas. I don't want to wash up, I don't want to read the cellulite stories in women's magazines, and I don't want to watch *When Harry Met Sally* again.

So I switch on my computer. And it's amazing. The entire world is awake with me. American junk mail people are busily sending messages like MAKE $$$ NOW ASK ME HOW into my e-mail tray, and when I try out Usenet, there are pie recipes, and requests for Oasis singles, and filthy conversations about David Duchovny going on.

Then my computer makes that funny kind of rooster noise which means someone's just mailed me. Thank God for that, even if it is more American junk mail. But it's not. It's Liam.

To: shep@mpx.com.au
From: liam@ozemail.com.au
Subject: R U OK?

Hi Victoria. Sorry you couldn't stay. I know I'm crap on keyboards, but. Anyway. I'll see you. Liam.

And then, lying on my pillow a few minutes later, something strange happens. I see Liam's face when I close my eyes. And it feels good, somehow. Not right, not at all. But definitely, very, very good.

Six

I wait for the clock to click over to 7.30 a.m., then I call Kylie. Part of me feels totally humiliated to be hanging on the every word of a twenty-two year old in a micro-mini kilt, but I have to know.

'She was about so high, a bit taller than your friend, whatsername, Hilary, and they were in the front window of the pizza place. Sort of pretty. Not as pretty as you, though.'

I ignore this. It's Queensland schoolgirl talk.

'Where?'

'On Oxford Street.' Damn, just near his work.

'And what did it look like?'

'It looked like – you know.'

'Like they were on?'

'Yeah. She had a tattoo on her arm.'

Oh no. Not the Tattoo Lawyer.

'What of?'

'A rose or something.'

A rose or something. God help me. It is Tattoo Lawyer. She worked with Dan years ago. She used to wear little denim shorts to all their big legal barbecues and tell everyone about how she chose to defend bikies and junkies, because they were the real people. Every time I was introduced to her, she forgot me five minutes later. Maybe I wasn't a real person, I don't know. And now Tattoo Lawyer is sleeping with Dan. Or at least having dinner with him, which means sex can only be a few days away. That's how it is with Dan. No patience.

So I call him. It's amazing how punching in a phone number – a pathetic little fingertip exercise – can make your heart bang as if you're on army assault course. But I need the contact. I have to hear him.

After the usual nervous kick inside when he picks up the phone, we go on to have one of those very boring, miserably inhibited conversations that only newly separated people can manage. Lots of information ('I've got onto the Internet, I saw a band. We won the game last Saturday.') but never any of the things you really want to know, like – are you going insane without me, any chance of you reaching the stunning realization that we must immediately get engaged, etc etc.

And I need to know about Tattoo Lawyer, I desperately need to know, I think I might die if I don't find out. But I can't ask. And I don't ask, because that's not what happens in these conversations. And when he hangs up, I feel such a huge sense of loss that I end up crying again. Then I wash my face, put on foundation, put on eye pencil, then look at my face in the mirror and lose it a second time. I'm getting *Clockwork Orange* eyes. I look like hell.

Then I do something I thought I'd never do. I find a magazine, and call up a 1900 psychic. It's $3.95 a minute. The advertisement shows someone with badly drawn eyebrows, a plunging silver dress and a silver choker. Who knows, she probably doubles for the 1900 sex lines too. Is this mad week? Am I beginning one of Hilary's mad weeks?

That's partly why I'm ringing, though. Hilary had to know about the librarian, and they told her. And I have to know about Dan, and I want to be told. In some weird way, I do actually think I want the worst.

When I read out my credit card number on the line, I'm so dazed I put in too many fives, then when I do it again I drop off a nine. Hopeless.

'We will be introducing you to Cara today. She is one of our very best clairvoyants working here at Krystal Connections. She is just preparing and will be with you in just one moment. Please hold the line, Victoria.'

So I hold, thinking it's never too late to put the phone down, except they've got my credit card number now and they're mindreaders anyway, so I'm in trouble if I hang up. Then Cara (why am I trusting my life to someone called Cara?) comes on.

'Hello, Victoria, now I'm a clairvoyant, not a tarot card reader, and we tend to work a little differently. I won't be asking you to do anything, we're not going to look at any cards, I just want you to relax, focus, breathe, and we'll start your reading for you. Please focus.'

And I do, as much as you can when you've just rubbed foundation and tears into your eyes.

'Now you seem a little bit upset to me, are you upset?'

'Yes.' (Croak.)

'You know, Victoria, if we look at things in five years' time instead of the present, we can see things a little differently. And what I'm being asked to tell you now, and I do have my guide with me, is that this is not the end of the line for him.'

'For Dan?'

'Oh, well that's interesting, my guide tells me his name is Don. But it's Dan is it, oh well. He's quite a fit sort of chap, isn't he, he needs that outlet from work, doesn't he.'

'He plays football.'

'And that's how he lost one of his teeth, isn't it.'

What?

'No.'

Then I remember. He chipped his back tooth at uni, when he came out of a scrum the wrong way. He had a crown put on years ago.

'Anyway, what I would like you to concentrate on is the fact that there are many, many different relationship journeys that Dan will be taking. The one he is with now is not his final destination.'

'So they're together.'

'The one he is with now is not his final destination,' she repeats, making it sound like an announcement from CityRail.

'Can you see anything about her?'

'She's not his usual type of girlfriend. There is passion, but it will burn itself out.'

'And anything else?'

'She has a picture of a rose on her arm . . . You know Victoria, what I need you to remember at this time is that Destiny has many different things in store for us, and life is often what happens to us when we are making other plans.'

Shit. He's not coming back.

'There's an interest in computers, isn't there. That's going to be important.'

'I've got a computer.'

'Well, you hang onto that, Victoria. Would you like to continue this call, love.'

I can always use the rent money from the teapot.

'Yup.'

'You might like to take notes, a lot of people do that. Just so you don't forget. You've got a nice pen there, with a daffodil on the top of it, why don't you use that?'

Oh my God. The pen I bought on Daffodil Day last year. I hope she can't see me with eye make-up all over my face as well.

'I *have* got a daffodil pen.'

'Yes, love. I know you have. You're surprised that I can see these things, aren't you? Well, anyway, now that we've got you writing everything down, I can tell you that your computer is going to be very important in the next six months. Am I going slowly enough for you?'

'Yes.'

'But it's not for work. I can see you meeting new people, some very nice new people, through this computer.'

I scribble down computer – not work – nice people.

'Someone's sending me e-mail at the moment.'

'Yes?'

'He's sending me letters on the computer.'

'Oh, well that's very interesting.'

'Is it?'

'Ye-es. Because my guide tells me that you will meet your soulmate through these computer messages.'

'My soulmate?'

'Yes, we all have a soulmate, and when we are ready to find them, we will meet them.'

'Dan wasn't my soulmate?'

'He was what I call a fellow traveller on your journey,' she says, sounding like a CityRail platform announcement again. 'But, Victoria, I am talking about your *real* soulmate. And he is yet to come.'

79

She pauses, and coughs, rather un-spiritually.

'Do you want to continue the call, love?'

'How much has it been?'

'I'll just transfer you.'

Then a robotic voice tells me 'Cost of this call has been forty doll-ars and thir-ty cents.' Which is more of my teapot rent money than I can afford. But I think I know all I need to know. Or maybe I don't – but I feel calmer than I have for ages. So calm that I actually manage to put my foundation and eyeliner on all over again and go to work on a near-empty train for once.

'I told them you were coughing up blood,' says Kylie helpfully, when I get in just before lunch.

'Thanks.'

'I'm sorry about last night. I didn't think you'd be so upset.'

'I thought you had a psychology degree.'

You can see this going tick, tick, tick in her brain, somewhere above her earrings, then she finally gets it.

'Sorry. Sorry, Vicki.'

Actually, Kylie doesn't have a psychology degree. She has something called a human resources strand tacked onto a communications diploma. I think that's why they've hired her to write about Breakfast Grits.

'I think Liam likes you,' she offers by way of compensation.

'Why?'

You will meet your soulmate through your computer.

'He looked really miffed afterwards when I told him you'd gone home.'

So Liam looked miffed. That's interesting. Actually, that's more than interesting. And he e-mailed me too. All of which means that those eyes, those very dark eyes, have been staring into space somewhere and thinking about me. He's been thinking about me. And

80

I'm going to meet my soulmate through my computer. I've been on his mind.

It's funny how a push from one side can tip the other side just over the edge. It happened like that with Anthony Anderson. He'd been around forever, a kind of fixture on the friends-of-friends circuit, when he got slightly drunk one night and told me I reminded him of Scarlett O'Hara. I got out *Gone With the Wind* for the first time in my life after that, and watched it all the way through, replaying the bits where Vivien Leigh looked most sexy, and wondering hopefully if it was that bit, or that bit, that reminded him of me.

The next time I saw him, I noticed things that hadn't occurred to me before. Like the way he was always making people laugh, and how much his friends in the scuba-diving group liked him, and how he had a funny way of pushing his hair back with his hands when he was concentrating. After that, it was only a few more friends-of-friends dinners before Anthony Anderson and I were rolling around on the carpet next to his oxygen tanks.

The push-shove thing happened the other way with Leon Mercer. For ages he ignored me, probably because I was wearing wall-to-wall Country Road in those days, and he was an army surplus and Clash T-shirt kind of guy. Then one night I laughed at all his jokes and leaned in a bit closer to light his cigarette and it was his turn to be pushed over the edge by me.

I'd hate it to be like that with Liam, though. I don't want to fall in love with someone just because it's con- venient, just because he likes me, just because Cara thinks he's my soulmate. I'm always stuffing it up. I want to get it right. I can't take any more risks.

Then I see him weaving his way in from reception, and I know I'm going, going, gone. I still love Dan, always will, even if it's over and Cara is right. I love Dan so much that if the Devil turned up now and told me one of us had to be shoved into the mouth of a volcano, I'd still stick my hand up first. I love Dan so much that I can loathe him and still love him, in fact. But Liam . . . now there's something. Only something faint at the moment, but I'm encouraging it all I can. I'm coaxing it along like a walk with Pistachio the poodle, if you must know. It's better than the pain, it has to be. Better than looking forward to the divorced fortysomething male army.

And Liam's looking so strokeable in his suede jacket now, with every other female head bobbing gently in its partition box like a daisy as he passes by. He comes near us. He's smiling. Then he rushes straight past, flapping a manila folder around, and not even looking me in the eye.

'Hi, Victoria and Kylie. Bye, Victoria and Kylie.'

What?

Kylie pops up behind her screen and leans her head over the edge, with her mouth hanging open, making 'Did you see that?' faces.

And he really has gone, just like that.

'It's because you stood him up,' she hisses.

'It wasn't a date.'

'You should have stayed. He was brilliant. AWFOS were brilliant. It was so cute, they played the Decore song.'

'Well, if you hadn't told me about Dan . . .'

'I had to tell you, nobody else is going to tell you.'

'Yeah, five minutes before the band starts.'

'OK, I'll keep my mouth shut then.'

And as I think about Dan and Tattoo Lawyer something comes to me. Dan used to have this word he'd use, just to annoy me, and it comes back to me now.

Pert. Some *Baywatch* bimbo would be on the TV and he'd say, 'Well, she's quite pert, isn't she, Victoria?' And I'd pretend to throw a cushion at him, or grab the remote control, or something. It was an old, couple-ish kind of half-joke back then. But that word just makes me sick now. He told Tattoo Lawyer she was pert once, in front of me and a few other people at lunch. Some of them laughed. I didn't.

It's all I can do to stop myself ringing Cara again, and for the rest of the afternoon I'm torn between common sense (she told you you're going to find your soulmate, what more do you need to know?) and total, Hilary-styled, Mad Week addiction.

In the end I make off with the office mobile and call Hilary from the car park.

She's doing time in the Children's Library.

'I'm very busy,' she yells, over the top of a bunch of screaming kids.

'Sorry.'

'No, what is it, tell me, it's just that someone's been sick in one of the beanbags. And it's not the vinyl beanbag, it's the frigging velvet beanbag. Anyway, go on.'

'I rang up a psychic.'

'Oh no, Victoria, you know what happens!'

'I had to.'

'Who was it?'

'Cara.'

'Never heard of her.'

'Cara said it was true. Dan's with another woman. As in *with* her. Not with her. You know.'

'Yes, I know what you mean. No, Jason and David, I'm talking. Sorry. Oh no, that's terrible. I wonder if he took magic mushrooms or something and just lost his mind? Maybe you should call him.'

'No! And I know who it is – the new woman.'

'Yeesh. Who?'

'Tattoo Lawyer. Do you remember me telling you about her? She was at a lawyer's barbecue we all went to, and she had a rose tattooed on her arm, and she kept bending over in denim shorts a lot.'

'Oh no.'

'Cara said Dan would break up with her, and he'd go out with more people for five years.'

'And then you'll get back together?'

'No.'

'Was she sure? Oh no, what am I saying, those psychics are always sure.'

'But I am meeting someone. My soulmate. On the Internet.'

'Jason, go and empty the bucket please. Don't show me where someone's drawn something rude in that book, David, just go and get Mr Murphy to rub it out. No, I don't care about it, I've seen one before, it's a very natural part of the human body. Sorry, Vic . . .' She comes back to normality. 'What does she mean, on the Internet? Ooooh, not Mr Boxer Shorts!'

'It might be.'

'But that's fantastic!'

'But he's not talking to me.'

'Ego. All musicians have ego.'

'He's not a musician. He just thinks he is. I just saw him. He hates me.'

'Send him an e-mail.'

'I can't!'

'Look, Victoria,' Hilary puffs at last, 'You won't call Dan, you won't e-mail Liam, how is anything going to get better? Look, I've got to go. We're doing *Thomas the Tank Engine*. Just do me a favour, all right? Ring Dan and make sure Cara or whatever her name was got it right. And don't ring any more psychics. I went bankrupt on the psychics.'

Wandering back to my desk, it occurs to me that she might be right. I can't spend my whole life tortured by gossip given to me by a twenty-two year old with furry monsters stuck all over her partition window, or spooky information from Cara of Krystal Connections. I mean, come on. I'm mature. I'm thirty, I can take it. I have to know how I stand.

So I ring Dan at work. Big mistake. Huge mistake.

'I've got someone with me.'

'Just tell me quickly, I need to know if I've got it straight.'

'Yes.'

'Yes, you're seeing someone?'

'Yes.'

'Lawyer?'

'Yes. I'll have to call you later.'

'That woman with the tattoo.'

'Look, can we do this later?'

So it's official, and I'm damned for the rest of the year.

Pert body, pert sex, pert nose probably, pert little laugh, and even though I know something she doesn't know – thanks, Cara – it doesn't make me feel any better. This is the kind of anger that makes you physically shake. Can't lawyers crossbreed, or are they only capable of doing it with their own kind? They're worse than golden retrievers.

Seven

I have a couple of weekends to recover from the psychic and the Tattoo Lawyer episode when we're all called into a meeting at work. The Breakfast Grits Frisbees have arrived at last, and everyone who's been involved with the three-prong attack has been invited to troop on down to the local park and chuck them around.

I hate these jolly outdoorsy things they arrange. They made us have a tug-of-war day once, so that we could all 'pull together' – get it? – and bond with each other. Then they made us go abseiling last Christmas and Kylie nearly killed me by unravelling her rope from the wrong end.

Liam's not there, and I didn't expect to see him. He hasn't answered any of my e-mail since the disastrous night at the Crow and, according to the girl in Accounts, he's been in Perth doing a catalogue for BHP. Apparently. He's probably just ignoring all of us, and maybe even me, especially.

So we all drive down to the park, with the usual cardboard box of beer and cheap champagne and the bags of cheese-flavoured chips also made by – but, of course – the Breakfast Grits Frisbee people.

For some reason, Bobbi, the American project manager, starts singling me out for a private session.

'Hey, Vicki!'

She hurls the frisbee which looks, as I predicted, like plastic vomit from a trick shop. I miss. And while I'm stomping around behind trees looking for it, she comes over.

'We're very pleased with what you've been doing on this campaign, Vicki.'

'Thank you.'

'Sit down for a minute.'

Oh, I can't stand this. A business meeting disguised as a frisbee throw. It's typical ad-land bullshit. You know, making *human connections* in a relaxed, casual environment.

'You know they want us to do their other stuff, too?' she says.

I nod. That's what we do in this job, we nod.

'Kind of interesting this time round, because it's Slim n' Smile.'

Wow, not Slim n' Smile! Good grief, what is she crapping on about?

'They like what you did with the frisbee, so – Slim n' Smile. Hmmm? And Dennis would like to build a campaign around real people.'

'Who's Dennis?'

'You know Dennis. Look.'

She points and I can see him sitting on a blanket under a tree, a sort of cross between Pavarotti and that bloke with the glasses from *Neighbours*.

'What real people,' I ask, 'does that mean fat people?'

She laughs. Bobbi laughs like the sort of woman who finds toilet roll ads with little puppies in them hysterically funny, which is exactly the kind of woman she is.

'We have some extremely good real people talent,

once a little heavy, now very much trimmed down, as a result of Slim n' Smile.'

'Kind of before and after thing?'

'Very much so. And we would like the story behind the person, too. Come on. I'll show you.'

We wander over to 'meet with' as Bobbi describes it, the mighty Dennis, MD of Breakfast Grits, Chuckle Chips and – yes, inevitably – Slim n' Smile. If that's what he calls his food, I wonder what he calls his children? But, let's not argue with a company which shifts ten trillion units a year.

He's got that big gut, blue suit, bad tie, mobile phone, shiny car and side part that goes with the job. He doesn't look very comfortable on the rug – he's a restaurants man – and he looks even less comfortable making what seems like very small talk with the four women sitting next to him. I can't believe it. They're all eating jelly from Slim n' Smile containers.

'Vicki, these are some of the people I was telling you about. Margy, Robyn, Nadia and Debbie.'

'You can call me Deborah or Debbie, I don't mind,' says Deborah/Debbie.

'And of course you know Dennis,' Bobbi adds.

We both know I can't distinguish him from a petrol bowser, but I suppose we were introduced once, and he likes my frisbee slogans, so I reach for his right hand, smiling, and he swaps his mobile phone over to shake it – not smiling.

Then Bobbi trundles off, stomping off over the grass in her black stilletoes. Leaving me, in fact, to fend for myself.

'What we're after, Vicki, is the human angle,' says Dennis. 'I suppose Bobbi's been explaining it to you. Margy over here has a story to tell, Nadia has a story to tell, Debbie – now there's a story!'

Debbie/Deborah beams.

'And Robyn *certainly* has a tale for us,' Dennis finishes.

'Slim n' Smile saved my relationship,' says Margy, who has obviously been practising because someone's told her she's going to be on TV.

'I was a size twenty-two and I went down to a fourteen in less than six months,' says Nadia, with a mouth full of cottage cheese.

'Me too,' says Robyn, 'and my fiance says he wouldn't look at another woman now.'

And I have to say, although I have now had three plastic cups of champagne and a frisbee game with Bobbi, I am now beginning to get it. What we're talking about here is like a happy couples bank ad gone mad. We are talking Slim n' Smile strawberry jam helped me find my man. And just thinking of it makes me want to crawl up a tree.

'Now, I hear you're a single lady, Vicki,' says Dennis.

'No, actually. I'm not.'

I mean, really. It's none of his damn business, is it?

'Ah, I've been misinformed.'

Is there anyone in this agency who doesn't know about my love life?

'Anyway, Vicki, these are real-life love stories,' Dennis continues, 'and we have gone to a lot of trouble to find these ladies.'

In a perfect world, Jodie and Didi would appear at this moment with a gang full of chainsaw-wielding women and large pit bull terriers, but alas, it is just me, Margy in her sandals and floaty floral frock, Nadia in her fair-isle sweater, and Robyn and Debbie/Deborah gobbling down Slim n' Smile lime jelly.

'So, Margy,' I venture, 'would you say that Slim n' Smile saved your relationship?'

'Oh yes,' she nods, 'definitely. I had split up with someone, but he changed his mind after he saw how much weight I'd lost.'

They all laugh at this. Like, really. Hysterically funny story, don't you think?

'He even left the woman he was with,' adds Nadia wonderingly.

'So he left this other woman he was with,' I find myself saying stubbornly and semi-drunkenly, 'and he broke her heart, left her in the lurch, and came trotting back to you because you'd got a smaller bottom or something.'

'Well, it wasn't quite like that.'

'Well, I do have to know the details,' I say, in my most professional Senior Copywriter's voice.

'Well, *I* think it was true love between them,' Nadia says.

'And how old was he at the time?' I ask.

'Thirty-seven.'

'So what we're saying is, he was a pathetic old thirty-seven-year-old commitment phobic. Then you stopped being obese, so wham, he dumps the woman he's with to come back to you. Don't you have an awful feeling this could happen again, Margy?'

'Well, I wouldn't have called myself obese,' she says, her voice trailing off.

I'm losing the plot, now. I can hear it in my voice. Bobbi has been selling me to good old Dennis as Young Vicki The Agency Girl Genius, and here I am letting the side down. What on earth is happening to me? I can remember a time when I would have rushed to do this campaign. Slim n' Smile is a huge account. One of the biggest in the country. It's the kind of thing that hurls you up the ladder and gets you on the sort of monster salary that makes lawyers with tattoos look like rank amateurs. My God. And I think I've even made Margy the ex-fattie cry.

It's not about Margy and her love life at all. It's about me. Two things about me, actually. Jamie Streeton, the baseball-mad American I used to go out with, and my anorexia episode.

Jamie used to have this thing about his ex-girlfriend. She was in the local women's hockey team, which a mate of his used to coach, and every Saturday morning over winter, I would be stuck at home ploughing into grated carrot, half a slice of dry white toast and two litres of water while he was at the game. She had great thighs. She used to wear a ponytail. It used to bounce up and down when she ran.

Nothing would stop Jamie turning up to all her matches. We used to go and see a film on Friday night, he'd come back to my place, we'd have sex, then he'd wake up the next morning, use my shower, use my shampoo, use my towels, pull his clothes on and drive off to her game – just for a bit of friendly support, ho ho ho – and how could you have a problem with that, Victoria? What are you, paranoid? Anyway. It was the match reports that used to get to me.

'How was it?' I'd ask lamely, trying to be cool about it and failing.

'Not a bad match at all, they're a fit team. Very fit. They wound down in the first half. But they re-covered.'

In other words, I used to think, miserably weighing tuna cans and adding up kilojoules, he's still in love with her. And she's got better legs than me. And what can I do about it? Nothing. Unless I want to come across like a screaming jealous harpie. They had a great double act. I saw it at a party once, a kind of gruesome baseball and hockey party. She'd give him a progress report on her latest boyfriend, in a jokey, matey kind of way and he'd say things like, 'Ha ha, guy sounds like a total loser' – also in a jokey, matey kind of way. You know. Meanwhile, as Hilary said, they were looking at each other like Romeo and Juliet on their death bed.

And was Jamie Streeton really in love with his ex, with the thighs and the ponytail when he should have been in love with me? There were Saturday nights he'd organize with her and not with me ('You don't have a problem with that, do you, Victoria?') and she and her friends used to act as if they were still together. But after all these years, though, I have to say no, I don't think he was ever in love with her. I think he was in love with himself at the end of the day.

Actually, that's a Jamie catchphrase too. I can hear him now, in his New York drawl, saying, 'At the end of the day, Victoria, the Yankees are useless without a good manager' and, 'At the end of the day, I'm just friends with her, nothing more.' So, at the end of the day, I think I can safely say that Jamie was so terrified of losing the delicious thrill of pulling the emotional strings of two women at once that he was happy to let me go on being miserable and grating carrots and half-starving myself while he gave her, you know, friendly after-match hugs in the pub. Did he ever notice that I was falling into an eating disorder? I doubt it. Not when the Yankees were playing the Boston Red Sox or something. Not when one of her hockey games was on.

Amazing. All these years later and it still kills me to think about it. Spending half of winter staring at pictures of models in magazines and hating myself. And being so pleased with myself for having this kind of huge ridge in my collarbone, sticking out a few inches below my throat. A true sign of progress, I thought, after a couple of weeks of celery and spinach soup (no salt), the occasional orange, a 5km jog, and a couple of litres of water a day. Borderline anorexic? Not me. Ha.

Bobbi is pounding over the grass now. She's not psychic the way Cara from Krystal Connections is psychic, but she has this kind of corporate nose. It's like a cat who automatically sniffs upwards when the fridge door opens. In her case, it's a matter of sniffing professional disasters from a distance of fifty metres.

'So, how're we doing, Vicki, I'm going to have to drag you away for a minute.'

'I'm not doing it,' I hiss, when we're far enough away.

'Well, I can see that. Why don't we sit here and talk about it.'

'In your car.'

'OK.'

Bobbi's not so bad, really, it's just that she spent the whole of her life watching vacant American TV in New Jersey. She smiles and puts her head on one side like Mrs Brady, and holds her eyes wide in surprise, like The Flying Nun, and puts her hands on her hips like the hard-rockin' mother in *The Partridge Family*. Kylie likes her, by the way. So do I. Or maybe I just feel sorry for her, sad old charming fortysomething that she is.

'Bobbi, I can't do it.'

'You don't have to do it, honey.'

'I just broke up with my boyfriend. No. He broke it off with me. He's got someone else. Actually that's got nothing to do with it, but. Oh shit, can I have a tissue?'

And I cry, and I cry. And she gives me some menthol-scented tissues from her glovebox, which I snort into until the mint goes up my nose and makes the tears grind to a halt.

'And I nearly had anorexia once,' I find myself

rattling on. 'Actually – whatever, I had it. I had anorexia. And my periods stopped.'

'Mmm.'

'I used to eat that shit they're eating. I'd have some of that Slim n' Smile jelly, then I'd do fifty sit ups and have stomach ache.'

'Yes.'

'I'm not doing it.'

'No.'

Bobbi pauses and sighs, and out of the front window we can both see Kylie, running and flapping her arms around, and tearing towards the car with a Breakfast Grits Frisbee in her hand.

Bobbi winds down the window.

'Busy, Kylie. We'll be right out.'

She puts her hand over the top of mine. It looks nothing like mine. It's got a tan, and a whopping diamond wedding ring, and long shiny red nails.

'My sister had an eating disorder,' she says. She pronounces it 'dis-order.'

'Well, then.'

'But you met these women, Vicki, they are happy.'

'Can't do it.'

'Well,' she says, 'somebody else will, you know that.'

And I do know that. But I don't have it in me to even go back up there and say sorry. I expect they'll give the job to Kylie. That's probably why she was racing over.

'Anyway. You clean up.'

Bobbi has a Chanel quilted cosmetics bag with tiny face-freshener sachets, I kid you not, and a matching Chanel powder compact which she generously lets me wallow in.

'Thanks.'

Then I get out of the car and find Kylie, who has

stopped flapping her arms and is talking to Liam. Liam! Who I had no idea I would be so glad to see.

I'm embarrassed about my blotchy face, so I fluff my hair around it – as much as a uselessly spiky red haircut can fluff, anyway.

'Does anyone want more champagne?' asks Kylie, and obligingly trots off.

Liam looks at me. Hard.

'You've been in Perth,' I say, uselessly.

'You noticed.'

I don't know him well enough to ask what's wrong, but I do anyway.

'Look at it from my point of view,' he says, chucking a frisbee rather aggressively in the direction of the pond.

'What? I sent you God knows how many e-mails . . .'

And I did, bastard.

'Did you?'

I look at his face, then I think about it a bit more. E-mail. Me. New computer. Technobimbo. Oh no.

'Well, I did write them, but if you didn't get them . . .'

'I ask you to the gig, you walk out, I don't hear from you, well . . .' he shrugs.

And then he mumbles something about always lusting after bitches, or maybe it was always lusting after sandwiches, and wanders off.

Eight

When you've spent most of your adult dating, bonking life getting used to the fact that around thirty per cent of men are incapable of calling back, it's quite a shock to realize that you can stuff them around too. And if I look at things from Liam's point of view, they look pretty bad. He asks me to the pub – OK, along with half the micro-mini kilt-wearing population of Sydney, but he does ask me – and I bail out. Then he doesn't hear from me at all, due to my technobimboism. From his point of view, I do indeed look like a cold-hearted bitch.

I owe him an explanation. Not just about the e-mail that never arrived, but about Dan, because if I'm ever going to start anything with Liam, Dan's going to have to be explained somewhere along the line. So I ring him, and after a lot of embarrassed mumbling and more Avon Lady-styled 'ha ha ha' from me, we decide to pick up some takeaway and have lunch in the Botanic Gardens. I'm not exactly sure if you can drink alcohol there, but we're definitely going to need it, so I pick up a bottle anyway.

He's late, and I'm early. So I have around twenty minutes to stare mindlessly at all the long botanical descriptions of various trees. How useful it would be if people came with the same classifications. Imagine. Daniel Hawker = Emotionus Cretinous. Jamie Streeton = Femalus Manipulatus. Phillip Zebruscki = Phallus Obsessus. Think how much time Hilary and I would have saved since 1982 (the beginning of our dating lives), if men had come with little metal tags on their heads, like trees.

Then he appears, and he's had the same idea about wine. And I don't know, maybe we should get pissed, perhaps that's the only way either of us is going to solve anything.

We sit under a tree, throwing bits of bread at the occasional ugly ibis, and a seagull doing ballet, and I have a plastic cup of his riesling.

'I'm sorry about all this,' I say.

'That's all right.'

'I did want to see you play. It wasn't that. But just before, Kylie told me she saw my ex out with someone else. And I lost it. I had to leave.'

'Ah. The ex.'

Something about Liam makes you want to tell him things, and I do. In fact, I can't stop.

'I met him through work. Before they got their own lawyer there, they had Dan. And I wasn't even looking for a relationship, I was too shell-shocked, I did this head count one day and realized I'd had five relationships and too many one night stands, and I just had to be single for a while. Well, that was the theory, anyway.'

'So you thought you'd be single.'

'And I met him. And I forgot about my friends completely, and went off on this incredible love affair. Relationship. You know how the first three months is the most insane?'

He nods, and it's hard to tell if he does or not.

'I couldn't let go of Dan at all. Just couldn't. The football club got this big bus trip together, and everyone went, and I spent the whole trip buried in his arms on the back seat, woffle, woffle, woffle into his shoulder. It was a primitive thing, like gorillas or something.'

'Woffle, woffle, woffle?' Liam asks.

'It was the way it's meant to happen. Bang, we met at this party, and within the first ten minutes I was totally hooked. And every party after that, I used to half kill myself trying to work out if he'd be there or not. It was like being a detective. I used to piece together all the clues, you know. If someone from this circle of friends is turning up, then that means this person will turn up, which might mean he'll be there.'

'So how did you get together?'

'Alcohol. It was the only way. It was just so obvious between us, every time we met up you could practically see this huge red arrow pointing to both our heads, you know – THIS MAN AND WOMAN MUST GET TOGETHER. And when it's obvious like that, you get too embarrassed about it, so you just don't do anything. Then we had a bottle of Scotch together one night, and I fell over and he picked me up.'

'How romantic.'

'I wish it were a better story. But that's really how it was.'

The pretence now is that Liam is a disinterested outsider, and I'm just telling him this stuff as a friend, in a very cool nineties male-female way, and neither of us have an interest in each other at all. Which is total bullshit, but almost every relationship I've ever had has gone through this little piece of play-acting. And, as I sit here telling Liam all this, part of me is wondering about how much more I should reveal.

We both know what we're really discussing. This is not lunchtime banter in the park. This is like a job interview. It's a relationship interview. I'm thirty, he's a few years on from that, we're beyond the stage where you can just stuff around and go to bed with people — or I think we are. This is what police might call the preliminary investigation. I'm trying to persuade Liam that I'm not a mad cow, and he's trying to suss me out. He's trying to persuade me that he's cool enough to be able to listen to stories about another man, and I'm trying to show him what I'm really like. Which is vulnerable, I suppose, particularly when riesling is swishing around in my bloodstream.

And then — let's be honest — I'm trying to conceal a lot of other stuff. The main story, in fact. Which is not so much how Dan and I got together, or even why we stayed together for such a long time, it's more about why he left.

I'm sure even the ibis would be shocked. Because I tried to get pregnant behind his back. That's really what it amounts to. Dan went off with his family to Bali, and I missed him like hell, and when he came back I screwed up the foil pill packet in a brown paper bag, put it inside another bag, and threw it in the bin in the bathroom. What did I think I was doing? I don't know. Maybe my hormones do.

When my period arrived I had the worst PMS I've ever had in my life — almost as if my body was acting out everything for me. And then I calmed down a bit, and actually thought about things, and went straight back to the chemist to pick up my next prescription.

For around two weeks, I could have had Dan's baby. Goodbye career. But at the time, I couldn't think of anything I ever wanted more. I had this little film running in my head — feeling sick at breakfast, going to the doctor, getting the result, turning up to surprise him at work. In the film, he always whirled me around in his arms and raced out to buy me flowers. And in real life? Well, you work it out.

I suppose most people would have forgotten all about it after that, got on with their lives, and Dan would never have known, and maybe our relationship would have trundled along quite happily. But two weeks before my birthday, we had a fight about something stupid that became a fight about something even worse – babies.

How do arguments escalate like that? You start with a bit of whining over the fact that he likes Quentin Tarantino and you think he's a jumped-up video shop attendant, and he thinks Pistachio is a great name for a dog, and you don't, then it somehow leads to 'Yeah, well, I threw my pills in the bin.' Funny about that.

Of all the arguments I have had with Daniel Hawker, that was the only one that didn't end up on the couch with a bra on the floor. Instead, it ended up never being discussed again. Ever.

Then not long after that, I got the birthday card with the little message about me turning into a wonderful old lady.

And with Liam sitting opposite me now, I can only think: I wonder how much crap we'll have to go through in the name of love? More importantly, can I do it again?

'So do you want any more of this?'

Liam's smiling at me, holding the wine up. He still looks great when he smiles, like the kind of man who is automatically your friend and could, with a little more imagination, become your lover too. But there's more to it than that these days, and I can't go back.

At twenty-two, I could quite happily go out with

someone like him, and turn up to see his band, and go for drunken picnics and bounce around in bed until the inevitable breakup. I have, however, been corrupted and I don't really think I can do it any more. At thirty, it's finally happened, I'm incapable.

'Liam, I have to tell you something.'

He nods.

'And I wouldn't unless I was pissed, which I am.'

'You're not that pissed.'

'It's just that I could go off and have a fling with you, and that would be fine, but I can't do it any more.'

'No?'

'You should have met me ten years ago, I could do it then.'

'What are you trying to say?'

'Liam, is there any chance you might be a relationship retard?'

'Of course I am.'

'You know what I mean, though, don't you?'

'What do you want, a note from my mother?'

'I can't – bonk.'

'What about a shag, then?'

'Oh, go away.'

And I march off to the loo, wondering vaguely if he'll still be there when I get back. Hilary always says the litmus test of drunkenness is talking to yourself in the toilet mirror, and I do, shocking an old lady who shoots out of the cubicle like a rocket and disappears.

'You've blown it,' I tell the mirror.

But when I stumble back over the grass, Liam's waiting for me, and he even squeezes my arm. We're lying together, side by side, in what Jodie would call Acceptance Body Language.

'Glad we had this little chat,' he says gravely. God, he's sexy.

'Tell me something,' I say at last. 'Why is this so bloody funny?'

'Because it is. Look, if we end up sleeping together, fine. You're doing this – thing. This analysing thing.'

'Am I?'

'Yes. Stop thinking so hard. And let's go and get a coffee and sober up.'

And we do, and I look at my watch and it's half past bloody three.

'I shouldn't say this,' he says suddenly.

'Yes?'

'I think you need to be careful at work. They're kind of watching you.'

'Oh that. I thought you were going to say something nice. You know.'

He laughs.

'Love tis of man's life a thing apart, tis woman's whole existence,' I quote, probably wrongly, and that's where we leave it. Where most men and women leave it at the beginning. Nowhere.

Nine

I'm supposed to meet Hilary for a shopping session on Saturday morning, and I completely forget. When she knocks on the door, I'm still in my grey dressing gown, playing with the computer. There's this thing called Find A Friend File which is the saddest thing I've ever seen in my life, but it's completely addictive.

There are five men seeking women in Afghanistan, and one woman seeking man in Algeria, and eighteen men seeking men in Australia, and a couple of lesbians in Aberdeen. So anyway, I click on Men Seeking Women, Age 21, just to see if I can do a Susan Sarandon and pursue the older woman, younger man scenario (which as everyone in Women's Circle knows is the way of the future, as they are more evolved, have feminist mothers, etc. etc.).

Anyway, they're all crap. 'I love a good time, if you like to party, get in touch . . .' That's from someone called Bronzed of Bondi. Gender, male. Race, caucasian. Star sign, Virgo. Body type, athletic. Looking for, woman for friendship. Occupation, atheist. What? Apparently, if I want to add him to my hot list I must become a member. There's also a thirty-five year old called Wildman who says he likes listening to Mike Oldfield.

'Wow, that's really wild, Wildman,' says Hilary, when she turns up. 'I suppose you know I waited half an hour for you.'

'Sorry. I'm really sorry, Hil. My brain's just turned to mush.'

'Anyway, let me have a go on it.'

That's one of the reasons Hilary and I have stayed friends all these years – her short attention span. She is pleased to see that the Find A Friend File has a woman-seeking-woman option, and wants to print it out to take back to the Circle (it's become the Circle now, apparently) where most of the women are, you guessed it, seeking women. Then she sees a 42-year-old man from Michigan and becomes thoroughly over-excited.

'He likes *Koyaanisqatsi* and *Powaqqatsi*, they're my favourite films of all time!'

'Yes, but he's a non-smoker. And he lives on the other side of the world. And he wants a woman he can be playful with. Did you read that bit? Playful.'

'Oh, my God. Go somewhere else.'

So we spend the next hour in the cosmetics newsgroup, arguing about the world's best waterproof mascara, and then we go to a CD site and order cheap US import copies of *The Best of Blondie,* and then we go somewhere else and register our names for automatic e-mail birthday greetings so we'll feel loved.

I send a message to Bill, telling him to come downstairs, but there's no reply.

'I don't think Bill exists,' Hilary says.

'You'll meet him.'

'He's just a cyber-hologram.'

Finally, we tear ourselves away from the Net and

take the bus into town to find Hilary a new navy blue jumper, as the old one has little knobbly bits on it, and me something under thirty dollars, which is all I've got left for fun money this weekend.

We end up, as always, in The Body Shop.

'I turned down a campaign for diet crap.'

'Good for you,' Hilary says, her nose stuck in a tester. 'Hey, smell this, it's great. Why did you turn it down?'

'That's men's deodorant you've given me. I turned it down because – you know why.'

'Oh, that.'

Hilary was part of the anorexia and Jamie Streeton winter. Hilary was the one who looked at me back-on in her bedroom, when we were getting changed to go out one night and noticed my spine had gone knobbly through my skin. She rang my parents.

'Do you think this face mask is any good?' she asks suddenly.

'Hilary, no.'

'Why not?'

'The love of your life will knock on your door and you'll answer it with a banana face.'

'What about one of these wooden massage rollers?'

'You'll never use it.'

'It's for a good cause. They make them in the jungles.'

'Just roll a piece of Lego over yourself.'

'Cellulite mitt?'

'Try liposuction.'

I feel sorry for men. They will never know what it is to have the free entertainment of The Body Shop, where you can spend thirty minutes trawling around with your nose stuck in a pot of marmalade body scrub, and unlikely looking green colour corrector all over your face.

Actually, men will never know the pleasure of shopping full stop. Oh, I know they make pathetic attempts at it, wandering around hardware stores looking for bolts, and loitering in secondhand record shops. But they seldom really enjoy the bliss of trying on, viewing and totally rejecting.

Hilary does it about eleven times while she's looking for her navy blue jumper. She puts ten of them back on the rack, on these grounds:

1) Makes boobs look saggy.
2) One hundred per cent acrylic.
3) Overpriced, yet sewn by Asian outworkers.
4) Looks like it could be HM The Queen's navy blue jumper.
5) Looks wrong in the light.
6) Strangling neckline.
7) Creeps up when she lifts her arms.
8) Looks like it might shrink.
9) Too scratchy.
10) Too sexy for the library.

Part of the fun of the viewing and rejecting is that you can voice all these objections in a very loud voice, thus taking revenge on the shop assistants who, as every woman knows, just get in the damn way.

We then go to the newsagency and flick very fast while standing up.

'Look, there's one of your ads, Vic.'

It's something I wrote for a yoghurt campaign so long ago that I can hardly remember if it was before Dan or during Dan, which is the way I measure time at the moment.

'Mmm,' Hilary says. 'I feel like yoghurt right now. Especially if it's DREAMY and CREAMY.'

'Oh, shut up.'

I end up buying an expensive English import copy of *New Woman,* just because I like the horoscope (Gemini: Expect an exhilarating rush in your sex life around the 27th) and then we slag off the fashion in some Italian magazine, also in very loud voices, which is almost more fun than baiting shop assistants.

'What – is – that – woman – wearing?'

'What drugs are these designers on?'

This is another part of life that men can never indulge in – look at their side of the magazine racks, it's all *Steam Train Monthly* and bad porn.

'Those pathetic "new man" magazines,' sniffs Hilary. 'What a load of crap, Vic, I hope your yoghurt ad isn't in them.'

'Am I hearing a Women's Circle discussion coming on?'

'Dirty old men in new man's clothing. Think they can run a few articles on testicle cancer and mountain bikes and it makes everything all right. Look at this woman with her tits out.'

'Exactly,' I sniff. Even though I know Liam buys them.

And so it goes. We whiz through Lush, trying not to eat the chocolate massage bars, and Hilary blows all her money on pink bath bombs with lotto numbers hidden inside them. Then we end up in one of those brasseries where the waitresses all have no make-up on, because they all have stunning skin.

And I'm just about to tell Hilary that we should go and eat somewhere else because the mushroom risotto is fourteen dollars ninety-five when I see Dan, by himself, reading the menu.

Ten

They say you can believe in parallel universes because, when tiny particles split, there is a fraction of a second when they haven't broken apart. They're in two places at once, in fact – a parallel universe. I know this because Bill the Boffin tried to explain it to me on the stairs one day.

And right now, I'm thinking about all the little universes that must be going on here. There's the world where I walk over to Dan and say hi. And there's the world in which I get up with Hilary and walk out. Another, less possible, universe sees Dan and me racing across the floor waving our arms around like Cathy and Heathcliff, knocking the waitress over. An unlikely option.

In the end, Hilary goes over and asks him if he feels like joining us, and he does.

Dan could never remember anything about Hilary or her life when we were together, and he can remember even less now we're apart. He concentrates on her as a way of avoiding me, but he asks all the wrong questions.

'How's the aromatherapy class?'

'I don't do aromatherapy,' she says, jamming her lips together.

It's so awful and strained that a few minutes later Hilary decides she bought the wrong navy blue jumper after all.

'If I go back to David Jones I can get there before it shuts,' she says. Which is rubbish because it's two blocks away and she has hours.

'Anyway, I'll be off,' she says finally, in the same kind of voice she uses when she's flushing kids out of the children's library for the day. And then we're alone if you can call it alone when the waitresses are hovering and the conversations around you are blaring.

'Still the same,' Dan says. He means Hil.

'She's my support system.'

'Well, you're lucky.'

'Tell me something. Is that why men do it?'

'Do what?'

'Race off with the first woman that comes along.'

'Meaning?'

'Oh, don't be such a lawyer.'

I wait for him to walk away. He doesn't. He sits, and stares, and smiles.

'You mean, do men need a woman because they don't have that support from their friends?'

'Yes.'

'That might be part of it.'

I think of that idiot in the football club who used to call him Dan the Man, and feel sorry for him. And I think of his brothers, whose main method of support seems to be clipping each other around the head. But most of all, I think about him with her.

'So, she's not with you then.'

'Well, in twenty minutes,' he says, looking at his watch.

Suddenly, it's all become sickeningly real. I wonder

what she's doing. Getting another tattoo? Having a chat with the Hells Angels?

'God, I hate Sydney.'

'Why? You used to love it.'

'It's so bloody small. Everyone I know lives in the same street, practically. I wish I lived in—' I try to think of somewhere big, and fail. 'I hate – running into people.'

I'm fighting the urge to cry now. And he's reaching out to me. What else can he do? He's not a bastard and never was. I tried to get pregnant behind his back, and it was the wrong thing to do, and there wasn't enough of the good stuff there for him to forgive me. That's it.

'I can't stand it, Dan.'

'Which part?'

'The jealousy. No, not that. The insult. I feel like I've come off a conveyor belt. You can just switch everything over to her, just like that?'

'You're very moral, aren't you.'

'Well there should be rules, there are rules.'

He shakes his head.

'Nope. No rules.'

'Do you love her?'

He smiles, and doesn't answer.

'I love you.'

An idiot waiter is hanging around with one of those big cracked pepper grinders for my sandwich, and Dan flicks him away, and I smudge off all my streaming black mascara with the side of my thumb.

'Come on, let's go.'

He propels me by the elbow to the counter, and somehow we make it up the street, past a Japanese tour group, past lots of people with big plastic bags which knock against my legs, and into the safety of his car.

Seeing it is another blow. It's a Rover with a dent in the front and football stickers all over the back window, part of our old life together, and something we laughed in, screamed in, listened to the Happy Mondays in, and had sex in. Cars have always reminded me of the men I've been with. I can tick off the list now – Greg Daly – white Volkswagen, Philip Zebruscki – green Honda Civic, Jamie Streeton – blue Mazda, Leon Mercer – old Holden that never left the kerb, Anthony Anderson – white Jeep.

Being in the front seat of the Rover now only makes me think of Tattoo Lawyer and I start crying again. He's already on his mobile phone, fixing it with her. He doesn't call her by name, but I know it's her. He has an utterly professional conversation – as if they were both talking about a client – and I'm guessing that she's guessing what's happened. And naturally, she's being very mature and understanding about it. Very cool. Very adult. I want to kill her.

'So you've both got mobiles then.'

'Yes. Aren't we wankers?'

'Can I just say one thing about her?'

He sighs. A heavy sigh. An 'oh, all right then' sigh which is so familiar it's almost like being back together again.

'I'm just surprised. Is it a reaction against me?'

'Erica and I have been friends for a long time.'

'Erica. Now I remember.'

'She's not that different from your other friends.'

'What other friends?'

'You know, Jodie, that lot. It's not a reaction against you.'

'Can't see her turning up to the football.'

'No, and it's not that kind of friendship.'

'Oh, it's friendship is it?'

'Yes.'

'That has to be the biggest piece of bullshit I've ever heard.'

'Yeah, well. It's accurate.'

'You are having sex with her and you both call that friendship, do you?'

'Vic, you're beginning to get a sound in your voice that you know I hate.'

'Tell me the truth.'

'We are not sleeping together.'

'But you will. So, that's not a friendship. Is it?'

He shakes his head at me.

'If you hate that sound in my voice,' I hear myself saying, 'let me tell you something, I hate that intellectual superiority pose you pull.'

And he doesn't even answer that one.

'You're so right, and I'm so wrong, you're so bloody sussed about everything, and I'm such a bimbo.'

'I didn't say that. It's just that sound in your voice, it's just very hard to talk to you when you . . .'

'LIKE THIS?' And I scream it so loudly that people in other cars with the windows down can probably hear me.

We drive in silence. And part of me wants to be back in the parallel universe where Hilary and I walked straight out, past his table, and through the door. There's an awful kindness about him, a terrible kind of good-humoured, patronizing, philosophical kind of thing going on. It's the mark of a man who's already got me in a basket marked, Dear Old Victoria, and I hate it, I hate it. It kills hope.

When we hover for a parking spot outside the flats, Bill is edging his car out.

'God, that guy's a shit driver,' Dan says. And he catches me off guard for a moment, and I laugh. Then

Bill looks at me through the window and quickly turns away in embarrassment, so I know I must look even worse than I feel. He waves Dorrigo-ishly, and drives off.

'Remember him?' I say, hearing myself sounding almost normal again. 'He moved in upstairs. Bill the Boffin. He's been helping me with my computer.'

'Someone should help him with that thing on his face.'

'His Elastoplast, there's no-one to rip it off for him, I keep trying to fix him up with Hilary but it's always going wrong.'

The words are rushing out of me, with little giggles. And Dan seizes the moment, anything to stop me crying. I'd forgotten how much he hated me crying.

'So, are you buying your first Porsche yet?'

This is an old joke between us, a very old joke, and it's not even funny. I had a crappy old bomb years ago, and I ran it into a power pole and it wouldn't go after that, so I left it where it stood, and the council fined me, and when I told Dan the story when we first met, I said very stupidly that I planned to buy a Porsche soon. So that's it. That's our old joke. That's what he's now resorted to in an attempt to – ha, ha, ha – cheer me up.

However. I'll have my little private torture alone in bed tonight, thinking about Erica's tattooed arm and wondering if other bits of her are tattooed as well. So I want him to feel all of my pain – preferably every bit of it – now. I won't be denied. I know Dan's terrified of me in a way, feels almost sick at my grief, but I won't be fobbed off so that he can feel better about himself.

We go up to the flat and I unlock it, feeling him watch my back and wanting him to reach out for me, but he doesn't. Rule Two of splitting up. No matter how much you want them to call, they never will. No matter how much you want them to grab you, they never do.

Then we're inside. You can see my unmade bed through the door and I wish like hell there was a blond, spiky-haired man leaning up against the pillows, but there isn't, there's just my usual mess and a packet of tampons on the floor.

'So, I've put off lunch with Erica,' he says finally.

'So?'

'So we can talk. About this. Maybe you can meet her one day, realize she's a human being.'

I snort.

'A yuppie pretending to be something she's not.'

He ignores me. I feel about six years old, childishly hurt now, and I suppose that's what's turning him into a sixty-something. He's wise, I'm demented. I wonder what would have happened in our relationship if I'd tried the act he's pulling now? Would it have ended with him pulling his hair out and having tantrums?

'Don't tell me you've never broken up and found someone new,' he says, finally.

And if I go back, back, back I suppose that might have happened, somewhere between Greg Daly heading off with Annalise the German Exchange Student, and me ending up in a tent, God help me, with someone else in the Wilderness Walks group, a man who smelled of roll-your-own cigarettes. But this is different.

That was a sleeping bag, and a bottle of Scotch, and a starry night. This feels nothing like it. In spite of Cara the amazing daffodil-pen spotting psychic, the only thing I can think of right now is Erica and Dan moving in together. Achieving what I used to think was the impossible, in fact. They'll have weird expensive paintings up everywhere. They'll have dinner parties. She'll find all my old letters to him one day and won't even care.

It's funny how few details you need to fill out a whole picture of someone. I can count what I know about her on one hand. She's a lawyer. She has a tattoo on the top of her arm. Her name is Erica. She used to make cocaine jokes and wear denim shorts at lawyers' barbecues. She thinks she's got a social conscience.

I leave Dan on the couch while I go to the loo, and think about her. I expect half the men in court lust after her. I suppose she left home when she was sixteen to backpack around Berlin, unlike me, whose greatest adventure at that age was a coach tour to the Hunter Valley with my Aunty Beth. I can see her holding forth brilliantly at dinner with Dan, arguing the case for the legalization of heroin. I expect she has another lover stashed away in New York somewhere. I suppose she gives half her salary to the Black Panthers.

I look at my bathroom. Toilet cleaner, terrible old pink plastic toilet brush, make up all over the sink, and a stupid shower curtain with dancing clam shells all over it. I can see her bathroom. Sunken bath. Aveda environmentally sound bath oil. Black silk dressing gown. Really, how can I blame Dan, he'd be mad to say no. But I do.

And when I go back in, he shuffles himself to the furthest corner of the couch it's possible to reach, just so that we won't be sitting – you know – too close to one another. This is how we started out, at other ends of my couch. But back then it was pure electricity that was getting in the way, not the kind of dead air that's separating us now.

'Victoria,' he says at last, using my full name, my proper name. 'I cannot watch myself not liking you any more, because I like you too much. Yes, I am fond of you. Yes, you do matter to me. You do.'

'Say that again, you can't watch yourself not liking me, because you like me?'

He nods.

'So this is liking, is it. I put all that energy in, and I end up with *like*. Is this the kind of like where you still see me?'

'You know that's not going to work.'

'So you like me too much not to like me any more, and you don't want to see me. Hmmm. How long did you spend working on that one?'

He gets up, and I think for an awful minute that he's going to leave, but he brings back a glass of water – one each, for both of us.

'I wish you hadn't just ended it like that on my birthday. That's all.'

'It had to end some time.'

'Why?'

'Because – why do you keep on with this? I don't feel right for you. You don't feel right for me. Why push it?'

'You do feel right for me.'

'Oh, so chuck your pills in the bin and try to get pregnant.'

He shakes his head again, looking at an old red wine stain on the carpet left by Hilary last year some time.

'I never talked to you about that,' he says, 'and I should have done.'

'It might have helped.'

'It would have helped end it sooner, yes, and that might have been a good thing given where we are now. It wouldn't have changed anything. I do want you to get that through your head. Our relationship didn't go bust because you decided in your wisdom to try and get pregnant behind my back.'

'What then?'

'Retrace your steps. No, you didn't end up pregnant in the end, but if you had, what do you think might have happened?'

'Tell me.'

'What were you expecting?'

'I don't know.'

This flat has seemed lonely to me in the past few weeks, it's been too quiet when I get home from work, and it's been grey and dark and deadly when I get up in the middle of the night. But right now I've never been more grateful that I don't have flatmates. This is the most desperately private conversation I've ever had in my life.

'I did want to have a baby with you.'

And he says nothing at all, just gets up and brings back a box of tissues from my bedroom – the bedroom where there is no blond spiky-haired man, just a chaotic mess and a photo of him on the inside of my wardrobe door that I still can't bear to take down.

'Here, blow your nose.'

I do, and half the green Body Shop colour corrector comes off on the tissue. I suddenly realize what I must look like to him. New red hair, new spiky red hair, red eyes, red and green face.

'So tell me again. What if I had got pregnant?'

'But you didn't. That's a non-question.'

'But if I did?'

'Your call.'

'Would you have had it with me?'

'Non question. But I can tell you this much. The fact that I don't feel passionately one way or the other, now that's a definite worry. And the fact that you hadn't even considered that – what do you think a baby is, a one-way street?'

And then it's his turn to rub out a tear. And in all the time I've been with Daniel Hawker, I can honestly say I've never seen it. What is it that we do to men that they lose the ability to cry?

I saw a mother doing it to her son in a ladies' loo once. He was still at the age when he could be dragged into the same toilet as all the women, and he was snuffling and crying while his mother kept pulling more and more toilet paper off the roll to mop his face. First she said, 'Don't cry' and then it became, 'Cheer up Nathan' and then eventually it turned nasty, and became 'Stop that, you're a big boy.' If she'd hit him, I would have said something, but she didn't, and I dried my hands and walked out, feeling like I finally understood something.

Boys Don't Cry, as Robert Smith used to sing on all my old Cure compo tapes. But here's the evidence, right in front of me, now. I'm looking at someone who I've loved, fought with, hurt and horrified by turns and although he's feeling something – it's better than nothing – it still adds up to one small tear rubbed out before it has a chance to become anything more.

'I'm sorry, Dan.'

'It's all right. You should be with a man who wants to have your kids.'

'You're not it,' I hear myself saying bravely.

'I'm not it.'

Our souls must look like lava lamps. Glug, glug, glug. And we sit there, for a silly amount of time, not touching, not looking at each other, just looking around at walls, and cushions, and all the books – some of them presents from him – on the shelves.

'So.' He smiles. And it's that good-humoured, kind-hearted, philosophical thing again. The deathly fondness that means love has been permanently cancelled.

I don't think I can stand it.

I get up and put the kettle on.

'Not for me.'

And the shock of him not staying, not even for a cup of coffee, is terrible.

He comes up to me in the kitchen and holds me tightly for a while. Then he kisses me on the head, and says goodbye, and that's it – over. It ain't over 'til it's over, thank you Lenny Kravitz, and now it really is.

When he drives off my ears follow the familiar, revving Rover sound until it goes forever. It's not forever, of course, we'll end up friends in the year two thousand and twenty and Tattoo Lawyer will have married a judge by then, and he'll be with a pert wife. I know all this. I know it. But I want to wallow, now. It's wallowing time.

Eleven

I don't know where I heard it, but someone once told me that when a shark bites your leg off in the water, you don't feel a thing — just a tug, rather than teeth ripping into your flesh. I suppose that's nature's way of being kind. And maybe that's why it takes me two days exactly to get over Dan this time.

I have The Cruel Dream first. You know the one. Your head is on his shoulder, and it's warm, and you're in love, and you wake up, and you realize it's crap, and you look in the mirror, and you have bags under your eyes, and you're still single.

But after this, a kind of miracle sets in. I go numb, and when I wake up on Friday morning, Dan's just not an issue. The washing up is an issue, the lack of clean, unladdered, available black pantyhose is an issue — but he's not.

Like drowning people who have hallucinations and shark victims who only feel a gentle tug, I am being spared the worst. And I'm not even on Prozac. And all I can think about as I rinse through the top pair of tights from the laundry basket is sex with Liam. Meaningless, temporary, sex. An emotionally uninvolved and mutual waste of time. A pathetic tryst for relationship retards. Everything I said I didn't want one week ago, in fact.

I'm even trying to mentally undress him, despite the fact that I've never understood how it works. You know, 'He undressed her with his eyes.' Well, I can't do it. I get as far as the top of Liam's head, and his sideburns (Kylie's favourite thing about him) and the suede jacket he wears, and then I get stuck. Men are such a mystery. Hairy chest or non-hairy chest? Legs? And yes, the obvious bit in the middle, The Unexplored And Distant Lands, as Hilary calls it. What about that? How the hell are you supposed to guess that bit right? Not that it stops me trying.

In actual fact, when I'm thinking about sex with him, it's more like a badly edited film. I can see his arms waving around in there somewhere, and I can imagine some of the things he might say, and I get a blurred impression of red boxer shorts – but that's it. I can see his eyes – like the inside of Mars Bars – and his smile – lethal – but that's about as far as it goes.

Nevertheless, I know this badly edited film will be enough to sustain me for some months to come, if necessary. Something I can take out and look at when life gets too bleak.

It's funny the way women prepare for single life. It's like those Victorian explorers who used to carefully stock up on provisions. If I really develop this Liam fantasy it should keep me going on weekdays, then I can have a Someone Famous fantasy for weekends. And, if all else fails, Alaska, because someone once told me there were eighteen men to every single woman.

Thinking about all this as I blast my black tights with the hairdrier is enough to get me humming one of the Elvis Costello songs Bill's pumping through the ceiling. All in all, I think, I'm not doing too badly. Imaginary sex with Liam. Total numbness re: Dan and Tattoo Lawyer. Hmmm. 'My aim is true,' warbles Elvis Costello. And I really feel quite cheerful.

Then I check my e-mail and nearly die.

From: liam@ozemail.com.au
To: shep@mpx.com.au
Subject: Dirty Weekend

Dear Victoria. Yes or no (please circle one). Liam.

Sex with Liam! Yes! Il est une miracle! Now I know how Jamie Streeton the baseball-mad American used to feel when his team won. I punch the air. I think I actually whoop. Then I put on wet black tights and get the crutch up as far as my knees before the whole thing rips around my legs.

I mean, who needs a fantasy? This is it. It's here. Liam, who I thought I had turned off for life, wants me, Victoria Total Bloody Relationship Disaster Shepworth, to go to a hotel with him. And suddenly, there are thirty-five sources of brand-new anxiety, beginning with:

1) Lack of clean black non-ripped tights
2) Unshaven armpits
3) Inferior fellating skills

and ending with:

35) Condom explosion

Then I sit down, have a cup of tea and wait for sanity to return. It does. I knew it would, eventually. Dirty

weekend? I am back in the land of shagging and bonking – all those words men use because they can't
handle love, the cowards – and I am betraying every
instinct I had not less than a week ago in front of Liam
and an ibis.

I am, in fact, selling out. And if I agree to this, I have
no excuses.

Then I have another cup of tea and think about it
again, hoping that by the time I go to work and step out
of the train it will all make sense, but of course it
doesn't. I'm seriously tempted to tell Kylie, too, in a fit
of smug 30-year-old triumph, but then I realize I'm
being pathetic.

When I finally get to work, in stale tights I've fished
out of the laundry basket, they've given me a brochure
for a landscape gardening firm. I know I'm going to be
useless, and I am. The client wants me to mention how
big their garden gnomes are, and all I can think about
is sex.

I finally allow myself to give up at lunchtime, when
I call Hilary and Jodie for an emergency summit meeting. We go to the place we always end up at, because
it's cheap enough for Hil, close enough to work for
me, and vego enough for Jodie. I can see the sun-
burst clock on the wall, and I can see the hands are
whizzing around to 2 p.m., but I'm beyond caring
any more. Hilary orders a pizza, and Jodie has a
caesar salad without the bacon, anchovies and
mayonnaise.

'I think that's just lettuce,' says the waitress.

'Are you sure you're OK about the timing?' Jodie
asks, stretching back in the spindly wrought-iron chair.

'The main thing is, did you reply?' Hilary says.

'I can't reply just yet. I don't know what I'm going to
do.'

Hilary rolls her eyes.

'Do it. He can be your transitional man.'

'Well, I don't think she should,' Jodie interrupts. 'It's so soon after Dan.'

What I really want is reassurance. I want to know that it's going to be OK, and this is going to be the beginning of something fantastic. And I've already decided to say yes.

'The thing is, I don't mind if it's just a fling,' I say, unconvincingly.

'Not looking for love?' says Jodie.

'Crap,' says Hilary.

'No, I really think I can handle it. Just fun. I need fun. Is there a law against fun, suddenly?'

'Well, at least he's not waiting for you to do all the organizing,' Hilary says, grudgingly.

'Only you can decide,' Jodie adds, in her most sincere Women's Circle-ish voice.

Then the waitress appears holding a huge bowl over her lettuce leaves.

'Parmesan on that?'

Back at work (2.28 p.m., I think, not bad at all) I close the landscape gardening brochure on the computer and open up a file which I call Breakfast Grits 2 to put Kylie off. Then I type in all the pros and cons of Liam in Helvetica 14 point, trying to stretch the pros as far down the page as I can. Then when I've done that, I do it in Ye Olde England writing. Just to make it look more official.

REASONS FOR BONKING LIAM

PROS
1. Dan is doing it with someone so why shouldn't I?

2. If he sees me and Liam together he may come grovelling back.
3. Liam is a sex god and I should let nature take its course.
4. I need some fun.
5. My horoscope said it would be OK.
6. Liam may be my last chance for several years, apart from the divorced fortysomething male army.
7. I do not need a serious relationship, I need a Transitional Man.
8. There is nothing else on this weekend anyway.
9. If we get married, he can design our wedding invitations for nothing.
10. Cara said I would meet my soulmate through my computer.

CONS
1. What if he's been with someone who could afford breast implants?
2. Liam may be HIV positive or have sexual perversions – eg, drawn to sniffing young girls' bicycle seats.
3. If I fall in love with him, it will be a total disaster as he has all the hallmarks of a non ringer-back.
4. Someone from work might see us.
5. If it is a disaster, none of my friends will have any sympathy left.

Finally, after an hour of staring at this on the computer screen, I wait until Kylie has gone to get a cup of tea, and log into my home account. After a few attempts at an answer, I end up sending this.

To: liam@ozemail.com.au
From: shep@mpx.com.au
Re: Dirty Weekend

Please note – I have circled the 'yes' option. Now what? Victoria.

Then, to my intense horror, I see both Kylie and Liam walking towards me holding mugs. She's laughing, and he's pretending to.

'Hi,' he says lightly, like a man in a casual slacks advertisement.

'Hi,' I say back.

Kylie looms like a gargoyle.

'Actually, I think I'll get a cup of tea too,' I say uselessly, and flee to the kitchen.

My face is burning so much I could shove it in the freezer and still feel the same. I am thirty years old and I feel thirteen. This is a groan situation, as we used to say at school. A triple groan situation, in fact.

And there's no way out. I am going to have to stay in the kitchen until he's gone, and if Kylie keeps up her monologue about last night's episode of *Friends*, that could be days.

Then Liam solves my problem for me by suddenly sticking his head around the door. For a minute, I just stand and stare, like a possum caught in car headlights.

'You got my message?' he says, looking at me strangely.

'Er, yes.'

'And I take it the answer is no?'

And you'd think, after fifteen years of practice, that I'd have some kind of handle on this male-female, relationship thing. But I don't. I'm as hopeless as I was at the Blue Light Disco in 1984, when Trevor McVie tried to stick his tongue in during a Cure song and I pretended my tooth had an abscess.

Why can't I be like a TV sex-witch bitch? Why don't I have heavy-lidded eyes?

Why can't I speak?

'No, I want to.'

'You want to.'

'I just sent you an e-mail. I want to.'

And there's a gap, a few seconds of silent staring and mindreading, and then he puts his cup in the sink and goes towards the door.

'I'll talk to you later then,' he says, and then he's gone.

When I go back to my desk, Kylie is typing furiously. I can tell it's the Slim n' Smile copy just by looking. Poor Kylie. Part of me can't help feeling smug, I suppose. But part of me also remembers what it's like to be twenty-two and single, and sometimes I suppose it must almost be as depressing as being thirty and single.

I promise God that if my dirty weekend works out, I'll find her someone to love. Maybe Bill the Boffin would be interested. Maybe one of Anthony Anderson's old scuba-diving friends, who I run into sometimes. Maybe I could enter her into the Find A Friend File on the Internet under M for Micro Mini Kilt Wearing.

Successful lust makes you feel like Santa Claus. I want to buy my friends presents, and throw parties, and bring lonely singles together, and find homes for small furry animals. A miracle has occurred, and I don't need to store up a Liam fantasy for a long, lonely winter ahead because I am getting a Liam reality. And, some time tonight, there'll be a phone call.

I can unravel the extension cord that takes the phone

from the dining room to the bedroom, and lie back on my pillows and talk total, rubbishy, flirty, coupley stuff until I fall asleep.

His Mars Bar eyes practically melted my shirt off in the kitchen. And I know it's just lust, I know the odds are against me, I know I'm on the rebound, I know all of that. But still, Liam is a graphic designer and I am a copywriter. He is single and I am single. Who is to say that I, Victoria Shepworth, might not be purchasing white suede shoes in a year from now, and booking a big bridal plait-weaving session at the hairdresser's?

Just to even things up the other way, I give him about three chances to change his mind when he finally calls me at home just after eleven thirty. I ask him if he's sure he's not too busy at the moment, if he's sure he's not too tired, if he's sure the hotel's not overbooked, twisting the telephone cord around my fingers, willing him not to bail out. Overall, though, he sounds very sure.

'Why do I get the feeling you've done this before?' I say.

'I haven't.'

'But you seem to know what you're doing.'

'I'm just going off old Seventies TV shows. You know. Ooh-er, let's book in as Mr and Mrs Smith.'

I remember again why I like him, and it's partly the fact that he always, reliably, makes me laugh. Maybe laughter is like sex, that's why.

'And what's the plan?' I ask, sticking my legs up in the air to see how hairy they are. Praise the Lord they haven't invented vision phone.

'I'll pick you up tomorrow after lunch,' Liam says. 'We'll drive there, get there by dinner.'

'And where is it?'

'In the mountains.'

131

'And what should I bring?'

'Nipple rings and absorbent sheets.'

In the end, I pack everything in the bathroom except the toilet brush and the plug. The bottle of Eternity, the old bottle of Poison with a few dregs left in it, fake tanning lotion, Evening Primrose Oil, the lot. Then I throw in my bunny nightie, in case I feel so comfortable with him that I can wear embarrassing old stuff to bed, and a white lacy body that goes up my crutch unless I suck my stomach in. Plus Old Black Faithful, the sexy nylon thing I bought during the Anthony Anderson years, and Superbra, which Jodie borrowed for last year's Mardi Gras and stuck sequins all over. Luckily, I made her pull all the sequins off. And will I end up wearing any of this? As if. As usual, it will be pants on the floor and shirt chucked over the other side of the room. Pathetic.

When he knocks on my front door, I feel like Anne Frank did when the Nazis arrived. I want to go and hide in my secret annexe, except there isn't one. The only thing that makes me feel slightly better is knowing that it might even be worse for him. Not that he shows it.

He's let his stubble grow back for the weekend. He smells of herbal shampoo. And I'm not sure who jumps first, but I think it's me, and suddenly we're kissing against the wall, with my back digging into the bookshelves.

Liam close up is something I couldn't have imagined, despite my weak attempts at a fantasy. You really can look into his eyes and feel as if you're being sucked into one of those whirly hypnotic wheels they used to have on *Batman*. I don't want to look away. And I don't want to let go of him either.

He's not Dan, and I don't care. And that seems to me

to be true progress. His not-Dan aura actually makes him feel all the more amazing, if I'm really going to be honest about it. He smells of sharp lime aftershave and his unshaven face feels rough against mine in a satisfyingly sexy and gritty way. And every time I pull away because my back is digging into the shelves, he pulls me back again and twists me round into a different position. He feels like he *thoroughly* knows what he's doing. What else can I do except give in gratefully?

Finally, after what feels like every Jilly Cooper I own has been indented in my spine, we go. 'I'm having trouble concentrating,' he says, when we clamber into his car (new-looking MG, sucked in Dan, and I don't care if I am a superficial bitch) and head off.

'Can I just say something?' I ask, winding down the seat and leaning back.

And he lets me, so I do.

'Thankyou, thankyou, thankyou, thankyou.'

Kiss the joy as it flies, some poet said. And after all the fleeting passion in my life, you'd think I would have learned. But why is permanence the first thing that rushes into my head when I get anywhere near a man or a bed, in that order? It's like a mania.

I suppose it began at school, as most things do. If you lent Trevor McVie your set square, that basically led to this conclusion: 'You love Trevor McVie.' And if, a few years later, you got a friendship ring from someone else, that was a kind of junior engagement. My God, I can even remember thinking I was going to marry Phillip Zebruscki.

I am 30-years-old and I am being driven to a hotel strictly for the purposes of sex. Possibly with a two-day cut-off point. I must, I must, remember this. That is all that has been promised to me, and that is all I am agreeing to. This is not *Pride and Prejudice*. This is not *Sense and* bloody *Sensibility*.

So, the Next Bit. The frightening bit. The bit where you both get out of the car, and should probably kiss or something – but don't – and end up walking into the foyer like two people on a business trip. The hotel receptionist couldn't give a stuff if we were single, married or dragging a conga line of naked sex slaves behind us. The only thing she wants from us is a breakfast menu with a doorknob-shaped hole in the top of it.

And the hotel is nice enough, I suppose. Beige. Not that I can notice anything right now, except my own nervous system. When I push the button for the lifts, I get a mild electric shock. It's one of those places with too much air conditioning, and nylon carpets and after that I feel as if I'm going to get zapped every time I touch anything. Including Liam.

In the lift, we both stare at terrible ads for The Palm Verandah Cafe, with the crappiest drawing of a palm tree I have ever seen, and a picture of a giant dancing pineapple announcing the $4.95 Kids' Special (pineapple chunks, by the look of it.) Then Liam walks ahead of me, checks the room number, sticks in the square plastic techno-key and we go in.

I race straight over to open the curtains, yanking them apart and ignoring the cord, as if it's the most crucial thing in the world that we see the view, right now. Then I pull open the fridge door to see if there's anything free and exciting in there, then I open the wardrobe to see what the coathangers look like, then I go to the loo, because I can't think of anything else to do except run screaming out of the hotel and back to Sydney.

Once I'm in there I flush the loo anyway, just so he won't think I'm completely mad, and look at myself in the mirror. Do I have time to take all my clothes off, inspect myself and put them all back on again? Unfortunately, I do not. Has my hair grown back at all? It has not. Is there any hair I've missed from under my arms? Probably. Are the wires from my bra poking out of the front again? Yes, I can feel them. Do my breasts look like two firmly poached and perfectly even eggs? Oh yeah, sure.

When I come back out again, he's lying on the bed – our bed – with his fingers locked behind his head, staring at the view. He's got all his clothes on. Thank God. I think if he was naked I'd probably start yapping hysterically like a hyena.

'Come here.'

And I do. Why do I get the feeling that he's amused by me? Probably because he is.

'It's worse for me, you know,' he says. 'I am the seducer, after all. Think of the pressure.'

Then he kisses me again, and it really is the most incredible thing in the world. I know men are like food processors and we don't know why we need them. But we do, we really do.

And is he, as Kylie would say, good in bed? I guess that depends on how you define it. There are some men who think that means something like cracking a safe or tuning a television in. You know, hands-on, practical skills. Magic fingers. Like jiggling a bent coathanger through a car window when you've locked your keys in the glovebox, or picking a lock. Liam's not one of them. Which isn't to say he's clueless, because he's not. Far from it. But there's something else there. And I couldn't put it into words, and wouldn't want to.

For me, good in bed means knowing that I'm doing something right, which I seem to be, and managing to lose myself in it, which I am. I hate that phrase anyway. 'Good in bed.' It reminds me of trying out for the netball team and being marked on your ball-handling skills.

Am I good or bad in bed? I have no idea, and at the moment I don't care. Greg Daly the bushwalker used to say I was, whatever that meant, and Leon the student radical used to stroke my hair afterwards and let me borrow his Clash T-shirt, which was nice. But now? I don't know. And it bothers me that I should care anyway.

I've bought into Liam's idea of sex as a bonk, a shag, a function. Otherwise I wouldn't be here. That's enough. It's not like entering cake decorations for the Royal Easter Show. I don't need a score card from the judges, and if he wants one from me, he's not getting one.

At some point – 2 a.m. maybe? it feels like that – I wander into the bathroom and brush my teeth and wash my face. Then I put my hands on my hips and look at myself in the mirror again. I can look at this situation two ways. I am either a sexually independent woman of the '90s, having some fun in a luxury hotel, or I am a hairy and emotionally confused single female, trading sex for love because there's nothing else going at the moment.

When I go back to bed, he's sitting up with the light on, rubbing his hand across his face.

'What's up?'

'Nothing. I'm fine.'

'You don't want a deep and meaningful conversation, do you?'

'No.'

'Well, that's a relief.'

And we begin again, in that half-interested kind of way people behave when they remember there are more chocolate biscuits left in the pack. And this time it's easier and lazier, somehow. Which is a problem, because I'm caught off guard, and for some reason, I start crying.

Oh no. The worst. The absolute worst. But I can't hide it, and part of me doesn't want to.

'Hey.'

More tears. I'm a very good silent crier, after years of practice, but they're still pouring down my face.

'Sorry,' I sniffle.

And I try to get myself back into it, remembering all the pros I typed in on the list at work, and thinking about breakfast in bed tomorrow, and trying to feel like I'm Having Fun With A Transitional Man.

But . . . no. The act of taking my clothes off has done something to me on the inside as well, and the more I try not to cry, the more I do cry. It feels all wrong, I suppose. Not just because he's different, and we're stuck in this plastic beige hotel room in the middle of the Blue Mountains. It's more to do with me. I'm conning myself and I've only just realized it. I'm not sure who I thought I was being this weekend. Tattoo Lawyer? Whoever it was, the only person I've actually managed to pack is me. And I'm useless. I might have woken up feeling numb about Dan a few days ago, but he's the only person I want holding me at the moment.

Liam gets up, as all men seem to do, for a middle-of-the-night glass of water. That's a Dan thing too. And it brings back familiar memories of thumping out of bed, running the tap, then coming back with two glasses — one each.

When Liam goes for the water, though, he only brings some back for himself.

'OK?' he whispers.

And I nod into the pillow, and mumble something,

and he leaves it at that. Dan wouldn't have left it there, I think, Dan would have done something about me, mess that I am. But he's not Dan. And why did I ever think he would be?

At some point, either I fall asleep or Liam does. But when I wake up in the morning, his side of the bed is empty and it looks like he's already read the newspaper, had a cup of coffee and gone somewhere.

Brilliant. Perfect. What now? I take the paper back to bed and prop the pillows up, trying to feel luxurious and mistress-like, but I catch myself in the mirror and I look like a bereaved old cow. My face is stupidly red and creased. My hair is sticking up all over the place.

And suddenly I think, long and glossy and auburn. That's the kind of hair I'd like next time. Abba hair. Hair which I can put up on top of my head, or let loose. I don't think I want to be red and spiky any more. It hasn't worked. As if I ever thought it would.

When I go to wash my face, I can see his razor, and his shampoo, and his toothpaste all neatly arranged on the left side of the basin. What am I supposed to do, pile up all my stuff on the right side? Then I throw a tissue in the bin and see two condoms, neatly knotted, among the rubbish.

If I'm being optimistic, and I really think I should try, then I can see another weekend like this some time. Perhaps, if I explain it very cleverly and wittily, he'll understand why I spent half the night crying into a pillow, and maybe it will be OK again, and maybe I can take him away next time.

But when he comes back to the room, I can tell there's not going to be a next time.

'Hi.'

'Hi.'

'I've just been for a swim.'

'Oh, I didn't bring my bathers.'

'Oh, well.'

'Peanuts,' he says, throwing the cartoon section across.

'I love that,' I say. I don't.

'Are you feeling OK then?'

'Bit tired.'

'Sleep on the way home.'

'Yes.'

'Shall we get going then?'

And that's it. We drive back to R.E.M. and he doesn't say anything, and I can't think of anything to say. When we get back to my flat, he gets my bag out of the boot, and puts it down on the pavement.

'Do you want to come up?' I say.

'Do you want me to?'

I hug him then, because for the first time it occurs to me that the whole thing might have been even worse for him than it has for me. And he hugs me back, which is nice, except it doesn't feel the way it did twenty-four hours ago.

'Come up and I'll make you a coffee,' I find myself saying. 'Not a hotel coffee.'

So we go up, and when I get back there are two messages on the answering machine, both probably from Hilary and Jodie, both no doubt requesting detailed reports on Liam, the universe and everything. And what can I say, really? We tried each other out, and it didn't work. I pretended to be something I wasn't, and I didn't even realize it until I was crying myself to sleep.

I bring back the coffee and sit next to him on the couch. That couch. I should ring somebody up and get it exorcized.

'I'm sorry about all that,' I say at last, 'you know it

wasn't you, don't you. It was me. I'm just upset. And tired. I don't know. Dan . . .'

'Not a problem.'

'Don't say it like that, "Not a problem." You make it sound like work.'

'Look. I had fun. Thankyou.'

'Are you sure?'

'Sure I'm sure.'

And I wonder, could I right all the wrongs right now, this minute, and drag him off to my bedroom? But I can't. Apart from the fact that the wardrobe door is still hanging open with its picture of Dan, the things that used to get me dreaming about Liam a few days ago no longer apply. He's the kind of man who arranges his things neatly on the left side of the sink. He's the kind of man who ties knots in his condoms. He's the kind of man who goes off for a swim when things get a bit too human for him.

When he goes, and he does, after the second cup of coffee, I play back the messages on the machine. I'm half right about them. One of them is from Jodie, and she wants to know how it went, and she hopes I had fun, and Didi chips in at the end saying, I should come over for some lentil stew, or something.

The other one is quite unexpected, though. It's from Kylie, and for a minute I think it might be about some terrible work thing I'd forgotten about, then I realize it must be something else – her voice is higher than usual. Squeaky. Upset.

'Hi, it's Kylie. Can you call me? Bye.'

For some reason I don't want to. So I unpack my bag and methodically put everything away, including the bra from hell, and the half-empty bottle of Poison I never used. Then I go back to the phone, curl up on the couch, and make the call.

Why do I know what she's about to tell me? I'm not sure. But it all comes out anyway. She rang his place, and one of his flatmates said he was in the mountains, and she worked out that it was with me. And she's upset, really upset. Not just because I'm having a fling with Liam and I haven't confided in her, and she always thought we were friends, but mainly because he's just taken me to exactly the same hotel they were in not so very long ago.

'Oh, Kylie,' I say.

'I'm not jealous, I don't want you to think that. I want you to be happy.'

And in a funny way, I know she's telling the truth.

'I had a shit time, anyway.'

'Oh?'

'Yeah, shit. He spent more time in the pool than he did with me.'

'Really?'

'Yup.'

'Did he say anything about me?'

And I wish he had, so I could throw her a crumb, but, of course, he didn't, and unless I e-mail him something nasty tonight, he probably never will.

'Kylie, you make me feel old.'

'Do I?'

'Old and cynical. But I know you'll get over him.'

'Do I have to?'

'Yup. Right now.'

'Oh.'

'And I have to go to bed. I'm sorry. I'll see you at work. Bye.'

Then I peel the photo of Dan off the inside of the wardrobe door, where it's been for far too long, and get into my good old bunny nightie, and fall asleep, alone, on the right hand side of the bed.

141

Twelve

Ages ago, when I'd just started at the agency and was feeling enthusiastic, I bought a home fax. I've used it twice. Once to fax through a pizza order, just to see if you could actually do it, and once to send through an urgent message to Bobbi saying I had suspected meningitis and couldn't come in when I was actually in bed with Dan all day.

I can remember every excuse I've ever used to take a day off work. Maybe years of escaping school PE classes trains you for it. If I had suspected meningitis last winter, I have to come up with some new ailment this winter – that kind of thing. So today, Monday, the worst of all possible days to go into the office, I have to come up with something so cunning, so original, and yet so believable, that I won't even need a medical certificate.

After I sit through an hour of Jacques Cousteau on daytime TV it comes to me. Seafood poisoning. So I write a masterful fax – not too long, not too short – and feed it through.

It's hard not to think about Liam, and I do. I'm not stupid enough to fall for the usual sad female scream of anguish – 'Heee's a baaastard and I still luuurve him'

– but it's almost impossible to kick him out of my head. Jacques Cousteau is holding his nose and dropping backwards off the edge of the boat while I do this, and it makes me think about Anthony the Bastard Scuba Diver as well.

In a way, Liam and Anthony aren't so different. They're physical creatures, good at understanding things like sex, and wine, and food. And what did Liam give me except exactly what he'd promised? A dirty weekend. There you go. He told me he was a relationship retard, and I can't blame him. But – funny about this – I do. And after I've chucked a cushion at Jacques Cousteau, I feel like kicking the TV in to finish it off.

The daffodil pen is on the table, next to a notepad with Liam's name doodled all over it with a little pattern of question marks and smiley faces. Bloody Cara. 'You will meet your soulmate through your computer.'

But it's funny how these things stick. I want it to stick, that's half the problem. But what if it really is Liam, and the dirty weekend disaster is just the course of true love never running smooth and all that? It's worth clinging to, sorry, thinking about.

I ring Hilary.

'What was the address of that tarot card thing on the net you were telling me about ?'

'Oh, no. You're having a Mad Week. I knew it.'

'It was a disaster, Hil. The whole weekend.'

'Really?'

'Yup.'

'Don't even want to talk about it?'

'Nuh.'

'But don't have a Mad Week, that's the last thing you want to do.'

'I think I have to.'

'Oh. Well, whatever.'

And she tells me the address, and I write it down with the daffodil pen, and rip out the sheet of paper with Liam Liam Liam all over it and chuck it in the bin on top of a pile of old teabags and snotty tissues, which makes me feel slightly better.

I can understand why Bill the Boffin spends so much time with his computer. It's like a little grey plastic life substitute. I suppose he thinks it is life. But I'm not that desperate. Am I?

If Liam could see me now. If Dan could see me now. If a psychiatrist could see me now. But I don't care. I've got the address for tarot readings online, and I'm going to use it.

Ping, ping, ping. No new e-mail this morning. Oh, what a massive shock. Then I go to tarot.spooky.com and breathe deeply, turn Jacques Cousteau off ('Meanwhile, back on the *Calypso* . . .') and type in the question.

IS LIAM MY SOULMATE? THANKS, VICTORIA SHEP-WORTH.

I wait. And I wait. Then my tarot card appears on the screen, line by line.

PAGE OF CUPS

A young man, maybe an artist – who is outwardly calm and inwardly passionate. He cares intensely for power and wisdom and is ruthless in his own aims. A message, invitation or proposition is about to be received. The opportunity for a new beginning is approaching.

I remember Hilary telling me, 'You read into it what you want to read into it', and I suppose I am. But this is looking a little bit strange. 'An artist (yes – well, a graphic artist, anyway) whose calm surface masks intense passion (well, it did for about an hour), caring intensely for power and wisdom (what?) and ruthless in his own aims (well, I got off lightly then).

The picture shows a tarot card with a jaunty looking teenager in tights, long boots and a kind of medieval floppy hat. 'A message, invitation, or proposition is about to be received. The opportunity for a new beginning is approaching.'

That's fine. Except do I want to take any messages, invitations or propositions from a ruthless, power mad graphic artist who has just gone through me and a twenty-two year old in a micro mini kilt in just over a month? Or indeed a man in tights?

But something drives me on. So I click on the other tarot card option, and ask the question again.

IS LIAM MY SOULMATE? THANKS, VICTORIA SHEP-WORTH

Once again, a card appears. This time it looks like a woman in front of a pair of scales, which makes no sense to me. And the next bit makes even less sense.

JUSTICE – The scales are evenly balanced in the end, as good will overcome all.

So putting that all together we have . . . I don't know. Total confusion. Does this mean Liam is my soulmate, or does it mean that I am playing with hidden forces I don't understand, or does it mean that every person who has just taken the day off work to play with the Internet is getting the same two tarot cards?

I'd like to ring up Cara but the teapot rent is looking dangerously low. So I do the next best thing. I ring up Helena Chettle, the only happily married and babied person I know. I've never thought of her as an oracle before, but somehow it makes sense to call her.

Whenever you ring up Helena, you usually get Mick, her husband, first. Primarily because Helena is usually up to her elbows in a washing machine, or clipping her maternity bra back on, or wiping Olga's baby goo off her shoulder. I went to school with Helena Chettle, all the way through from Littlewood Primary to HSC. I have no idea why we still know each other, except it has something to do with her Christmas cards and my guilt.

Helena and Mick met at the same Blue Light Disco where I used to spend the evenings running away from Trevor McVie. They started their relationship in the standard way – Helena sitting on Mick's knee in the dark – and when they got married a few years later, they even played Nutbush City Limits, that old Blue Light Disco reliable, at the reception.

It's quite a shock to ring her number and not get Mick first. But then I remember. It's Monday. Normal people are at work.

'Hello Victoria, how are you?'

I can hear Olga in the background, making that standard 'Waaah' kind of noise. It's funny. I've never heard a dog go 'bow wow' and I've never heard a cat say 'meeow' but all babies really do go 'waaaah.'

'I need some advice actually.'

I can tell Helena is a bit shocked at this. She is, after all, a wife and mother and as my life bears about as much relation to hers as Mr Spock's does to . . . I don't know – something normal, anyway – she can't quite take it in.

'What is it?'

'Well, I've taken the day off work.'

'Oh.'

'It's not serious. It's just . . . a guy.'

'Oh. Do you want to come over?'

'I don't know. Are you busy?'

And this really is a stupid question, because I don't know anybody who is busier than Helena Chettle. The last time I went round to her house, she had the sprinkler system going, the tumble drier revolving, the taps running and Olga sucking furiously on her nipple like some kind of hydraulic pump.

In the end, she talks me into it. Actually, it doesn't take much persuasion. The Chettles en masse might be the last people you want to get stuck next to on a long plane journey, but they are exactly the kind of people you want to see in a time of crisis. They're the kind of family you could wave down on a wet, dark night if your car had broken down. Helena is the sort of person you'd long to see if your drink was spiked with LSD one night and you ended up thinking your spaghetti had turned into a snake. You know, that kind of person. Helena Chettle, of Mick And The Kids fame. Secure. Solid. Sensible. Makes cakes.

Her two other kids apart from baby Olga are junior athletics champs and jazz ballet trophy medallists. They love her to death, and when I saw them with her about a year ago they had gaps between their teeth and were saying things like 'Mum, can we go to McDonalds' while Helena kept saying 'No' – on rotation.

The other funny thing about Helena is that her life actually looks like a TV advertisement. All the crappy old ads I write for detergent and dried milk powder are seriously the way she lives. If Helena runs out of milk, she really does reach for the – hey, lucky I've got some – dried milk powder. I don't know anybody with dried milk powder. I don't think single people know what it is.

Sitting at her kitchen table, drinking tea, it's hard not to take notes for some campaign of the future. And when Helena puts on her oven glove and lifts the tray of shortbread out of the oven, I almost want to photograph the look on her face, because it's that kind of 'Aaah, home-made shortbread!' look that we spend days trying to recapture in all the ads.

'Hello Olga.'

The baby is making snotty, chuckling sounds in its pen, clutching and unclutching its fingers in a way that reminds me a little bit of the jellyfish on Jacques Cousteau this morning. There are photos of its brother and sister up on the wall, next to a gigantic mobile with cross-eyed wooden ducks hanging off it.

'Work keeping you busy?' Helena murmurs, pouring tea into matching mugs with yellow roses on them.

'I had a one night stand with someone.'

'Oh.' She laughs. I can't blame her really. I suppose I do sound as if I'm trying to be funny.

'I work with him. That's why I can't go in. In fact, I'm wondering if I can ever go in.'

'Do you think he feels the same way?'

'I don't actually think he's that sensitive. To tell you the truth.'

She nods.

'Some people are like that, aren't they,' she says, after she's had a bit of time to think it over.

'He's also been having it off with someone else. Ten years younger. At work. You know.'

'Ah.'

And just as I'm sure she's about to say something

profound and insightful, Olga belches and brings up the usual white stuff.

'Can you tell me something?' I ask Helena, while she's mopping and patting and simultaneously putting shortbread on a wire tray.

'Mmm?'

'How do you do it?'

And I suppose she could laugh her way through this one too, or suddenly have a coughing fit, or fob me off. But for a good minute, Helena Chettle stares through the kitchen window at her own Hills Hoist, with Olga over her shoulder, and gives it more thought than I've ever seen her give anything in her life. Except her vows to Mick. That was like watching the last scene in *Camille*.

Finally, she turns around. And she asks me a question instead.

'Why didn't you follow it up with Trevor McVie?'

'Oh, eeeugh.'

She smiles.

'Trevor lives in Perth now. He's got two little girls. He's separated.'

'Trevor McVie?'

It seems impossible to think of him having girls, for some reason. And really, the last time I saw the man was at the age of sixteen, reaching halfway down my tonsils while the DJ played Cure songs you couldn't dance to, even if you had been drinking Coca Cola shaken up with Disprins all night in a pathetic attempt to feel like you were on drugs.

'He's a nice guy,' she says thoughtfully.

And she keeps on patting Olga, and turning taps on and off and unscrewing jars, smiling and waiting for me to say something.

'I can't marry Trevor McVie,' I say finally.

'You pretended you had a tooth abscess, didn't you, when he tried to kiss you.'

'I know.'

'I think he was a bit upset about that. He told Mick.'

'Oh no!'

'Oh, it's fine. He's not that different to Mick, you know. He's a good bloke.'

'I couldn't.'

And she puts Olga down, still smiling, and takes half the shortbread and puts it on a paper plate with Gladwrap stretched over the top.

'There you go.'

'Oh. Thanks.'

And I suppose that's it. The oracle has spoken. Helena Chettle has told me the meaning of love and life, and it amounts to the fact that Mick Chettle and Trevor McVie are both good blokes, and if I hadn't been such a lying cow and pretended I had a tooth abscess when he tried to stick his tongue down my throat in 1984, I'd be a happy woman today. But I take the short-bread anyway. As you do.

Thirteen

In the end, I don't have a Mad Week at all. I manage to restrict it to a Mad Day. And that may be because of Helena Chettle's calming influence, or it may be because Bill decides to show me there's more to the Internet than tarot cards.

He comes down one night, when I'm so sick of agonizing over Liam and Dan by turns that I resort to ringing him up for a bit of boffin help.

Actually, the truth is, I can't stand being alone in the flat any longer. And I feel utterly alone at the moment. And when Bill galumphs down the stairs and does his double-knock on the door, it's actually a relief to see him.

He looks relieved to see me, as well. Or maybe it's the fact that I'm not wearing the dressing gown that shows my nipples this time.

I make us coffee, and then I notice that his Elastoplast has gone. In its place there is a small scar, still quite pink.

'Your thing's gone.'

Strangely enough, he seems to know what this means, and runs a finger along his jaw. His not unattractive jaw, I remember to tell Hilary.

'Yeah, it finally healed up,' he says, shrugging as he switches on my modem.

We've got to that stage where he treats my computer as his own, and I spend the whole time hanging back in a chair, peering over his shoulder.

'So what happened?' I say, being nosey.

'Oh,' he shrugs. 'Someone threw something at me.'

'Really?'

The idea of anyone throwing anything at Bill is mindboggling.

'This woman I used to live with. At home. It's a long story.'

And, all in all, I suppose I'm speechless. I can usually come up with something to say to Bill the Boffin, no matter how uncommunicative and shy and Dorrigo-ish he's being. But this time, zilch. Absorbing these two amazing facts – a) That someone felt passion-ate and angry enough about him to chuck something at his face, and b) That he has recently been living with a woman – is enough to silence me.

'You been having a good week?' he says, with his back to me, in the wobbly director's chair I always make him sit in. And for an awful moment, I think he might have heard the various weeping sessions and long, therapeutic phone calls to friends which have basically kept me afloat since Sunday.

'Oh yeah. No. What about you? My life's a piece of shit, actually.'

'Oh.'

He turns around in his chair and smiles at me then, and it's a nice smile, a kind of singles' solidarity smile, and for one strange moment I actually feel that I might have something in common with him. Then he turns back to concentrate on the computer, and becomes Bill the Boffin again.

'Here,' he says, after a few minutes of tapping and mouse-sliding. 'This is IRC.'

'Oh, yes.'

'Inter relay chat. Like talking to people, but you type it, you don't say it.'

'Mmmm.'

Honestly, this makes about as much sense to me as my Internet tarot readings, but he seems to think that IRC is something I should know about, so I'm not about to disagree.

'Look. These are all channels, that one's obviously New Zealand, Kiwi Line, and then you've got . . .'

'Oh, yes. Orgy Online. That sounds good.'

Looking at the back of Bill's head, it's possible to see his circa 1945 ears, and the back of his well-clipped neck turning raspberry red.

'Then you've got Channel One Australia,' he says, as if nothing's wrong, 'and Seinfeld.'

'Not really him?'

'No. Fans.'

'Really?'

'Do you want to go in?'

He makes it sound like I'm being dropped by a helicopter or something, but I say I do, and he asks me to think up a nickname.

'Why can't I just be Victoria?'

'Well, you could be. But most people use nicknames.'

'All right then. Technobimbo.'

When Bill laughs, even slightly, his shoulders move up slightly. I suppose if he's really amused, he just falls off his chair.

'OK, so we type in your nickname, Technobimbo, and then you can put in your message.'

'Aaagh. What? What am I going to say?'

'Well, hello would be a start.'

He points to the screen, and as I follow each sentence down the page, I can see some kind of conversation about a Seinfeld episode going on. Four people look as if they're involved. Someone called Ziggy, someone called Phantom, a woman (or is it a man, how can you tell?) called Tina and a guy called Dave.

'And they're really typing?'

'Yes.'

'And they could be anywhere?'

'Yes. You're watching this with a slight delay. Type in now. Should take a second to come up.'

So I do, feeling slightly exposed, and I wait until their – excuse me – 'conversation' slows down for a minute, then rush in to type

TECHNOBIMBO – HELLO HOW ARE YOU?

'Now wait,' says Bill. And I do, watching in total horror as it comes up on the screen. The sentences now look like this.

ZIGGY: My favourite episode is the Soup Nazi episode.
TINA: Yeah :-)
PHANTOM: No way, The Contest. Definitely the best Seinfeld of all time.
TECHNOBIMBO: Hello how are you?

'Now wait again,' Bill says. And we do, until this appears on the screen.

PHANTOM: Who the hell are YOU?

Bill turns around again and smiles at me.

'Very polite. Do you want to answer back?'

'No! Yes! No!'

We keep watching, and more lines appear on the screen.

ZIGGY: Hello Technobimbo
TINA: Welcome Technobimbo

And for the rest of the night, Bill and I crane our necks over the computer, taking turns to bring back coffee from the kitchen while we continue the conversation. And I suppose that's what it feels like, a very strange, very stilted, but totally addictive conversation.

'And how many channels are there?' I say finally.

'Hundreds, thousands.'

'And this is people from all over the world?'

Bill gets up, yawns, stretches, scratches his chin where the Elastoplast used to be, and flicks off the modem.

'Yeah, and not just boffins either.'

Then he's gone, just like that, and I'm left alone again with a strangely flickering computer screen. And a strangely flickering brain. Does Bill the Boffin know he's secretly called Bill the Boffin, and if so, how? Or am I just being paranoid?

Fourteen

I don't expect to hear from Liam again, and I'm right. No e-mail in the tray, no matter how many times I log in, and no calls on the machine, no matter how many times I check it. In the meantime, Kylie and I invent a nickname for him. Macrame Man. It turns out he tied knots in the condoms with her as well, and it's the least we can do.

This is every man's secret fear. Finding their vital organs and/or sexual performance the subject of common discussion among cackling females. But who cares? If he's going to behave like a cliche, so are we. So am I, anyway. Kylie feels guilty about trashing him. I'm older, I've had more chances to become bitter and twisted, and I couldn't care less.

Just to prove to myself that I haven't entirely given up on romance, though, I decide to organize the Bill and Hilary summit meeting/dinner.

We're wasting time on the Internet, checking out the Site of the Day at my place, arguing over who has to sit on the wobbly director's chair, when I broach the subject.

'Bill was round the other night.'

Silence.

'Oh, yeah?'

'He's quite nice.'

'Mmmm.'

'Not into it?'

Another silence.

'Can we turn this off?' Hilary says, finally. And scuttles into the kitchen to put the kettle on. She makes a kind of Steven Spielberg production out of finding the teaspoons, asking me if I want Jodie's herbal teabags or normal tea, and rinsing out every last thing in the sink.

Then she comes back with two mugs, sits down on the couch, and says, 'Actually I've got some other things going on.'

'Oh?' I'm pleased for her. Really pleased. 'Like what?'

'I met someone in the group.'

'What group?'

'You know.

'Hil, you're in about a thousand groups.'

'Women's Circle.'

A mental picture of a sensitive new age guy with a Byron Bay tan and a bicycle appears in my head. Nice. Obviously relates to women. In touch with his female side and all that. About time Hilary got lucky. Then she breathes in very quickly and says this:

'She is a woman, actually.'

What?

After years of exposure to Jodie and Didi sticking their hands down the backs of each other's jeans in public, you'd think I'd be shock proof. But this is something else. This is Hilary. A librarian. Wears navy blue jumpers. Likes men.

'I've been feeling guilty about not telling you, actually,' she says, after she's allowed me to sit and

160

stare at the wall for a bit. 'It's been on for a while.'

'Are you sure?'

'Well, yes, as sure as you ever are.'

'Sorry.'

What do you say? What do you do? I feel like I did the day I tried to head one of Daniel Hawker's footballs and half concussed myself.

'I'm fine about it,' I say at last.

'Are you sure?'

'Yeah. Fine about it.'

And I even manage to say this, with a reasonable smile on my face. 'Do I get to meet her?'

'Well, Jodie thought she could organize a barbecue.'

'Oh, a vegetarian lentil barbecue.'

'Yeah, right. Throw another turnip on the barbie.'

I do my ha, ha laugh. But something's wrong here, and we both know it. Normally, if Hilary or I had a new man, we'd cross-examine each other until the second or third mug of coffee. We'd be merciless with each other. Suddenly, though, I seem to have entered an atmosphere of political correctness. I've entered a no-man's land – quite literally – with someone I've known since we were both wearing fudge-flavoured lipgloss.

'Just because it's a woman,' I say finally, 'is that – does that have to be – more private?'

'Well, it's new. It's a new thing. What do you want to know?'

'Well, the big question has to be, is this going to be the rest of your life?'

'That's like me asking you if Liam was going to be the rest of your life.'

'No. I don't mean that. I mean, being gay. Are you gay?'

'No,' she says quickly, then corrects it. 'I don't

know. Maybe. But – I like her. I really, really just like her.'

'Do I get to hear what happened?'

And she goes all girlie and embarrassed and pleased at once, just the way you do when someone's just asked you about a potential new man, and all this nose-pulling and hair-twisting looks very odd considering that we are talking about a woman. Nevertheless.

'We have to go off into pairs for some of the exercises.'

'Oh, yes.'

She shrugs. 'She always chose me. Her name's Natalie. We had one hundred and forty-seven cocktails one night in Paddington.'

'And she jumped you, or the other way around?'

'Of course she jumped me. You know it's always other people jumping me first.'

Then she picks up the newspaper and starts flicking through the real estate guide, a sure sign that the conversation is now over. I suppose this is what's known as Coming Out. I, Victoria Shepworth, a woman of the '90s, have witnessed my first Coming Out. For some reason I start plumping up cushions on the couch. I swear, I have never plumped up a cushion in my life. Is this what happens?

'Anyway, I can have dinner with Bill if there are other people there,' she says after a while. 'You know. But I don't want a set-up.'

'Oh.'

'Thanks, anyway.'

'So.' And yet, and yet, I can't leave it alone. 'Does Jodie know?'

'Oh yeah.'

And I feel hurt about that.

'There was some fear about my reaction, is that it?'

'No. But you need the right place and right time, don't you? You've been busy, I've been busy. It's not like Jodie and Didi and me keeping it from you.'

'Except you have.'

'Why so pissed off, Vic?'

And what she thinks, but doesn't say, is that she hoped I'd be happy for her. And because there's nothing more to say — because I can't trust myself to open my mouth without offending her, anyway — we change the subject, and find a film in the paper, and head off to see it.

You know how you remember some films just because of the mood you were in at the time, and the people you were with? I can tell instantly that this is going to be one of them. We are buying tickets for *The Full Monty* and all I can think of is, this is the film I saw when Hilary told me she'd turned into a rampant lesbian.

I find myself thinking, is Hilary relating to this any more? Is Hilary offended by this? What does the future hold for our mutual movie-going? No more films with naked men in them? Or does she think I've deliberately chosen this film to be patronizing?

But when the lights go up, she's the same old Hilary. Apparently. Moaning on and on about the price of movie tickets, and how she reckons Robert Carlyle must be really short in real life, and how popcorn never fills her up, and she doesn't know why she bothers.

If I was a better friend, I'd be hoping that Natalie, or whatever her name is, would turn out to be The One. Or, at least, It. But then again, I've never been ideologically sound. Leon Mercer the student radical could tell you that much. I was the girl who stuck her hand in the Socialist Workers' Party raffle tin so I could go and buy Toblerone. And today I am the woman who has witnessed one of her best friends coming out, only to find myself praying like hell that she goes straight back in again.

Fifteen

One of the things I've only just discovered about the Internet is that it keeps a little list of all the sites you've visited. After I spend most of Sunday morning on line (oh how good it feels to use impressive non-techno-bimbo terms like on line) I check the list.

Tarot of the Cat People
The Rider-Waite Tarot
Ask Mystic Molly
The I-Ching Page

It's amazing. There must be one billion websites out there, using the most advanced technology known to woman or beast, and the only thing I want to use it for is childish, perverse fortune-telling thrills while I sit on a pile of cushions on the wobbly director's chair. Then again, what does everybody else use the Net for?

No matter how many times I ask, though, I never get the answer I want. Liam's not coming back. Dan's not coming back. Repeat after me . . . I suppose this is Mad Month, then. I swore it would never happen to me, and now it is happening to me. First a Mad Day, then a Mad Week, now a fully-fledged MM. It's got beyond the

Hilary stage. It's now fully-fledged Loony Tunes froth-mouthed behaviour, in fact. All I need to do now is start picking the marshmallow bits off biscuits and living in a terry-towelling dressing gown for a month.

Then I find something called Kurt Cobain's Talking Eight Ball and catch myself getting excited about it, and feel like I've really hit rock bottom. 'If you've got burning questions about some of life's mysteries,' the site announces, 'you may find the answers through the Kurt Cobain Talking Eight-Ball. The Punk Poet of Grunge is standing by on the other side, ready to help you tackle the big questions. What would you like to ask Kurt Cobain?'

I suppose the sensible answer to that would be what he thinks of Courtney Love's new haircut. But, having come this far in my aimless Net wanderings, I feel obliged to type in this:

WILL I MEET MY SOULMATE THROUGH THE INTERNET?

And then something really weird happens, quite apart from the fact that my bottom has gone totally numb after hours of sitting on badly arranged cushions. The screen freezes and the little throbbing N for Netscape in the corner of the screen stops moving. Actually, let's be honest, it's not weird at all. Bill says this happens about ten times a day when you're on the Net. But maybe Kurt Cobain really is trying to tell me something. Not to be such an obsessive cow for a start. Or maybe to use the Net for something truly worthwhile, instead of making pathetic attempts to contact dead Seattle rock stars who only wish to be left in peace.

Curse you, Cara of Krystal's Connections. I wish I'd never heard of you. Hilary was right, it is like an addiction. 'You will meet your soulmate through the computer.' I've still got that written down somewhere. I've still got the evidence. But now, when I look, I can't find it anywhere. It's not under the pile of string, sticky tape, loose staples and other rubbish in the old cupboard I inherited from my mother. It's not in my bedroom. And even though I occasionally shove things like photos and love letters (ha!) in my old leather notebook, it's not there either.

And what can you do, really, when you're lovelorn, disgusted, bored, dazed and confused all at once – and you still can't give yourself permission to eat a family block of fruit and nut chocolate? There is only one answer, I suppose, and it's an old one but a good one. Two pillows under my head, Teenage Fanclub on the stereo, a bag of cashew nuts (I bought them from the health food shop so they must be good for me) and *Wuthering Heights*.

And I'm just getting up to the bit where the ghost of Cathy is scratching at the window when something odd happens. The piece of paper with all my notes from Cara on it falls out of the back of the book. And it's still all there, written in my scrawl. Computer important next six months. Not for work. Meet nice people. Meet soulmate through computer messages. There. Not for work. See? Liam = work. Soulmate = not work.

Then again, something nags, as I keep flicking pages, if Cara's such a brilliant old spook, why didn't she warn me about Liam? I mean, she could have done me a favour. Just a brief warning – 'I see the Blue Mountains. I see beige bedspreads. I see knots in condoms, I see total disaster' – that kind of thing, you know.

Anyway. I take the fact that I found the note again as

a kind of omen, and think vaguely about trotting off to the shop for the banned family block of fruit and nut chocolate when the phone rings.

'Hi. It's Liam.'

'Oh! Hi!'

Damn the surprise element in life. I've run through this so many times in my head, this call. And I was always going to be cool, serene and at one with the universe. A universe that didn't include him, incidentally. Instead, what have we here but the Victoria Shepworth frantic, panting Avon Lady routine all over again. 'Oh! Hi!' For God's sake get a grip . . .

'I just thought I'd call,' I hear him say, 'see what's happenin'.'

Why do men use really bad, fake American accents and drop the g off everything when they're feeling embarrassed? Or, more specifically, why does he?

'Well, what's happenin' is that I'm reading *Wuthering Heights* and eating cashew nuts,' I say.

And then I can't quite believe what he says next, but he says it anyway.

'Dja miss me?'

And I'm not sure if it's the sudden elevation in my blood sugar levels thanks to the three hundred cashews I've just eaten, or Emily Bronte's good influence, or even one of Cara's spooky guides hanging over my shoulder. But suddenly, amazingly, I find myself saying all the right things. For a change.

'Liam, I know you only promised me a dirty weekend, as per 70s sitcom, ha ha ha. But the point is, I didn't know you'd recently been having sex with Kylie. That would have put me off, you see.'

'Mmmm.'

I think he may be speechless. Good. Excellent.

'Yes. And she's been quite sad about the fact that you

decided to have sex with me, too. Actually, sad, angry and obsessive. Pretty much where you left me as well. This is the effect you have on women when you try to have sex without emotion.'

Big pause.

'Like a sprinkler system. Are you aware of that?'

'Look . . .' he tries.

'No, you look. When you go back to your mothership and give your report on earth women – I'm assuming you are, after all, an alien from an outlying galaxy – can you just tell them this? WE-CRY. WE-GET-JEAL-OUS. WE-EMOTE. All right?'

When he hangs up, which of course he does, my heart is rocking in my ribs like one of those clacky executive toys. And I'm breathless, scared, panting. It's awful. But . . . I've done it. And even though Bill upstairs is going to think I'm mad, I jump, literally jump, in the air and yell 'Yeeharrgh!' and run into the kitchen and have glass of water, then run out and do it again. I think I may be shaking, in fact, I'm fairly sure I am. I feel like I need medicinal brandy or something, and I absolutely desperately need the family block of fruit and nut chocolate. But – never mind the fact that Women's Circle would stick a medal on me for what I've just done, never mind that I stuck it up him for Kylie as well, it's the sheer kick of blasting him out of my system that's making me feel so great. And I do. I feel great.

Later, when I've calmed down a bit, and I'm back to the bit in the book where Heathcliff is losing his mind, my thoughts wander off the page and back onto Liam. This time, though, I feel very philosophical about it. Very wise. Very un-Victoria Total Bloody Relationships Disaster Shepworth, in fact.

The tarot card was right. He is ruthless. And it was

right about the message, invitation or proposition as well (I'm sure he had all three in mind). What it didn't say, though, is that until you spell it out to people like Liam, they just don't get it.

I'm well aware that some people might see this as unfinished business. Bad karma between a man and a woman, to grow and fester for another day, or maybe another lifetime. But for me, it now feels complete. When he rang up and said, 'What's happenin'' as if nothing had – excuse me – been happenin', as if life was casual and fun, and he was casual and fun, I suppose he expected me to play the game. And I've done it before, it's not as if I haven't had practice. Everyone I know has done it. You just push an everyday, happy kind of sound into your voice, and shunt all the painful, terrible things to the back of your brain, and smile, smile, smile.

Here's what Liam wanted to hear.

Him: What's happenin'?
Me: Oh, nothing much.
Him: Dja miss me?
Me: Ha ha ha.
Him: Feel like going out?
Me: Oh, maybe.
Him: Sorry I've been busy lately, haven't had a chance to call.
Me: Oh, that's all right, Liam.

And so on. Ad nauseum. And it really is nauseum. What we have here is a pathetic, stunted old thirtysomething who thinks life is like a seventies sitcom where you all bonk each other in hotels, and have a few – you know – laughs, and if anybody dares to have a crying session because she's feeling a bit fragile about her ex, you just go for a swim until she cools off.

And I love that stuff I said about aliens. I can't quite believe it was coming out of my mouth, but I can't wait to tell everyone. And what did he say then, Victoria?

Yes, I have added to the wall of fear and loathing between man and woman. No, I don't feel guilty. Why? Because the next time he is lying back on some hotel bed with his fingers plaited behind his head, waiting for some other Kylieish person to trot out of the bathroom, my words will be singed on the front of his brain with a cattle brand. I know very well I'm going to be this year's neurotic bitch in his books, but I am also going to be his conscience, well beyond the next 100 neatly knotted condoms. And another thing. I'll never have to sit through another night of AWFOS playing wacky Vegemite jingles at the pub ever again.

And then I think, you wanker, Victoria, and chuck *Wuthering Heights* back on the shelf and go to check for premature chocolate blackheads.

You will meet your soulmate through these computer messages. OK then, Cara. Deal. Every spare moment I get, at work or at home, I'm going to be looking for him. And you don't need to be psychic to work out that somewhere out there, on a billion web sites, newsgroups and IRC channels, there is going to be a bloke for me. Not someone who puts tennis balls in the washing machine to keep his puffy outdoorsy jackets puffy. Not someone who thinks sex is a physical function. Not someone who'll lecture me on socialism.

None of that. It's over to you, Cara. I'm looking for my soulmate this time, and even if I go blind from staring at a screen, even if my Internet bill eats the rent, I'm going to do it. Besides, it has to be my soulmate. If I have another breakup I think I'll have to become a radical celibate, or a radical halibut, or whatever they are.

Sixteen

It feels strange going to Jodie and Didi's barbecue by myself, and it takes me ages to get ready. Normally Hilary and I would arrive together because, after all, we live fifteen minutes away. But I don't feel like interrupting her new relationship. Reasoning it all out, if she was with a new man, I wouldn't suggest we all turn up like some Brownie pack. So I leave her to make her own arrangements with – say it, Victoria – Natalie, and spend about an hour doing my girlie rituals.

Why so long? I'm not sure. But something about this whole exercise makes me want to put on more Eternity than usual, and more lipstick, and brown eyeshadow, and even some dainty crystal beads I've had forever and never wear. I normally don't bother for a Jodie barbecue, because the odds of discovering what Hilary used to call an Eligible (in the good old, pre Women's Circle days) are practically nil. But hey, if I'm walking into the land of dykes on bikes, I want to feel like a girl. And I'm horrified to hear myself thinking that, but it's true. To hell with political correctness, it's like my oldest friend has just been abducted by green things with tentacles on their heads.

Then I wander through Jodie and Didi's house (front

173

door open, as usual) past all the black and white photos of Frida Kahlo in the corridor, past the bathroom with the aroma-therapy burner wafting away on top of the loo, and into the garden. And I see Natalie and Hilary together and all my prejudice and niggling fear goes out of the window.

They're both sitting in the shade, under Jodie's avocado tree, and Natalie has long, brown ringlets and a long, brown Laura Ashley-ish dress on, and bare tanned feet. She's somewhat porky. And Hilary is giggling at her — actually giggling — and looks exactly the same as usual in her tracky pants. No bull terrier. No mirror shades. No studded leather belts.

Hilary sees me, and waves me over.

'This is Natalie.'

'Hello.'

And I'm about to launch into my well-prepared, oh so casual, oh so lighthearted and amusing spiel about the irony of vegetarian barbecues (I have to have something ready for this moment of horror, don't I) when Natalie cuts in ahead of me.

'I just saw my ex-husband in the supermarket, can you believe it? He was buying soft loo paper. When he was with me, we never had soft loo paper. And it had flowers on it!' She makes a face of mock-horror, with her mouth hanging open, gulps in a breath, and then goes on. 'Anyway, I was glad to see he had the trolley with the stuck wheel, I'm normally the one who gets that. I had to check to see if he had a single chocolate eclair in his trolley, because that's the secret bachelor signal, isn't it? But all he had in there apart from the toilet rolls was a can of sardines. For the cat. Never cooked sardines for us, but the cat, that's a different story.'

As Natalie reels all this off, Hilary is watching her,

half-laughing, half biting the top of her finger that means she's a bit nervous, and a bit excited all at the same time. And I suppose you have to like Natalie – how could you not? And I guess if Hilary is going to start her epic voyage into lesbian land – dwelling permanently on the Isle of Lesbos, you might say – she might as well begin with someone like her. Someone who's done the man thing and given up on it. Like her.

'Look,' Natalie says, after five seconds of oxygen. 'They've got that potato salad we had on the first night, you know.' She prods Hilary in the arm. 'It's got all those spring onions in it, or are they pickled onions, I can't remember.' Then she turns back to me. 'I've heard such a lot about you, isn't that a boring thing to say, but I have, Jodie says you've got the Internet on, and I wanted to ask you about that, because apparently there's a little page that tells you how to make your own worm farm, and I think a lot of my problems would be over if I had a worm farm.'

How do you look for signs of great love? Is it the fact that Hilary and Natalie both have their legs crossed in exactly the same way, sitting on Jodie's rockery wall, or should I be searching for something else? Something tells me, though, that this isn't it. It reminds me of the time Hilary went to Italy for a holiday with her Italian language class. While she was in Florence, she used to write me endless letters about how cheap it was to buy a place in the country, and how great the people were, and how fantastic the weather was, and how she never cared if she saw Australia again. Then, when she got back to Sydney, Italy got mentioned less and less. The outrageous T-shirts with the sequins all over them she'd bought in Rome got shoved to the back of the wardrobe, and she stopped chucking little Italian words into her sentences, and the pasta stopped, and even her tan disappeared.

Looking at Natalie now, I have a feeling she'll turn out to be a little like Italy. And – I shouldn't hope this, but I do – lesbian lust for Hilary will turn out to have been a nice place to visit, rather than a permanent residence.

In the meantime, Didi is handing around what, at a distance, look like sausages – but turn out to be marinated eggplant things cunningly disguised as meat. Jodie's not far behind, offering the various women (and the two men, and four dogs) strawberry daiquiris. As usual there aren't enough plastic chairs to go around, but there are so many yoga aficionados there they actually seem quite content to sit cross-legged on Jodie's crazy paving garden.

There's a woman there I know neither Jodie nor Didi can stand, but she's always invited to things because she knows someone on the documentary film funding board. For a moment I consider doing the chicks a favour and wandering up to her for a casual chat about *Love and the Female Experience,* or whatever it's called (surely an improvement on *My Grandmother's Feet,* don't you think?) but then she turns and looks at me owlishly and scares me away. Honestly, is there some rule that being involved in the Arts means you have to wear big goggley glasses like Brains out of *Thunderbirds*?

Jodie drags me back to the kitchen.

'Come and help me do the next one, Vic. It's a banana fizz, with Cointreau. Yum.'

Jodie is wearing what appears to be an old bra and a pair of Didi's jeans, and she looks about twenty-one, just as she always does.

'I feel like I haven't really seen you for ages,' she says. 'Sit down.'

So we do, at the table, and although I'm well aware why we're sitting down, I go along with it. Surprisingly, though, at first, she doesn't want to talk to me about Hilary and Natalie. She wants to talk about Liam.

'Hilary told me. What was he, Macrame Man or something?'

'Yeah. Tied knots in his condoms.'

She laughs, and then rubs my shoulders, being the touchy-feely old naturopath that she is.

'How are you, though, really?'

'Oh, not so bad.'

'I feel guilty. I should have stopped you. I had a bad feeling about him.'

'Oh, it wouldn't have stopped me. You know.'

'So who's on your mind more? Or are none of them on your mind?'

'None.'

'Good.'

She begins to whiz bananas through the blender.

'And you met Natalie?'

'Yeah.'

Something about the mention of her name makes us both half-laugh, and I suppose that's what most people who've just met Natalie do. She's A Character, is what we're both implying, but she's nice too.

'She was married, you know.'

'She said.'

'Then, she just got it. Like that. She's been in a few relationships, nothing serious.'

'It's interesting how you can go from a man to a woman,' I say, more to myself than to her.

'Mmm.'

Jodie, of course, has known about girls since she was at school and she went from a crush on a horse to a crush on a blonde, in a very short school uniform, called Cheryl. She still has photos of her and Cheryl together, wearing love-heart T-shirts and holding hands. Their mothers didn't mind, because their mothers didn't know.

'I think Hilary's having fun. She's happy.'

'She is, actually.'

'She was worried about it, it took a while for her to feel OK.'

'And do you think it's for good?'

'I don't know.'

Jodie smiles her fish-face smile, and starts pouring a stream of Cointreau into the jug.

'Maybe she's just into people,' I hear myself saying. 'Maybe that's it.'

'Yes. Natalie's not that different from that Indian guy, remember him?'

'Oh, God. Yes. Never shut up.'

'Well, exactly.'

'But Natalie seems a bit more together.'

'Yes.'

'Like, she'll return your calls.'

And we laugh, and she brings me out into the garden as her apprentice cocktail waitress, and I recognize people I haven't seen for a while, and everything seems OK – especially after a few drinks, when I even manage to sit down cross-legged on the crazy paving as well.

If I stand back from the whole situation and think about it, it shocks me. Will I tell my mother, who has known Hilary since she was a teenager? Will I mention it to Dad on the phone next time he rings up? I don't know. Maybe – if it lasts. Then again, perhaps the rest

of the human race – and I include my parents in that –
is just more advanced than me. She's just into people.
Remember that, I tell the mirror when I lurch drunkenly into Jodie's loo, and you've got the whole thing
sorted.

Seventeen

On Saturday night, when everybody else is seeing films in units of two, and reserving tables for two at restaurants, and ordering two rounds of drinks at the bar, I lie on the couch like a zombie for an hour, alternately getting teary-eyed and watching *Hercules*, then I decide it. If I'm going to seriously start looking for my soulmate, then I may as well start here – and punch the word SOULMATE into every single Internet search engine I can find.

Somehow I think I'm going to be here a long time. So I put the cushions back on the wobbly director's chair, prop up the computer on the Sydney A-K *Yellow Pages*, and make a huge pot of Jodie's disgusting herbal tea. Then I change the screen saver to something more interesting than grey – a picture of dancing teddy bears, in fact – and log on.

When I try my first search engine alone, 5076 matches for the word soulmate come up. I take the first ten. In order, they are:

1) Kutie's Kittens Drop in to our website or our stall at Animal Kingdom. We can find you your own animal soulmate.

The net is full of aberrations like this. But I'm not giving up.

2) Starcrossed Lovers Astrological Soulmate Dating Service.

Well, yes. But Dan was an Aries, and I'm a Gemini, and we were supposed to get on, and we didn't. So they can stuff it.

3) Soulmate Photographics Inc Matching heart-shaped photographic frames for you and your soulmate on that special day.

Please, a plastic bucket. But then, scrolling down the page I see—

5) Good Enough To Eat Bachelors. Match the man to the pan! We have the best-cooking, best-looking men in sunny Australia and recipes for all!

And why not? I mean, it's Saturday night, and nobody's watching me, and I can't get out *When Harry Met Sally* again, can I, so . . . why not?

When the site appears on the screen, it looks even less promising than the legendary Friends File. There are several blurry photographs of men posed in front of a variety of objects. Sometimes the objects actually obscure part of their head. They are posed around, in front of, or behind, vases of plastic flowers, tractors, and nightclubs. I wonder who took them? Or did they set the timer and run? If you click on the box, you can sample the merchandise, according to the people who run the site. And they say it like that, too. 'Sample the merchandise.'

Apparently there are hundreds of men, plus their recipes, to choose from. I guess someone at mission control thought it would be an ice-breaker to introduce you not only to – Glenn, fortysomething – but also Glenn's raisin and apple turnovers.

So I check him out. And Glenn has an apron on, and he's smiling, and I suppose one day a woman will click on this site and feel something stirring in her heart, or even her bra, but it's not going to be me. Glenn doesn't even make me want to stir my coffee. But he is a human being, and he's looking for love, and he deserves a break, I suppose. He says he loves playing his guitar to people and making them smile, and he doesn't mind children, and he likes horses and spa baths.

Anyway, I download his recipe for raisin and apple turnover. And then there's Neil, who wants to be a film director although he's actually an accountant, and he's fond of fine wines, and another extremely boring thing that most other people on the planet would be fond of – I don't know, sleeping, or eating, or washing under his armpits or something. His recipe is Anzac Biscuits. I suppose his mother gave it to him. In the photo, he looks as if he's about to cry. Or about to come out of the closet.

There's another one called Dan – oh, the irony – but his ideal woman loves relaxing and hanging out at the beach, and she doesn't stress out about relationships, and she hates fighting. So, Dan of Adelaide with your recipe for Chicken Maryland, I bid you farewell. And I only just got here.

I can't imagine how many women must have checked into this website. I wonder if any of them are frantically cooking Bob's turnover at the moment? And more importantly, I wonder how long Dan and poor old Neil and the rest have had their photographs up there.

It's amazing. Nothing that these men want is offensive to me. Nothing that they enjoy in life can I honestly say I have not enjoyed. They don't appear to be married, in jail, or otherwise unavailable. But it's not enough, is it? What I want to know is, does he get a funny crinkle at the corner of his mouth when he smiles, and can I make him laugh until he falls sideways off the couch, and will he make up stupid nicknames for me and program them into his mobile phone? I couldn't care less about the horses and the spa baths. I'm not interested in the fine wines.

So. Back to the search engine, back to the teapot full of fungal-smelling herbal tea, to look up SOULMATE yet again. And here's my next option . . . Christian Dateline! Where Happiness Is Just A Phone Call Away!

It makes you wonder about God, really. What can he have been thinking of in the first place? Having come up with Noah's Ark, he has since produced Christian Dateline! Where Happiness Is Just A Phone Call Away! and . . . yeah. Good Enough To Eat Bachelors.

I think I remember going to church. They used to drag us along at school, and I even bothered to pray properly when everybody else had their eyes open, and for a minute I think I may have even wanted to light a candle.

If I thought prayer would work now, I would pray. But so far, God – whatever that might be – has managed to produce me, alone, single, miserable, desperate – and let's not forget, having a Mad Month – on a Saturday night. With my computer propped up on the *Yellow Pages* for company, and – that's it. Thankyou, God, for letting me become my own worst nightmare, a cross between Glenn Close in *Fatal Attraction* and some sort of social leper geek woman.

And look at the rest of the world – another series of cosmic stuff-ups, all courtesy of God. Bill, upstairs, with a scar on his jaw where his ex-girlfriend threw something at him, who spends his Saturday nights out with various male computer types with beards, going to *Star Trek* films. You can tell Bill's lust for life died ages ago. And my parents, who looked so happy in their wedding photos – that was all done in church, wasn't it, so what went wrong there?

And what about Hilary, who has given up on the male species so completely that she's ended up sleeping with a divorcee called Natalie who can't stop talking and whose husband loves the cat more than her. Then there's Jodie and Didi, who everyone knows want to have kids, except no man will ever do the honours for them. And then there's Greg Daly, wherever he is, and Phillip Zebruscki, and Jamie and all the other failures in my life. I mean, well done, God. Great job.

If God had any brains, he would have invented a world without arguments about Socialist Workers' Party raffle tins to break everything up. Or was that Satan's fault? Anyway, whoever is responsible should show themselves, now. If I look at my bookshelves I can see *Men Are From Mars, Women Are From Venus*. I can see *The Joy of Sex*. I can see *Women Who Run With the Wolves*. And where has it got me or the rest of the world? Nice one, God.

Round and round my brain it all goes. Why, why, why? What's happening to the world? It's gone so single suddenly, it's looking like some gigantic cheap wine bar – except nobody's talking to anybody else. We're all stuck in our flats, alone, wondering when something's going to happen, wondering why it went wrong last time, and scared stupid in case it goes wrong again.

At five minutes to midnight, I'm still trying to get my head around this little list:

1) Maybe All Men Are Bastards. But while (statistics: Hilary) it's mostly men who do all the raping, murdering and molesting, it's also men who commit suicide more often, and die younger, and have their penises cut off by angry females with names like Bobbitt. So there you go. You can't really blame men, can you. Or are all those things connected?

2) The World Is Over Populated And Needs Singles. This is actually a Jodie argument, and it's not so bad. The theory goes, Mother Nature is trying to save the planet by making men and women repellent to each other. Celibacy = more ozone layer to go round, I suppose. And we, the thirty-something generation, are going to do it.

3) It's All Germaine Greer's Fault. Well, probably. But without her, we'd still have Miss World, and then where would we all be?

Bill gets back a bit after midnight, and I wonder if I should ask him down for a mug of Milo and chuck the stinking tea in the sink. But I've got the obvious-nipples grey dressing gown on again, and I can't be bothered changing. The clumping sound of his Doc Martens going up the stairs does remind me of something else, though. The IRC thing. The talking and typing to people thing.

'Bill,' I yell through the door.

'Yeah?'

'Tomorrow night, can you show me IRC again?'

'Yeah, sure.'

'Thanks.'

Clump, clump. Up the stairs go the Doc Martens. That's the good thing about Bill. He's so laid-back. You can do things like have whole conversations through the door, and he doesn't mind. If I ever have a kid (a possibility that looks more remote with every new, single day) I think I'd like it to grow up in Dorrigo.

At the moment, after a night of single hell, I can only think I'm going to end up like Carrington and Lytton Strachey. I'll have a really bad haircut, a platonic relationship with an ugly, bearded man, and then blow my brains out.

Eighteen

IRC, when you've practised it a few times, is simple. Bill makes me do it two or three times (I'm standing up, he's got the wobbly chair back) until I've got the hang of logging in, and then he generously gives me the chair and stands behind me with his arms folded while I type in emoticons. You know, a hash key, plus a star key, plus a few other things makes a drunken, yet happy, face. That kind of thing.

'That has to be a male invention, emoticons,' I say.

'Why?'

He slides the A-K *Yellow Pages* out from under the computer, leaning across me, and I get a whiff of squash court shower gel. It's familiar, and yet strange. Then I realize why. It's the stuff Dan used to use. Mixed with Bill sweat, I suppose.

'Computers don't like balancing on phone books,' Bill mutters. 'You need to raise the height of the desk, not the computer.'

'It's not even a proper desk,' I say.

'No. What is it?'

'Something Jodie thought was a massage table, but it wasn't, so she gave it to me.'

He humours me.

'I've got some bricks upstairs.'

And he galumphs up to get them. Of course, you'd expect Bill to have something like bricks hanging around his flat. I wonder what else he's got up there. Combine harvester parts?

Then he slides around on the carpet on his stomach (God I wish I'd vacuumed in the past six months, it's so embarrassing), propping up the desk legs while I watch.

'Anyway,' he says, in a lying-on-the-floor voice. 'Why are men responsible for emoticons?'

'Well. Lack of emotion. You know. Making a bracket and two full stops look like a smiley face. Sorry. I know you are one, but that's what they're like.'

I suppose this is as personal as conversation with Bill gets. Maybe that's why his ex threw something at him.

'There's something stuck in the carpet,' he says, coming up for air.

I look. Old chocolate. Typical.

'Sorry. Were you lying in it? Do you want some tea? Not herbal. Proper tea.'

'In a minute. Let's try finding a channel first.'

So we get into our normal positions, me standing in front of the computer with my legs bent like Charlie Chaplin because it's never the right height, and him stretching out his long legs in the chair behind me. Every time I make a mistake or hit the wrong key, his chair creaks. It's a funny, comforting sound in a way. The sound of Bill the Boffin cringing at my stupidity, then Dorrigo-ishly holding himself back each time. I suppose I've become used to it. And anyway, computers? What are they? Glorified typewriters.

'I don't think I want to join any of these channels,

they're all called things like Vampire Club.'

'Start one.'

'Can I?'

'Yeah.'

He reaches over, and the lemon shower gel smell squeaks past my nose again.

'Just call it – I don't know, what do you want to call it?'

'Actually,' I hear myself saying slowly, 'I'm trying to find a man.'

He laughs. I knew he would.

'I know it's pathetic,' I say.

'No, it's not,' he says quickly. 'Lots of women are doing it like that.'

Then the worst, smoked-salmon blush I have ever seen creeps up past the neckline of his T-shirt and up, up past the 1945 RSL Club photograph ears, and almost to the top of his head. Then I start blushing too. I have to put my face in my hands, it's so bad.

'Why am I so embarrassed?' I almost yell at him, as if that's going to make everything better.

'Anyway,' he says, recovering. 'What do you want to call it?'

'You won't tell anyone. About me being pathetic. Will you?'

'No. And I won't tell them you had your computer balancing on the *Yellow Pages* either. That's worse you know.'

'OK then. I want a group called . . . I don't know, something about being single. I don't know, Global Singles Solidarity or something. Is that all right?'

'Sure.'

And he types it in, and steers me through it, and I wait. And wait. But nobody's interested. Then finally, after I've trotted back from the kitchen with a pot of real tea, I see Bill pointing at the screen, and it looks as if someone's taken the bait.

'Only one problem, though,' says Bill. 'Wrong sex.'

Her nickname is Sleepless Sue, and she says she lives in New Zealand, and she's been single for two years. Bill and I take turns at typing in questions and answers. It's OK – nothing special. Like getting stuck with someone at a party when you're not drunk enough to really find them interesting.

'Anyway,' says Bill, getting up to go. He still has fluff from my carpet all over his T-shirt.

'Thanks,' I say, still typing and feeling vaguely guilty about neglecting him. Hilary was right. Computers are anti-social.

'You'll have to tell me if it works out,' he says.

'I will.'

And he's gone, Doc Martening his way up the stairs again.

Sleepless Sue signs off not long afterwards, and there's another long wait. Isn't the Internet supposed to be crawling with singles? Or maybe they're all so depressed that a group called Global Singles Solidarity is too much for them. Maybe I should change it to something else. X Files groups seem to have about 25,000 people logged in. Then it comes to me, in the same way that ideas for Breakfast Grit Frisbees still occasionally come to me. The Ex Files. Perfect. Not too sad and pathetic. In fact, possibly considered witty by some eligible males out there. I'm sure somebody else thought of it before me, but who cares.

But before I can change the name, someone called Pierre Dubois logs in.

PIERRE DUBOIS: Greetings, in the name of Global Singles Solidarity.

Pierre Dubois? What is it about that name . . . ? Then I remember. French classes at high school. That stupid book with the bad drawing of two spotty boys on bicycles pointing at fruit and vegetable stands. All those sentences – 'Bonjour, je m'apelle Pierre Dubois. Ou est le fenetre?'

So I type this in, really fast.

TECHNOBIMBO: I know where you got that name.

And the reply comes back.

PD: Oui, bonjour, and I also have a bag of onions and a beret.

So I keep it going.

TB: So you live in North Sydney, right, and you've never even been on a day trip to Calais?
PD: English, Madame.
TB: Really?
PD: London, England. But I live in Paris now. Where are you from?
TB: Sydney.
PD: Ah, the world famous Gay Mardi Gras. Is that why you are in Single Hell?
TB: Too easy. No.
PD: Something to do with men?
TB: That's a bit obvious isn't it?
PD: Something to do with you?
TB: Permit me to use an emoticon :-) Are you really in Paris? What time is it there?
PD: I don't permit you to use an emoticon. Yes, I am in Paris. Near Clichy. It's early. Are you really in Sydney?
TB: Yes. In a flat in Newtown.

PD: Never heard of it :-)

TB: Well, I've never heard of Clichy :-) :-) I've never even been to France. How do I know you're really there?

PD: More importantly, how do you know I'm a man?

TB: If you're not, go away.

PD: I am. Sorry. Trust me. Definitely male. Have this on my chest: / / / / / / / / /

TB: I should tell you. I'm looking for my soulmate.

PD: FOBL

TB: What?

PD: Fall Over Backwards Laughing. It's an Internet thing. You wouldn't understand, Madame Techno-bimbo. That is, if you really are a TB. How do I know you're a woman anyway?

TB: I have a crap love life and cry a lot.

PD: Ah.

TB: R U a computer nerd?

PD: Non, je suis Pierre Dubois.

TB: Yeah, right. Anyway, what's Paris like? I *can't* believe I'm talking to you all the way over there. Sorry, typing to you.

PD: Paris is great. Better without my ex girlfriend in it.

TB: I was going to change the name of this to The Ex Files, as a matter of fact.

PD: Very clever.

TB: I make bad puns for a living.

PD: Graffiti artist?

TB: I write commercials for frisbees.

My fingers have been racing across the keyboard so far, in the same way that you find yourself clicking with people sometimes and just spend the whole night raving on to them after the first hello. But now I find myself wondering what Pierre Dubois looks like. If he's lying about the ex. All of that. Then it occurs to me. This is the Net. You can say anything. So I do.

TB: What do you look like, how old are you, are you really single, are you straight?

PD: Sigh.

TB: Well, come on. If we're going to continue this conversation . . .

PD: And what's your favourite cheese, and can you play table tennis, and do your ovaries work?

TB: Pierre, I'm shocked.

PD: OK. What are you really worried about?

TB: I've never done this before. Here I am talking to you and you could be anyone.

PD: Je suis Pierre Dubois. Je suis single white male seeking single white e-mail.

TB: Can I be honest?

PD: What is le Internet for?

TB: I can't help thinking you're fat, forty and you've got a beard.

PD: You left out halitosis.

TB: And?

PD: My forty-seven children and gambling debts.

TB: In Australia, we have this word – spunk.

PD: Go on.

TB: Are you a spunk?

PD: I'm C of E, if you must know.

TB: Are you a dag?

PD: A what?

TB: Do you wear socks and sandals?

PD: Only during sex :-)

And so it goes. Backwards and forwards we type, and

it feels like playing ping pong or something, click, click, click. Most of all, I feel like a fisherman who's found something decent on the first cast. Not a bottom-dwelling gudgeon, but a proper catch. And amazingly – by myself. Without Bill the Boffin assistance.

We keep typing friendly rubbish for a while, and I shift around in my chair at some point, only to find that my entire right leg has gone to sleep. And so has the rest of the world. Peering through the window, I can only see two square chunks of light in the opposite block of flats, instead of the usual eight or nine.

PD: I hate to leave you when the conversation was getting interesting.
TB: But you are.
PD: My lunch break is over, Madame. In fact it was over an hour ago.
TB: I know the feeling. What do you do?
PD: C'est une mystery, Madame.
TB: Hang on. I have to find out how late it is.

And when I run to my bedroom and flick the alarm clock around, it says 1 a.m. I've been talking to Pierre Dubois – surely I can't call him that, the boy with the onions in the French language books – for an hour.

TB: It's 1 a.m.
PD: Merde!
TB: I have to go. I have to *work* tomorrow.
PD: Your secret is safe with me. Come back again tomorrow night.
TB: Yes?
PD: Same place, same time. Do you want to make this a private chat room?
TB: ?????

196

PD: A chat room for deux, Madame Technobimbo. Nobody else can drop in. Log in 7 p.m. your time.
TB: OK Pierre. Can't I call you something else?
PD: My real name is Vincent Scrotum.
TB: You slay me.
PD: OK. Good night TB from PD. Sweet dreams.
TB: Good night.

And for some reason, I have no idea why, I leave him a x. Just a lower case x, but a x nonetheless. Maybe Mad Month has softened my brain.

Nineteen

The application form Jodie filled in for her documentary application for *Women In Love* (as it's now called) is something I've never quite managed to forget. 'Who will follow genius New Zealand female film director Jane Campion into the future if we don't?' I mean, really. But this morning, sitting next to the chicks at their favourite vegetarian cafe, a place where they serve you eggplant that looks like dried up dead mice, I can't help but feel proud to know them.

'Remember our doco, Vic?'

'How could I forget.'

Didi giggles.

'Anyway, so we're doing it,' Jodie says, trying to be cool about it. But she can't help herself, though, grinning from one silver Indian earring to the other silver Indian earring. Then it occurs to me. This must be the first proper job Didi's actually had in two years. No wonder she's so happy.

'So, do I get to be in it, then?'

'Sure!'

'I mean, I am the Queen of Love Gone Wrong. You know that, don't you. If you're going to make a film about the female love experience, then you have to interview the female love disaster zone.'

'Actually,' says Jodie earnestly, sticking her chin forward, 'it would be really good.'

'As a thankyou for helping us,' Didi says, 'we thought we could take you out for a big fat juicy steak.'

And I can tell they've been working on this joke for at least two days, because they're squirming and giggling like two five-year-olds in Hilary's library who've managed to wee in the velvet beanbag without being discovered.

'Wow, red meat with blood dripping all over it. Thankyou. Would you like to watch?'

'We wouldn't have got the money without you,' Jodie says.

'Shucks, it was nothing.'

'We would like to film you, though,' says Didi, biting her lip.

'No nudies.'

'You know it's not about that,' Jodie says, putting on her 'let's talk about it' Women's Circle voice.

'What then?'

'Just Love. Sex. Being a girl. What does it mean to you, that kind of thing.'

'What is love?' Didi muses, staring wistfully out of the window in the manner of a creative, unemployed street puppet theatre person. Which in fact she is.

'Thirty years' experience,' I say. 'I'm the expert. And you may as well interview me while I'm halibut.'

'What?'

'Halibut. Celibate. You know. All the young people are saying it, it's the hip expression for the nineties, Kylie told me.'

And I can tell I'm never going to get a steak out of those two, but part of me is quite pleased to be in the film anyway. Not that they'll get anything out of me. Ha.

I suppose I should tell them about Pierre Dubois, but I don't. I'm not sure why. It's not embarrassment, because I'm beyond that. It's something else. Not wanting to talk about something until it becomes a bit more real? Anyway. I let it go.

When I'm back at work and finishing things off later on in the day, I find myself hopping around a bit. It's a vague, almost, but not quite, excited feeling.

'You going out tonight?' says Kylie, noticing me.

'Of course not.'

And it takes me a few minutes, and a few slurps of cappuccino to get my head around it. It's not the sort of feeling I had when Liam used to walk past our cubicles with his sideburns and brown suede jacket looking gorgeous, and it's nothing like a Dan-and-footy-bus love madness feeling. But it's definitely . . . oh I don't know. Have I really got the energy any more? I mean, we're talking about a computer.

I don't know who the hell Pierre Dubois is, how old he is, if he's married, if he's a pervert . . . He lives on the other side of the world for God's sake. But still. Seven is hammered in to my brain and at 5 p.m., with a superannuation brochure still in front of me, it seems hours away. Maybe in the pathetic, desperate, boffin-girl new world I am inhabiting, IRC a deux counts as a kind of a date. Maybe that's the feeling.

'Kylie?'

'Ye-es,' she says, on the other side of the screen with the furry green monsters all over it.

'If you were a gorgeous, eligible single English guy in Paris, would you be using the Internet to meet women?'

'Joke.'

'No, serious question.'

'No way. I mean—' she makes a face.

'Yep. OK.'

'Don't even THINK about it,' she says absent-mindedly, flicking through her Slim n' Smile folder. 'I mean, why would you? But maybe he can't speak French. Maybe that's why he's desperate. Nobody will talk to him.'

'But let's say he can speak French.'

'Yeah, well.'

She shrugs, and leaves it at that. So. Guru Kylie has spoken. But why is it, that when I'm strap-hanging home on the train at six o'clock, whole chunks of my conversation with PD come back to me? 'What's your favourite cheese, and do you play table tennis?' And 'Sweet dreams.'

Nice. I'm being stupid, I know. But at the moment that feels seriously nice.

When I get home I look at the piece of chocolate stuck in the carpet, under the desk with the bricks, and decide to vacuum. Bill's going to hear the noise all the way through the ceiling, but it gives me something to do from 6.45 to 7 p.m. Then, as the time comes closer to log in, I do something even more unusual. I iron my underwear. The last time I did that was in the Phillip Zebruscki era.

Then it's only three to seven. What else can I do? Wash my windows? Put on a Body Shop face mask? The computer is sitting there with its great, grey blank face looking about as exciting and sexy as a bar fridge. Funny, then, that I can almost hear myself breathing slightly faster when I sit down in front of it. And here we go, I suppose. Except for one thing. I can't get through. The modem makes its usual strangled noise, three lights go on, and then . . . nothing.

I try, and I keep on trying. Click, ping, ping, disconnect. Click, ping, ping, disconnect. DAMN my el cheapo service provider. Bill was right. For every dollar an hour you save, you have to suffer agonies. Not so much surfing the net as getting bogged in quicksand.

Finally, at 7.30 I admit defeat, give up, and ring them up to complain. The line's engaged there as well. Hopeless. So then I do something even more constructive. I ring up Dan.

Why do I ring up Dan? I don't know. Maybe it was that dream I had this morning, the one where we were swimming together with our arms around each other's necks in the North Sydney pool. If I want to stop myself from ringing, of course, all I have to do now is seize my own right hand and jam it under a large object. But hey. Here I am. And there's the phone.

So I ring up Dan, thus instantly turning myself into one of those warped females that other women write into problem pages about. You know the kind of thing – WHEN HIS EX WON'T LET GO. Except it isn't Dan who picks up the phone, is it? It's Erica.

'Hello?'

She's got that slightly posey kind of voice which means you're meant to think she's read Dostoevsky, but she's still cool. It's not pearls and polo Australian, but it's different. Warm. Rounded. Different from my whine, anyway. And I find myself whining now.

'Is Dan there?'

'Who's calling?'

'Oh, you know.' And my voice is really disappearing now, squeezing in my throat so that I sound like a vomiting cat. *Oh you know.*

'Doesn't matter,' I hear myself saying, as if it's all one

word. Then I put the phone down, and wait for my heart to stop clanging.

Oh, God. Dan, Dan. Can I cry now? But I can't, it must be the shock and horror of actually hearing her voice, and picturing her floating around his house. So I finish ironing my underwear, and adjust all my bra straps, including Super-bra, and switch on the TV, and switch it off, and try my computer again, and give up, and have a shower and go to bed.

It's just been a bed lately. Somewhere to collapse, in fact. But now it's turned into Haunted Bed again. The place where I used to have sex with the man who is now having sex with Erica the Tattoo Lawyer.

Oh, well. Insomnia Central, here we go. And if the mysterious Pierre Dubois and I ever meet up again in cyberspace, which we probably won't, because he's given up on me, I suppose I'll have something to talk about with him. Daniel bloody Hawker. Still Daniel Hawker after all this time, in fact . . .

At about 2 a.m., I give up. Pink bubble isn't working. Jodie's alternate nostril breathing isn't working, it's just irritating me and suffocating me by turns. Thinking about myself on a deserted beach on a beautiful island isn't working either. Every time I picture the sand and the waves, I see a bitch in a bikini with a tattoo on her arm sprawled on a sand dune.

Maybe I should think about washing the windows again. Very quietly, and thoughtfully. Surely a gentle swishing sound wouldn't wake up the street? Or . . . I don't know. Try the Net again? Just to see? I get up in the bunny nightie and sit on the wobbly chair. And fall off it.

Ping, ping, squelch, fizz, silence. The modem glows like green fairy lights on a tree and I'm through at last. I find Bill's scribbled instructions and I follow the sequence. Do this, do that, yup, yup. Then it occurs to me that I'd better close the blinds. My reputation is sad enough in this street, after all the Dan dramas, without the neighbours seeing me playing with the Internet at two o' clock in the morning.

I know Pierre Dubois from Paris will have given up hours ago. But it's worth a try. Better than Find A Friend File, anyway. Better than Men Who Cook Apple and Raisin Dumplings, or whatever it was.

As usual, the whole world is awake. There are even more IRC channels online than I saw with Bill the other night. The rest of the world has woken up while Australia's going to bed, I suppose. But nothing called Single Solidarity or even Ex Files. Nothing.

A hope, just a faint hope, sends me to Lycos. If he's been using the Pierre Dubois name with me, maybe he uses it in other groups as well. So if I do a search . . .

I type it in. And I get back French bread roll companies, and pottery students in Grenoble, and all kinds of typical Net strangeness. But not my man in Paris.

Maybe he's fallen into another IRC channel. Maybe if I just pick the right one, I could log in and find him again. The odds of that, I suppose, are about fifty to one, but I can't sleep, and if nothing else this will bore me into sliding off the wobbly director's chair, and onto my nice clean carpet, and at least I'll get my six hours.

The screen's so bright I can almost feel my eyes shrinking into my head. But I scroll down the screen yet again, past channels for ageing punks, and single parents, and karate masters, and people who like doing it with small animals. Then I see it. Global Single Solidarity. It's there.

About the only decent thing they taught me at high

school was speed typing, and I use it now, racing in to log on at a rate that would have won me a gold typing star in Grade Ten. And he's there.

PD: Bonjour, Madame.
TB: PD! Sorry I couldn't get in.
PD: I knew it.
TB: I didn't think you'd wait :-)
PD: I thought we said no emoticons :-)
TB: Sorry :-)
PD: Lucky you got me. I just checked back on the off chance.
TB: Sorry, sorry.
PD: Stop saying sorry. Anyway. How are you tonight?
TB: Traumatized.
PD: And???
TB: Do you really want to know?
PD: Je suis Pierre Dubois, I always want to know.

And for the first time, I understand what people are always going on about. You know, the freedom of the Net. Yes, if I think about it too hard – typing in stuff about my personal life to someone I know nothing about on the other side of the world – it could worry me. But I don't know. There's something true about the freedom of being able to type in absolutely anything to absolutely anyone. And more importantly, there's something about PD. Instant trust? I don't know. Anyway. He's in Paris. And he thinks my name is Technobimbo. And for all he knows, I could be a toothless old crone with a tartan shopping trolley and a moustache as well.

TB: I just called my ex.

PD: Braver than me.

TB: I got *her*

PD: And?

TB: I hate her.

PD: Give me the worst five things.

TB: Voice, tattoo, thinks she's ideologically sound, oh I don't know.

PD: More information please, Technobimbo.

TB: My ex is a lawyer. She's a lawyer.

PD: Don't tell me. She only takes on serial killers from underprivileged backgrounds.

TB: You got it. She picked up the phone.

PD: Ow.

TB: I made a dick of myself.

PD: That's a *quaint* Australian phrase you've got there. I'm sorry :-(I think I know what that feels like.

TB: Am I allowed to hate her?

PD: For about a year.

TB: I'm supposed to be over him.

PD: Who says?

TB: I had my Transitional Man.

PD: Your what?

TB: Have you ever done that? Transitional Woman?

PD: If I ever meet one I'll let you know.

TB: Maybe it's just me.

PD: And what was wrong with Transitional Man?

TB: I cried when we had sex and he went for a swim. And he puts knots in his condoms.

PD: You're not really laughing about this, are you?

TB: How did you guess?

And it's funny, but it's making me cry. He's making me cry, this complete stranger. His sympathy, I suppose. It's so cold, this grey computer screen, and it's so strange, watching the words flash down the page from someone out there – in the ether. But I'm tired, and Dan's in bed with her when he belongs to me, and I'm fed up, and if you really must know, I'm losing it. Really losing it. I can feel a tear itching down one side of my face.

PD: Are you OK now? I worry about you, Technobimbo.

TB: Yes. No. It's about two-thirty here.

PD: I *know* the feeling – can't sleep?

TB: Nope.

PD: Maybe we should change the subject.

TB: It's OK.

PD: How about hyenas. Did you know the female of the species is developing male genitalia?

TB: No, let's talk about your love life.

PD: Like Greta Garbo.

TB: ???

PD: A mystery wrapped inside an enigma wrapped inside a parcel of fish and chips wrapped inside a great dark thing.

TB: I told you mine, you tell me yours.

PD: She wanted space, man.

TB: I hate it when they say that.

PD: I said, find an astronaut.

TB: No you didn't. You cried, I can tell you cried.

PD: You just want me to say that.

TB: You can tell me.

PD: No, I didn't cry.

TB: You should. You'll feel better.

PD: And you have, and you do?

TB: Maybe that's a crap theory too.

PD: Yes.

TB: Anyway, Pierre . . .

PD: You have an Anyway for me?

TB: Anyway, at least you didn't throw your pills in the bin.

PD: You did?

TB: I may as well confess.

PD: Why?

TB: I feel like telling you. I'm probably *mad*.

PD: No :-) You're not mad. Tell me if it helps. Why did you throw them in the bin?

TB: Isn't it obvious?

PD: Sorry.

TB: If you really want to ruin your relationships at any time in the future I could probably give you lessons.

PD: You're so hard on yourself, ma cherie.

TB: What does that mean? My cherry?

PD: Yes. My cherry. Didn't they teach you anything in your French class?

TB: I'm tired.

PD: You must sleep.

TB: Yes.

PD: We must do this again some time.

TB: Yes.

TB: Tomorrow? What if I can't get through.

PD: What's your e-mail?

TB: shep@mpx.com.au. What's yours?

PD: It changes too much.

TB: Why?

PD: Work.

TB: Ah, the mysterious work :-)

PD: I'll e-mail you first, OK?

TB: OK.

PD: Sleep well. And can I say something?

TB: Yes.

PD: It's a very, very old James Taylor song.

TB: My mother loves James Taylor.
PD: You know the one?
TB: Yes. Thankyou. I think so.
PD: Good night. Sweet dreams again.
TB: Bye.

How incredibly corny. James Taylor. *You've Got A Friend*. When my mother used to put that on at her fiftysomething dinner parties Hilary and I used to swipe it off immediately and put on the theme from *Shaft* instead (her only other record, let's face it.) But tonight, I don't know, I'm glad I can remember the words to that song, even if I do have to fill in some of the verses with bla bla bla. And I know I'll be checking my e-mail again tomorrow.

Twenty

At work, I manage to put in about an hour on the superannuation brochure when I'm hauled off for a chat with Bobbi. You generally smell Bobbi before you see her – a blast of Chanel, and then you look down and see black patent leather heels, and she's just . . . there. Like something out of Greek mythology, if I think about it. Or an episode of *Hercules*. She just kind of appears, and then you feel as if you've met your Fate.

'Hi, Victoria.'

'Oh, hi.'

I suppose Kylie couldn't make excuses about me coughing up blood for ever, and let's face it, I was half an hour late today, and everyone knows I'm way behind on an advertorial that should have been in last Tuesday. I follow Bobbi down the corridor, past the photocopier slaves who are shunting out piles of evil-smelling paper, and into her office.

'Now.'

'Bobbi, has anybody ever told you that you smile exactly like Sally Field being blown over the rooftops in *The Flying Nun*?'

Of course, I don't say that.

'Now . . .'

I bite my lip. 'I think I know.'

'Yuh.'

'I'm sorry.'

She nods, repeatedly – and for too long a time – like Mrs Brady. 'You know we have the three-tier warning system in this company?'

'Yes.'

'OK, and we have you on tier one. But on a personal level . . .'

Oh please no, not the personal level.

'I do understand what you're going through,' she says, suddenly switching to Mary Tyler Moore. 'I realize that you are going through a – difficult – situation in your personal life, and we take that into account whenever we consider the people here making a creative contribution, in particular.'

Thank God. The creative = neurotic theory. Saved again. Even if she is completely wrong, and the photocopier slaves have more hysterics and dramas than I'll ever have Toblerone.

'So this is just your one tier talk, I guess. But I do have to know about your commitment here as well, Victoria. We can take you through a temporary situation, but that underlying faith and mutual sense of commitment is very important.'

'I'm happy with the job.'

'Happy?'

Damn. I think my mouth formed the word happy at the same time that my eyes did a kind of Edward Munch Scream thing.

'It's a good job, and I don't want to lose it,' I say, all in one breath.

'That's good. We wouldn't want to lose you either, you know that.'

'It's not about the Slim n' Smile thing as well, is it?'

'No.'

It's a weird one. I can count on one hand the number of people in the world who know about my world famous anorexia episode, and she's one of them. You can understand the others. Parents, Hilary, Dan, Anthony the Bastard Scuba Diver. But it feels strange to know that someone called Bobbi is the other one. Then again, maybe that's why she's being so nice to me. Perhaps I fascinate her on a personal level. Umm, do I fascinate her on a personal level?

'There does need to be an attitude adjustment. I have to make that clear.'

Damn, I don't fascinate her.

'I'll adjust it.'

'Yuh.'

And I'm out, out, out of there. And I would kill for a triple-strength flat white now, on top of the cappuccino I already had, and the last thing I feel like doing is sliding back into the cubicle next to Kylie and hammering out more scare-tactic superannuation waffle. ('Would you like to be eating Pal meaty bites when you're sixty-five years old and rubbing Tiger Balm on yourself to keep warm just because you spent all your money on gorgeous shoes?') However. Attitude adjustment. Yes. First Tier Warning. Totally. When you're Victoria Total Bloody Relationship Disaster Shepworth you can't afford to be unemployed as well.

Twenty-one

'This interview will go into the part of the film we want to call Love and Weddings,' Jodie says. We're sitting in her kitchen, because it's the darkest room in the house, with a few of Didi's old batik sarongs gaffa-taped to the windows.

Natalie, next to Hilary on the couch, has been told to shhh repeatedly since the film started, so she's starting to wriggle now. And Didi's perched on top of the kitchen table like one of those cross-legged Irish leprechauns people hang from their wing-mirrors, wearing a pair of 1950s cat's-eye glasses so that she can actually see things for a change. And one of the women Jodie's been interviewing for the film is lying on the floor right in front of the projector, hanging on her own every word as we all look on. It's a very strange little viewing panel Jodie's found. But then, maybe *Women In Love* is the kind of film which will always attract strange little viewers. So maybe it's just right — perfect, in fact.

Jodie's in charge of the projector, and you have to admire her. She wrote the application, she's been filming the whole thing, asked all the questions and now she's even made little celery boats with ricotta cheese in them to hand round to the audience.

'What did your wedding day mean to you?' we hear Jodie saying in the film, out of sync.

'Death,' says the rather scarey-looking woman she's interviewing, also massively out of sync.

I find myself lazily wondering what Pierre Dubois would make of this. It's the kind of thing I can imagine us having a very long and silly conversation about. If I'm ever allowed to call this net thing a conversation. And, yeah. I still haven't told anyone.

Jodie's voice-over sounds very clear, very solemn and a bit shaky.

'Is it any coincidence,' her voice booms, 'that the same place that a woman marries in is the same place she will die in?'

She's taken random footage of a bunch of bored-looking funeral directors wandering down to the pub at lunchtime for this bit. Nobody says anything. Then, of course, I do.

'I LIKE WEDDINGS,' I say loudly.

And you know what Jodie does? She only stops the projector, switches all the lights on and rushes at me with a camera while Didi points a microphone, that's all.

'So, you're saying you like weddings, Victoria. I wonder if you could explain that to us?'

Oh give me a break. I mean, really.

'I just like them. They mean something.'

'Even when one in three marriages will end in divorce?'

'Yup. I don't care.'

'Even though your own parents are divorced?'

'Oi, that's a bit personal.'

And it goes on, and on, until I pout Hollywoodishly and say, 'That's enough.' I know they'll only use about one sentence anyway. I've been in Jodie's documentaries before.

When I finally return home after an eternal wait for the bus, the first thing I do is flick on the modem and check my e-mail, way ahead of putting the kettle on, even way ahead of checking my answering machine. And it's there. My Pierre message is there. It feels like Christmas. Oh God. Is this what my life has come to?

To: shep@mpx.com.au
From: pierre@netshop.com.fr
Re: Superannuation Brochure.

This must be the reply to the other reply I sent after my little talk with Bobbi. So I scroll down the page, and read:

Dearest Technobimbo,
I've been thinking about the superannuation brochure you're writing (somebody has to). I can see why you don't want to scare people by threatening them with having to live on dogfood on toast in their old age. But the other idea is even worse. Promising young people golfing holidays in their old age as a reward for their canny investment at the age of 25 is just going to make them feel depressed and frightened. Even more than the thought of eating dogfood. If you don't believe me, take a survey. Eating meaty doggy chunks in your old age, or wearing tartan slacks and spending 20 minutes sizing up a golf shot? PS: There is no charge for this information. PPS: Have you recovered from talking to the tattooed lawyer from hell yet? Pierre.

I send this message back.

217

To: pierre@netshop.com.fr
From: shep@mpx.com.au
Re: Tattooed Lawyer From Hell Recovery Program

Dear Pierre,
Thankyou for your useful suggestion for my super-annuation brochure. You are right, having a picture of old people playing golf will only frighten and upset the twenty-five year olds whose money they are trying to grab. Now, to the important thing. My feelings about Erica the Tattoo Lawyer.

And I stop right there. I have to. I mean, my feelings about Erica. Am I really expecting some guy whose real name I don't even know to really understand this? He's asked me to write it down, and I know he's being kind, and I know it would be good for me, but the way I'm feeling at the moment this could turn out to be a whole day's work, not a quick e-mail. Then again, if PD's around right now and he's looking at his computer, I could just reach him in time to ask him permission before I begin my verbal splat attack. So I type this in.

Is it OK if I go on about this for a few pages?
Cheers, TB.

It takes him the equivalent of one cup of tea, one reapplication of eye pencil and one cushion re-arrangement on my couch (Sydney time) to get back to me.

To: shep@mpx.com.au
From: pierre@netshop.com.fr
Re: Uncork your Soul

Dear Technobimbo, feel free to write as much as you want. Your friend, Pierre.

But it's funny. When I have to put it all down on the computer screen, it's really like a letter to Dan, not to Pierre. Or maybe it's a letter to her as well. I don't know.

To: pierre@netshop.com.fr
From: shep@mpx.com.au
Re: Soul Uncorking

Dear Pierre,
Thankyou for your kind offer. As you know, I am unable to talk to my friends about Dan any more due to the following reasons:

A) They are bored with it, and have already had to listen to Transitional Man (Liam) crap as well. Consequently, I feel I am out of relationship chronological order and should get over it, blah blah. In fact,
B) It has been so long ago that one of my old schoolfriends (Hilary) has gone gay in the mean-time, which means
C) How can I talk about the man dumps woman thing anyway? Or even woman wants to kill woman scenario, which is very anti Women's Circle (I am sure they have them in Clichy, you know the kind of thing, they massage each other's feet, too cool to use the word sisterhood but might as well, do graf-fiti with female symbols all holding hands together on walls).

ANYWAY Pierre. Life has come to a pretty pass

when I have to do gut spillage with someone I've only just met, and even then not in the flesh. But I do feel as if I know you. Sort of. Well, you seem to understand me anyway :-) (Ha! Emoticon!)

OK, so here it is. The twenty reasons why I would like to see Erica Tattoo Lawyer publicly hanged with Dan's jockstrap, and I don't give a shit about the sisterhood, if you must know.

1) She wore denim shorts to a lawyers' barbecue averaging twenty degrees celsius when other people (eg: me) were wearing big woolly jumpers with reindeers on the front. And why? Because she has fabulous legs and was pissed off at having to cover them up in court all the time.

2) She laughs at every pathetic joke – or even jokette – made by any male, whatsoever, in fact anybody with a penis, in the immediate vicinity. However, when women in the surrounding area are genuinely funny (example: self, Pierre, as you know, a wit and raconteur from way back) her face becomes brick-like.

3) She uses her mobile phone to ring Dan's mobile phone. When he was with me he used to call that a wank. Now he's with her – not a wank, apparently.

4) I have been introduced to her three (3) times and she has never bothered to so much as NOD IN RECOGNITION or remember my name. Ever.

5) She is in the social pages all the time with exactly the same kind of photo – eg, laughing with her head back and clanging around with these big bracelets on her wrists, and showing off her tattoo. And she never shows her fillings when she laughs either, probably because:

6) She doesn't have any as she only eats raw foods and wholefoods and

7) She loves nothing better than a nice slice of orange for lunch, and

8) She's never felt the need for chocolate and can't imagine why other sad women like it because

9) She's a saint.

10) Not that I want to push the point or anything, but when she wore the denim shorts to the lawyers' barbecue she spent about fifteen minutes longer than necessary bending over with her bottom stuck in the air to look in the Esky for her bottle of mineral water which

11) She consumes at the rate of two litres a day, but only if it's

12) Evian (eg: French, Pierre), despite the fact that she

13) Craps on for hours about Pacific nuclear tests which

14) She is an expert on, because

15) She does legal work at a *special rate* for Greenpeace which

16) Amazingly enough, the whole world seems to know about, despite her

17) 'Modesty' and 'Cool attitude' about it, according to Daniel Hawker, who seems to think

18) She's a saint (again) thus enabling her to have

19) Hairy armpits which

20) I never got away with, not for a moment.

As you can see, Pierre, I'm not over anything. I wish I was, and I thought Liam (Transitional Man, you remember) would do it for me, but all it took was her picking up the phone for a minute, and I seem to have lost the plot. Or I've got a plot, but the plot's like a bad episode of Dynasty. In fact, I feel like Joan Collins. What am I going to do?

And can I tell you about my worst case scenario fear as well? The one where I turn up to see Jodie and Didi's Women In Love thing at the Sydney Film Festival, and Dan and Erica are both there, and she's wearing the denim shorts again, and I'm by myself, and they sit there listening to me talking about weddings for five minutes, right in front of me, with their arms around each other, nearly killing themselves laughing.

I don't think I told you about the weddings thing. Sorry PD. When I was watching Jodie's trial run of her film, I made a foolish comment about actually liking them as opposed to thinking of them in connection with coffins, corpses, cremation, rotting and death. You know. Anyway, they made me talk about it in front of a camera and now I've got a horrible feeling Jodie's going to use it. In fact, I know she will, because I am the only hetero she's managed to get for the film so far.

What else can I tell you? I'm surprised you've read this far Pierre. But thanks anyway. I guess I'll hear from you. Technobimbo (Maybe in the year 2020 we can reveal our true identities. Ha.)

As soon as I'm off the net, the phone rings. For an insane moment I think it's him. Pierre. Then I realize someone must have been trying to get through for ages. They have. It's my mother.

'Every time I ring up there's a strange sound.'

'Sorry. It's the Net.'

'The what?'

'The Internet.'

'Oh. The Internet.'

I know she'll change the subject immediately, and she does. I've noticed this a lot in people who have consumed too much information over a 40–60 year life span. Having stuffed so many things into their brains over the years – The Cuban Missile Crisis, Marilyn Monroe, The Beatles, The Moon Landing, The Pill, Pauline Hanson – they reach a point where no more information can be allowed to enter. I think Johnny Rotten finally did it for my mother, in 1977. He was the last straw. The last bit of new information she could take. One more little thing like punk rock and – bang – that was it, her brain shut down completely.

Some things still get through the filter, of course. Bloody Ralph Fiennes, there's one. But don't even think about Gianni Versace, Nine-inch-nails or teppan-yaki. Not that I think about them either, but you know what I mean.

'Anyway, I'm ringing up about this film, your friend's film. Jodie.'

'Yes?'

'She rang me. She said they wanted the voice of a strong, older woman.'

'Just the voice, then?'

'No-o.'

'I forbid you.'

'Why? She seems pretty desperate, Victoria, I don't think she would have rung me otherwise.'

'I'll kill her.'

'What harm can it do? She says you're in it.'

'Mum, trust me, it's not your kind of film.'

'What sort of film is it then?'

'Put it this way. Shirley Maclaine wouldn't do it.'

'Oh.'

End of conversation. I knew the Shirley Maclaine factor would do it for me.

'It's a very different sort of film. Not your cup of tea.'

'Aah.'

And I almost feel like telling her about Hilary and Natalie while I'm at it, just to make completely sure that Jodie's mad idea about putting my mother in a film isn't going to see the light of day. But that's yet another information overload I believe I should spare her. As you do.

Twenty-two

Perhaps because it's Friday night, singledom seems worse than usual. I can hear little gaggles of twenty-somethings shrieking in the street outside – some girl's giggling 'Norman! No! No! Norman!' and you can tell she's enjoying herself, whoever or whatever Norman might be. There's nothing on TV. Helena Chettle mumbled something about having me over for dinner, but it doesn't look as if it's going to happen – well, certainly not tonight. Carrie the pisspot architect, who was a Dan friend too, has mysteriously disappeared from my life, and she was always a good Friday night bet. And even *Wuthering Heights,* a Teenage Fanclub CD and cashew nuts aren't going to do it for me right now. It's Friday night. I'm thirty. I'm alive. Why aren't I out somewhere?

When I catch myself thinking that I should have been nicer to Liam after all, I really start to worry. And although I've been steeling myself not to even look at the computer, not to be a sad Net junkie, not to be a geek girl with a guilty secret, I find myself flicking on all the switches, and watching the dancing green lights on the modem in the same mad, staring way that old ladies look at poker machines in RSL clubs. That's it.

I'm an addict. I have no hope and dignity left.
There's an e-mail. From him. Thank God.

To: shep@mpx.com.au
From: pierre@netshop.com.fr
Re: Dinner tonight (your time)

Dear Miss Technobimbo,
If you're not doing anything this Friday night, per-
haps you'd like to have dinner with me. I know a
nice place down the road, BYO. Maybe you could
bring some wine? Anyway. If you're there, let's
make it 8pm. It's about time we got to know each
other better (emoticon, emoticon). Pierre.

Silly cyberwanker. Honestly, is this what my life has
come to? And I can't even pick up the phone and run
his message past Hilary, because Hilary's not there any
more, she's out with Natalie. And anyway. I still
haven't told them. Haven't told anybody.

Maybe I should, but it's just that I have a feeling they
might tell me to stop. It's unhealthy, this. Total nerd
behaviour. And anyway. As if. Ha. Dinner in cyberspace, I don't think so. This isn't how Helena Chettle
would behave. And look at Helena Chettle. A happy
woman. I want to be Helena Chettle.

At ten minutes to eight, I log into the channel. Our
channel. And I pull down the horrible old cask of red
from the top shelf in the kitchen, and find a glass, and
sit down. Stupid. Really, really stupid. And he's there.
As if I thought he'd be anywhere else.

PD: Hi. You're early.
TB: Better than being late.
PD: You look great.

TB: How the hell would you know?

PD: Come on, play the game.

TB: I'm wearing an old grey cotton dressing gown that shows my nipples. It doesn't look great. It's got egg down the front.

PD: That's OK. It's that kind of restaurant. Sorry, I just realized you typed in the word nipples. Give me a moment.

TB: -----

PD: Thanks.

TB: Do we eat while we do this?

PD: I've already ordered for you.

TB: Is it my imagination or are you being sleazier than normal tonight?

PD: If we were really having dinner you wouldn't say that.

TB: No.

PD: Well, behave.

TB: Tell me honestly. Do you think I'm sad and desperate?

PD: Am I?

TB: I don't know, that's what worries me.

PD: OK. I can tell it's going to be that kind of night.

TB: Do you realize I'm drinking wine here?

PD: Good. So am I.

TB: Really?

PD: Beaujolais.

TB: Australian cask red.

PD: Better than nothing. So, to answer your question, am I sad and desperate? No I am not sad and desperate. I am a long way from home. I have moved to a place where people speak a different language, and my ex girlfriend wants so much space she can hardly stand being in the same ten kilometres as me. I happen to like IRC and one night I met the most interesting woman I have found in almost a year.

TB: Oh shut up

PD: So does that make me sad and desperate?

TB: I wish you'd tell me your real name.

PD: Later, Madame.

TB: So there is a later in all of this, is there?

PD: Well, *I* certainly hope so.

It's a very weird sensation, drinking red wine while tapping into a computer. And looking at my desk (well all right then, Jodie's old massage table) I can't help thinking it looks like one of those quizzes they used to have in the cartoon sections of the newspaper. Spot the difference. One of these things doesn't fit, what is it, kids? Oh yes. The big cask of red wine among the computer discs, paper clips, pens and piles of paper.

TB: Will I ever get to know what you look like?

PD: Is it really important?

TB: Yes.

PD: I can't do these things. I'm a man, for God's sake.

TB: Handlebar moustache?

PD: No.

TB: Goatee?

PD: No.

TB: Sideburns?

PD: No.

TB: What sort of nose?

PD: Gerard Depardieu.

TB: Really.

PD: Average. TB, do appearances matter so much to you?

TB: Get off it. And don't tell me you haven't wondered about me.
PD: Beautiful on the inside.
TB: Sleazebucket.

Slurp, slurp. The wine is disgusting, but I'm at that mindless knock-it-back stage now. And down the page the words creep, so that I find myself falling into a steady rhythm of drinking and scrolling down. Slurp, scroll, slurp, scroll. It's outrageous, the way we flirt. Like two stags locking antlers. Or something. God I think I must be drunk already.

TB: Pierre, this cask wine is very potent.
PD: The interesting thing is, will you start slurring your words?
TB: Are you really drinking over there?
PD: Yes. This is Paris.
TB: Do you think you'll ever come to Australia?
PD: Will you ever come here?
TB: Only if Breakfast Grits launch Le Grits de Breakfast frisbee.
PD: Maybe we could meet in the middle.
TB: On the Equator.
PD: I'll be the one with the big nose.
TB: I'll be wearing my dressing gown.
PD: Madame, this is really embarrassing.
TB: What is?
PD: I have to go to the Gents.
TB: Well, this is a cyber restaurant so feel free to go to the cyber loo. Or the real loo, even. I think I've had too much wine, Pierre.
PD: Back in five.

And he disappears from the screen, almost as if he

really was leaving the room for a while, all of which makes this seem very — I don't know. Very real? Like actually having a dinner date with someone? Or maybe it's just very bloody bizarre, I don't know.

Jodie and Didi had this very earnest discussion once about soulmates, not long after they'd started going out together. Didi said she thought that people were joined by a kind of invisible silver cord, like an umbilical cord, and even though they could be living miles away from each other, sooner or later the cord would tug them back and they would meet each other, just as they'd been destined to since birth. I think she might have been rubbing her stomach as she explained this theory, all of which makes me feel like rubbing my stomach now. Invisible silver cords. Yes.

It is a bit like that with him, and I know I'm drinking horrible cask wine, but I seem to be making sense to myself here. I can't see PD, I can't smell him, I can't hear him, I can't touch him. I don't know who the hell he is, or where he works. But there's a kind of cord thing in there somewhere. What Jodie always calls (in capital letters) A Connectedness. I really do know him. I hardly know him, but I know him. So — cheers? Did Cara the psychic get it right after all? While he's in the loo I fantasize about us meeting ITRW (In The Real World, nerd girl speak I'm ashamed to say I've just learned in the last two weeks.) Maybe, just maybe . . .

While I'm gazing at the screen, he comes back.

PD: Thanks for waiting.
TB: I hope you washed your hands.
PD: Anyway, I forgot. Here's the first course. Poached salmon, asparagus, pommes frittes.
TB: Thankyou. If you keep on talking like this I

really will have to go and get some food.

PD: It's a good restaurant, though.

TB: Very discreet.

PD: I'm surprised you were free on a Friday night, actually.

TB: I have no life.

PD: Why, thankyou.

TB: Sorry.

PD: This *is* life. Don't insult me.

TB: Yeah, well.

PD: How can you deny that this is life too? What's the first thing you do when you get home?

TB: Check my e-mail.

PD: Me too.

TB: It's just – you know.

PD: Have you told your friends?

TB: No.

PD: Me neither.

TB: Why does this feel as if I'm having an affair when all I'm doing is staring at a computer?

PD: I'm glad you feel like that.

TB: PD, I've just had a horrible thought.

PD: What?

TB: You've done this before. You've done this with somebody else before me.

PD: ????????

TB: Have you?

PD: No, as a matter of fact. And permit me an emoticon but that makes me feel :-(

TB: Oh God, sorry.

And I really do feel sorry. I might only be staring at words on a computer but I think I just felt that lurch inside him all the way down the lines from Clichy, Paris.

TB: Really, really sorry PD.

PD: It's OK. But no, since you ask, it's my first time. Catch me thinking about an Internet romance.

TB: There, you've said it.

PD: So we're admitting something here, is that what you're thinking?

TB: Well, are we?

PD: If you want.

TB: But I hardly know you.

PD: You hardly knew the world famous Transitional Man if I remember correctly.

TB: Yeah, all right. Anyway, I've got a confession.

PD: ???

TB: A psychic told me about you.

PD: How?

TB: She said I'd meet someone on my computer.

PD: What do you mean, someone?

TB: OK then, under the influence of alcohol, can I just say this. My soulmate. She said I'd meet my soulmate on the Internet.

PD: Well. I'm glad you're under the influence of alcohol. Good night.

TB: What, that's it?

PD: Only joking. *Thankyou* for telling me.

TB: Well don't you have an opinion on it?

PD: What?

TB: Don't embarrass me. The soulmate thing.

PD: Good night Madame Technobimbo.

TB: Do you think we'll meet one day?

PB: Do *you* think we will?

TB: Only my psychic knows:-)

TB: Good night.

PD: Good night.

And can you believe it, just like a gooshy farewell in

the real world, neither of us can end the conversation. Like some old couple – like Charles and Camilla on that Camillagate tape, if you can believe it really happened – we're incapable of signing off. In fact, it takes us a good ten minutes to do it. It's like bedtime on *The Waltons*. 'Night John Boy', 'Good night then', 'Yeah, well good night.' I mean, really. But part of me thinks, very romantic as well. And I need it. I said as much when Jodie was interrogating me for her film, and I may as well admit it. I'll take it from anywhere these days. Even from a computer screen.

And I'd love to talk to someone about this, I think I practically have to or I'm going to spontaneously combust. But how do you begin? 'My name is Victoria Total Bloody Relationship Disaster Area Shepworth and I am having a Net fling with a total stranger in Paris.' Well, you try it. So I do the only thing I can do, at this time of night. After four glasses of cheap wine on an empty stomach, I throw up.

Twenty-three

Kylie and I are ploughing through some extra lines for the dreaded superannuation campaign, laughing hysterically at the fact that neither of us actually has any, when the office mobile rings. Whoops. I gave Jodie the number ages ago as an emergency option, and I shouldn't have done. But anyway.

'It's for you,' says Kylie, handing it over.

Fortunately the office mobile has also become a kind of Batphone for conversations between Kylie and her mother in Queensland lately, so I don't think there's going to be a problem. To be on the safe side, though, I take it into the kitchen just in case Bobbi sees me and feels moved to have another conversation about tiers, or rungs, or whatever it is.

The person whose strawberry yoghurt has been such a source of controversy has now put another piece of paper up on the kitchen fridge. It reads IF YOU WANT SOY MILK BUY YOUR OWN. Exclamation mark, exclamation mark. Why is it that I always feel a sick lurch of guilt whenever I see those fridge notes? I mean, I don't even like soy milk.

'Jodie, you haven't been breaking in here and stealing the soy milk have you?'

'No. What are you talking about?'

'Well you're the only person I know who drinks it. Anyway.'

'It's about your mother being in the film. I thought I'd better—'

'Look, I'm really not into it.'

'Is this a bad time to talk?'

'No, this is a good time to talk. I don't want her getting involved.'

'This is a bad time to talk, I knew it.'

I can see, but not hear, Didi in the background, biting her lip, and waving her hands around making 'later, later' signals.

'Look. I'll be really pissed off if you go and interview my mother about her love life. OK? Mostly because it's going to involve my father. EG, Jodie, my parents.'

'But you should see the footage, Vic, it's amazing. Just see the footage. Please.'

'Oh, so you've got footage.'

'When the camera stopped rolling, and we stopped recording her, she said it was cathartic.'

'When did this happen?'

'This morning. She just rang and said, come over.'

My mother. How does she find the time? She's supposed to be an accountant, works from home, blah blah blah, so busy she has to get someone in to wash up for her (a job that was once offered to Didi, which she declined) and now this. Being interviewed for documentaries all over the place.

'So did she talk about Dad?'

'Yes.'

'Great.'

Yet more free entertainment for Dan and Erica when they front up to the Sydney Film Festival. The entire Shepworth family exposed, for all to see. Me burbling on pathetically about weddings, and Mum going on about how Dad was a root rat (her favourite expression: 'Your father is a sensitive man, but he's a root rat'), and all the rest of it.

'Jodie, I'm serious about this.'

'But Vic!'

'No way.'

'Look, your mother wants to be in it.'

'Well, take me out of it.'

'Oh. OK. Look, maybe we'd better talk about this later.'

'And don't ring me on the mobile. It's not mine. It belongs to the office. I'm on the wrong tier at work as it is.'

'What?'

Click. Goodbye Jodie. Mad old cow. I suppose it's something that happens to these Hollywood film directors. They get a crazy glint in their eye, and the scent of ambition in their nostrils, and then they go behind your back and interview your mother when you're not looking. Anything to get into Cannes. As if. Anything to get into some silly women's art thing on the Central Coast in a boy-scout hall, if you ask me.

Then Jodie turns up to work at knocking-off time. I knew she would. Kylie gives her a slightly interested, slightly horrified stare. I'm so used to the John Travolta T-shirt and the smudged kohl around the eyes I forget that Jodie has the power to terrify and/or fascinate total strangers.

'Is everything OK, Vic?' she says, purringly.

'Not OK.'

'You look as if you could do with a massage.'

'No I don't.'

'Your shoulders look knotty.'

'My head is knotty.'

This is typical Jodie. Trying to calm troubled waters which she churned up in the first place. But anyway. It's keeping Kylie entertained.

Since the Macrame Man incident, she and I have reached the stage where we can't even be bothered pretending we're not eavesdropping on each other any more. So she sticks her head up over the screen to check out Jodie, and asks me if I'm all right.

'Yeah, I'm all right.'

What she means is, do I want her to get security onto this mad-eyed woman with the bad haircut (but admittedly fabulous 21-year-old looking vegetarian body) and have her thrown out. But I don't. I don't know, I just don't. Infuriating as Jodie can be, I'm used to her. And when your life has turned into Cyclone Tracy, you need to be around people you're used to. They're like trees you can strap yourself to when it all starts to go wild and dangerous.

'Come on, let's go.'

I wave to Kylie, pick up my bag, steer Jodie out of the corridor, wave at the photocopier slaves, stomp past Bobbi's office and down the stairs. As we clatter down each step, me in my heels, Jodie in her weird purple ballet shoes and jeans, the words tumble out of me.

'I don't want to ruin your documentary, I just don't, and I can't stop Mum, and you can leave me in if you want to, but just don't show it anywhere Dan might see it, all right? Or Dad. Like, don't show it in LA.'

Jodie catches me up.

'It's not going to be in America. I don't think so anyway. Look,' she shrugs, pulling her fish face, 'It's just an experimental thing. About love. Something for Didi and me. Something we need to find out about ourselves. It's not like a film film. You know. Anyway . . .'

'Yes, convince me some more.'

'What if Dan does see it?'

And for a minute, I have to stop. What if he does? Good point. Me, rambling on about weddings in a low budget documentary – what does it have to do with him? What does anything have to do with the Loathsome Lawyer from Leichhardt any more? And for the first time in ages, I can use his nickname, just like that, and almost but not quite mean it.

'I've made a new friend,' I say.

'Yeah?'

'On the Net. He's English. He lives in Paris.'

'Cool.'

And that's all I want to say about it, and that's all I do say about it.

Twenty-four

A series of e-mails between Pierre and I, on the subject of – what else? Relationships.

To: pierre@netshop.com.fr
From: shep@mpx.com.au
Re: Voodoo dolls

Dear Pierre,
Today I was in one of those novelty shops when I saw a voodoo doll. Would it be wrong to buy it and draw a tattoo on its arm and make a little pair of denim shorts for it? Best wishes, TB.

To: shep@mpx.com.au
From: pierre@netshop.com.fr
Re: Good news

Dear TB,
This is good news. Your sense of humour has come back – eg, You are definitely making excellent medical progress. PS: Do not buy voodoo doll though. Au revoir, Pierre.

To: pierre@netshop.com.fr
From: shep@mpx.com.au
Re: Good News

Dear Pierre,
What do you mean, making progress and good news? I feel like dying at the moment. Or haven't you ever felt insane obsessive jealousy? PS: Find it hard to believe you won't be jealous when your ex in London gets a new bloke. Best wishes, TB.

To: shep@mpx.com.au
From: pierre@netshop.com.fr
Re: I don't get jealous

Dear TB,
When my ex gets a new man in her life, I will have fantasies about disembowelling him. Or even both of them. But until then, I am not jealous. Anything you can conjure up in your imagination is always much worse than the real thing, TB. Anyway, whoever gets her next will have to put up with her snoring. How's work going anyway? And the film? And your crazy friends? I'm missing my usual TB bulletin. Au revoir, Pierre.

To: pierre@netshop.com.fr
From: shep@mpx.com.au
Re: Snoring?

Dear Pierre,
How bad was the snoring? You know you can buy a little rubber beak thing from the chemist now. But maybe it takes more than that to save a relation-

ship, PD. Anyway, re: crazy friends, I haven't heard from Hilary for days. Natalie's repainting her kitchen and she's helping her. This is what happens when you hit thirty, your friends substitute home improvements for alcohol and they begin to find painted finishes sexually arousing. Work is too boring and I don't want to talk about it, except I think I might be back in Bobbi's good books again as they're doing Breakfast Grits Frisbee Mark Two (bigger, better, browner) and she keeps walking past my cubicle deliberately talking about it to other people and watching for my reaction. But I'll tell you something else. I found one of Dan's and mine old argument notes today. We had this big fight in a car park and I stuck it on his windscreen. I wrote LOVE IS NOT A DIRTY WORD, WHY DON'T YOU TRY USING IT SOME TIME? And he wrote WHEN YOU FIND OUT WHAT IT MEANS GIVE ME A CALL. I hate lawyers. TB.

To: shep@mpx.com.au
From: pierre@netshop.com.fr
Re: Love is not a dirty word

Dear TB,
I am shocked that you broke the cardinal relationship rule. The word love should never be mentioned except in dire emergency situations. As a woman of the '90s I thought you would know that. You only scare people and it's not good for them. By the way, my ex girlfriend *did* have a rubber beak because of the snoring. I have to admit, it contributed to the break-up. Cheers, PD.

243

To: pierre@netshop.com.fr
From: shep@mpx.com.au
Re: Love

Dear Pierre,
The word love should be used as soon as you feel it. I'm over this cool 90s thing. The next time I fall in love with a man I'm going to tell him right away, and I think you should too (with a woman, of course, I think we've already established that you're not gay, PD). As soon as you find your man, or woman, you should tie them up, brand them and rope them, Pierre. It just means you'll get the wedding cake and white suede shoes faster.
Best wishes, TB.

To: shep@mpx.com.au
From: pierre@netshop.com.fr
Re: Love

Dear TB,
I was joking about never mentioning love. PD.

To: pierre@netshop.com.fr
From: shep@mpx.com.au
Re: The problem with men

Dear Pierre,
The problem with men is, you are *always* joking. Why do you think Dan and I used to have so many fights? He never took anything seriously. Except footy. Very serious business, sport. I think you're lying about the love thing, anyway. I bet you never said it to rubber beak. TB.

To: shep@mpx.com.au
From: pierre@netshop.com.fr
Re: The problem with men

Dear TB,
Frankly, TB, I'm a little disappointed you're falling back on sexist stereotyping so early in our relationship. PD.

To: pierre@netshop.com.fr
From: shep@mpx.com.au
Re: Relationship?

Dear Pierre,
This isn't a relationship. And you didn't answer my question about rubber beak. TB.

To: shep@mpx.com.au
From: pierre@netshop.com.fr
Re: Since you asked

Dear TB,
Define relationship. And since you asked, I told rubber beak I was in love with her as soon as it happened. She snorted (not snored, snorted) if I remember. By the way, there is a difference between love, and being in love. I'm surprised you haven't spotted it, TB. Pierre.

To: pierre@netshop.com.fr
From: shep@mpx.com.au
Re: Don't patronize me

Pierre. I am well aware of the difference between in love and love. I loved Dan, I was in love with

Liam. But what men don't seem to understand is that if you say either one of them, it does not automatically mean that
a) You want them to propose immediately
b) You want them to impregnate you immediately
c) You want a mortgage
d) You want to become like one of the family
e) You want half his assets
f) You want matching baseball caps.
I am sorry she snorted when you told her you were in love with her. PS – Do you think you loved her as well? It doesn't sound like it. TB.

To: shep@mpx.com.au
From: pierre@netshop.com.fr
Re: Apologies

Dear TB,
In reply to your question, I don't know if I loved rubber beak or not. I was obsessed with her once, but I'm happy to let her go her own way in life now. And even though the first guy she chose to sleep with was a friend of mine, I don't want her to fall under a truck or anything. So. What does that mean? (You sound like the expert.) PD. PS: Did you and your man have matching baseball caps?

To: pierre@netshop.com.fr
From: shep@mpx.com.au
Re: Sorry

Dear PD,
I'm so sorry she went for your friend. Why didn't you tell me before? More importantly, how did you get over it? I think you are a guru and I should

worship at your feet. What's the secret, Pierre, did you read The Celestine Prophecy or are you an emotional no-hoper, too numbed by your stereotypical male upbringing and bad James Bond films to register pain? Anyway. Sorry if I'm crapping on, but I'm in a crapping on mood today. To answer your question, Dan and I didn't have matching baseball caps, but I know his girlfriend before me did – she bought one for her, and one for him. So is that love? Ha. I don't think you should be asking me to tell you if you loved rubber beak or not. That's pathetic, Pierre. Don't you know by now? As you think I'm an expert (I'm not, why do you think I'm still single?) I'll tell you what I think love is. Just so you can work out if you ever had it or not. You and rubber beak are standing at the top of a live volcano. The boiling lava rages below you. Satan is about to push one of you in. The choice is yours – who will it be, you or her? If she goes, your life is spared but you must live without her. If you sacrifice yourself, you will die a horrible and agonizing death. That is love. Think about it. TB.

To: shep@mpx.com.au
From: pierre@netshop.com.fr
Re: Boiling hot lava

Dear TB,
I knew you would help me. After a terrible night full of bad dreams about drowning in melted rock in the mouth of a live volcano I decided I would get Satan to push her in. It is a big relief to me to have sorted this out, I can't thank you enough. Just before you accuse me of being a typical man and never taking anything seriously – whenever I get

your e-mail I feel as if you know me better than rubber beak ever did. PD.

To: pierre@netshop.com.fr
From: shep@mpx.com.au
Re: Ex Files

Dear Pierre,
I know when I first started up the channel I was going to call it The Ex Files. But I don't think we should talk about our exes any more. I mean that. TB.

And why did I end up saying that to him? Not because I think there's anything wrong with discussing your love life with a total stranger. In fact, my e-mails to Pierre have done more for me than a whole year of therapeutic moaning could have achieved with Hilary. No, it's more the fact that I don't want to hear about his ex girlfriend. That's all.

And I'd never tell PD this in a million years, but that for me has always been a bit of a love indicator, all by itself. The first rumblings of jealousy, disguised as 'I don't want to think about her/I don't want to talk about her/Just shut up about her.'

How can it be? I mean, I don't even know the guy.

I give in and ring Hilary. By a small miracle, she isn't painting Natalie's kitchen ceiling, and she's home, and she's in a phone mood.

'I knew this would happen,' she says.

'What?'

'You'd find a little love bunny on the Internet. That's what I knew would happen.'

'Is love bunny something Natalie says?'

'Don't be such a bitch. No. Yes.'

'Am I fooling myself about this then?'

'Yeah, you might be. Has he sent you a photo?'

How can I explain, though, that asking him for a photo – or having him ask me for one – would spoil everything? That it would make me feel as if I was a contestant on *Perfect Match,* or *Blind Date,* and turn what we've got into some revolting meat market?

'I don't want to know what he looks like.'

'Oh, come on.'

'I've imagined what he looks like, and that's enough. I could be wrong, but I don't know. Whatever he looks like, I've just got an idea it might not be so different from what I imagined anyway.'

'So what do you think he looks like?'

'I dunno. Sort of tall. Not bad looking. Nice.'

'Oh lordy, Vic. You'd better be careful.'

'Why?' I shoot back.

'It's OK, I'm not on the attack. I just don't know how seriously you should take this thing right now. At this stage.'

'But I'm jealous of his ex, a bit, and that's the first sign isn't it?'

She sighs.

'Are you sure you don't just want to be in love with love?'

Damn her, old librarian mindreader.

'I don't think I am, though. I like him, and he likes me, and I don't think it's like that.'

'Well, OK, but you have gone from Dan to Liam, and that's like going into the wok from the waffle maker. What about some time for yourself?'

'But I don't want to be siiiiiiingle!'

'Why not? You can go home when you want, you can wake up when you want, you can eat cereal out of the box—'

'Oh shut up. I never believe those lists. Anyway.'

'Anyway what?'

'Oh, I can't talk to you.'

'Because I've got someone?'

'Yeah, if you must know.'

She sighs again, sounding like the long-suffering friend I suppose I've turned her into.

'I would be saying exactly the same thing to you if I was single.'

'I know.'

'Say sorry.'

'Yeah, all right. Sorry.'

But I make a point of saying it 'Swwy', just the way she always says it to me. Cow.

Twenty-five

When I was growing up, one of my mother's favourite TV shows was *The Mary Tyler Moore Show*. Perhaps it was because she was thinking about leaving Dad then, and seeing a programme about a happy single woman in culottes and a beret was like a fantasy practise run.

It must have been on its third repeat when it finally hit Sydney, because even as a sad ten-year-old in corduroy jeans and lacy white shirts, I remember thinking Mary's wardrobe was just too much. How did she get all those men interested in her when she was wearing ponchos and cacky pink lipstick? Anyway, my mother used to watch it religiously.

Mary Tyler Moore had a fantastic flat, and a glamorous job, and a friend who was fatter than her called Rhoda, which must have made her feel better, and even her boss loved her. And my mother, married to my father the sensitive root rat, must have looked at all of that and just thought 'Yes.' Even at the age of ten, some part of me must have thought that's what it would be like too. Single life. So good you just want to run through the streets of Minneapolis, laughing and chucking your hat up in the air.

Perhaps it's my flat. If only I had some huge open-plan penthouse, with a kind of conversation pit (how my mother used to envy Mary her coffee table conversation pit) my life would be better. When I look around me I see a massage table masquerading as a desk, a horrible wobbly director's chair, a haunted couch, a bed I don't want to sleep in, and a stupid shower curtain with dancing clam shells. There's chocolate in the carpet that I can't get out, and an answering machine without any messages on it.

Maybe if I had a glamorous job too, like a TV newsroom chick, or nice bouncy hair (the Mary Tyler Moore bob, now that's a thought) or a tennis club membership, then things would be different. And by different, I suppose I mean better. Better than coming home every night to switch on the computer like a woman possessed. When I wait for an e-mail from Pierre to turn up, I feel like a seagull looking for scraps of Kentucky Fried Chicken on the beach. I mean, what are the odds of me ever making it to Paris anyway? Or Pierre flying into Sydney for an in-the-flesh meeting? Hilary's right. I'm kidding myself as never before. How long has it been now? How many little IRC chats and e-mails have we sent? And still he won't tell me his real name.

I could check to see if there's a new message from him, but I'm not going to. He can bloody well forget it.

Then, on a Saturday afternoon, just when I'm feeling totally hopeless and useless, something rather bizarre happens. Hilary and Natalie bang on the door, and breeze in with a cat in a straw basket.

'Yoo hoo!' says Natalie. Honestly. I didn't think people said yoo hoo any more. Hilary's out of breath from carrying the cat, which is so angry now that it's shooting its paws out of the side of the basket like the disembodied hand in *The Addams Family*. The paws are ginger and white.

'It's a cat,' I say stupidly. And she's off. Natalie's off.

'It's just a possibility, you see the ex has now decided to take off to Adelaide and no arrangements for puss, nothing, didn't even call the RSPCA and I thought well, it's my responsibility, I don't mind, but this place I'm in is right on the main road and I thought puss would rush straight out there and get knocked down. Hilary said there was a slight possibility you might be interested, and I am willing to pay for his keep. Just until we find him a home.'

'You like cats,' Hilary says.

Natalie opens the lid of the basket and something maddened, yowling and furry shoots past me, into the bedroom, and under the bed.

'I'm not allowed to have cats,' I say.

And it's true. Ages ago, I promised myself that I wasn't allowed to have a cat. Why? Because if you are a single woman and you have a cat, you may as well get a wispy grey bun, a tweed suit, a pair of glasses and start calling yourself Miss Marple. Single woman plus cat equals bad cliche. Men are repulsed by it. No, no, no.

Natalie puts down her shopping bag and I can just see the cans of sardines poking out of the top.

'Really?'

She looks at Hilary. Hilary stares, hard and meaningfully, at me.

'If Roger can't stay here then we're going to have to take him to the pound. You know they only keep them for a few days now, don't you.'

Oh, my God. Roger.

'All I can say is, he treats animals like he treats me

and the kids,' says Natalie, a little sadly and quietly for her.

'Why did you call him Roger?' I can't think of anything else to say.

'It's his eyebrows.'

Do cats have eyebrows? I suppose for the purposes of the conversation I should really crawl on my stomach under the bed and drag him out to see. But I've done this cat-under-the-bed thing before. When my parents had one, a Siamese. They deliberately crouch in the furthest, darkest corner they can find under the mattress, so that all you can see is a horrible pair of glinting, catty eyes. Then, if you try to flush them out with a broom, or even your arm, they attack.

'You remember, Vic,' says Hilary, trying her special-effort voice on me. 'Roger Moore used to say his acting skills consisted of raise left eyebrow, raise right eyebrow.'

'So he looks like Roger Moore.'

'His eyebrows do,' says Natalie.

'Do cats have eyebrows?'

Perhaps because nothing else is working on me, Natalie starts fussing around in her purse and finds a little roll of mustard-coloured fifty dollar bills which she's put inside a rubber band. And I'm ashamed to say, the first thing I think is wow, fantastic, and amazing in that order. And even worse, my next consecutive thought is, I wonder if I can get away with feeding it no-name brand catfood while I secretly eat the sardines?

Roger is a mind-reader. Roger looks at me as if he wants to kill me, shoots out from under the bed, past my legs, and into the bathroom.

'Oooooh no,' says Natalie. 'I think I know what *that* means.'

When we troop in there, he is squatting over the shower drain, weeing frantically and nervously with wild, staring eyes. In a funny sort of way, this makes me warm to him. Disgusting though it is. I too, in times of stress and crisis, ask to go to the toilet. I know how he feels. But I'll tell you one thing. He's not staying here beyond a week. And he's not going to be called Roger either.

'No, don't be silly,' I say heroically, refusing to even look at the money Natalie's holding in her hand.

She checks my face. It takes about a second.

'Are you sure?'

Then the little roll of wonderfully crispy-looking cash goes back in the purse, still with a rubber band around it.

'Anyway.'

She hands over a couple of twenties. Lobsters, my father used to call them.

'Roger says buy yourself a little treat. Don't you, Roger?'

When I look he's scratching the shower drain with his paw in that stupid, completely useless way cats do to clean up after themselves. I mean, there's no soil there, what does he think he's doing?

I have deliberately avoided Hilary's eye throughout this whole feline disaster experience, because I know that if I look at her for more than a split second, I will want to smash a can of sardines over her head.

This is exactly what always happens with her. She gets into a relationship, and bang, she becomes a sort of assistant to the person she's with. I've been down this road with Hilary before. The librarian from the Adults' section got her to ask me if he could borrow my Walkman once, to take on holiday with him. I never got it back. All I can think is, wait until I get her by herself.

I offer to make a cup of coffee and they make going noises. Apparently Jodie and Didi are interviewing a nun today and they've been invited to hang around and hold cables.

'What would nuns know about love,' I say. 'They're celibate.'

'Halibut,' says Hilary.

'Oh I like that,' says Natalie.

When they go, Roger creeps out of the bathroom and starts the usual purry, furry flirtation business, banging his face against my ankles and snaking his tail around in the air. It's a bit of an awful feeling, actually. There's nothing wrong with the way he looks – and Hilary's right, damn her. I do like cats. Even when they piss in my shower. It's just that he belongs to someone else, that's all. A strange man. Natalie's husband. Who knows, he may even have been in bed with Natalie's husband, which is almost like being in bed with Natalie, and that's the worst thought I've had all week.

What does Hilary see in the woman anyway?

'What does Hilary see in her?' I ask Roger.

Then I catch myself doing it, and feel an awful lurch. It's happening already. I'm talking to the bloody cat.

Later, Hilary rings me up.

'We thought you might like to come out tonight.'

'I can't. I've got to feed the cat.'

'Vi-ic.'

'What was all that about, anyway?' I ask.

'Look. You're there by yourself.'

'So are you.'

'I don't like cats.'

'What makes you think I'd automatically like Roger?'

'I know you.'

'Yeah.'

'It's only until we find him somewhere else to live.'

'It's just that I swore it would never happen.'

'It's only a cat, Vic.'

'You don't get it, do you? I'm single. I'm white. I'm female. I live by myself. I have a cat. Do you know how much that scares men?'

'Not the sort of men you want in your life. You wouldn't want a man who thought like that. Would you?'

'At the moment, Hilary . . .'

In the end, I meet her and Natalie at the Frog, where you can order lots of little things and share them around. It's not just the two of them, though. It's everybody.

And by everybody, I mean almost everyone who was there at my birthday. The night of the Dan dropping. The night before I decided to cut all my hair off and dye it red. There's Kylie, there's Helena Chettle, who must have farmed the kids off to Mick for the evening. There's Jodie and Didi, looking blissfully stoned and handing poppadums round to everybody. There's the blonde threesome – Kerry and Olivia and Nicki, who always travel as a pack, and who I've known since Socialist Workers Party raffle days. People I thought were Dan's friends, not mine (after all, he introduced us) have turned up. And even though they're all pretending to ignore me and are cracking apart poppadums, I can tell what this is about. It's about 'Oh my God, we're really worried about Victoria.'

'So, how's it all going?'

They've even dragged out Quiet Kevin, my old gay friend from my first agency job. That's quite an achievement.

'Not bad. How about you?'

'Jodie said you're on the Net.'

I mean, is that the only thing people can say about

me these days? But he means well, I suppose. It's just that I know Jodie and Didi well enough to read right behind every line this evening. And I can just imagine the phone calls.

'Look, Victoria's been having a hard time lately, we're a bit worried about her. Yes, she's become an Internet addict.'

Or am I being paranoid? Then I think about it. Roger the cat. It all makes sense. These two incidents – the big, friendly dinner and the big, ginger and white cat – they're related. This is a rescue operation.

When Hilary goes off to the loo, I follow her.

'Oi.'

'What? Talk to me in there.'

So we do Cubicle Chat for a few minutes, which is always rather restricted by the fact that you know someone else in the third cubicle is hanging on every word.

'I'm fine, you know,' I say through the walls.

'Nobody said you weren't,' Hilary echoes back.

'I know what you're saying.'

'What?'

'I don't have a life.'

She flushes straight after me, and as we both start to wash our hands, a rather nervous looking woman in high heels clacks straight out. You can't blame her. The vibes in this toilet are distinctly icy. Nancy Kerrigan and Tonya Harding icy, in fact.

'Every time I ring you these days, you're on the Net.'

'I got it for my birthday.'

'This bloke . . .'

'If you're going to start talking to me about that kind of thing again, then I am going to start talking to you about Natalie. All right?'

'I mean, I can see you don't like her.'

'I do like her.'

'She was hurt about Roger.'

'I've got him, haven't I?'

'She meant well.'

'You mean, she thought having a cat would stop me from being so lonely. Yuck.'

'That's not what she said.'

'Oh, stuff it.'

And I walk out ahead of her, back to the table, where they are dithering over the menu because the usual bad combination of vegetarians and carnivores has turned up. Quiet Kevin is giving way over the dahl, which is quite noble of him because I know he can't stand it. Then, someone else turns up. Bill the Boffin.

Hilary squeezes up to make room for him, and although I can't hear what she's saying, it must be enough to give Natalie something to go on, because the next time I look up Bill's nodding a lot while a Niagara Falls of blather is being poured into his ear. Poor Bill.

It occurs to me that I should tell him about Roger. I'm going to have to hide him if anyone from the real estate agent's comes around (Hilary got it wrong, I checked the lease again and despite her mad optimism, I'm definitely not allowed to have cats). I'm sure Bill would be a good Rogerminder, given his experience with cows and sheep in Dorrigo.

'Bill.'

We look at each other for a minute across the table. And it's a funny feeling. Different. What is it? Maybe we've crossed some kind of line these days. His eyes are meeting mine in a softer, steadier way. Or maybe I'm just starving hungry and hallucinating.

Natalie's still going on about something – probably the cat, now I think about it. Poor Victoria, blah blah, she's become such a computer nerd we thought we should give her Roger the cat to look after, oh dear Bill, you don't work in computers do you?

Bill says something to her – it must be nice though, she's beaming – and he jostles his way around the table to me. Then Quiet Kevin goes off to get something from the bottle shop and suddenly we're sitting together. Not so strange when you come to think about it, but this must be the closest I've ever got to Bill the Boffin. I think our thighs are even touching for the first time. He smells of the shower gel again. The same thing that Dan used. I wish he wouldn't. It's confusing me.

'So you've got a cat.'

'She told you.'

'Don't worry, I won't tell anyone.'

'It's only for a week. His name's Roger.'

'She told me that as well.'

'He's got eyebrows like Roger Moore.'

He smiles Dorrigo-ishly at this.

'How's work going?'

'Good. All right. I have to do another frisbee campaign for them. How's yours?'

'Good.'

And that's about as far as we get. Bill never tells me very much about his job, possibly because the last time he tried to explain to me about software design and hardware components I started staring into space and dribble started forming in the corner of my mouth.

As I listen to him going on about his squash game, I can't help but compare our conversation to the kind of conversation I have with Pierre. Actually, that's not fair. It's not just Bill, it's everybody here. Normally, I'd be hopping around the table gossiping my head off. But whenever people start talking to me, all I want to do is creep back to my computer to tell PD about it all. Maybe Hilary and Natalie are right. I have turned into a nerd. What next, do I lose the use of my mouth?

Jodie comes over and grabs Bill's elbow.

'Sorry, Vic. Bill, can we talk to you for a minute?'

Oh no. Don't go there, Bill. But then again, maybe he'd feel flattered to be in a documentary called *Women In Love.* Even if he is the only heterosexual white male in the film.

At about ten-thirty, I make my excuses. You can tell it's a bad evening when you wait for your watch hands to reach a nice, round number so you can have a reason to go. Bill said he'd give me a lift, and he's tired from work anyway, so it seems to work out. When we get up to go, everyone waves, in that silly, floppy-handed way, for some reason. I bet as soon as I'm out of there they'll start talking about me.

Bill reverses the car, and nearly backs into a motor-bike parked behind him.

'Sorry.'

Then he switches on some music – Luscious Jackson apparently – and we talk about the price of CD's for a bit, then neither of us say anything. It's not a problem though. I think we've become used to each other, Bill and I. All those long nights of answering machine repairs and Internet instructions have taught us how to sit together in silence – in a comfortable, nothingy kind of way, I suppose.

I suppose I should show him Roger, but I can't be bothered. I just want to go to bed. Actually, no. I just want to boot my computer and switch on the modem. And I don't care what anyone says. Pierre, Pierre. I need you, PD.

I sigh and make an attempt at conversation.

'Jodie wasn't asking you to be in her film, was she?'

He looks embarrassed, and gives a half-laugh.

'I'm in it already.'

I look at him.

'You're not!'

He shrugs and turns a bad corner.

'When she asked me it was hard to say no.'

'Oh.'

After that it's even harder to talk. I mean, what on earth can he have found to say to them? All I can think of is, Jodie and Didi must have really been desperate for a white heterosexual male subject. Or maybe he was the only one tame enough to go along with it.

Eventually we get back to the flat, and I get out.

'Thanks for the lift.'

'See you later.'

Back in my flat, I can only think of one thing. The fact that I now know what it feels like to be a chronic masturbator. The guilt is terrible. The way I have to close every curtain and shut every blind, just so the tell-tale flickering of the computer won't hit the street. And the way I go into total denial until the very last minute, giving Roger some sardines, doing a bit of stray washing up, checking my answering machine (no Liam, no Dan, bla bla, nobody cares, nobody loves you, you're siiiiiiingle) and flicking through the TV guide.

Then, finally, I'm ready. Two cushions on the wobbly director's chair, a mug of tea, and I've even made sure I go to the loo first so I won't have to get up and interrupt things. Terrible.

But one day, I can't help thinking, one day when we actually meet face to face, I'll be glad I raced home from a restaurant to do this. I'll be glad I rushed Bill out of the car and up the stairs, just so I could reach the computer quicker.

Maybe one day I'll get to the stage where I don't care what it looks like to everybody else. I'm even getting to the stage where I don't care what it looks like to me, either. What's the difference? During the war American GI's wrote love letters to women in England they'd never even seen. What's so awful about this, an Internet friendship that feels like it could be something more? Hey it's the nineties, isn't it?

Ping, ping, ping. I get through without any problems, probably because every normal human being is where I should be on a Saturday night – clubbing, eating, drinking. And it's there. Our channel. Global Singles Solidarity.

TB: Pierre, are you there?
PD: Oui, Madame

And I think it, but don't type it – thank God, thank God.

TB: I've just been set up by my friends.
PD: How?
TB: They think I'm a sad old single woman, so they got me this cat and they organized this dinner for me.
PD: To get you back into the human race.
TB: Yeah. Because I'm always on the Net.
PD: Because of me?
TB: Maybe.
PD: What else do you use the Net for these days?
TB: Nothing. I gave up on Kurt Cobain's Magic Talking 8 Ball.
PD: And what did it say?
TB: The screen froze.
PD: Don't worry, TB, you *know* you'll find your soulmate through the computer.
TB: Very funny. I wish I'd never told you that.

And then, out of nowhere, a terrible clanging alarm sound rips through the building and Roger flies out of the bedroom like a furry cannonball. Shit. It's so *loud*. Why do they make alarms this loud? And forgive me for being Miss Stupid, but if you've never heard a fire alarm go off in your block of flats, you probably wouldn't know what it was at first either.

I can hear people go clattering down the stairs. And then suddenly, it sinks in. Serious. FIRE. Serious! HELP!

And it's only a few minutes later, when I'm down in the garden in my dressing gown with everybody else, gasping for breath, that I realize I have just left Pierre Dubois hanging on in Clichy, Paris, in the middle of cyberspace, without apology or explanation.

The man who works in insurance who lives on the ground floor has taken it upon himself to become our fire officer. Then I see Bill, in a T-shirt and shorts and bare feet, and run over.

'What's going on?'

'They think it's in flat five.'

He's out of breath too.

'Flat five?'

'But they're not there,' he says in a rush, 'They've gone away for the weekend.'

'Where's the fire brigade?'

'On the way.'

And then it hits me. Roger. I did the right thing, didn't I, when I shut the door behind me. That's what you're supposed to do. But I've shut poor little Roger in too.

I swear, and Bill jumps.

'What's the matter?'

'I've got to get the cat.'

One reason I suppose you should wear a bra to bed

264

is that if you are ever caught in an emergency situation in a nipple-revealing grey cotton dressing gown, your boobs won't jiggle all over the place. As I run past everyone and up the stairs, it's all I can think about. I'll never be able to look any of them in the eye again. Not that I ever knew their names in the first place.

There's smoke in the stairwell, I can smell it. And for the first time, I feel scared. Roger, Roger. Poor little Roger.

God, I'm so unfit. Even without the smoking, I can hardly make it up my own stairs.

But when I get there, my front door's still hanging open. Damn. I should have remembered, from my days of arguments with Dan, that whenever you think you've slammed it behind you, you haven't.

I look frantically, but I can't find Roger anywhere. He's not under the bed, he's not in the kitchen, he's not in the shower. He just can't be anywhere else, my flat's too small. Unless he's panicked and gone up the stairs to the top floor. Where did Bill think the fire was again?

This time I make a point of really shutting the door properly. But by the time I come out the smoke's worse. What did they tell you at school? Wet hankies or something. Or crawl down on the floor where the oxygen is. My eyes are starting to sting.

Every door is shut. Flat seven next door, flat nine, flat ten. Then finally I make it up the final flight of stairs to the top landing, and see it. Bill's door. Wide open. It's the only place he could have gone.

'Roger, Roger, Roger!'

What a bloody stupid name to give a cat.

'Puss, puss!'

Maybe he's crawled under Bill's bed as well. And as I go from one room to the next making stupid cat noises I can't help but noticing that he's finally put up a few paintings and photographs. At last. Oh look, there's one of his ex. Must be. On the mirror. Blonde, freckled, countrified looking girl.

And then I see it. His computer. Still on, still flickering. And I look up and read this.

PD: Don't worry, TB, you *know* you'll find your soulmate through the computer.
TB: Very funny. I wish I'd never told you that.

Bastard, bastard, bastard. But I know one thing. That's the last thing Pierre Dubois the Englishman in Paris is ever going to write to me.

Twenty-six

My father has always had an amazing sense of timing. And when he rings, at 6 a.m. Sydney time, God knows what in LA time, I'm just about to successfully fall asleep. The phone jerks me awake, in that horrible, sick, heart-thudding way a loud noise always does when you're really tired.

'Dad.'

'It's not early is it?'

Bugger him. He's never got the time difference right, never.

'You won't believe what I've just gone through.'

'Are you all right?'

'Well, I've still got the cat.'

'What cat?'

And I tell him. About Roger, and about doing my madwoman in a fire act, and then eventually finding the cat cowering under Bill's kitchen table. And I tell him about everyone being really pissed off with me, and the annoying insurance man from the ground floor who thinks he's a fire officer giving me a lecture while staring at my obvious nipples dressing gown, and all the rest of it.

He's psychic, though, my Dad. A bit like Bobbi and

Cara of Krystal Connections, if you must know. Although my opinion of Cara has dropped somewhat in the past twenty-four hours. Dad has this ability to zoom in on what you don't say, rather than what you're actually telling him. You can try and keep vital information out of the conversation if you want to, but sooner or later he'll get you. One of the reasons he got away with being a sensitive root rat for so long – I'm sure – is that he was always one step ahead of my mother. Telepathically, anyway.

'Man trouble?'

Oh I love the way he calls it that, too. It's like car trouble. But I may as well tell him. It's his fault anyway. I mean, who gave me the computer in the first place?

'The guy upstairs is a stalker.'

'What?'

'No, not a stalker. A hacker. Whatever. I'm really tired. But you know what I mean, he's just a creep or something. He got to know me on IRC, then we started sending e-mail and he pretended his name was Pierre and he was living in Paris, and he was English, and of course I got sucked in, and we've been writing to each other for weeks. When I ran upstairs in the fire, his door was open and I saw the computer. Saw the whole thing. It was all on there. The entire conversation I thought I'd just been through with Pierre. And it's just been him the whole time, creeping around upstairs, tapping away on his computer. It makes me sick even thinking about it.'

'What has he said to you?'

'Nothing. He doesn't know I saw it.'

'He doesn't know?'

'I can't face it. I just want to forget about it. I just saw what was on his computer and came straight back downstairs with the cat. I just said I found him in my bedroom. It was a fire, Dad. I haven't slept. They didn't let us go back in until about two in the morning.'

After that, my mother calls. It usually happens in sequence like this. The telephone companies do really well out of our family.

'Victoria. Are you all right?'

'Did Dad tell you?'

'Yes, this man. How revolting. I remember you telling me about him.'

Revolting. Well maybe he is. I don't know. I'm so tired, and my flat smells of dirty smoke, and I can't face any of my neighbours any more after that embarrassing fire safety lecture on the lawn, and I feel as if I don't know anything. Plus – they all know I've got the cat now. All of which means I'll probably be chucked out of here next week anyway.

'Mum, if they find out about Roger can I come and stay there?'

'Who's Roger?'

'Sorry. The cat.'

'What about Dan?'

'No, I'm not talking about men now, I'm talking about cats. What about Dan? Nothing about Dan.'

'And has Bill apologized to you?'

'Bill doesn't know I found out.'

'Oh.'

'I told him Roger was hiding under my bed the whole time. He doesn't even know I went into his flat. He's got a photo of his ex stuck on the mirror. She's got freckles.'

And that piece of irrelevant information, over and above everything else, is the thing that makes me cry, and cry, and cry.

'Come round for a bath.'

269

The answer to everything — the bath. But she's right. I stink. It's probably exactly what I need.

'Bring Roger.'

'Stuff Roger.'

When I fall into a taxi in a pair of jeans I've just pulled from the laundry basket, I try to get beyond the initial shock, beyond the first blow to the head. The taxi driver's got on inane breakfast radio, one of those programs where women and men are mock-fighting with each other, and it's all supposed to be incredibly funny. I ask him to turn it down. Normally, Sydney cabbies pretend they haven't heard if you ask that kind of thing. But one look at my face (red hair, red eyes, red skin) and he does.

As the shops on King Street flash past me, I let my shoulders flop, the way Jodie's always telling me to, and try to make sense of it.

If Bill and Pierre, separately, have been such good blokes for the last few months, then maybe Bill and Pierre, in one body, also constitute a good bloke. But when I think about everything I've told Pierre/Bill, all the stuff about Dan and Erica, all the stupid talk about the meaning of love, all the little private jokes we've shared, and even that ridiculous romantic 'dinner' with the red wine, I just want to hurl.

What's wrong with him? Sicko. He could have come down the stairs any night of the week, any long and lonely Friday night, or any crap siiiiiingle Tuesday. He could have made his move long ago, long before Liam. (And, oh God, I told him all about that as well. The knots in the condoms, the whole thing.) I've been here, the whole time, waiting for something. Waiting for someone. And he's never even got it together to take me out for dinner.

Bill is intelligent, he's sensitive, he's single. He

thinks like Pierre and he looks like Bill – which is not bad looking at all. I mean, if I think hard enough about him standing there in his T-shirt and shorts last night, and the things he's been writing to me all these weeks. Well, let's be objective and add it up here. If I can stand back from this, and be Miss Super Detatched for a minute, we are talking about different bits of the same man, which separately, add up to something I'd quite like. SO WHAT THE HELL IS WRONG WITH HIM? But more to the point, what's wrong with me?

When I get there, Mum doesn't understand it. Not so much the fire, and Roger, and all of that. But she really doesn't understand the Internet side of it all. I knew she wouldn't. Too much information. And while I'm trying to sink into her big yellow bath, watching all her funny little blue starfish bath things dissolve, I find myself trying to explain everything through the door. Loudly.

'But how do you know it was really him?' she hoots from the other side.

'We had a private IRC channel. Nobody else could get in.'

'But what if he snooped around,' she says, attempting her version of 90's techno-chick speak, 'and hacked in?'

'Ask Didi. Ask anyone. The odds are about ten squillion to one. But fixing up a false e-mail address is easy. Going into an IRC channel is easy too, with a nickname. That's why he wouldn't give me his e-mail at first. He was fixing one up with a French service provider as fast as he could, just so he could bounce all his letters from Paris and make me think he was really there.'

'Oh well,' I hear her say lamely, wandering off downstairs to make me breakfast, 'I suppose that must have cost him some money, anyway.'

After that, I dry off, get dressed and sit around drinking tea until some of the tiredness and shock starts to melt at the edges.

'You can stay here if you like,' Mum says.

'Nah. I might go and see Jodie. Is that OK?'

'Oh, good. Jodie's good.'

'You never used to think that.'

'Oh, well.'

When I go round there, Didi's half asleep still, so we make some camomile tea and end up decamping to their bedroom, sitting on the edge of the futon while Didi goes cross-eyed trying to make sense of what I'm saying.

'Oh OK,' she says at last. 'Got it. He set up the channel with you first. At your place.'

'Yeah, and then he went back upstairs.'

'And he logged on. You never thought of doing a Who Is on his nickname?'

'No. I don't even know what a Who Is, is.'

'Oops. I should have told you about that.'

Jodie starts rubbing my shoulders absent-mindedly.

'It's not like Bill's really a computer nerd, is it?'

'But he is a computer nerd,' I say. 'That's the whole point, he's doing revolting – that's what Mum said – *revolting* computer nerdy things.'

'But at dinner . . .'

'Oh, that's just because you wanted him to be in your film, and you were making him into something he isn't. Look at him. He can't talk. He can't talk about anything except squash. I don't even know why you wanted him to be in the film. I mean, his ex girlfriend hates him. That's always a sign isn't it? I should have known.'

'Oh, that's right. The Elastoplast,' Jodie says.

'Yeah. Chucked something right at him. So work that one out. And he told me she snored. Can you believe that? Telling a total stranger all about your ex girlfriend's intimate sleeping habits?'

'But Vic,' Didi says yawning, 'you're not a total stranger to him.'

And I suppose that's it. Bill really knows me. Better, in a way, than even Dan did. I think I typed in things to Bill/ Pierre that even I didn't know about before we met. Stupid little dreams I've had. Things about my childhood. Everything.

'The thing that gives me the creeps,' I hear myself saying, all in a rush, 'the thing that really, really makes me feel sick is knowing that he was just waiting to hear me come home, waiting to hear me switch the computer on every time. Even that night that I couldn't sleep and got up really late. He must have just been waiting to see the lights go on in my flat.'

'It's sexual harassment,' Jodie says, which – let's face it – has always been her answer to everything.

'It's an invasion of your space,' Didi adds, automatically.

We sit there for a while, Didi with her elbows behind her head in her bedtime sarong, and Jodie gently swigging herbal tea around in the pot.

'Vic,' she begins, 'can I ask you a question about this?'

I nod.

'Did it ever get – you know. Was it more than a friendship?'

And I suppose what she means is, did Bill turn it into a sex thing, and was he getting off on it. Well, it's

273

a fair enough question. And looking at it from the Jodie world-view, I suppose it makes sense. If he'd been using the IRC as a kind of extended obscene phone call, then I could take it to the police. I mean, I've kept every e-mail Pierre Dubois ever sent me. I've kept every word. But no. Bill never did try anything remotely cybersexual, if that's a word, and somehow, the fact that Jodie feels moved to ask about it makes me wince.

'If it turned out to be harassment, then you could sue,' she persists.

'What am I going to do, suing someone? I can't even house-train a cat. No. It wasn't like that. Anyway, it was consenting adult friendship. I think. I voluntarily went along with it.'

'But still, false pretences.'

'Yes, but I was asking for it. Oh, I don't know.'

One thing I do know, though, is that when I finally get back to my flat late that afternoon, that Roger will have left a little surprise for me, and sure enough he has. Fantastic. Thankyou Roger, for your massive show of support in my time of crisis. I grab a bottle of evil-smelling pine detergent and start scrubbing.

Workmen are downstairs, too, hammering away at the mess that used to be Flat Five. The people are on holiday in the Dandenongs, apparently. I think I remember them now. He used to look as vague as all hell, I'm not surprised they left the oven on.

It's awful coming into this building now. Just knowing I'm going to have to turn on an Oscar-winning performance with him the moment I hear Bill's Doc Martens clumping down the stairs is killing me. I know Jodie wants me to have it out with him. I know Hilary and Natalie won't be far behind, lecturing me on the phone, hassling me for the next six months.

But you know something? I can't do it. Bill's problems are Bill's problems, I reckon. Bill's weird life is Bill's weird life. And as far as I'm concerned, all I have to do now is ring up my service provider, pay my fees up until today, and disconnect right away. Jodie can have the modem. And she can have her massage table back as well. It's served its purpose. And while I'm at it, I might as well get rid of the haunted relationship couch.

I'm over this flat. It's too small, and Roger (funny that, how he seems to be here to stay) doesn't like it. More importantly, the rest of the tenants don't like Roger. Maybe I should move out before they chuck me out. And naturally, it would remove that other little problem. The one upstairs. The one that makes me start crying if I'm stupid enough to let myself think about it.

When I ring up and cancel my Internet account, they give me my final bill. Seventy-two dollars for the past two and a half weeks. Enough to book me at least one long session with Cara the daffodil pen-spotting psychic. But who cares, anyway. 'You will meet your soulmate through the computer.' I should ask for my money back. Bloody old charlatan.

Better still, if I hadn't spent half my credit card on Internet bills and telephone psychics, I'd have enough money to go back to the hairdresser's. I haven't split up with Pierre. I never even got going with Pierre. But I want something else, now. I'm over this short, red thing. A Mary Tyler Moore bob, maybe (it's been on my mind) just so that I can get myself a huge penthouse apartment with a coffee table conversation pit, and run around the streets laughing and being successfully single and chucking my beret up in the air.

Lying on the couch with Roger purring next to my

feet, I find myself wondering where things would have gone if I'd never gone up there and found him out. All things considered, it must have been pretty tricky for Bill. Sooner or later something would have happened. I might have been on IRC one night and had a computer problem, and I might have heard him playing his Elvis Costello or something, and gone up, and then he wouldn't have been able to answer the door. And if it had happened enough times, who knows, even me – gullible me – might have suspected something.

Perhaps Pierre Dubois would have found out something about me and my life that Bill the Boffin couldn't ever possibly know. And maybe Bill would have let it slip one day, when we were talking about squash, or the weather, or work, or whatever other drivel he always forces us to talk about. Honestly, it's like being in a bad Agatha Christie video. And on top of it all I've just spent the last half an hour cleaning up cat shit. No really. This is it. *This is the life.*

But why? Why, why, why? I just don't get it. I know Pierre/Bill isn't a loser. I know he isn't, because I've become his friend. I've got to know him. We share stuff. Same sense of humour, same way of seeing things, same ideas on life. He said it himself. Talking to me made him feel as if we really knew each other. More than his ex had ever known him, anyway.

Then again, I, Victoria Total Bloody Relationships Disaster Shepworth, am the same woman who thought it would be a really good idea to go off to the mountains to have sex in a hotel with Macrame Man. So what would I know?

At some point – thirty, maybe, it's a nice round number – you just can't shove everything onto men any more. It's fine for me to say that Greg Daly was more interested in bush-walking than he was in women, and it's fine for me to say that Anthony Anderson was a bastard scuba diver who never remembered any of my friends' names. Right now, though, I know perfectly well that Greg is very happy in Tibet with Annalise, and Anthony is living (successfully) with a corporate-looking woman. So.

Maybe there's just something about me that Bill can only enjoy at a distance. Maybe I'm OK for e-mail, and OK for little sympathetic late-night chats on IRC, but that's as far as he ever wanted it to go. He can't have that photo of his ex still stuck up on the mirror for nothing. I mean, how stupid am I? Half the time we went online, we were talking about her. The snoring nose clip woman. The one who wanted more space.

The lies he told me really scare me. Living just outside Clichy. His ex being in London (I mean, really, Dorrigo to London, you work it out). This is super male inadequacy we're talking here. Not just a bit of fun. Not just a little trick.

If he'd done it the first time, just for a joke, and if he'd come downstairs afterwards and told me – well. But maybe it did start out as a joke. Nobody wanted to talk to me on my Singles Solidarity channel, and he probably felt sorry for me. I just wonder, when did it start to get interesting for him? At what point did he think it was worth fixing up an e-mail address, all the way over in France, just so he could spend the next few weeks encouraging me to believe he was something he wasn't.

More accurately, he wanted me to believe he was somewhere he wasn't. Like it or not (and I don't) the real Bill is the real Pierre. And now I'm remembering something else. Something important.

The night Jodie and Didi fell asleep, and Hilary got drunk and sent that stupid message to Liam about doing a survey on men's underpants . . . I mean, how drunk were we? How loud were we? Loud enough for him to hear us through the door when he dropped his squash racket? Especially when I said 'What's wrong with Australian men?' And possibly loud enough for him to hear 'I want an Englishman next time.' All that crap Hilary talked (or maybe it was me) about all the different types of men, and what a waste of space they all were. Ferals and *Footy Show* men and inner city boys with Triple J promotional condoms, and men people from Bondi who wear sunglasses that make them look like blowflies. What if he heard that? It would have been enough to make any man crawl off and want to pretend to be somebody else.

He knows we all called him Bill the Boffin too. That night he said something about not having to be a boffin to understand things. He must have been listening through the floor. And it gives me the creeps to think of him watching me coming back with Dan, crying in the car that time. And watching us laughing at him while he did his usual bad Dorrigo parking in the street.

Then Roger jumps off the couch and starts meowing, and as I get up to open more sardines, I turn it around and look at things again. If Bill really wanted to get at me, if Bill really wanted to stuff up my life at the moment, I don't think he could have done anything better than this. At least with Liam I had a target to hit. At least something happened, even if it did end up with a 'How's it goin'?' phone call a few weeks later. This is something worse. This is like being deceived by someone who doesn't even exist.

Pierre Dubois may have something to do with Bill, but forty-eight hours ago I also thought he was a nice, funny, kind-hearted, romantic Englishman on the other side of the world, in Paris, the most romantic city in the world. The kind of guy I could build up my hopes on the Christmas holidays for. So – nothing to do with Bill after all. Just someone Bill dreamed up, because that's exactly who he'd like to be. Loser.

It gives me some satisfaction to think that he'll be logging in tonight, only to find I'm not there any more. And I wonder how long it will take him to find out that I don't even exist as an e-mail address?

When I see him, if I'm unlucky enough to run into him, I'll just tell him the Internet bills were too high and I had to give it up. You know how it is. And maybe he'll guess one day, and maybe he won't. Right now, though, there's only one thing I want to look at, and it's not a computer screen. It's that back bit of the paper where a woman like me, one cat, stable income, can still hopefully find a flat to call her own. And the further away from here, the better, to be honest.

Twenty-seven

It feels strange not having the Net any more. The computer looks half-full without it, and my life feels even emptier than that. TV is no substitute. Roger is no substitute. And for a moment, I weaken, reasoning that I can still go and visit Withnail and I sites and Exploding Pop Tart sites and bypass the rest of it. But it's no good. Bill's tainted it for me. Ruined it, even. The Net has to go.

I suppose it's not very practical. If I'd hung on for just another day I could have used all the newspaper classified sites to find myself a home. Apparently there's a place you can go to now where you just type in the rent you want to pay, the area you want to be in, and the number of bedrooms you want. For something which has stuffed up my life, I have to admit the net can still be what Bill Gates wants me to think it is.

Saturday mornings are usually loud Elvis Costello mornings for Bill. He gets up at around 9 a.m., and he'll put on an album while he's going up and down the stairs with his laundry. I can even tell you this much – sometimes he'll drop a pair of boxer shorts, or a sock with a hole in it, on the stairs. And he'll make a kind of 'shh!' sound which is almost swearing, but in a Dorrigo kind of way, not quite.

This morning there are no Bill sounds at all. I suppose he's worried that there's a chance I might be doing my laundry as well (although I'm usually an 'Oh my God, I forgot' Sunday night kind of washerwoman.) Well, good. I'm glad he's cowering in his flat with the mousepads and the photo of the girl with the freckles. I hope they find a dusty skeleton in a crouching position in the corner in twenty years' time.

I go out, I don't buy croissants (they're for couples) and I try not to notice everyone in the local cafes, all in their units of two, separating sections of the newspaper for each other, and ordering big plunger pots of coffee. Saturday night is couples' night, but for me it begins on Saturday morning too. Want to know when you feel most single? When you catch yourself staring at the only other lone male person in the cafe, only to find he's picking his nose and has a woolly hat on.

It's funny how some couples dress up for breakfast. *He'll* have ironed beige shorts on, and a belt through the loops of his shorts, and a pair of those yachting shoes that nobody actually ever wears on a yacht, and a Ralph Lauren polo shirt, and a pair of Raybans perched on top of his head. *She,* meanwhile, will be wearing a dazzling white tracksuit, with dazzling white sandshoes, and blowdried hair, and probably perfume dabbed behind each knee as well. You can never hear what they're saying to each other, but if you got in close you could probably lip-read.

Coffee, darling?

Thanks, darling.

Or am I getting it all wrong, and are the groomed Saturday morning, gently murmuring couples all collectively headed for some terrible divorce? According

282

to the paper today, there were 15,984 of them here last year, the second highest figure ever.

I've been through this mindless cafe-staring thing before. It usually happens when you're two years into singledom, not just a few months, and I have to admit it worries me. It's bitter and it's twisted and it's wrong. I need a coffee, though, and I'm not going to hang around the cafes of cosy coupledom to have one.

At home, I disembowel the paper. I mean, why do they put that cars thing in all the time? Why do they?

I leave the Real Estate section until last, deliberately, in the same way that Didi used to leave the Employment section until last.

In the end, I rush it. Flats To Let. Newtown. And as I suspected, the rents all start at something which could buy you a new washing machine. Every week of your life.

Upstairs, Bill still hasn't moved. No Elvis Costello. No laundry. No sock-dropping. Oh well, let him suffer.

Going down the page with a biro I find myself circling completely stupid options. Something called a Studio Apartment which I know will have one of those bathrooms where the shower is just a drain in the tiles, and the loo is next to it. A sofa-bed kind of place. You know, you turn around with a saucepan full of potatoes, and you smash into your own wardrobe. After five minutes of serious thought, I cross it out again.

Bondi Beach. Could I live there? Especially when the men wear sunglasses that make them look like blowflies? Anyway. I've got a sick feeling that's where Tattoo Lawyer might have her glamorous single pad with the black shower curtains, so no, I don't think so.

There's a flat in Waverton, which is miles away, which is cheap because it only has a three-month lease. So I ring. And the phone is engaged for hours, and then when I finally get through there's a woman's voice on the answering machine saying 'Thankyou for calling. Unfortunately . . .'

Clearly, I am going to have to ask Bobbi for a raise if I'm ever going to find a flat. Clearly, she won't give me one. All of which leaves one, last, shuddering option.

And here it is.

SHARE ACCOMMODATION
NEWTOWN Prof. person required share 2 others.
Veg preferred. Non smoker.
NEWTOWN 2 br, share male, broadminded pref.
NEWTOWN No pets. No veg. Share couple.

And then we have this:

RANDWICK Come and share our happy household!
Randy, Bella and Mo are looking for a cool guy/gal to
share a cute 3 bedroom terrace.

All of which means Randy must be in a bedroom with Bella, or Bella must be in with Mo, or maybe they're all bonking and bedding on a horrible smelly futon in one room together and they're actually looking for two more flatmates. *Kinky* flatmates. Anyway, if they want a cool gal for a happy household, I'm just not their woman. Why won't anyone advertise for a miserable old single with a cat, I ask myself?

In the end I circle the least scarey five options, brush my teeth, gargle with Dettol, wear something that won't say anything about my personality whatsoever, and stride out. Lucky I've got the agency mobile ('It must never leave this office, people, never' – yeah, that one) with me.

The first place is a terrace in Paddington. I ring up

and the man on the other end sounds OK. Not great, OK. But then, you never can tell anything from the phone.

When I get there, the front door is wide open and there's a guy going out as I'm leaving. He gives me a blank look.

The house has those polished floorboards that make your foosteps echo. And when I walk in wearing my black boots, I sound like Frankenstein's monster clumping around in a castle. Crash, crash, crash.

A man in a grey tracksuit, with Clark Kent glasses, shoots out of the kitchen. He is holding a glass bowl with some grey sludge in it.

'Pate?'

Then I see the bowl of crackers on the kitchen table. He's all prepared. Then he shows me a clipboard with a computer printout clipped onto it, headed POTENTIAL HOUSEMATE SURVEY. Wow.

'Please sit down. You must be the air hostess.'

'No, I'm the advertising person.'

'Oh. Do you know Simon Reynolds?'

'No.'

He looks amazed at this.

'Did I say have some pate? Help yourself. It's chicken liver.'

Yes, and he hasn't put it in the blender long enough to get rid of all the little livery looking bits. But I eat it. Perhaps it's one of the categories on the POTENTIAL HOUSEMATE SURVEY. Will you eat my crap home-made pate? Tick yes/ no.

'Now then.' He crosses his legs.

'Could you write your name and age in that box there, please. You don't have to tell me your whole age, just a clue – you're thirties are you?'

'Yes.'

So much for Estee Lauder Advanced Night Repair Protective Recovery Complex.

'And then, see where I've put PARTIES? Could you write down if you're a party person, not a party person, or sometimes that.'

'I think I'm sometimes that.'

There's a shy knock at the door.

'Oh hang on.'

He gets up.

It occurs to me I haven't even seen the place yet. I mean, I've seen him – whatever his name is, I can't remember it any better than he can remember mine. I've seen his nasty pate. I've seen his survey. But the room?

The *new person* is getting a look at the room, apparently. He's being led straight upstairs. I can hear them clattering around in what sounds like the attic. So I quickly fill in all the other boxes on the computer printout, ticking all of them the way you do when you have to fill in a customs sheet, only leaving it until the last box to write NAME: EVITA PERON. Then I just run away. Until I get halfway down the street and realize I've left my mobile phone there – except it's not my mobile, is it? Damn, Starsky and Hutch.

When I go back, the man in the grey tracksuit is standing up in the kitchen, waving his arms around, spitting dry crackers all over the room-seeker, who is looking at him with a nervous-laugh kind of face.

I dash in, digging my thumbnail into the side of my finger, which is my time-honoured technique for any unpleasant situation (dentist, injections, social embarrassment). Grey Track-suit hardly notices me.

'Oh hi!'

'I left my mobile. Sorry.'

'I loved what you wrote!' he calls after me, as I pelt

down the corridor. 'Are you interested in seeing the room?'

Well, really. So I get on the bus, and get as far away as possible.

The next place is SUMMER HILL: Fem. to share with smoker and cat. Foxtel.

When I get there, I can hear the Foxtel. Once again, the front door is wide open. Probably because of the smoke, I guess. I see the cat as I come up the front pathway. It is a Siamese with shaved bits, a red-studded collar and wild staring eyes. Roger wouldn't like it.

A woman comes to the door. She's a bit older than me. She's got a sapphire wedding ring on her finger — it looks like something they give away on quiz shows. She also has bits of peach face mask still crumbling on her chin. I thought she might have a fag in her hand to lend her share accommodation ad more authenticity, but she doesn't.

'Are you by yourself?' she asks me, waving me in past the TV set (gigantic) which is blaring out an old *Doctor Who* episode. One where the daleks have gone grey and white.

I tell her I'm by myself.

'I'm by myself,' the woman says.

And that's the last communication we have for the entire (five-minute) house inspection. My room, I judge from her hand gestures, will be the one next to the bathroom, which smells of face mask and those yucky sticky yellow round things men have on top of the urinals in public toilets.

The room has yellow smiley stickers stuck all over the ceiling, and a round dolphin rainbow sticker peeling on the window. There are four blue tac marks on the walls, right where a poster of a unicorn probably was. Downstairs, Doctor Who is yelling, 'This is evil!' which I think is probably right.

When we go back downstairs again, she gives in, sits down and lights up a fag. You have to admire the woman for holding back for the duration of the house inspection. Doctor Who gets turned down, and then she stares at me. For about another five minutes. That's what it feels like anyway.

'I was married, he moved out,' she says at last. 'Were you married?'

'No.'

The fact that some poor cows have never even made it up the aisle even once seems to cheer her up, so I give her my phone number – actually I give her my old work phone number, the one we changed by one digit about six months ago. She doesn't say goodbye, but waves instead, from the front doorstep. The bald Siamese with the studded collar just stares. It's hard ambling casually up the pathway when I really feel like breaking the record for the four-minute mile.

Anyway, I tell myself as I find the bus stop. Roger wouldn't have liked it.

There are three more places to go after that, and it's well past lunchtime, and I haven't eaten. I don't think you can afford to eat when you're looking for share accommodation, though. The next place is a long, long bus ride away. This one is BILGOLA: Huge room in Spanish-style beach villa. Gorgeous views. Entertaining area. Why not try something completely different.

It's half my salary, so I don't know why I'm bothering, but maybe I can get a second job as a waitress if I really, really like it. And maybe I should be a bit more upwardly mobile with my life. You know, do some entertaining. Then I wouldn't keep on attracting perverted PC users from obscure New South Wales country towns.

This time the door is closed. Good sign. And nobody is leaving, or arriving, as I'm ringing the bell. Another good sign. A woman who looks like a ballerina, with a tight bun pulling her entire face back, answers the door. She smiles sweetly, like Audrey Hepburn.

'Oh, I'm sorry. It's gone.'

This time I catch a cab. To hell with buses. This is *my* Saturday. *My* Saturday, and it's bloody almost gone. Shouldn't I be in my mother's bath using the blue starfish aromatherapy oil thingies? Shouldn't I at least be in bed eating cashews and trying to finish *Wuthering Heights*?

The cab driver sees my newspaper with blue biro rings all over it.

'You doing any good?' he asks. It's amazing, this man must have been in Australia since the 1950s and he still looks and talks like Marcello Mastroianni just before he died.

'No,' I say.

'You gotta move in with your friends,' he says helpfully.

'No, I don't think so.'

He looks sideways at me. Damn, now he'll think I've got no friends. He does.

'You just got here, to Sydney?' he asks me.

'Yes,' I lie.

He shakes his head.

'Everyone's coming to Sydney.'

'Are they?'

Then he swears at someone cutting him off in the next lane, just before he's about to get to his 'It's a wunnaful, wunnaful place' speech. Which, at the moment, I could do without. It might have been wunnaful when

289

you could get your own place for one hundred and fifty dollars a week, and the home-made pate lifestyle hadn't been invented yet.

He offers me a Mintie. Maybe my breath smells, despite the Dettol. Perhaps the ballerina woman in the villa was lying to me. The room hadn't been taken at all, she was just overwhelmed by my breath.

I make up my mind that this place, my last place for the day, is going to be The One. I don't care what it takes, I'm going to be happy here, and it's going to give me a whole new life, and I'm going to have a sunny little room with a big white mosquito net hanging over the bed, and a tree in the garden that Roger can live in.

It's going to be a tough call, but I think I can do it. This is it:

CITY FRINGE Unusual w/house style aprt. Christians welcome. No pets. Suit music lover. Shr. one male.

I stare out of the window sucking my biro thoughtfully (Hilary always says this is evidence of poor breastfeeding when young) making up a suitably good spiel.

'Wow, I love your apartment. It's so unusual. How clever, it used to be a warehouse, now look! I really admire Christians, there must be so much temptation around you. And did I tell you I love anything from Elton John and Kiki Dee to Wagner? And how I'm allergic to cats?'

I can give Roger back to Natalie. She'll understand.

The driver drops me off with a gloomy look on his face. I'm not surprised. It's a very gloomy warehouse. The aprt. is up a flight of stairs, no lift, and the owner has drawn a very tiny happy face on the bit of paper sticky-taped to his doorbell button.

Yes, it's true. It would suit a music lover. I can hear someone playing 'Bohemian Rhapsody' on the piano. And singing.

I don't like to interrupt when anybody's got up to the Beelzebub part of that song, I think in the original video clip it was the part where the four disembodied Queen heads suddenly started opening their mouths and shutting them very quickly. It's a very demanding part of the song, I've always felt. However. I knock. Loudly.

A man comes to the door looking absolutely normal. After a day of pate-gobbling anally-retentive males and sad divorcees in face-masks this is a complete shock. I almost say 'I'll take it' on the spot before I remember he's the one who's supposed to decide.

He beckons me in.

'Sorry, I've got a mouthful of carrot cake,' he says, with a mouthful of carrot cake.

The place is huge. Big enough to have housed at least one thousand sweaty women with headscarves, toiling away on gigantic hydraulic sewing machines. Before some old 80s yuppie bought it and the architect moved in and started waving his arms around and sniffing the air.

'You look as if you could do with a cup of herbal tea,' the man says. He reminds me that he's Graham. I think he's noticed that I don't know.

I look for the Queen sheet music on the piano, but what do you know, Graham's been playing it from memory. And when he brings back the herbal tea from the kitchen, which seems to be about 5km away at the other end of the room, it's actually real mint leaves, squashed up inside a little silver infuser thing.

He's got beanbags too. With shiny silver plastic covers. I must tell Hilary. It would create a revolution in her management of the Children's Library. She could just hose everything down at the end of the day.

'Wasn't it sad about Freddie Mercury?' I say stupidly. Then I think, perhaps he's one of those Christians who think AIDS is God's way of saying 'No you mustn't'.

'I'm a big fan of early Queen,' he says.

'What, not Fat Bottomed Girls?' I shoot back, then stop. I don't think I should be talking about bottoms either. Honestly, Christians. It's like being around Japanese people and trying not to mention the war.

He asks me lots of questions, and I dress my life up to sound better than it really is, and I leave out as many references as I can to lesbian friends, drunken debauchery and bizarre Internet relationships.

Then I ask him a few questions – about Queen, which seems to be the only safe topic there is, and he tells me how he bought a pair of white clogs because one of the guitarists in Queen had white clogs.

And we chat a little more, and I turn down more nice fresh peppermint tea, and then he drops his bombshell.

'Well, Victoria,' he smiles. 'Shall we leave it there then?' And faster than you can yodel 'Galileo, Galileo', he's opened the door for me – wide.

You know how you know when a man's checking you out from behind? Well he is, I can feel it.

'Sorry it didn't work out flatmate-wise,' he says. 'But I'd like to see you again some time for a cup of coffee. Would you mind if I gave you a call some time?'

And Starsky and Hutch-it, he's using the real estate columns as his personal conversion agency. He's got my proper number too. Yet another reason why I'm going to have to move out. I wonder if he knows about Christian Dateline! Where happiness is just a phone call away!

Twenty-eight

When I get to work on Monday, Kylie is going around collecting money. For herself. It's her birthday, and apparently she is the only person who has remembered she is supposed to be getting a big fat chocolate cake for afternoon tea.

I don't mind giving her $5, although nobody thought of mine either. From memory, I ended up crooning 'Happy birthday to me' in a pathetic little wheedling voice in my cubicle. It's amazing how long ago it seems now. All that. My birthday, and the break-up with the Loathsome Lawyer from Leichhardt too.

This morning I have to finish writing copy for a competition where you can win three years' supply of school shoes. Really. What sort of deranged young mind could possibly be interested?

Because it takes me about 0.05 seconds, I allow myself time to sneak out and find a card for Kylie, and maybe a present, if I'm feeling generous – or more to the point, if someone's selling a new kind of furry, blobby stick-on monster she hasn't got yet.

Maybe I should take the phone with me, in case Jodie or Hilary rings. Then again, where is it? Oh yes. I've had it all weekend, haven't I. So . . .

'KYLIE!'

'What?'

'I've left the phone, I have to go home, I don't know what I've done with it, oh my God.'

'Yeah, someone was looking for that,' she says calmly.

'Can you tell them I've gone out to see a client?'

'Ye-es.'

'You know I lied for you in a previous life, don't you?'

She sighs. But who knows, I consider, as I rush outside the building and wave down a cab. Maybe Kylie and I were both in the French Resistance and I told lies to protect her under threat of terrible torture from the Nazis. That may well be the reason why destiny has put her in the terrible position of continually having to tell Bobbi I am coughing up blood or recovering from seafood poisoning, or seeing clients, when in actual fact I am either weeping over my pathetic love life at home, or looking for stolen office property.

When I get to my flat at last, I'm in such a rush to get out of the cab that I do a Fergie, and get out crutch-first, with my legs about as far apart as a woman in the last stages of labour. Instinctively, I look up – just to see if Bill's been looking out of the window the whole time. But then again, stuff him. I don't care any more. Let him look.

When I open the door of the flat, Roger is very surprised to see me back so soon. It makes me wonder what he's been up to. No doubt using the phone to make calls to Krystal Connections to find out if I'm going to have him put down or not.

And *there's* the phone. Lucky I had the presence of mind to leave it somewhere sensible – like on top of the ironing board, next to a blazing-hot iron which has been on since 8 o'clock this morning.

And then I'm nearly out of the door again when I hear it. The strains of Elvis Costello, filtering down the stairs. It has the same effect on me that the sound of choppers probably has on Vietnam Veterans. In a word, I run.

It takes me ages to find another cab, but eventually one turns up, and I collapse into the back seat. All these cab fares are costing me a fortune, but then again, it does give you time to think, I suppose. If it's at all possible to think when John Laws is booming out of the speakers.

I wonder what it would be like to be someone's mistress? That way you could spend the entire day at home, lying on the couch, picking fleas out of your cat's fur and watching people trying to sell you all-in-one bathroom cleaner on Bert Newton. It was nice, sneaking home like that, in the middle of the morning. Like a quick re-entry into the womb. Pity I have to go to work though.

Oh hang on. Kylie's birthday card.

'Stop here please.'

There's a newsagent about five minutes up the road, not too far from work, where I know for a fact they sell particularly offensive and unfunny penis joke birthday cards, which is exactly what Kylie likes best in the whole, wide world.

And – wouldn't you know it – it takes me about another half-hour just to scan every card they've got. Including time for gift-searching. In the end I take up a card with a picture of Michelangelo's *David* with a real rubber balloon stuck to where his genitals are supposed to be, and a chocolate heart wrapped in red foil, probably left over from Valentine's Day, but the only approximation of a $10 present this newsagent's got.

It's only when I reach into my jacket pocket for my purse that I realize I've left it in the taxi. And not only that. The mobile phone too. Oh, thankyou God. Is this my punishment for rejecting Graham, the man who welcomes Christians?

It's embarrassing enough to have to hold your head up at the cash register and hand over a card with a rubber balloon stuck on a man's groin, without realizing you can't even pay for it.

'I'm sorry, I've left my wallet in the cab. Can I come back and pay for this later? It's for my friend.'

The man behind the counter gives me a look which says he believes none of these three separate statements.

And then it's back to work — half-jogging in my heels, and panting all the way. But I don't know why I bother. According to the clock above reception, this whole escapade has taken two hours as it is.

When I finally wheeze into my cubicle, I find out the cab driver's got there before me. With my purse, and the phone.

'He was really sleazy,' Kylie hisses, 'he kept looking up Bobbi's skirt. She wants to see you, too.'

'Really?'

'Yeah, like she *really* wants to see you. And I'll tell you something about Accounts, as well, they all mucked in and came up with $20, so divide that by five people and work out who the scumbag is!'

'Yeah. Terrible. Tch.'

She lets me go. Clearly my mind's not on her problems, it's on my problems. And why shouldn't it be? Bobbi is going to disembowel me.

I tap on the door. Why does she always keep it closed? It just ups the terror quotient.

The mobile phone is on her desk. I suppose in a

police report it would be 'the offending mobile phone.' Actually, Bobbi's looking at it as if she finds it pretty offensive, too.

'Now.'

Oh no, the three-tier warning system. But actually, she gets straight to the point. Like Mrs Brady in her best, brisk, no-nonsense mood when someone's stolen a chocolate brownie.

'You will be required to make up the missing hours in overtime, and use of the phone will no longer be available to you.'

'Thankyou.'

'The client has accepted your school shoes competition copy.'

'Oh, great.'

'If I have to see you again on any point at all, Victoria, you will be asked to leave immediately. Your possessions will be packed in a box and sent by courier to your home.'

'Sure!'

'Thankyou.'

When I crawl out, Kylie is still doing the rounds of all the little cubicles, begging for that extra five dollars that will turn a boring old chocolate cake into a much more exciting Black Forest Cake.

'Did she do it?' she yells, across the top of the partitions.

Up pop the heads, like those flighty little desert animals that you see in Walt Disney wildlife documentaries.

I shake my head. I suppose if everyone really liked me here, there would be a resounding cheer, but there isn't. They just want their mobile phone back, that's all.

At just before 1 p.m., everybody evacuates the

building for lunch. I stay at my post. Not only will I give Bobbi overtime, but I will give her *under* the overtime. Then again, what's the bloody point if she's vanished to the Bayswater or somewhere for squid ink pasta, and she can't even see me?

At 1.30 p.m. I'm starving and my stomach is making weird noises that sound like evil spirits talking in tongues. Fortunately, someone's left a packet of instant noodles in the kitchen cupboard. Actually, I've known about them for some time now. Whoever owns them thought they would be safe tucked away behind a series of plastic canisters, right at the back of the cupboard underneath the sink. Unfortunately, that's where I used to hide my chocolate chip biscuits, so I know all about it.

I wish they were normal noodles, but they're something from the health food shop, made from special wheat, in a miso sauce. Disappointing, but when you've got something that's good for you versus starvation, you have no choice. I pile them into a coffee cup I can't even be bothered washing up, I'm so hungry, and basically drink them. As I thought, they are wholly disgusting.

Just before 2 p.m., the dutiful people start trickling back in again, then finally at 2.20, Kylie turns up. She's waving an orange velvet scarf. One of her sisters took her out to a Japanese restaurant, and the other one gave her the scarf, it turns out.

'I meant to get you a present, but that was when I left my wallet in the cab,' I say, sounding pathetic.

'Doesn't matter.'

I can tell it does.

'Oh, by the way—' she says.

'Yeah?'

'Breakfast Grits wanted a copy of your final script. I

298

couldn't find it so I just did a search on everything on your computer with Grits on it and sent it through. Sorry. I had to. You weren't here,' she says, meaningfully.

'No, that's OK.'

Except it isn't OK, because about half an hour later, Bobbi comes stomping up to see me in her shiny black patent leather heels, waving a fax in my face. It's from Mr Breakfast Grits. The fat one. Whatever his name is. Apparently Kylie's sent him a document file headed REASONS FOR BONKING LIAM – or, more specifically, 𝕽𝕰𝕬𝕾𝕺𝕹𝕾 𝕱𝕺𝕽 𝕭𝕺𝕹𝕶𝕴𝕹𝕲 𝕷𝕴𝕬𝕸.

I resign five minutes before she sacks me. Oh, and they were her noodles as well.

Twenty-nine

It's been years since I woke up unemployed. The last time was just after I left Uni, day one after I got my BA. Actually, I think we all woke up unemployed that morning. I've never really done it by myself before.

Apparently, Hilary tells me on the phone, this means I've become a slacker, which is very groovy. I don't know where she finds out these things. Reading *Dolly* on the sly in the Children's Library, I suppose.

'Actually, Vic, you always were a slacker. It's just that you had a job so nobody knew.'

'Do you think I could become a librarian?'

'But you don't read.'

'All you have to do is put books back, isn't it?'

'Try and be nice to me, thanks, six months from now you could be begging for a job.' Mmm, hosing down the children's beanbags.

Then again, do I really want a proper job? Maybe this slacker thing is me after all. Maybe I've finally found myself. But I wonder what slackerdom really involves? It sounds as if you just lie around all day in a pair of baggy pants, playing with the ring in your pierced navel until you get a septic infection.

It occurs to me that I don't know what the dole is

worth either. So after breakfast, I ring up. It's a bit like ringing up to get the lotto results, except when they tell you, it's not quite as exciting. I'm so shocked at the amount I'm going to be living on that I can't help myself.

'Is that it?'

'*Yes*,' says the voice on the other end.

Actually, I've just thought of a job for me. I could get a toy xylophone and play the hold music on the dole enquiry switchboard. Or I could be a human number pad. 'Press 1 to find out if you are on the poverty line, 2 for the Salvation Army Soup Kitchen or 3 if you are really, really stuffed.'

I go to the newsagency after lunch – which is the same as breakfast, a big bowl of muesli – and gather up an armful of ad-land magazines, and newspapers for every state of Australia. I'm sure there's less competition for school shoes copywriters in the outback. I also look in vain for a magazine called *Slacker Lifestyle,* but it looks like they're all too lazy to put one out.

Roger sits on the bits I want to read when I lay them out on the bed.

'Why do you do that? You could sit on THIS bit, the business bit, but you sit on THAT bit, the employment bit. I hate you.'

Then I catch myself talking to him, and clam up. I am becoming a single sadwoman. Against my will, I am becoming a single sadwoman.

There are some great jobs. Glamorous, exciting, highly paid. I'll never get any of them. I circle the key words in the ad, so I can do that thing where you look them up in the thesaurus, find a substitute word, and cunningly stick it in your application letter so you can play with their minds and get the job.

'Small, go-ahead agency seeks motivated self-starter. Must be a team player with good client communication skills.'

OK. 'Dear small, go-ahead agency. I am a self-starter with *driving force, spring, mainspring.* I also like to think of myself as a *cooperator, team-mate, yoke-fellow, sympathizer, fellow-traveller, fifth columnist.'*

More importantly, I will not nick your boss's health food shop noodles, even when they are cunningly hidden behind a stack of Tupperware containers in the bottom cupboard underneath the sink. Nor will I walk out with your collectively owned mobile phone. Especially if I have been told it must never leave the office, never.

Sitting up in bed, with all the magazines and newspapers around me, I start to get cappuccino cravings. I suppose this is the first hurdle slackers must face. Round about now, Kylie will be trotting out for a cardboard six-pack tray, bringing back hot little white polystyrene cups of froth for everybody. Damn. Kylie.

I ring her up.

'It's me.'

'Who?'

'How quickly you forget. Victoria. I'm ringing to say I'm getting you a birthday present, all right? I haven't forgotten.'

'Is that really why you're ringing up?'

'Yes!'

'Bobbi's told me not to tell you anything about anything.'

'What does that mean?'

'Like, work things. She thinks you're going to go to a new agency and tell them what we're up to.'

'Yeah, really. Like lethal inside information on

landscape gardening catalogues. Wow, what a loaded weapon that is.'

'Anyway, she's really cracked down on personal calls since you—'

'You'd better go.'

'Yeah. See ya. I'd like a bottle of that Chanel nail polish that's nearly black.'

When I put the phone down, this takes some minutes to sink in. She, Kylie, employed, is asking me, slacker, unemployed, to buy her Chanel for her birthday? For that, she gets that nasty blue pot pourri Jodie gave me last Christmas, which I haven't unwrapped.

'I mean, stuff her.'

Oh no, I'm talking to the cat again.

I read the paper. I don't think I've read it from cover to cover since they had one of those competitions where a little dollar bill is hidden on each page, and you have to write down all the page numbers so you can win a car.

It occurs to me that quite a few things have been going on while I've been immersed in my pathetic love life. For a start, we're supposed to be turning into a republic. Whoops, missed that one. Somebody's put in a suggestion for a new flag, green and gold, like those old packets of cheese and onion chips you used to be able to buy at the tuckshop.

Embarrassingly enough, the only news I really seem to be up with is of the Liz Taylor hip operation variety. And the Spice Girls split rumour? Pshaw! I knew it *months* ago.

There's an article in the features section about the health department being alarmed at new statistics on teenage girls on diets, and how half of them are heading for a heart attack because they're too unfit, and the other half are just wasting away. They're going to launch a campaign to persuade the girls not to base their ideal height and weight measurements around the cast of *Friends,* apparently.

'About time,' I tell Roger, who is now in the roast chicken position, with his legs stuck behind his head, just waiting for a white paper noisette to be shoved on each paw. And yes, I *know* I'm talking to the cat now, and I just don't care.

Then it occurs to me. In that way that makes you feel like slapping yourself on the side of the head, except that it would hurt too much.

'Yes!'

It's not very slacker, but a good idea is still a good idea. Like a driving force, a spring, a mainspring, I turn on the computer and finally do something constructive with it for the first time in months. I write a letter selling myself to people who could actually provide me with gainful employment. People who might want someone like me – a tragic old dieter from way back – to write ads for girls who live on grated carrot sandwiches.

Then I leave the flat and walk (yes, walk – a bus fare is enough to get me a noodle lunch these days, you know) round to my mother's place.

She's doing someone's tax return. They look relieved to have me interrupting them.

'Sorry, I just wanted to get into the garage,' I say, standing in the doorway.

'Oh! Not at work?' my mother says, clambering up to find the keys.

And that would take at least half a day to explain, wouldn't it, so I don't say anything at all, I just mumble something about a project for the health department, and how I need to find some of my old books from uni which I've packed up downstairs.

'Is that a tax dodger?' I ask her, as she lifts up the rusty sliding garage door.

'The window's open,' she says in a low voice.

'Sorry.'

'There you are.'

She waves a hand at a pile of cardboard boxes, horrible old green armchairs and tea chests which contains most of her married life, and most of my school days. It's funny how people always have the same things in their garages, my mother included. Macrame owl pot plant hangers. Round orange plastic lampshades. K-Tel record selectors. And piles of *Women's Weekly* with pictures of Princess Anne, coming down the steps of a plane with her hair up in a bun, on the front cover.

When Mum pushes off at last, I go looking for my diaries. Or what passes for diaries. I've never been very good at keeping them. People used to give them to me for Christmas, and I used to make half-hearted attempts at filling them in. That's all. But somewhere in one of those boxes, I know there's a copy of my anorexia winter and Jamie Streeton diary. And I'm going to need it if I talk them into letting me work on this health campaign. So.

They're in an old straw laundry basket, next to neatly labelled cardboard boxes with all Mum's old accountancy course notes. They stink, mainly because of the mould that's beginning to creep in over the fake leather-look cardboard covers, but also because at some stage I seem to have chucked in half-empty perfume bottles too. The perfume you buy when you're eighteen, my God. It's all called stuff like Razzy! and smells of men's urinals. No wonder my boyfriends dumped me.

My whole life is stuffed in the laundry basket.

There's Humpty Dumpty in there, looking sick and pale – even though he was a lurid pink when he was first given to me. And there's a really disgusting plastic trophy, supposed to look like a silver cup, with WORLD'S BEST GIRLFRIEND written on it. Greg Daly gave me that.

There are old photos of me and Hilary standing in front of a tent, on the same school camping trip where Christine the Maths Genius embarrassed herself playing Spin the Bottle. There are toe socks too – toe socks, aagh did we really wear them? – and even a Boomtown Rats poster, with Bob Geldof in a pair of huge sunglasses.

I'm not sure if anyone knows that all my lovelorn adolescent diaries are in here. Perhaps the fact that you have to push your way through Humpty Dumpty and toe socks to get to them is enough to put snoopers off. I know it's putting me off. But there it is. 1990. The year I turned twenty-two, the year of Jamie Streeton, the year I went on the amazingly successful grated carrot sandwich diet, and the year I gave up writing diaries for ever.

There's a bit about that in the margins, too. It's all coming back to me now. In the entries for June, right in the middle of it all, I've written in capitals, WHY AM I THE ONLY PERSON WHO CAN'T STICK FINGERS DOWN HER THROAT?

It's not the endless kilojoule additions and subtractions, or the boring recipes (Orange and Watercress Salad) that get to me, though. It's the stuff about Jamie.

On the 5th of July, I've written this: 'I think he was going to tell me that he loved me today. We went for a walk at Whale Beach and I knew he wanted to say something, but he couldn't do it. Maybe he thinks it's too soon.'

And – this is the really embarrassing part – at the bottom of every page since our first date, there's a tally of days that we've been together. Not quite hours and minutes, but definitely days.

So, Victoria Total Bloody Relationship Disaster Shepworth, nothing's changed, has it? On reflection, most of my things with men have been two parts imagination to one part reality, and here's where it all started. He wasn't going to tell me that he loved me. If he wanted to say something, but he couldn't, it was probably about the fact that I looked like something out of a concentration camp when I got into the water in my bikini.

I do remember him kicking around a bit of seaweed on the beach that day, as if it were a football. That was Jamie's way of dealing with things. Hitting inanimate objects.

It's Dan's way, too. The day he drop-kicked the furry green alarm clock that Dad gave me out of the window was the day I told him I'd thrown my pills in the bin.

Asking myself what's wrong with them all isn't really the point. I'd be better off trying to find out what's wrong with me. Trying not to make up my love life in my head might be a good starting point. It makes me cringe, now. I was twenty-two years old, dieting – that's embarrassing enough – and coming up with crap like, 'I think he was going to tell me that he loved me today.'

And eight years later, what am I doing, except falling for my own fantasies about English men in Paris called Pierre who don't exist – except in Bill's head. And no-hopers like Liam, who I fondly imagine might want more than two days of sex in a country hotel, but never do.

In a way, I wish I was back in toe socks. At least life

was simple then. I used to make things up in my head, but they were mostly about people like Bob Geldof and David Soul. Nobody I was ever likely to have a relationship with. Or even run into in Woolworths.

I wonder what's happened to David Soul?

Thirty

I'm not sure what the protocol is when you're unemployed. Is it like a death in the family? Do you just ring up everyone and say 'Are you sitting down?' or do you not mention it at all?

Having my third consecutive muesli lunch in a row, I think about the likely reactions.

Jodie and Didi – Thrilled for me, over the moon.

Mum – Likely to offer me a job as her cleaner.

Dad – May send money.

The Loathsome Lawyer from Leichhardt – Likely to say 'I told you so.'

Then, after lunch, something wonderful happens. A woman from the health department rings me up and says she likes my letter. She also says she doesn't know what the budget is, and she doesn't know if they'll employ freelancers, but my brain shuts off at that point, and all I can think of is doing some kind of victory dance in my black socks (third consecutive day in a row, also.)

Because I've hardly spoken to anyone for seventy-two hours, I start gabbling.

'It's just that I had anorexia when I was younger, and

I even went and got all my old diaries yesterday, just to give me some ideas, and . . .'

'Well, Victoria, I'll ring you as soon as we know where we're up to on this.'

By the sound of her voice, she's secretly wishing there was some xylophone shut-up signal she could ping in my ear.

As soon as I put the phone down, though, I feel like I'm Cathy Freeman breaking some kind of record. Yes! As far as I'm concerned, that's the end of my unemployment. More cautious women than I might wait until they received something more definite – like another phone call, maybe – but as far as I'm concerned, this is my excuse to celebrate.

So I go into town and get my hair done. Expensively. At a place called Do. As you do.

When I get there, they all have DO written on their black rubber aprons. They also offer me flat white, decaf, peppermint, camomile or water, which means they must be good. Perhaps one day hairdressers will offer you alcohol as well. God knows you need it. I get introduced to everyone – the woman who's making the tea, the woman who'll shampoo my head, the man who'll do the colour, and the man who'll do the cut.

His name is Shy. I'm not kidding. His name is Shy and he works at Do.

Shy has an incredible curtain of hair hanging over the left side of his face, which he's streaked white-blond. The rest of his hair is shaved up the right side, and it's jet black. He's got so many earrings in his ear it looks like a curtain rail.

'Are you into Goth Revival?' he says.

'Mmmm.'

I mean, really. What does he think I am? I'm thirty

for God's sake. But anyway. Long years of experience in hairdressers' has taught me to say mmmmm to anything they ask you, because if you don't, they'll scalp you.

'Can you put on Blood Cult Suckers?' he asks his girlfriend, who's there for moral support. She troops off in enormous red leather boots – clack, clack, clack – and soon something which sounds strangely like Roger with his bottom shut in a car door is blaring out of the speakers. When the girlfriend comes back, there are bits of salon hair stuck to the side of each red boot. Maybe she and Shy will pick it off later and do something Goth Revival and ritualistic with it.

'I love your hair,' Shy says. 'Ooooh.'

'Thanks.'

'I thought I'd put some layers through.'

I nod. Do hairdressers ever do anything except put layers through?

The Bloodsucking Freaks, or whatever it is, gets turned up again. I have a feeling that Shy's snipping in time to the music, too.

'Between jobs?' he says nosily.

I nod. Well, it *is* the middle of the day.

'Try not to move your head,' he says. 'What do you do?'

'I write about Breakfast Grits Frisbees.'

'Ooooh. You're kidding me. We love them!'

'Do you?'

Maybe I have been contributing to the betterment of humankind after all.

'Is that all you do?' he says.

'I write about anything, actually. I'm in advertising.'

'Maybe you should speak to Neville, then.'

'Maybe I should.'

Who the hell is Neville? And how can Shy possibly

see what he's doing when he's got a huge hank of hair covering his left eye?

He calls Neville over and a kind of giant with curly hair and a three-day growth appears, wearing a rubber apron, except his is white. In the Star Trek scheme of things, I suppose this means Neville is the captain of the ship. Actually they all look like the elves in Santa's workshop. Or a lot of butchers.

'What's your name?' Shy asks me. I thought we'd gone through all that when someone was hanging up my handbag.

'Victoria.'

'Neville, Victoria is a writer. In advertising. She did Breakfast Grits Frisbees.'

'Heeeeey!' Neville says, looking wildly excited.

What is it about those frisbees?

'They're the ones that look like chuck,' he continues, answering my question.

'That's what I said in the meeting,' I hear myself telling him. 'They look like that plastic vomit you get from joke shops.'

'We love them,' Shy repeats, snipping around my ear.

'We want someone to do our stuff,' says Neville. 'We're doing a new brochure. How much do you charge?'

'I work for cat food these days.'

Neville laughs at this, and spits on me a little bit.

'We had something really crap last time,' he says, standing behind me and talking to my reflection in the mirror. 'This brochure that said WE CAN DO YOUR DO AT DO. It sounded . . .'

'It sounded like someone was singing an Abba song,' Shy interrupts. 'Do dee do dee do. It was stupid.'

'With a name like Do,' I say, trying to sound serious

314

and professional, 'you don't really need a play on words.'

'Well, no, that's what I thought,' Neville says. Then, true to his trade, his short attention span calls him away. I suppose someone's just drowned in the sink.

'Woo-ee,' says Shy. 'Got yourself some work, girl-friend.'

Then the colour man drags me off and gets rid of the last bits of red from the post-Dan cut, and paints in a few strands of blonde at the sides.

Someone's surrendered *Cosmo,* so I grab it and read my stars.

'Uranus is broadening your horizons, and anything is possible,' the colour man reads over my shoulder.

'Is that you, too?' I ask him.

'Yeah. I'm a Gemini. Are you a Gemini?'

'Yes.'

There doesn't seem to be much left to say after that – after all, we appear to have absolutely nothing in common except for the fact that we both like reading our horoscopes. But then the colour man says something that makes my jaw clang.

'I suppose I am broadening my horizons,' he muses. 'I'm going freelance. Actually, this is my first day. First day of freedom!' he snickers.

I wondered why he wasn't wearing a rubber apron like the rest of them.

'That's a coincidence,' I hear myself saying, slowly. 'I've gone freelance too.'

'Oh, well, there you go then. I'll just leave you with the heat lamp on for about twenty minutes, and then Shy will finish off. Tea or coffee?'

I look at myself in the mirror. Freelance. Broadening my horizons. Freelance. I wonder if they still have that Businesswoman of the Year competition?

It's really a total joke. So far I've scored slight, faint, possible interest from a government department – and a brochure for a hairdresser's called Do. But I like the label I've just stuck on myself. It makes me feel as if this whole Bobbi episode hasn't been a disaster after all. It makes me feel as if I'm doing something right for a change. And – this is the weirdest thing – I don't mind so much about being by myself any more.

When Shy does his finishing off, blasting me right, then left, with the dryer, then making me hang my head upside down over the chair, I think about it a bit more. This is the one thing that everyone in advertising said I should never, ever do. Everyone knows it's insecure. Everyone knows the cheques are always three months late. But it's something about that word freelance. The fact that it's got free stuck at the front of it, probably. Freelance. It's me. I'm it. It's my horizon, broadening.

'There you go.'

Shy's finished. His girlfriend obligingly holds up a mirror on one side of me, and he holds up a mirror on the other side. I look soft and fluffy, like a little brown dog who's just had a bath. I smell of herbs. I'm not red and spiky any more, and to be quite honest with you, it's a relief.

When I get up to leave and find my handbag, Neville rushes back over.

'Have you got a card?' he says.

Oops. Business cards. Now there's a thought. How very un-freelance of me not to have any.

'Sorry, I gave my last one away,' I lie.

'Here's ours.'

It's black, with black shiny writing on top that you can hardly read.

'Give us a call!' he says brightly, leaving me to begin

my new, exciting, broad-horizoned, fluffy brown-haired life.

Then somehow, on the way to the bus, I find myself thinking that I might need some new clothes to go with my new, exciting, fluffy and freelance life too.

All the clothes I'm standing up in were bought with either Dan standing behind me peering over my shoulder, or for Liam-seduction purposes. You can tell, too.

My top half is very Dan – pale blue linen shirt, stupidly expensive leather belt – and the bottom is pure Liam-grab. Short blue-pleated skirt, a la school-girl fetish fantasy, and shoes with heels designed to lift, elevate and kill. Basically I look like a prostitute trying to get a job interview with a law firm. Not very freelance at all.

The shop assistant bawls out 'HOW ARE YOOO?' from the other side of the shop, so I yell back 'OKAAAY!' and shoot over to the furthest corner I can find. As usual there are five pairs of black pants in size 8 and nothing else except a horrible selection of shiny mustard-coloured satin shirts.

Moving right along to the purple row (I know they want you to call it claret, but it's still purple to me) I find a skirt that would look great on Shy's girlfriend, a jacket that Hilary could probably wear to librarian conferences, and – at last – a top that I'd kill for, except it is designed for a woman with the chest of Marilyn Monroe circa 1958.

Then it occurs to me. I'm doing this all wrong. Every single time in my life I try to make my obligatory Fresh Start, what have I always done first? Exactly. Spent $150 at the hairdresser's, and double that on new clothes.

The only difference today is that I also happen to be

unemployed while I'm doing it, which adds a certain frisson of excitement at my own insanity, but not much else.

With the money I'm about to spend, I could improve myself from the inside. I could sign up for one of those weekend seminars with someone from LA with a moustache, and a name like Doctor John Bobenschloss Jnr. Hell, I could blow it on a holiday. Yes, a holiday by myself, but so what? A holiday is still a holiday.

I scoot out of the shop before the assistant can wave something from the green (sorry, sage) rack at me. I feel like telling her that I've discovered the meaning of life, so that she can find daily fulfilment from something other than a brown jacket with a toning beige scarf.

I'm being a wanker. All I've discovered is that I've got the willpower not to blow my credit card on new clothes when I don't need them. But then, that's it. I don't *need* the bits of fabric to tell me something about myself. Unlike Australia, I don't need something new in green and yellow to fool me into thinking that I know who I am.

Back at the flat, I think of a few other things I don't need too. I start counting them off on the fingers of one hand, then I move to the other hand, and then I run out of fingers so I end up writing it down. This is the list.

Greg Daly
Phillip Zebruscki
Jamie Streeton
Leon Mercer
Anthony Anderson
The Loathsome Lawyer from Leichhardt
Macrame Man

And when I hear Bill going up the stairs later on, I

318

work out that I don't need Pierre Dubois either. I left it until last for some reason, and it's been bothering me that I couldn't just write his name down along with the rest of them. Until now. So here it is.

Pierre the bastard Dubois.

There. Then I add some more things to the list:

I don't need to make friends with Tattoo Lawyer because it will make the world a happier place.
I don't need a proper job.

At bedtime, I'm still going. I don't need *Men Are From Mars, Women Are From Venus,* I don't need telephone psychics, I don't need to change my hair any more because I think it will change my life . . . It's amazing. By my calculations, I don't even need thirty per cent of my life at all these days.

Thirty-one

Didi rings a few days later. She's in a flap.

'Can you come and help us with the mushrooms?'

I'm not sure what she means. What mushrooms? And why does she want me to help with them? Is it because Hilary told them I've become a slacker, and they think they can just treat me like a kitchen hand?

Waiting for Didi to explain anything is usually a waste of time, so I have to ask.

'Why do you want me to help with your mushrooms?'

'Because Jodie's got to fix the projector and I have to go up to the shops to get more parmesan.'

'Right.'

'You are coming, aren't you?'

'What?'

'Our film premiere.'

Oh right. *Our film premiere.*

'Your mum's coming,' Didi says.

'Oh, good.'

'We sent you an invite.'

'Didn't get it.'

'Oh. Well, we sent it. It had confetti inside the

321

envelope. I painted old copies of the phone book pink and cut them up.'

'Well, thanks anyway.'

Maybe Bill the Boffin's been stealing my mail. It's the kind of thing I wouldn't put past him. Not that I've seen him of course. In fact, if it wasn't for the fact that I could hear Elvis singing BLOOD and CHOC-o-late down the stairs last night, I wouldn't know if Bill existed or not. Not that I care. Ha. I wonder if he's worked out that I'm off the Net yet?

Sometimes even I have to admire my false bravado. But I've wasted enough time crying over the boffin upstairs, thanks.

Jodie's frantically fixing the projector when I arrive.

'Why don't you ring up the man?' I say. I'm not sure which man, or who. It's just an automatic reflex in our family, and always has been. If something gets tricky, you just Ring Up The Man.

'No, I'll do it,' she says, rather snappily for her.

'We'll just work in here,' Didi calls from the kitchen. She's managed to scam some parmesan from their long-suffering neighbour so we start chopping.

Jodie nods. Her John Travolta T-shirt has great big wet patches under the arms, and she looks a bit like a mad professor today, with her head buried in an instruction manual.

While we stuff mushrooms one by one, Didi tells me about Bill. For no reason, apparently.

'I don't want to take it out of context,' she begins.

'No, no.'

'You have to see the whole thing of people speaking, and the music and the whole vibe of the film. You know?'

'Mmmm.'

A lot of Didi's conversations begin like this. It's like

coming in halfway through some bizarre Danish soap opera on SBS.

'You can put more garlic on that if you like. Just that – I don't know. What Bill has to say isn't the whole film, you know?'

'But he is the only heterosexual male in it,' I say, prodding her. What on earth is the woman on about?

'Ye-es. I guess.'

Long pause.

'Well, what did he say then?'

'I dunno,' Didi huffs and puffs.

'I'm not pissed off with you any more,' I lie.

'What for?'

'Asking him to do it.'

Jodie is making projector-fixing noises in the next room, but I have the distinct impression she's eavesdropping.

I go into the lounge and turn up the volume on Enya and come back.

'I think he might have been talking about you in the film,' Didi mutters.

'About me?'

'He said love is the fear that you can't reveal yourself.'

'Really?'

'He was good,' she chirps, eating a stray piece of mushroom. 'He just came out with this stuff. I thought it must have been about you, though. About not revealing yourself. With the Net and all that.'

'Bastard,' I say, absent-mindedly.

'Bastard,' she repeats, out of habit.

It's the world's most boring word, and I swore I'd never use it again, but here I am – just look at me. I can't help myself.

So. *Love is the fear that you can't reveal yourself,* I

323

think, chopping a mushroom stalk off with undue savagery. But then again, he might just as well have been talking about his ex. The long-suffering rubber beak.

I keep chopping.

A couple of hours later, once everything's done in the kitchen, Jodie and Didi disappear for a joint in their room, leaving me to scan their invitation list, stuck on the door of the fridge. It looks like all of Women's Circle are coming, followed by Hilary and Natalie, me and my mother. Then I think of something terrible.

'Jodie!' I yell into their bedroom, through the red sari hanging over the doorway.

'Yeah?'

'You didn't invite Bill, did you?'

'Vic! What do you think I am?'

I stick my head round the sari just to make sure she isn't offended. Their bedroom looks and smells like the back of Janis Joplin's tour bus, circa 1967. Very frightening. But the dope seems to have fixed her bad mood, and judging by the serene look on Jodie's fish face, all is well again.

She even lets me borrow her clothes. Or rather, their clothes, because Jodie and Didi are both the same size and they merged wardrobes long ago. But when I look through the rack (which seems to have a disgusting mouldy orange stuck with cloves dangling from every hanger) all I can see is cheesecloth pants which look like big nappies, and Jodie's T-shirts with sweat rings all over them. Even though I stink of mushrooms, I decide to stay in my jeans and stripey top after all. Old me clothes, for the new me.

There's a Goddess calendar hanging on their noticeboard, and every second Tuesday is circled in red. I think for a moment Jodie's periods must be going ballistic, then I realize it's Women's Circle day.

The phone rings. Under a copy of a book called *The Angels Are Speaking To Me*. I think for a moment they might be, but it's only Hilary.

We talk about what we're going to wear – she's in a dress, thank God, so we won't be doing our usual identical twins number – and then I put Jodie on – Hilary wants to ask her about bringing drinks – and go off to have a shower.

Jodie and Didi have one of those showers with the sort of water pressure that could knock Kate Moss sideways off a catwalk. It makes you want to stand there for ever, perhaps taking time to read the feminist version of the Desiderata which is stuck on the opposite wall.

When I get out, it's nearly time apparently.

'It's nearly time,' Didi whispers, while Jodie pretends to be cool, calm and collected, arranging batik sarongs over the back of couches and tweaking the parsley on top of all the vegetarian dips.

Hilary's first to arrive. As usual. What's not so predictable, though, is the guy hanging off her arm. That is – *guy* – shock number one, and – *hanging off her arm* – shock number two. He's pretty sexy. He looks like a young Andre Previn.

'This is Paul,' she says, looking smug. He smiles and nods.

What?

Jodie's fish face goes into overdrive – so much so, she looks as if she's going to sprout gills or start spouting water all over the rug. But she quickly recovers.

'Paul, hi. Would you like a drink?'

Didi gets him one, and we all sit down together in

the garden, slapping mosquitos away as the light begins to fade.

'Paul's just been away,' Hilary says. 'White water rafting.'

'Nice,' says Didi diplomatically. And after that we all just sit there in silence. All I can think of is Natalie. What happened there? What's going to happen when she turns up? Or is this something they've already worked through in Women's Circle? Transitional man acceptance therapy. Honestly, nobody tells me anything any more.

I want to talk sideways out of the corner of my mouth, like Jimmy Cagney, and ask the cunning old cow a) Where she got him and b) What happened to the old dwelling on the Isle of Lesbos. But Paul just won't go away. In fact, he seems to be positively clinging to Hilary's side.

I wonder if he knows what he's in for? When Didi drags Paul off to help her with the drinks, I can't help myself any longer, and lean over for a quick interrogation.

'Does he know?' I hiss.

'Know what?'

'About Natalie.'

'No. Shut up. Don't say anything.'

'Does she know?'

'No. I don't know. Shut up.'

'So does this mean you've gone back to men permanently?'

'Shhh.'

When Didi comes back, it's with lavender-scented candles, which she informs us are supposed to induce calm. I think we're going to need it. In fact, if Natalie is about to turn up to this film, then we're definitely going to need it.

More people are trickling in now, and Jodie's started to play hostess and film director with a vengeance, wearing the strange cheesecloth pants that look like nappies. Oh well. Then Natalie arrives. Much to my amazement, she spots Hilary and Paul, waves cheerfully as if she is thrilled to see them, then disappears in a huddle of Women's Circlers.

I look at Hilary, who is refusing to look at me. Paul, I notice, is looking through Jodie and Didi's CD collection. Probably wondering why there's so much Joan Armatrading in it.

Then my mother arrives. And also waves, then disappears into the Women's Circlers' huddle. Really. Have I become boring or something, since my new slacker lifestyle? Which reminds me. Now might be the time to tell her I've lost my job. Before Didi accidentally tells her first.

Before I can do anything, though, Jodie starts waving her arms around and shouting at people.

Before she became a film director, she never used to care about punctuality. Now, for some reason, she's become manic about it.

'Well, it's been half an hour, everybody' she says, standing in front of the projector. 'I think we might make a start. Yes?'

'Yes! Wooo hooo!' shouts an over-enthusiastic hippy.

And all I can think is: no, no, no. What the hell is going on? I mean, stop the film. Come on somebody, stop it! There's going to be so much stuff about me in this documentary it's going to be like the episode of *This Is Your Life* from hell.

Then Jodie claps her hands.

'Well, here we go. Working title, *Chicks, Lies and Videotape*!'

'What happened to *Women In Love*?' yells the same hippy – obviously under the influence of my mushrooms. And everyone laughs, yok yok yok, and claps, and Didi turns the lights off and the titles flicker up on the sheet on the wall.

The first shot is Didi without any clothes on.

'Quel surprise' mutters Hilary.

And I suppose most people could guess the general story after that. Lots of shaky camera work, lots of rambling interviews with Women's Circlers and poor old people they've found sitting on park benches, and every so often some curly handwriting Didi's done with a calligraphy pen appears over a graphic, announcing a new theme. One of them is TIL DEATH DO US PART, and that's where I come in.

There's a massive blackhead on my nose, and I never realized my eyebrows were so badly plucked.

'Weddings are like footy finals,' I watch myself say, with a microphone poking in my face . . . I remember now. I was thinking about Dan when I said that.

'How?' you can hear Jodie saying, in a slightly stupid voice.

'Well, someone always loses. You know. And we all know they're going to lose. But that doesn't stop people turning up for a good look.'

And that's it. Honestly. That's all they used. And I look crapulous.

But no, hang on. After a few shots of close-up flowers – red roses, purple irises, very poetic, more of Didi's curly handwriting – it's back to me again.

'Do you think you're swimming against the tide?' Jodie asks dramatically.

Oh no. I remember now.

'What do you mean?' I say, sounding and looking like a total fool.

'One in three marriages fail. Aren't you a walking anachronism, a true believer in love when society says love no longer believes in you?'

Whose documentary is this anyway? But you can see me blinking a bit at this, and getting ready to say something. A defining statement, if you like. But if only, if only, I hadn't said this:

'If I don't get a wedding before I'm forty I'm going to top myself.'

And then more lovely film of lilies, and pansies and hibiscus.

I notice Paul looking at me with a mixture of horror and fascination. Fair enough, I suppose. He's only just met me. And Hilary's refusing to look at me at all, shaking with laughter like one of those big wobbly plastic castles kids jump up and down on.

Then it's my mother's turn to be on. She, of course, looks fabulous. She was probably lying in the bath with a face mask on for hours before they turned up. She certainly looks as if she got Mrs Thing, the hairdresser, round for a home visit before they started filming.

'How have things changed for women today?' asks Jodie's disembodied voice again.

'As an accountant,' my mother begins (Oh no . . . please . . . not that) 'I have to say that women have more financial independence. We just don't need to be in an institution with a man any more.' (She makes it sound like a loony bin, for God's sake.) 'No, I think it's better than it was. Even if we do have this serial monogamy. We've got the freedom. Haven't we?'

'Are you talking about yourself?' asks Jodie, who knows damn well she isn't.

'I was thinking of my daughter, actually,' Mum says brightly. 'You know, Victoria might not have her man any more, but she does have her freedom. And men are like buses, I always say. If you stand around long enough, one will come past sooner or later.'

'Wasn't that true the first time, too?' Jodie asks – rather nastily for her.

Mum sighs, off the microphone.

'I married a man who was a sensitive root rat. It was a mistake.'

'And do you think your daughter is happy being single?' Jodie continues, in the same disembodied voice.

'No. But what really worries me is the way she's become so addicted to the Internet,' she says gaily.

Oh. My God. Isn't it amazing how you can still blush all the way up your arms, your neck and your head, even in total darkness?

And there's more of course. You can probably imagine it without trying too hard. Didi in the nude again, talking about how bras make her feel trapped in her own body, and Jodie questioning herself very seriously about her true motives for making the film. ('Why, I ask myself. Why did I, as a film-maker, want to tell this story?')

I can think of a few reasons.

Then it's Natalie's turn to come on.

'Are you in a relationship at the moment?' Jodie's voice asks, creepily.

'Yes,' Natalie says, and you can tell it's one word that's just been chopped from about 147.

'Is it happy?' Jodie asks.

'No.' They've cut her again there.

'Why not?'

'Well, I feel a bit as if the relationship thing is more like a student with a teacher, and at the moment I just feel like the teacher.'

'Thankyou.'

And then they cut to yet more footage of flowers. It's not unlike watching *Gardening Australia* with nude segments.

Then there's the sound of someone getting to their feet. Thank God, I thought I was the only one dying to go to the loo. It's Hilary. And she's stomping out. *Whoops.* A few seconds later, she's followed by Paul, falling over everybody's legs. And then, after that, Natalie, and the door slams. It's a mass exodus.

And then, just when I'd forgotten all about him, Bill comes on at last. He's wearing a very, very familiar red T-shirt.

'What is love?' Jodie asks him. She's got him standing in the local park, because I recognize the duck pond. 'And is it the same for men as it is for women?'

And it's so weird, thinking that this was all happening before the night of the fire, before the whole thing collapsed on me.

'I like the French word better,' Bill says. And I can hardly breathe now, listening to him. 'You know? It sounds like what it's supposed to be. L'amour. I think that sums it up. Both sides of love. Being in love, and loving someone. And yes, it is the same for men as it is for women, since you ask.'

I can't help smiling to myself in the dark. Then I catch myself thinking he's nice all over again, the way it was at the beginning, and I have to stop in disgust.

'I guess it's not being able to reveal your true feelings,' Bill carries on. And he now looks as if he's forgotten Jodie altogether, and he's talking to himself. 'Love is putting yourself up for rejection. I think that's it. Cut.'

More, more. I need to see more. But it's back to my mother after that, rambling on about women's financial

331

independence again, and then there's a bit more of a Women's Circle meeting, and Natalie talking about her ex-husband liking Roger more than he liked her (My cat! Mentioned in a major motion picture!), and then it's all over. Jodie's given herself credits as writer, presenter, producer and director. Didi's just below her as writer, sound recordist, creative producer and caterer.

I go out into the garden, followed by my mother.

'I didn't really realize what I was saying to her,' she mutters.

'Oh, well, these film-makers, they just make you say things, don't they,' I reply.

'I didn't mean that about the Internet. I think the Internet is a good thing for you.'

'Well, I got rid of it anyway.'

'Oh.'

'And I got sacked as well.'

And with that, I march off to find Hilary. Serve her right, disloyal old parent.

Hilary is sitting in a bush with Paul's head in her lap. They are both furiously smoking her cigarettes.

'Where's Natalie?'

'She left.'

'Oh, well.'

'It was mutual.'

There's a bit of a gap after this. I wonder what Paul thinks of it all? I hope to God this isn't their first date.

'Bill said something interesting,' I hear myself saying. 'You should go back and see it.'

But I can tell Hilary's got other things on her mind – or in her lap, anyway – so I leave it. When I go back inside, Jodie and Didi are smooching in the kitchen.

They don't seem interested in knowing what I think, but I tell them anyway.

'It was good,' I lie.

Jodie rubs my shoulder.

'Thanks.'

'We will take you out for that steak,' Didi adds.

'By the way, great crowd tonight,' I say nastily. I can't help myself.

'Yeah?' Jodie asks.

'No really. Hilary, Paul, Natalie – the walking bisexual love triangle. My mother. And thanks so much for asking Bill to be in your film behind my back.'

'We thought he would have told you!' protests Didi.

'Ha!'

Jodie rubs my shoulder again.

'Don't be stressed about it.'

'No, really, I'm not stressed.'

And I light one of Hilary's fags which I've just managed to pinch – OK, it's in the house, but I'm taking it out of the house aren't I – and go home.

Thirty-two

In the morning, I look at the Share Accommodation ads
again. It's a weekday, so maybe there'll be less competition. The only real option is CHIPPENDALE 2 br,
sunroom, share prof. female, so I ring up. There's a
message on the machine saying the woman will be
home at lunchtime. Is this another chain-smoking
divorcee with a bald Siamese cat? It's hard to tell.
But this time, I know one thing. I'm not going by
myself.

I ring the library.

'Can I have Hilary please?'

She's panting when she picks the phone up.

'I had to run all the way from Biographies. Yeah?'

'Are you free for lunch?'

'Maybe.'

'Come and look at a house with me.'

'I didn't even know you were moving out.'

'Well, I didn't know you had a boyfriend.'

'Why are you moving out?'

'Because of Bill. I just can't live there any more. And
because I can't afford it. Why are you going out with
Paul?'

'Maybe we should have lunch,' she sighs.

There's a cafe a few streets away from the Chippendale house, so we meet there. It's one of those places where the manager seems to think that foccacia, scones and caramel milkshakes might be a good combination.

'So anyway,' I start.

It's like letting a horse out of the box on Melbourne Cup Day.

'I met Paul after Women's Circle one night. I'd seen him round for ages, thought he was gorgeous—'

'Hang on. So you'd been going off Natalie anyway. Or just going off women?'

'All of it. The whole thing,' she says, flapping me away 'Anyway, let me finish. Paul was doing this white water rafting evening class, just down the corridor from Women's Circle on Tuesday nights, and I just started talking to him one night. And then I thought I'd ask him to see Jodie and Didi's film.'

'Without telling Natalie.'

'She wouldn't have minded.'

'Like, really.'

'No, it wasn't that sort of relationship.'

'Did she mind when Paul stuck his head in your lap?'

'That was afterwards. Anyway, she rang me this afternoon. It's all sorted out. I've forgiven her for saying that thing about me in the film, the teacher-student thing, and she's fine about Paul. So. Enough about me.'

'So you don't want to go into detail.'

She sighs.

'It's hard to explain.'

'To me.'

'Yes, to you.'

'Can I just ask one really basic question?'

'Maybe.'

'Who was the dumper, and who was the dumpee?'

Big pause.

'She dumped me. All right? After the film. She rang me up. Paul had walked me home. I was by myself at home, and she just rang up and said she didn't think it was going anywhere. So maybe we'd better call it quits. You know.'

'Weird.'

'Why?'

'I always thought you'd be the one to leave first.'

'And why would that be?'

And I can't really tell her, can I, that it's because Natalie's not as good-looking as she is. I mean, call me politically incorrect and superficial, and hang me upside down on a pole from the Gay and Lesbian Mardi Gras, but that's really what it comes down to. The old rule we always knew from school. Someone is always Top and someone is always Bottom in any relationship, and you can bet a million dollars it's always Bottom who's first to go.

I swirl the coffee around in my cup.

'Remember the old Top and Bottom thing?'

'Vic, I can't believe you still use stupid stuff from high school as a kind of rule for living.'

I shrug.

'Well, I do. Maybe that's why my life is such a joke.'

She nods.

'Anyway, you never really told me about the lesbian thing,' I say at last.

'Bisexual thing,' she corrects me.

'Whatever.'

She sighs. 'OK. I will try to do this in a simple way that explains it.'

'Because I'm an insensitive moron and I'm politically incorrect.'

'Because it's bloody complicated, if you'll listen to me.'

She waves at the waiter and points meaningfully at her empty cup, making a 'More, please' face like something from *Oliver Twist*.

'You don't have to explain it if you don't want to,' I relent.

'It's just that you're sitting there with your tongue hanging out like some voyeur.'

'Sorry.'

'There's nothing juicier about me and Natalie than you and Liam. You know?'

'I know.'

'It's just that for the first time in about a year, I had someone chasing *me*, I had someone being nice to *me*, you know?'

'Yup.'

'And I never thought she was the love of my life, and she never thought that about me. But I'll tell you something, being with a woman has—' she nods, backing herself up, 'all the advantages you'd expect.'

'Hmmm.'

'Not that crap about sex, either, though that's all you ever hear.'

'I wasn't thinking that.'

'Anyway, it was good if you must know.'

'Well, I wasn't asking.'

'I'm telling now—' a new pot of tea arrives, and she nods at the waiter. 'Something about the fact that you've both got L plates on in bed, and you *know* you both have and it's *OK* – well. That can feel like a holiday.'

'Better than pretending you know what you're doing.'

'Exactly. With some man who lives his whole life like *Nine and a Half Weeks*.'

'So.'

'So. That's it. I don't know if it was the moon that night, or what we had to drink, or the fact that she'd just been staring at me the whole time . . .'

'What I don't understand is . . .'

'What?'

'Why is it I feel I'm going to be an outcast of political correctness any time I say anything on this subject?'

'Stop being paranoid.'

'What I don't understand is, why her? I understand why *it* – I'm sure *it* is a good thing, and yeah, everyone's doing it.'

'OK, look at this minute.'

'How?'

'Imagine me saying to you, why Liam? Why Dan? I mean . . .' she puts on a patronizing voice, 'I can understand it – heterosexuality – absolutely everyone's doing it darling, but why Dan? You said it yourself, he's the loathsome lawyer from Leichhardt.'

'I fell in love with him.'

'Yeah, and it was the moon that night, or what you had to drink.'

'Well, OK. I get it. I mean, *hello,* I get it.'

'*OK.*'

Big pause. Long pause. Longer than the pause at the altar during Helena Chettle's wedding vows.

'Well, anyway, I looked for houses last weekend,' I begin.

'Why don't you get your own place?'

'Can't afford it.'

'Oh.'

I think she's forgotten, as employed, non-slacker people do, that in one month from now Roger and I will be living on government handouts, thus making Darling Point mansions a little out of our reach.

'I looked at loads of places, they were pretty bad.'

'Well, you should've told me.'

'Why?'

'The funny woman downstairs is moving out. In the bedsit. The cheap smelly one.'

'Oh, the cheap smelly one.'

'Well, you could clean it up.'

'How much?'

She tells me and it's not much more than the pate man wanted.

'Can I have a look?' I ask.

'I dunno. I suppose if I speed all the way over there and speed all the way back. I've got to go back to work, you know. You seem to forget.'

'Do you mind?'

'What about the place in Chippendale?'

'Don't worry about it. She'll have about a million people turning up anyway.'

We pay our bill and leave. For some reason, any acceleration at all in Hilary's car makes it five times as noisy. It's like being in an air raid. And as usual, her passenger seat belt won't clunk into its metal holder.

'SO ARE YOU PISSED OFF WITH YOUR MOTHER?' she yells above the racket.

'NO, BUT I'M PISSED OFF WITH JODIE,' I yell back.

'YEAH, THAT FILM!' she booms back. 'BUT WHAT ARE YOU GOING TO DO ABOUT BILL?'

'NOTHING. I'VE JUST FORGOTTEN HE EXISTS.'

And that's about all we can be bothered with at that volume, until the car hurtles around the roundabout and into Hilary's street.

The smelly bedsit is hidden around a corner on the ground floor of Hilary's block. There's a cleaning cupboard next to it, so I suppose it must have been the caretaker's place once.

Hilary knocks on the door. It's opened by the funny woman, who is wearing a turquoise quilted-nylon dressing gown and a pair of yellow slippers that must have been white once. She's watching Oprah. Poor thing.

'I heard you're moving out.'

Hilary puts on her sweetest, talking-to-the-parents-in-the-library voice.

'Yes, me nephew's putting me in with them.'

'Oh, that's good. My friend, Victoria, was wondering if she could have a look.'

'Yeah, come in.'

We shuffle in, and the three of us take up the entire room. There are two lovebirds in a cage eating a bit of pantyhose for some reason – which is probably why it smells – and the woman's also got not one, but three, toilet brushes on the floor next to the loo.

It's amazing what passes for desirable real estate in Sydney, though, and I blurt out 'I'll take it' before I realize the woman in the turquoise quilted-nylon dressing gown is not really the person I should be speaking to.

'Do you have a number for your agent?' Hilary probes gently. 'Is it the same as my agent?'

The funny woman says that it is, so we mumble apologies and creep back up the stairs to Hilary's place, leaving her to the TV.

'That's me in twenty years,' I whisper as Hilary opens the door of her flat.

'Don't.'

I sit down on the couch, moving Virginia Woolf out

of the way, while Hilary puts the coffee on the stove.

I haven't been in here for ages. There are a few new Virago paperbacks on the floor, where she usually chucks magazines, but otherwise there's not much evidence of her new Women's Circle lifestyle.

'So do you think you'll take it?' she asks.

'I'll sleep on it.'

'The toilet brushes . . .'

'I know. But I could paint it.'

'That's what I said when I got this place.'

She's right. I know that if I move into the funny woman's bedsit, it will be exactly as it is now, plus a few posters, a dancing clam shower curtain and Roger. And maybe a bit of Mr Sheen.

'She's only moving out on the weekend so it won't be advertised yet,' Hilary advises me.

'And you wouldn't mind?'

'Tch. Why would I mind? Better having you down there than her turning the TV up to fifty decibels every night.'

'Poor woman.'

'Poor woman.'

Now that Hilary's got Paul, I find myself thinking, she's well out of it. But for me and every other 30-year-old single female, that's the future out there. Two lovebirds and three toilet brushes, and – if you're lucky – a nephew taking pity on you.

'Stop thinking about her,' warns Hilary. 'Now, I meant to tell you more about Bill.'

'What about him?'

'I was on the phone to Jodie this morning, and she said they've got all this extra film of him, and it's basically a one-man tribute to Victoria Shepworth.'

This takes some time to sink in.

'Really?'

'Yes. I dragged it out of her. She didn't want to tell you because she thought you'd be upset.'

'Well, maybe I am upset.'

'No you're not, you're interested. I can tell.'

'I am *not* interested!'

Good grief. Just because a miracle has occurred and Hilary's got some white water rafting man who looks like a young Andre Previn sticking his head in her lap, she wants to pair off everyone else as well. Well, I'm not having it.

'Bill is a pervert.'

'Yes, but he says some very nice things about you. Anyway, I've got to get back to work. Want a lift?'

I haven't even begun to drink my coffee, but slackers can't hold up the public library system. So we hurtle back to my flat, crashing around every roundabout, and over every speed hump Hilary can find.

When we get there, there's a huge removal truck blocking the entrance.

'Typical,' tuts Hilary.

'Hang on a minute.'

Two removalists are carrying what appears to be Bill's desk, followed by Bill's computer.

'Oh, he's moving out,' I hear myself saying slowly.

'Oh well, there's another flat for you then. Who's moving out?'

'Bill's moving out.'

'Oh.'

She chews her lip. We sit there for a bit.

'Sorry, Vic, I know it's not the time, but I really, really have to go. They kill me if I'm late back.'

'No, it's OK.'

And she waves and zooms off, leaving me standing in front of the truck as a series of boxes with his squash rackets sticking out of them, and his clothes in green garbage bags, go up the ramp and into the back.

I go up there. I mean, this is stupid. I've got to say something to him now, haven't I?

But his flat is almost empty, except for a pile of dust and a broom in the corner, and when I ask the men, they say it's all going into storage. Nobody's here.

'Instructions to store,' says one of the men, grunting, as he lifts up what used to be Bill's one and only arm-chair.

'Did he say where he was going?'

'You might want to ring up our reception on that.'

And I do, but they won't give me the forwarding address. As I expected. He's probably been planning this for weeks. Ever since Pierre Dubois tried to e-mail Technobimbo and found she no longer existed.

Thirty-three

Jodie's at a friend's place for dinner, so Didi sets up the projector for me. She's actually quite sweet, Didi, when she's not part of the two-headed film-making monster known as JodieandDidi.

'Can I get you some water or anything?'

'No, it's OK.'

'Hilary said you were moving into her place.'

'No, I'm not any more. Bill moved out—' I make a face at her. 'So I don't have to.'

I lie on my stomach on the floor, while she puts up the screen again.

'I feel like a royal,' I tell her.

'Why?'

'Private screening. Isn't this what the Queen Mother has?'

She doesn't get it. I knew she wouldn't get it. Oh well. After what seems like ages, the film is finally ready to go.

'The thing is, I have to hang around to do this,' Didi says. 'Like, I have to work it for you. So it can't be really private.' She bites her lip. 'Sorry.'

'No, I don't mind.'

'Yeah.'

The film goes through its 5, 4, 3, 2, 1 bit, and the suspense is terrible. But then there he is again, in the park on a sunny day, up on the screen in his red shirt, with his hair falling into his eyes the way it always does. You can even see the small dent on his jaw.

I'm not sure what Didi is doing with the camera after that. One minute there's some very shaky footage of the sky, then a tree seems to shoot sideways past the lens. Eventually she gets it right, though, and it settles on Bill – or rather, his head and shoulders. He swallows nervously a couple of times, then Jodie moves in.

'What is love? And is it the same for men as it is for women?' she demands.

Pause. Long pause.

'Er, sorry,' he says eventually, 'I'm not sure. I might have to think about it.'

The screen goes black at this part.

'That's where we turned the camera off,' Didi informs me, standing at the projector.

'And then what happened?'

'Jodie took him behind a bush and they lit up a joint.'

'You're joking.'

'It worked, though.'

'Did it?'

'He was like a lamb after that.'

'But isn't this supposed to be a fly-on-the-wall documentary? I didn't think you were supposed to manipulate your subjects.'

'Well, we had to,' Didi says blankly. 'He couldn't talk otherwise.'

The camera wriggles around a bit more, going from the sky, to a passing duck on the pond, and back to Bill's face again. And yes, I must admit the little session behind the bush seems to have improved things. Now, the main problem seems to be that Jodie can't shut him up.

'What you said about love,' Bill begins. 'I like the French word better. You know? It sounds like what it's supposed to be. L'amour. I think that sums it up. Both sides of love. Being in love, and loving someone. And yes, it is the same for men as it is for women, since you ask. It's l'amour, and that's the only way you can explain it. If you have to explain it.'

'Is l'amour easy?' Jodie poses, dramatically.

'No, or it wouldn't be what it is. The whole point is, you have to be prepared to feel that way about someone even though you know she's never – they're never – going to feel the same way about you. And you hope that they might change, but you don't know. And maybe if you had more sense, you'd walk away from it, but you don't.'

'Why?'

'Because part of you thinks you might be able to help them, and do things for them, and that's what keeps you going,' he says at last.

'Isn't that martyrdom, though?' Jodie cuts in.

'Well, that's part of love in my book. If it comes to that.'

'And do you have anything *else* to say about love?'

'I saw a story going round on the Net,' Bill says, after a minute. 'It's about a sailor in the war, an American sailor who starts getting letters from this woman he's never met. A girl called Poppy. It's like a penfriend thing, and for three years they write to each other. And something happens. He starts to depend on her letters. And almost without realizing it, they fall in love. Then, the war's over. And it's time for them to meet up. So they arrange to meet at Grand Central Station, at 5 p.m., and she says she'll be wearing a red poppy in her buttonhole. Then it hits him. He's never seen a photo of her. He doesn't know how old she is. He doesn't know if she's ugly, pretty, fat, thin. So he's waiting on the corner of Grand Central Station, and the clock chimes five, and there she is. A woman with a red poppy in her coat buttonhole. She's about sixty-five years old.'

'Oh, no!' Jodie says on camera, despite herself.

'And he could turn and walk away, but he doesn't. This is the woman who has been writing to him the whole time he's been at sea, sending him Christmas gifts, keeping him going. And she deserves more. So he walks forward, holds out his hand and introduces himself. And you know what?'

'They get married and live happily ever after,' Jodie says, back in cynical film director mode.

'No, she tells him he's got it wrong. She tells him that Poppy is the woman standing *behind* her. And he turns and looks, and there she is. His age. Beautiful.'

'And?'

'The old lady tells him that Poppy asked her to stand there wearing her flower, and that if he was to turn and walk away, that would be the end of it. But if he came forward to meet her, then the old lady could show him the real Poppy and tell him the truth.'

'Hmmm,' says Jodie unconvinced. 'So you found this story on the Net?'

'You find a lot of things on the Net,' Bill replies, not really listening.

'So beauty is more than skin deep, is that the moral of your story?'

'No, the moral of my story is that love is the fear that you can't reveal yourself. And love can go in wearing a disguise,' he adds, as an afterthought . . . 'And even if it's a really bad disguise, it doesn't matter.' He pauses for a beat. 'I guess it's not being able to reveal your true feelings,' he says at last. And he now looks as if he's forgotten Jodie altogether, and he really is talking to himself. 'Love is putting yourself up for rejection. I think that's it.'

'Cut.'

'Aaaah,' says Didi from the projector. 'We take a break here, because something went wrong with the camera.'

'Maybe it collapsed under the weight of all the emotion,' I reply. Really. Bill crawls into a bush with Jodie and has a joint, and that's the kind of rubbish he comes out with. As if.

Still, something won't let me stop watching. So I lie on the floor on my stomach again, while we wait for the film to re-start.

'Here we go,' Didi says.

This time both Bill and Jodie are in the shot. They've moved to the edge of the duck pond, now, so the background quacks have become foreground quacks.

'What do you think of women today?' Jodie asks.

'You should ask them what they think of us first,' he replies.

Long pause.

'You sound as if you have some more to say about that,' Jodie prods, meaningfully.

'Well, I get the feeling they're looking for something we can't give them. Or I can't give them.'

'Like what?'

'I don't know. But . . .'

Jodie waits. I suppose the truth drugs must have been wearing off at this point.

'I guess I'm just saying that women today don't seem to like men very much,' he sighs. 'They see getting one as almost like buying a car. And not even a car that they really want. I mean, they think they want the car, but in the end, if the paint job's not right, and the name's not right, and the engine's not right – well.'

'They don't want the car,' you can hear Didi shouting from behind her camera. Then Jodie tells her to shh – I don't think the camera operator is supposed to turn into the interviewer, somehow – and the interview ends.

Didi gets up to turn the lights back on, and I crawl up from my stomach to see Jodie stand behind us. I'd been so engrossed, I hadn't even heard her come in.

'I had to see it,' I say.

'Sure.'

'He's pathetic, isn't he?' I ask hopefully.

'I thought it might upset you, that's why I didn't think you should see it,' Jodie says.

'Well, I'm glad I did. At least I know the effect a tiny bit of marijuana has on him now. God!'

'Oh no,' Jodie says, shaking her head. 'It wasn't drugs.'

'Didn't you go out for a smoke, though?' Didi says.

'Well, I wanted him to, because I thought it would relax him. God, he just wouldn't *talk* . . . But he wouldn't touch it. Said he never had and never would. Which I respect,' she continues, frowning in her most sincere fashion. 'Anyway, that's all Bill, if that's what you mean. Sober and straight.'

'Camomile tea?' offers Didi.

In the end, though, I just go home. To a flat without Bill. And with a head full of nothing else, just for the moment.

Thirty-four

The health department finally rings back. They want to know my fee for doing a poster, a sticker and the back of a brochure. On the spur of the moment, I tell them my exact rent for the month, then immediately regret it. Starsky and Hutch–it, a proper freelance advertising copywriter woman of the '90s would have a rate card, wouldn't she? But I don't. I don't even have a business card.

'That sounds within budget,' the woman says.

'Oh, fine.'

'Why don't you come in for a meeting on Tuesday?'

'Fine.'

'Is 3 p.m. OK?'

'Fine.'

And she puts the phone down. All of which means, thanks to an unusual piece of luck on my part, I've officially done my last Breakfast Grits Frisbee campaign. *Very* fine. I can't stop smiling, even if I did just make a dick of myself over the phone.

No proper freelance advertising copywriter, slash, woman of the '90s, would ring up everyone she knows to tell them. But of course I do. Mum sounds relieved. For a moment, I guess, it looked very much as if the sensitive root rat in LA would have to start paying child support.

'And I'm doing a hairdresser brochure as well.'

'Oh, that's good.'

'It's called Do.'

'Oh well, they have to call these things something, don't they,' my mother says.

Lying on the couch at the end of the day, though, there's a nagging feeling that the person I really want to tell isn't there any more. It's not Dan, and it's not Pierre. It's Bill.

For hours in bed last night, when I was supposed to be sleeping, I was replaying the dreaded girls'-night-in-with-Internet scene in my mind. In my imagination, we laughed like deranged hyenas, and were drunker than Oliver Reed. *Women today don't seem to like men very much.* Oh lord, and no wonder he thought that, because I bet he heard every word.

Maybe he was standing outside my door that night, back from squash, ready to knock, ready to drop in and make a neighbourly visit. Maybe he was returning something I'd given him to fix. I can see it now. Bill, shy, homesick, standing on my doorstep – and me, raucous, pissed out of my brain, yelling about Ferals, *Footy Show* men, inner city boys with Triple J promotional condoms, criminals, paedophiles, people from Bondi who wear sunglasses that make them look like blowflies, and men who wear their baseball caps backwards. *Love can go in wearing a disguise.* Yeah, well maybe it had to. Maybe I sounded like the kind of demented female who wouldn't let it approach any other way.

Damn. I pick up the phone and call Hilary.

'Yes?' She's with Paul. He must have his head in her lap again, because her voice sounds weird.

352

'Can you think of a way, any way at all, I can find Bill? Without calling the police?'

'Er. Hang on. I'll ask.'

Mumble, mumble, mumble. She's asking Paul, of course.

'We can't think of anything,' she says at last.

I knew they wouldn't. They're not even trying.

'What about finding him on the Internet?'

'I tried,' I sigh. 'I rang up his service provider and they said he'd pulled out.'

'Couldn't they still trace him for you, though?'

'They did a search on his name for me and they just got Bill Bryson, Bill Clinton and Bill Cosby.'

'Oh well.'

'I just don't think he wants me to find him.'

'No.'

'No.

'Sorry'

'That's all right.'

Then she thinks of something.

'We're off to Byron on the weekend. Want to come?'

'Not if it's just you. I mean, both of you – and me.'

'Oh no, us, and Jodie, and Didi, we're all going up for the Byron Bay–' she stumbles to get the name right – 'Women's Short Film Festival.'

'But I thought you hated the film?'

'Well, I do. But they don't care, they think it just means it's controversial. But a free holiday is still a free holiday. Didi's driving everyone up in the combi.'

'I'll feel like a single.'

'Oh, bring the cat.'

'He's not my sexual life partner, you know.'

'Why don't you look for Bill up there, anyway?'

'Yeah, right. Combing the beach.'

'He's from Dorrigo isn't he? Well, it's on the way.

Kind of on the way. If you ask Jodie nicely. Maybe his parents are still there. Someone would know him.'

'Yes.'

'So are you going to come?'

She's right, as usual. And it takes me about five seconds to decide.

'Only if I don't feel too single.'

When I put the phone down, I find a map of New South Wales. It dates from Anthony Anderson days, and it's still got chocolate marks all over it from the times when he'd drive us out to some godforsaken scuba diving spot, and I'd eat serial Flakes out of sheer boredom.

I don't know why I'm doing this. I have a perfect opportunity here to let sleeping golden retrievers and dalmatians lie. He's out of my life. He's conveniently moved hundreds of miles away, thus giving me the chance to get on with my life without any more dramas. I can now forget the whole humiliating PD and TB fiasco ever happened, and get on with things. Things like writing brochures for DO, and not changing my hair ever again, and being single.

But there's unfinished business here, and it's nagging at me. I suppose I thought one of us would break the silence at some point or other. I just didn't know when. And now he's disappeared, there's too much I have to say. Some of it violently abusive, agreed, and using a series of four letter words. But now I've seen the film, in a funny way I understand him a bit better as well. I don't like him any more for it, but I am starting to get a glimpse of what might have been going on in his poor, overworked, boffin brain with all its cogs grinding and its lights flashing.

Dorrigo is inland. Miles from Byron. But if you're feeling kind, and you're not in too much of a rush to get to your festival, and you don't mind stopping at a country town for lunch . . .

I ring Jodie.

'Wow, Didi just told me about the anorexia campaign. Congratulations!'

'Thanks. Um, do you feel sorry for me at the moment?'

'Why?'

'Are you in a rush to get to the Byron Bay thing?'

'Why?'

'Have you ever considered having lunch in Dorrigo?'

I don't know if it's guilt because of the havoc her documentary has wreaked, or a spirit of sisterhood, or just the accumulative effects of too much dope – but somehow, Jodie agrees. On Saturday at 5 a.m., we are all going to pack ourselves, our sleeping bags and our herbal teabags (well, her herbal teabags anyway) into Didi's old combi van, and drive up to the Byron Bay Women's Short Film Festival. Via Dorrigo.

And no, I'm not taking Roger as my partner.

Thirty-five

I'm taking Roger. My mother has acquired a new boyfriend, who she insists on referring to as her 'friend', and he's an asthmatic who's allergic to cats. Also air freshener and hair spray, but mostly cats. He's also staying the whole weekend with her. Starsky — and indeed, Starsky.

'Couldn't your neighbours feed him?' she says.

'I'm not even supposed to have a cat.'

'What about one of those girls?'

'They're coming too.'

'What about that other girl who had all the children?'

'Helena Chettle's already got a cat. And a dog.'

'You mean she's got a family *and* a cat and a dog?'

How times change. I can remember a year (say, 1972) when that would have seemed quite normal to people like my mother.

'So where did you find this bloke anyway?'

'We made friends at Jodie's party.'

'At the film.'

'Yes.'

'I didn't see him.'

'His ex-wife was in the film.'

'Which one?'

'The one who was on at the very end. The one who said men were like buses because they create air pollution and never turn up on time.'

'And he didn't mind all that stuff you said about men being like buses, and if you hang around long enough, one will turn up?'

'No, he thought it was terrific.'

'Oh, right.'

On reflection, what with Bill comparing women to cars, and my mother and her bonk-in-law comparing men to public transport, Jodie's documentary is beginning to remind me more and more of a bad episode of *On the Buses*.

At 4.30 a.m. on the day of the big journey, I still haven't found a suitable container for Roger. Every time I try to jam him into the cardboard box I dragged home from the supermarket, his paw (claws out) shoots out of the top, followed by his head with his eyes all slitty like Mickey Rooney in *Breakfast At Tiffany's*, and the whole thing collapses. He won't even go near the straw basket he came in, at least, not without sinking his fangs into my wrist.

Half an hour later, the chick mobile turns up. Hilary has been sent to come and get me. She looks tired, and ill, and old at this hour of the morning. But in love, nevertheless.

'You're not taking the cat *free-form* are you?' she says, horrified.

'Well, he won't stay in the box, and I can't get him in the basket.'

'Haven't you read James Herriot?'

'No.'

'Well, I have. Lucky for you I'm a librarian and we've got five copies of *All Creatures Great and Small* in large print. Now, what you do is this.'

She pulls a blanket off my bed, gathers it up into a bundle, and then throws it over Roger in much the same way that the Leyland Brothers used to throw nets over crocodiles. Then she scoops him up, with him boxing furiously inside the blue blanket, and whirls him round and round like an Egyptian mummy until he's in a cocoon, with only his head poking out.

Roger is very, very angry.

'James Herriot is also good if you ever have to deliver a calf,' she says.

When we pile into the van, everyone's in a surprisingly good mood considering I've kept them waiting, and it's a horrible hour of the morning.

Paul is looking even more like a young Andre Previn than usual, with baggy eyes from lack of sleep, and craggy lines running from the corner of his nose to his mouth. I notice he's got one of Hilary's never-ending navy blue jumpers on (a particularly baggy one from some years ago) but I don't say anything.

Meanwhile, Didi has surrounded herself with crystals, a bag of carob drops and a stack of Enya tapes for the long journey ahead. Jodie is in the front passenger seat, wearing her Byron Bay Film Director's outfit. No nappy this time, just a pair of mean sunglasses, Doc Martens and a black sundress. She must be freezing.

'James Herriot,' Paul says, immediately, when he sees me with Roger wriggling in his blanket cocoon. Hilary looks at him with love. So – I don't know. Maybe they are soulmates after all.

We get as far as the bridge, and Roger starts making a noise which sounds like he's holding his nose and screaming while somebody jabs him repeatedly with a sharp instrument.

'Come here, baby,' Jodie says, and takes him.

He immediately wriggles free, and shoots over to the back of the van, skidding all over the place when Didi floors it at the lights, and making even more howling noises.

'Come here,' Paul says. Roger bites him.

Finally, somewhere along the Pacific Highway, he just shuts up and collapses. Then Didi puts Enya on, and the whole ordeal starts again. So Enya gets switched off, and peace returns.

'I don't think there's anywhere in Byron that takes cats,' Hilary says, as an afterthought.

'They take babies, don't they?' I reply.

'You're not thinking of passing him off as your babe in arms?'

'Well he could get away with it.'

'Bloody hairy baby.'

I must say, I haven't really thought about where I'm going to stay so far. Maybe this is just a reflection of the new, freelance woman of the '90s. Or is it just unemployed slacker? I suppose we'll end up doing what we did the last time we went on a road trip, and check into the cheapest caravan site, then fight about who gets the best beds.

Roger and I can have a caravan, Jodie and Didi can have a caravan, and Paul and Hilary can have a caravan. Perfect. How coupley.

Time passes in that blurry, headachey way which means a) You've still got further to go than you thought and b) Yes, you did wake up too early. Jodie starts a feeble attempt at a game where you to have to think of a female politician for every letter of the alphabet, but we get stuck at Benazir Bhutto.

Finally, I give up, steal Roger's blanket and fall asleep. When I wake up we seem to be driving past a cricket match.

360

'This is Bellingen,' Hilary says helpfully. Paul's head is in her lap. Again. And he's asleep too.

We keep going, and then we find the sign. Dorrigo. I lean my head on the window and breathe in the air, rushing past. It smells of nothing, which is the way air is supposed to smell. I think I've forgotten what that's like.

'Did you know Roger nearly jumped out of the window one hundred times when you were asleep?' yells Didi from the front. He starts howling again, and skidding around on the floor.

Finally, we're there. And it's pretty much the way I thought it would be. Trees in different stripes of green backing up along the hills, the threat of scones approaching, and one main street with so few people on it that it looks like one of those miniaturized landscapes that model-makers produce for architects, with tiny plastic people dotted in funny places holding shopping bags.

There's a milk bar with a home-made poster in the front window, held up by an old Chiko Roll sticker, asking for volunteers for the local ladies' soccer team. There's a dead bird in the gutter. And there is — yes — an Information Centre.

While everyone else piles into the milk bar, I go and tackle the woman behind the desk.

I think I'm the only person she's seen this hour.

The shop sells postcards, so I buy one in the hopes that it's a good political move. It isn't. She could not care less.

'I don't think I know a Bill McGinley,' she says, flicking over the front page of her knitting pattern.

It must be the first time I've ever used his proper name with anyone. Even Didi still thinks his name is Bill Boffin. In fact, if I'd never sneaked a look at his mail, I never would have known.

'What about just McGinley?' I say.

'Well, there are McGinleys, but there are five of them, and the furthest ones are way out where. About what age is he?'

'Thirty, thirty-one, thirty-two. Maybe thirty-three.'

She looks at me as if I'm a total moron, but I let it go.

'Sorry I can't be more specific.'

Then I notice it, behind the postcards. A computer. With a throbbing N for Netscape in the corner that I feel I haven't seen for about one hundred years.

'You're on the Net!'

'Yes.'

She sounds and looks insulted, and I can't blame her. I suppose I look and sound like the worst kind of Sydney tourist.

'Have a go if you like,' she relents. And I suppose she thinks I want to find a hotel, or a scenic drive, or something. But all I really want is the credit at the bottom of the page, because something – maybe it's my Dad's psychic ability rubbing off at last – something is telling me it's going to help.

There it is. The official Dorrigo Tourist Website. Page design copyright 1998 Bill McGinley.

'The person I'm looking for is the one who did this web page,' I say, very slowly and wonderingly. Because it feels like the finger of fate now, it really does. Jabbing me in my ribs until I give in.

'The one who did that? I do know who you mean now,' the woman says. 'But he moved away. Or – no, he came back for a bit, I think. I saw him out with his mum a while ago. I don't know if he's still here. They're the McGinleys with the farm nearest to town.'

'Could you give me directions?'

I mean, I hate to sound desperate, but then I am desperate.

In the end, because I'm obviously not taking anything in, she draws a map in biro on the back of the postcard I've just paid for. It's about 5km away. Closer than I thought. In fact, all of this has, suddenly, become much, *much* closer than I thought.

I go back to the van, waving my postcard. They're all inside eating ice cream, except for Didi, who is dutifully popping carob drops into her mouth. Someone, probably Hilary, has bought Roger a chocolate cornetto, which he's eating off a paper plate on the floor of the van. And spreading over the floor of the van.

'I've found Bill!' I say, waving the postcard in the air.

And wouldn't you know it, Roger throws up all over the floor.

Thirty-six

To give her credit, Jodie doesn't complain about this extra diversion. I'm going to make us all so late for our Byron Bay caravan site that we'll probably have to sleep on the beach, but she smiles beatifically and takes the wheel when it's time for her and Didi to officially swap seats.

Didi map-reads. It's all a bit like watching *Thelma and Louise,* except they're too peace-loving to rob a service station.

We set off down an unsealed road.

'Next left,' Didi commands, 'then right, then according to this, you see a sign saying McGinley. Hang on, why is there a duck crap farm there?'

'What duck crap farm?' Jodie fires back.

'Look, they're selling big bags of it. It's called Scrooge McDuck's Quack Quack Crap. That sounds like the sort of thing you write, Vic.'

'Thanks,' I say, looking out of the window.

'Good, let's buy some,' Hilary interrupts from the back.

'No, look Jodie,' Didi says suddenly, 'you must have taken a wrong turn at the service station.'

'That old thing!' Hilary hoots. Paul's fallen asleep in

her lap again. I don't know how her bladder takes the pressure. He might look like Andre but his head is at least twenty-five per cent bigger and heavier than Mr Previn's.

Finally, Jodie and Didi work out that we're going to have to head back to town, and start again, from the last scarecrow at the stagnant creek, or whatever the landmark was.

And then it happens. Just as Hilary is gaily announcing that it's time for I Spy in Dorrigo, we see a car I've seen a million times before, a car currently smashing the local speed limit to smithereens, a car containing . . .

'BILL!' Hilary yells out of the window.

And then Roger leaps into Jodie's lap, gets shoved onto the floor, and wedges himself on top of the accelerator pedal. Five seconds later, we are in a ditch and Bill is spinning horribly off the side of the road.

Paul reacts first.

'Get out!' he yells.

'What happened?' Hilary asks, foggily.

'Everyone get out now,' says Jodie briskly, 'because the van might blow up. All right?'

One by one, we crawl out. First Paul holding Hilary, then me, then Didi frantically massaging Jodie's shoulders as she's trying to open the door of the van, then Roger. He looks fine, for the record, and wanders off.

Bill's car has lurched sideways, with one of its front wheels wedged up on a rock, and what used to be the headlight has smashed into a pile of orange and white plastic. I can smell petrol, even from here. This is not a road where a man who cannot drive should be breaking the speed limit while trying to squeeze past a combi van driven by a power-mad female film director in dark sunglasses coming the other way. Basically, I think, it's a road for ducks. Probably ducks toddling home after a hard day's work at Q.Q.C enterprises.

This is typical of me in shock. I can never take anything seriously. I've always suspected that I might be one of those hysterical gigglers who need slapping in the face, and I can feel something coming on now.

Bill gets slowly, slow-ly, out of the car, and the first thing I notice is that his hair's grown longer. The second thing I notice is that his face has turned completely grey-white and his arm is bleeding.

'Bill!'

I race over.

Suddenly, I think he's my friend, and he's hurt. I don't care about anything.

'Hi,' he manages, blinking at me. Then he half-falls, half- sits down in the grass. 'Dad's going to kill me, he's just serviced that,' he says automatically. He's holding his arm up like a glass that's going to break.

'I'm sorry!' Jodie yells, stumbling over the grass in her purple ballet shoes. 'The cat got under my feet, I know it was my fault.'

Recognizing the well-known director of *Women In Love*, working title *Chicks, Lies and Videotape,* Bill seems to go even whiter. And this silly thing keeps running through my head. *I want to hold his hand.* He looks so lost and frightened. *I want to hold his hand.* But I can't.

'Are you all right, mate?' Paul asks manfully.

Hilary is about to go into bloke-to-bloke introductions, I can see, when it occurs to me that we should do something a bit more useful.

'Are you hurt?' I ask. I mean, I know he is.

'A bit. I knocked my arm.'

'What do you want us to do?'

'Get Dad would be the best thing.'

'Well, let's drive you home then,' Hilary says.

Good, I catch myself thinking. She's handling it.

I still want to hold his hand. Or do something. But when he staggers to his feet, it's Paul who helps him get up.

We clamber back into the van, Roger complaining in Hilary's arms.

'Where's the blanket?' she asks me.

I find it, and uselessly put it over Bill's knees. Hilary immediately leans forward and tucks him in properly. I suppose it's one of those librarian first-aid courses coming to the rescue.

And then, as we bump along the road (Didi's driving and in control of the map this time) I just think, I don't care. So I change seats and sit next to him, and take his hand under the blanket. Bill manages a smile. And although everyone else in the van is politely looking the other way, I catch Didi's eye, just for a minute, in the driving mirror.

'I'm not just running into you, am I,' Bill manages, after a few bumpy minutes.

'We came up to look for you. We were worried about you,' I say. Using 'we' makes it safer somehow.

I mean, what can you say, when someone is bleeding to death under one of your own blankets?

Thirty-seven

We finally get there and, of course, we'd already passed it once on the way up. There's a hand-painted sign saying McGINLEY and a postbox made out of a petrol can, and a rocky driveway that seems to go for miles. Roger starts skidding around on the floor again.

I hope Bill's parents don't think we're a band of travelling clothes-peg makers who have come to sell our wares. I'd better try to keep the cat under control. It might give them the wrong impression if Roger leaps out first. Like we've come to kidnap theirs, or something. I can see it now, Mrs Fluffy or something, a big black and white thing, sitting on top of the porch. Bill used to tell me about it sometimes. I realize now, looking at all of this, how homesick he must have been.

Roger's looking at Mrs Fluffy now, making weird snickering noises.

'Better keep your cat back in the van,' Paul says.

Hilary gives him a doting look.

Bill's parents wait patiently at the top of the driveway while Didi tries to park the combi, dodging various boulders painted white, and what looks like bits of old barbecue. His parents look nice. Not like the beasts who spawned a computer pervert at all. Mr

McGinley has a nose a bit like Bill's, and you can see where he got his RSL Club photo big flapping ears from. Mrs McGinley looks like herself, but smiles like her son. I suppose they must be used to all kinds of crises in their rural lifestyle, too, because when I jump out of the van first with Bill, still looking as white as a sheet, and Jodie in her Byron Bay film director outfit, they don't even blink.

His dad works out Bill's OK just by looking at him.

'I knew it. You had a prang didn't you?'

Everyone forces a smile at this, but then Bill's mother immediately hustles everyone into the house for tea, and says she doesn't care if anyone argues with her, she's going to get the doctor.

I'm glad she is. How fantastic it is when other people take over. Because I was holding one of Bill's hands under the blanket, I could see the other one clenched into a fist. Instinctively, I know he's being too brave for his own good.

They live in a weatherboard farmhouse with family photos hanging up along the entrance corridor – they must be Bill's sisters, they've got the RSL Club ears too – and white net curtains that look like they get washed in dew.

It smells of Sunlight soap, sponge cakes and – funny, this – Bill's lemony shower gel, the same stuff that Dan used to use. It's a smell from *then* not now, and it confuses me.

'Everyone sit down and I'll put the kettle on,' Mrs McGinley says. 'And I'm going to put a pack on your arm until the doctor comes, Bill, all right?'

He nods.

I notice he's doing the thumbnail-digging thing into his hand.

'Where's the car?' Bill's dad says, looking appropriately worried about the practical, mechanical side of things. Maybe he thinks his damn fool son has run it into the front window of the local milk bar, and their reputation in the township will be ruined.

'Back out near Travers' place,' Bill manages from his armchair. His father grunts, and goes off to find a phone.

For some reason we've all separated ourselves into boys and girls. It's very strange. Maybe it's the traditional country air getting to us. Jodie, Hilary, Didi and I are squashed on one couch like the four musketeers, and Paul and Bill are in the big armchairs. I suppose they've always been the men's chairs in this household.

'What was the cat doing in the van?' Bill says at last.

'No-one else could look after him,' I almost whisper. I could tell him about Mum and her new asthmatic boyfriend but I don't. It's that kind of house, you feel you can't break the calm because the sound might physically shatter the windows. No wonder when Bill came to Sydney, he couldn't speak.

But looking at him now, still pale and grey, I can't help thinking *this is Pierre*. The man who wrote, 'I am a long way from home. I have moved to a place where people speak a different language, and my ex girlfriend wants so much space she can hardly stand being in the same 10 kilometres as me.'

Mrs McGinley comes back in with a tea-towel and a plastic bag full of ice for Bill's arm, and asks us if we want anything to eat. Hilary says she does, which is typical. When Bill's mother shoots back into the kitchen again, I jam her with my elbow.

'She asked us so I said yes,' she protests.

'Gives her something to do,' Bill says, backing her

371

up. And just for a moment, I get a glimpse of the old Bill again. The one who was at dinner at the Indian restaurant that night, looking at me across the table when Natalie was pouring blather into his ear.

Then we hear a car pulling out of the driveway.

'Well, it sounds like he's gone to get the tow-truck for you, so we might as well start,' his mum says, coming back into the room with a plate full of biscuits.

Clearly, Mr McGinley is a man of few words, too.

'I called up the doctor but he's over at Pascall's,' Mrs M tells Bill, talking across the rest of us. She doesn't sound very pleased about this.

'The Pascalls are hypochondriacs,' Bill explains.

'They're not the people who run Scrooge McDuck's Quack Quack Crap enterprises are they?' Hilary blurts out.

Then there's an awful silence.

'Wow, lot of videos,' Didi says, sounding amazed.

Everyone turns to look, and there are about a hundred of them, all individually marked in biro with the legend Blue Heelers Episode 1, Blue Heelers Episode 2 and so on. Everyone stares at them for as long as they possibly can, making murmuring noises of wonderment, until the moment has passed.

Then Bill gets up. Big mistake.

When he tries to get from his chair to the door, he almost falls on top of us, squashing the four musketeers to oblivion. Immediately, his mother springs up to make him sit back down again.

'If you have to go, I'll take you,' she says.

I suppose she means the loo. Bill is going a familiar smoked-salmon colour at this.

'No, I'll go later,' he mumbles.

Then it occurs to me. This woman has absolutely no idea who we are.

'I'm Victoria, and this is Hilary, and this is Jodie and Didi,' I say. 'And that's Paul.'

'Well, I'm Sylvia McGinley, and this is Bill,' she says, trying to make a joke. 'You did introduce yourself, did you, Bill, when you'd nearly run them off the road?'

'No, we ran him off the road,' Jodie protests, halfway through a biscuit. 'It was our fault because Victoria's cat sat on the accelerator.'

By the way Mrs M is looking at Jodie, I think she's just twigged that she might be a clothes-peg seller or cat kidnapper after all. Or possibly on her way to a drug rehabilitation centre.

'Mum, I know them,' Bill says at last.

She blinks.

'They came up to look for me. This is Victoria. The one downstairs.'

'Oh, Victoria!'

And I'm not sure if this is good or bad, so I quickly take a biscuit and start making 'Mmmm, scrummy' noises.

'So has he told you a lot about Victoria, Mrs McGinley?' Hilary begins, wickedly, and Bill blushes again. He keeps going from white to pink, like an English backpacker on his first day at Bondi.

More silence.

'I might try that doctor again, see if he's left Pascalls yet,' his mother says, getting up.

Then Jodie looks at her watch, and uses a word that I don't believe the McGinleys would ever have heard on Blue Heelers. Luckily, I think Mrs M got out of earshot just in time.

'We're gonna be late,' she says. 'We'd better move it.'

Paul, for one, looks relieved. Maybe it's because his position in the opposite armchair is achingly far from

373

head-in-lap proximity. But anyway, everyone jumps up and makes going noises.

Everyone, in fact, except me.

Hilary stares at me.

'Victoria might be good for Bill to have around for a bit,' she says cheerily to nobody in particular. 'Save his mother having to hang around. Then we can pick her up later.'

'No, we can't,' says Jodie.

Saved.

'Or she can take the train,' bats back Hilary.

Not saved.

Then again, why aren't I protesting more? Why can't I get out of the chair? Why does my left hand still have the imprint of his right hand, half an hour later?

Yet more silence. And we can't possibly all start talking about their fine video collection again.

'I don't mind,' I begin, 'but . . .' I look at Bill. He looks back at me. Bloody Hilary. I could pick her up and shake her like a rat. Why does she think she always knows best. Why? Ever since the fudge-flavoured lipgloss and herpes episode, ever since . . .

'You can stay if you want,' Bill shrugs. 'You kind of came a long way to drop in, so . . .'

'And then Vic can get the train from Urunga up to Byron tomorrow,' Hilary says brightly. 'It's not far, I looked it up on the map on the way up.'

Mrs McGinley comes back into the room.

'No, he's still at Pascall's,' she says gloomily. 'I think I'll have to go and get him myself.'

'It's all right,' Bill says, 'I can wait.'

'No, I know you.' She sighs. 'Like your dad. You say it's all right and then you pass out in front of me.'

Bill goes redder.

'Victoria says she might like to stay,' he begins.

'Oh, well, you're very welcome,' Mrs McGinley replies. 'You can all stay if you like, I won't be long.'

He tries again.

'Maybe stay overnight. In Emma's old room. Then get the train back to Byron tomorrow.'

'Oh, well, yes, that's easy. The room's made up.'

And I hate to say it, but not only is Mrs M completely oblivious to the horrible embarrassment creeping up the chimney, she looks absolutely thrilled at the prospect of me sleeping in her house. Maybe Bill hasn't been slagging me off after all. Or maybe it's just the prospect of making me vats of porridge and griddle cakes, or whatever it is farmer's wives do in the morning. Maybe she wants a spare pair of hands to hoik on the udders at milking time.

I can't even look at Bill now. This whole thing is just too horrible for words.

'We'll look after Roger,' I hear Paul say. Honestly. Is he in on it too? Hilary with an *assistant* is even worse.

Finally, they just give up on me and go, trundling out in single file with Jodie at the front, making a very theatrical show of looking at her watch the whole way.

'If you follow me as far as Pascall's and get out, I'll show you from there,' is the last thing I hear his mother saying, as they trail up the corridor and close the front door. I hope Didi's driving for that bit.

Then it's quiet. Cow and country quiet. And it's just me and Bill now, staring at the walls (Monet print on the left, Manet print on the right, very democratic. I bet his mother sent away for them).

'Thanks for holding my hand,' he says at last. I still can't look at him, but I can hear the half-laugh in his voice.

'I might go for a walk,' I say, in return. 'I feel a bit funny.' And believe me, I do.

'OK.'

'Do you want more tea or anything?'

'Er – yeah. Sugar would be good.'

'For shock.'

He shrugs. 'Because I like sugar.'

I go into the kitchen, and gaze at the view while I wait for the kettle. Even washing up would be a blissful experience in a house like this. You can follow the top of the washing up liquid bottle in a straight line, out of the window, directly onto blue hills and pink sky streaks.

I wonder what time it is? It seems ages since we had the accident.

When the kettle boils, I open the cupboard doors (the old-fashioned kind, with fly screens) looking for the sugar. There's a mug with Emma written on it in flowery writing – that must be his sister. I think there's another sister too, from memory. A married one. Then there's a big mug with Microsoft written on it. That must be Bill's. Very boring.

I pour too much tea in, and have to carry the mug back carefully, one step at a time. It must have taken me longer than I thought, though, because when I go back into the living room, he's fallen asleep, bent sideways over the armchair.

I leave him to it and go for a walk.

Thirty-eight

I suppose the whole point of getting a farm is having the freedom to throw your bits and pieces all over it. As I wander behind the house and up to two gigantic barns, I can see rusty tricycles (I can just imagine Bill as a kid, crashing his tricycle into anything that moved) and tyres painted white to look like swans, and even some old game of Totem Tennis with a bit of dirty rope hanging from the top.

I think it's going to rain. And then it occurs to me. My bag.

'Starsky and bloody Hutch!'

Hilary's grand plan for me didn't include getting my bag out of the boot, it seems. Oh please, God, let her have remembered by the time they got to the hypochondriac Pascalls and given it to Bill's mother.

Somehow, though, I know it won't have happened.

I have one dress, one pair of pants, one bra, one pair of shoes, no jacket, no umbrella, no toothbrush, no hairbrush, no Estee Lauder Advanced Night Repair Protective Recovery Complex, no make-up and not so much as a tampon for emergencies. All I've got is me and my purse, basically.

As I walk up the hill, it starts to pour. In a minute,

my little floral frock, so perfect for my afternoon arrival on Byron Bay beach, is going to turn into a see-through nightmare. In fact, it's going to make the obvious nipples dressing gown look like the height of modesty. I run for it.

The last time I ran up a hill in pouring rain was in 1984, during school cross country. It shows. By the time I make it to the first barn, I can hardly breathe.

To get in, you have to crawl under a half-door, bolted and padlocked at the top. It's dark inside, and the rain – now starting to hammer down – is deafening on the roof. Helena Chettle told me a terrible story once, about going into a barn somewhere in the country and finding a huge big snake hanging from the rafters.

And where's the light switch? Damn, do barns have light switches?

Eventually, though, I can see the way the place is organized. Even though half the barn is stacked with snake-enticing hay bales, the rest of it seems to have been turned into a rabbit's warren of storage rooms. In fact, at the top of the ladder at the back of the barn, I can see someone's turned the loft into a kind of makeshift office.

A makeshift office with a computer, it turns out, when I get to the top of the ladder. I wonder how he operates it? Pedal power?

It's a real hiding place, though. I can see why Bill might have missed it all these months. Shakily, I step off the ladder and walk in.

Thank God it's warm up here at least. And I'm out of the rain. Then I look down at myself. Thought so. I look like I'm wearing Gladwrap with a flower print.

Maybe if he's got his computer, and all his old books from school, and his purple swimming pennants up here, he'll have some old clothes up here too?

I find them eventually. They're in a box with a couple of old, smelly music magazines with his beloved Elvis Costello on the cover, and one of those long, stripey scarves that girlfriends used to knit for their boyfriends in sewing class. I wonder if rubber beak knitted that, or some other long-gone girl?

I put on an old windcheater with tight wristbands that grip halfway up my arms, and on top of that a denim jacket with a big, round Life Be In It badge on the front. Funny, that. I can't imagine Bill being a Life Be In It campaigner, even as a spotty schoolboy.

The rain's still beating down. I'm going to have to go back in the house some time. And then I see it. I suppose part of me knew I would. A shoebox with rubber bands around it, right on top of the tea-chests he's piled up in the corner. Even with bands on, the lid still doesn't fit properly, and I can just make out a stack of letters piled on top.

I stand on my tiptoes in my soaking, wet, black shoes and half-knock it down. As I thought. Letters from rubber beak.

There's a photo of her in one of them. From the same camera, the same day and time, that the one in his flat came from. He obviously liked this one less. Maybe because her freckles show less.

Then I hear a car rattling up the hill below, panic, and bundle everything up again.

Should I go down there? They'll probably think I've gone missing. Bill asleep in the chair, me nowhere to be seen. It probably looks like I've poisoned him.

I scale the ladder, watching for snakes, and make my way out. There's some rule in the country that you're supposed to leave doors open, or leave doors closed, but I can never remember which, so I just leave it hanging. Then I skid down the hill again.

It looks like Mr M finally found the tow-truck, and the tow-truck finally found Bill's car. He's done more damage to it than I thought, though – all the panelling along the front at the left side has been bashed in.

He sees me, and waves me over. It's still pissing down.

'Doctor's about half a mile behind me,' he says, thumbing somewhere down the driveway. I nod, and rush into the house. I don't think Bill's dad is easy to talk to at the best of times, but in the middle of a flood zone, it's probably impossible.

When I go in, the denim jacket I pinched has already gone from old white stonewash to dark blue, and the Life Be In It badge has dropped off. Bill's still asleep in the armchair.

'Bill.'

He opens his eyes.

'The doctor's on the way and your dad's got the car.'

He looks down and notices his tea-towel ice pack has melted all over his T-shirt, and the chair.

'Shall I get you another tea-towel?'

'No. Sorry. I just worked out why you're here. Why is that – what is that? Mum got you my jacket out.'

'I got it out. Sorry. I had to. Hilary's got my bag. It's raining.'

'Right.'

He nods. He looks completely dazed. And I want to tell him that I found the shoebox full of rubber beak's letters, and that I didn't read any of them, but I don't.

'Do you want some more tea?'

Maybe it is the country air. I'm acting like his mother.

'No thanks.'

Eventually, we hear more cars going up the driveway, more grinding of gears, and then a few minutes later everyone piles in. The doctor (big black umbrella – not wet), Bill's mother (no umbrella, soaking) and Bill's dad (practically drowned).

Isn't it funny the way people become noisier when it rains? There's a lot of tongue-clicking, and fussing, and 'Ay ay aying' from Mrs McGinley, and the doctor keeps going 'Phew!' a lot, while even Mr McGinley is making more noise than usual hanging the doctor's coat up on the stand in the hall.

'I was going to say, do you want some of my things?' his mother says, looking at my bizarre combination of wet shoes, bare legs, soaking wet flowery frock, over-tight windcheater and tiny denim jacket.

'Oh no, I'll be fine.'

'Emma's got some old stuff in her wardrobe,' Bill manages.

That's typical, I think, as his mother shoos me into Emma's old bedroom. He's lying there with his life's blood draining away, with his car completely wrecked, and all he wants to do is organize *me*.

The Life Be In It campaign must have swept the entire McGinley family at one stage. There's another old badge, with a rusty pin, stuck in one corner of Emma's old cork noticeboard.

'Now, she's got some things in here–' Bill's mother opens the door on one side of a gigantic old oak wardrobe –'then some other things in here–' the other side is groaning with long, full-length party dresses. Wonder how I'd look in red velvet at the moment?

'Is Emma older or younger?' I ask, to be polite.

'Younger. Only 17. Doing her HSC at the moment.'

'Aaah, the HSC,' I say pointlessly.

'Anyway,' his mother says, preparing to leave me alone at last, 'you sort yourself out in here and let me know if you need anything. There's towels in the cupboard and you know how to do the electric blanket, don't you?'

Well, if I do it's about the only thing I do know how to do at the moment. Which reminds me, I really must sort out that brochure for Do. She trots out.

At some stage, I must have decided it was safe to lie down on the bed, because I seem to have fallen asleep, and it seems to have gone awfully dark and quiet. Then I remember. Not being able to think of anything for the Do hair brochure, and lying down for inspiration. I must have just crashed.

I can't breathe. Why can't I breathe? Then I realize the wet windcheater must have physically shrunk around my ribcage.

Emma's got one of those lamps in the shape of a woodland forest scene that eight-year-old girls go ga-ga over. The only trouble is, there are so many badgers and ferrets and weasels and spotted toadstools all over the bloody thing, I can't find the switch. I fumble for about five minutes, give up, get out of bed, and fall over.

'Shit!'

Somebody's left a pile of mini shampoo bottles and soap on the floor. Oh no. That'll be the guest toiletries. And it also explains the terrible smell of synthetic apricot hanging around the bed.

I cannot believe this. It's dark, I'm wet, I'm cold, I'm wrapped up like a mummy in a wet denim jacket Bill probably wore when he was fourteen, and I've just brained myself on some apricot hair conditioner.

Finally, I find the main light.

When I switch it on, I see a furry woodland folk alarm clock, handily stationed next to the furry woodland folk lamp. It's about twenty past two in the morning.

What happened?

The weasels and other assorted woodland folk on the lamp reserve the right to remain silent. It's shock I suppose. I mean, it was Bill who smashed his car and stuffed his arm, but we ran off the road too. I remember the sleeping thing from the last time I had a car accident – that time I ran my crappy old bomb into a power pole. You just sleep and sleep, for some reason.

I peer inside the wardrobe looking for something vaguely nightie-like so I can peel off the disgusting wet dress, windcheater and jacket. If they haven't shrunk to the point where I can't get them over my head.

The only thing that I can a) get into and b) imagine wearing at all, is Emma McGinley's old red velvet evening dress. Help. I suppose she must have worn it to her year 10 dinner. As I put it on, I try to remember what I wore to mine. From memory, something yellow and satin with padded shoulders that made me look like a camp American football player.

Then I hear something. Track two, side one, *Mighty Like A Rose*. Bill's third favourite Elvis Costello album. Nice of him to play it at about 2 a.m. on his stereo.

I lean forward out of the doorway of Emma's room, slapping the wall softly, trying to find the switch. No switch. I'm going to have to make it up the corridor assisted only by the chink of light under Bill's door, and the soft pink glow thrown by my very good friends, the woodland folk.

I knock.

'Yeah. Come in.'

He's sitting up in bed, wearing a pair of blue and white stripey pyjamas that *must* have belonged to his

383

grandfather, with a cacky flesh-coloured crepe bandage going from his elbow up to his thumb.

'Oh, hi.'

I suppose he thought it was his mother.

'It's just me.'

'Shh. Come in.'

I close the door quietly behind me and creep forward. There's nowhere to sit, and I'm not sitting on the bed, it's all too close, so I stand.

'What are you wearing *now*?'

I suppose it must look funny. First the wet windcheater and schoolboy denim jacket ensemble, now the red velvet evening dress.

'It's Emma's.'

'Yeah, I know it's Emma's.'

I knew it.

'How are you?'

'Good.'

'That's good.'

'Did I wake you up? Sorry. I thought I had it on low.'

'Good old Elvis Costello.'

'Yeah.'

'Are they your pyjamas?'

He looks at himself in surprise.

'Why?'

'They look like they belonged to your grandfather.'

'No, they're mine.'

'Oh. Sorry.'

'Unlike you, I don't go round nicking all my family's old clothes.'

'Sorry.'

'No,' he half-laughs. 'Sit on the floor if you like. There's blankets under the bed.'

So I peer under his mattress, no doubt looking very elegant in my red velvet evening gown, and find an old grey blanket, the spiky, hairy kind that nobody likes, so it's permanently packed away. I sit on it, and itch.

'I'm not good at expressing myself,' Bill says, sticking his jaw out and staring at the wall.

'I know you're not, that's why you thought you had to lie to me and pretend to be some bullshit Englishman in Paris. Is it because you went to boarding school? An all-boys' school, is that the problem? I don't blame you, they say it makes it harder to relate to women. Well, Hilary says that anyway, and she'd know, she went out with some bloke from Kings. I just don't see why you had to do the worst possible thing to me at the worst possible time, that's all.'

He doesn't say anything for a bit.

Then finally he looks at me.

'One of the reasons I find it hard to talk to you is because you never let me talk.'

'What?'

'You talk for me. You don't let me talk.'

'But I always let you talk! You just never say anything. Well, you never have so far.'

Except on the computer, I think.

I play with the velvet pile on my dress sleeve, smoothing it one way, like Roger's fur, then the other way.

'What if I let you talk for the next hour, uninterrupted?'

He smiles, and scratches his jaw with his good arm, near where the dent is. It occurs to me he'll now have two scars to show off.

'I'll still find it hard to express myself. And I've been practising saying *that.* All tonight. I thought we'd be doing this talk tomorrow.'

'So you knew we had to have a talk, then?'

'That's why you came up.'

I nod.

'I saw the film Didi and Jodie took of you. The whole thing, not just the bit they ended up using.'

He shrugs at this.

'Well, it was your little secret message to me, wasn't it, whether you knew it or not. And I did get it. The old lady at Grand Central Station wearing the poppy in her buttonhole. All that stuff about love wearing disguises.'

'Can I tell you, then?'

'What?'

'Everything.'

And forgive me for not leaping forward in gratitude, begging him to reveal all, but I just don't know if I want to hear it. Maybe because, whatever he says, it's going to be final. It's either going to lead to the end, or a beginning. And I don't know, maybe the idea of a beginning is even more terrifying.

I shuffle my knees up under the blanket and lean back against the wall. Where his sister has a woodland folk lamp, I notice, he has one in the shape of a cricket bat.

'So anyway.' He sticks his jaw out again, and sighs. 'I felt sorry for you.'

'*You* felt sorry for *me*? Oh, sorry.'

I'm talking over him again. He's right, I can't help myself.

'I saw you talking to yourself when you put out the rubbish. Or you were talking to God.'

'I don't believe in him so I can't have been.'

He looks at me.

'I won't interrupt again.'

'Well, you were talking to someone. I just thought, "She's had a break-up. Like me." And then you kept giving me things to fix, and asking me to help with your computer. Well, I *paid* to get the answering machine done . . .'

Because I'm not allowed to talk I just make a horrified face at this.

'Then I heard you and all your friends saying stuff, and I worked out I was the boffin man. And every other guy in Sydney was a loser, according to you. So I just thought, stuff it. I gave up. At this stage my ex was still writing to me. It looked a lot easier than you. Her name's Beth.'

He goes quiet for a minute, and scratches his arm under the bandage.

'Beth really was in Paris, and really was staying in Clichy. That's why I thought of it. I should have come up with something better than that, but you didn't give me time to think. I just ran upstairs and did it – bang.'

'And why did you?'

'Oh, because I could tell nobody was going to log into your channel, and I didn't want to think of you staying up all night just waiting by yourself. And then it kind of happened. It just went of its own accord. The more you wrote to me, the more I wanted to keep writing back to you, and it was like having freedom all of a sudden. Like . . .' he shifts on the pillows '. . . the girl you think you're beginning to fall in love with, just by looking at her, the one you're starting to think about instead of your ex. Well. Instead of going through the whole thing of not knowing if she feels the same way, and worrying that she really hates you – well, yeah. Suddenly, there she is with you on the computer, and it's *easy*.'

It's amazing, the change in him. He's talking now like he talked in Jodie's film. Weirdly, it's almost like talking to Pierre – and not just tapping into a computer either – really *talking*.

'But after the first night,' I say, 'didn't that make you want to just tell me it was you, set me straight? At least we could have gone on from there.'

He sighs and looks straight through me.

'We wouldn't have gone anywhere from there,' he sighs, 'and don't tell me you'd have coped with it. Anyway, after that I got a grand romantic vision.'

'And what does that mean?'

'I bought you a ticket to Paris.'

'What?'

He shrugs, and readjusts his arm again.

'I already had one of them. For me. I'd bought it because I had this crazy idea I was going to go over there and win her back.'

'Rubber beak.'

'Yeah, Beth. I liked it when you called her Rubber Beak, it made it less – I dunno, *big* in my life. But she'd left by then, gone on to Germany with some guy she met travelling. So I had one ticket. I was going to get a refund. And then I thought . . .'

'Mmmm?'

And somewhere inside my head, one of the woodland weasels from the lamp is squealing *He bought you a ticket to Paris! He bought you a ticket to Paris!*

'Well,' Bill sighs. 'That was going to be it. An invitation from the very charming, mysterious, fascinating Englishman Pierre Dubois – a hell of a lot more interesting than me – to join him for a romantic weekend on the left bank, and then you'd find out it was me at the airport, and I'd have this big bouquet of roses, and we'd . . .'

He can't even bring himself to say live happily ever after.

We sit there for a bit. Then finally he says something else.

'I realized it would never work.'

'Right.'

'Because I worked it out.'

'Right. What was that?'

'Because you weren't looking for love, you were looking for a wedding. Any wedding. Any man. Just as long as he wasn't, you know, a paedophile, wearing his baseball cap on backwards, too old or whatever. And you had to be no older than thirty-nine and eleven months of course.'

I feel like he's just slapped me.

'You *listened*!'

He shakes his head and sighs again. 'I *heard*. By mistake.'

And I think of myself opening the shoebox in the barn, and look the other way.

'Well, we were drunk,' I say, through gritted teeth. 'I'm sorry. We're old friends, we drink, that's what we do.'

'But not just that. It was what you wrote later, too.'

'Like what?'

'As soon as you find your man, or woman, you should tie them up, brand them and rope them, Pierre. It just means you'll get the wedding cake and white suede shoes faster.'

I get up.

'You bloody bastard.'

'Shhh!'

'OK then, I'll whisper it. You printed that out, and you've kept it all this time just so you can use it against me.'

'Well, you tell me,' he says back, in a normal voice, 'why are all men bastards to you? And then Jodie tells me one night what you say in this film, about topping

389

yourself or something, if you don't get your wedding by forty.'

'Oh, shit aren't you a genius then. It was a *joke*, you moron, a joke. Well, you can just . . .'

And that's it. I'm shouting now. And yeah, I do slam the door. Even though it's past 3 a.m. and it's not my house. It's finished. Over.

Thirty-nine

It's not hard to stay awake all night when you're basically curled up on a pile of old damp clothes, on a hard wooden floor, in a barn loft.

Well, I'm not staying in Emma's room.

And the way I see it, if Bill's arm is in a bandage he's not going to be able to follow me up a ladder, is he. So I'm safe – relatively. At least until the sun comes up in this godforsaken rural hell-hole and I can hitch a ride to Urunga and wait for the train (probably one, once a day, but I don't care) to come by.

I'm not going to Byron Bay. I'm going home. I've had it. If it wasn't dark, and wet, and freezing now – and if I wasn't wearing this stupid red velvet evening dress – I'd even begin walking now. Anything, just to get me away from Bill Boffin Brain McGinley.

I thought I'd seen it all from men. Commitment-phobes. Sex addicts. Compulsive liars. But this – this is the Olympics of relationships. And what do you know, I've never even kissed him. I can't cry and won't cry. I refuse. I'm too tired. And I begrudge myself the bodily fluids. It's just not worth it.

To keep myself awake, I work my way through an old pile of his Richie Rich comics, using a big rubber torch he's left up there. I'd forgotten those great Sea Monkey ads they used to have in the back of Richie Rich. And what about those halcyon days when a girl could sell packets of gardening seeds to her family and neighbours, thus earning herself enough points to get a hairdrier, a blow-up submarine, a basketball hoop?

This is supposed to be a diversionary tactic to prevent me from crying, but it goes the other way. Going back to childhood in my head makes me want to go back to childhood right *now*. It was safe then. The Bionic Woman had the Six Million Dollar Man, and you knew that one day you'd get the love of your life too.

I wonder if Bill's fallen asleep yet? Probably. I saw a packet of painkillers by the bed, with any luck they'll knock the stupid *bastard* out until some time tomorrow. Then that's it. Back to Sydney, and he'll never see me again. I can't even face keeping the flat on. I'll take the funny woman's bedsit with the three toilet brushes. Anything, rather than creep around my own flat knowing that whoever moves in upstairs now can hear every bloody word.

If only Roger was here to talk to.

'How *dare* he?'

I suppose Bill's right, I do talk to myself. Then again, I think, furiously trying to wriggle into a comfortable position under his old clothes, it's his fault for listening.

What did he mean he felt sorry for me?

And the way he just took every single thing out of context. I am not a wedding junkie, I am not. Ask Dan, ask anyone. Well OK, don't ask Dan. But ask Liam. I made it through a swinging dirty weekend in a hotel, didn't I? I don't think I mentioned proposals of marriage, did I? And what about Leon Mercer, mature age student radical? He'll stand up for me in court. If I remember rightly, we'd already worked out a deal about de facto polygamy in Nimbin by the time I was twenty-five.

I will get perspective on this terrible night, I *will*.

And grinding my teeth over all of this takes me through until about 5 a.m., when the local roosters – or is it a stray pack of renegades from Scrooge McDuck's Quack Quack Crap Emporium? – kick in.

I've got my purse, I've got my red velvet evening dress and I've got my soaking wet black shoes. I mean, what more does a freelance advertising copywriter, slash, woman of the '90s actually need? The sun's up, I can see where the hell I'm going, and I'm sure some dickhead in a truck will give me a lift. Be brave, be strong, pretend you're Joanna Lumley in *The New Avengers*.

I clamber down the ladder. I don't even care about the snakes.

Part of me can't help cringing as I duck out and under the barn door. Is Bill lying in wait for me? But no, the house is still and quiet, and as long as their cattle dog – no, don't tell me, they've called him Blue Heeler – doesn't start up, I should be able to slip out, out and away from the McGinley farm, with grace, style and dignity.

Then I trip over a tyre painted white in the shape of a swan, and fall knees-down into the driveway.

'Starsky and bloody Hutch!'

Ow. Then it starts to rain. No, really. As both Queen and the Christian-loving Graham might say at this point, Beelzebub has a devil put aside for mee-e-e.

Maybe that's it, I think, as I'm traipsing down the long road back to Dorrigo in Emma McGinley's red dress. Clearly, all my problems in life are a direct result of the night I was allegedly putting the garbage out, and allegedly saying some kind of prayer out loud. Basically, I shouldn't have been allegedly putting out a bag of old catfood cans and other evil-smelling rubbish while taking the Lord's name in vain. Not that I can remember, of course.

Trudge, trudge, trudge. I'd like to think I look like a Thomas Hardy heroine at this stage, of course, but then why did a panelvan just whizz past me with what appeared to be a man's naked bottom pressed against the window?

I hate Dorrigo. I hate the country.

Finally, somewhere between Quacky McDuck's crap farm, or whatever it is they call it, and the road sign to some stagnant creek, I hear the miraculous sound of a car slowing down. A car with a woman in it, because I can hear her squeaking something as she winds down the window.

Thank God, even if he has been so mean to me. I blink the rain out of my eyes, pull up the sodden evening dress, and trudge over.

'Do you need a lift?' the woman says. She looks motherly. 'I think Emma McGinley wore that to her school dance.'

Five kilometres later, still driving in pouring rain, I find out she's one of the hypochondriac Pascalls.

'You're joking,' I say.

Then I realize the only people who actually live here are either McGinleys, McGinleys or Pascalls, so the situation really isn't bordering on the occult after all.

'Lucky you got me,' the woman says. 'I'm just off to get the milk.'

'I didn't think the shops opened for hours.'

That's good, I can buy myself a towel.

'No, up at the farm.'

'Oh, right.'

She seems too mild-mannered to jab me in the ribs and chuckle, 'Tch, you townies' but I can tell she secretly wants to.

'*You're* making a getaway,' she says.

'Well, I am. Actually.'

She waits for me to say something else.

Then I think, stuff it.

'Bill McGinley just insulted me so I'm going home.'

'Not Bill, Col.'

'No, Bill.'

'I thought Bill was so quiet!' She starts laughing. '*Col's* the one they normally have a go at.'

'Yeah, well. Like father like son.'

Then I shut up. I'm just too tired to talk any more.

Finally, we reach the train station. I think the whole journey must have been about 40km out of her way, but I can also tell she's going to dine off this story for weeks. Well, good. I hope Bill blushes until he dies. I hope the entire McGinley family is ostracized and their womenfolk banned for ever from playing for the Dorrigo soccer team. I hope the Quacky McDuck Crap Emporium staff round them all up and lynch them.

The hypochondriac Pascall waves through the window, and drives off. Then it's really just a matter of waiting for the train to Sydney in a wet red velvet evening dress, with an equally damp Richie Rich comic to entertain me. Paris? I mean, pshaw, who cares.

After a minute, I find a phone box and ask Directory Assistance for The Byron Bay Women's Film Festival. Much to my amazement, she says 'Hold the line please', which must mean it's not being administered from a tree house after all.

The message on the croaky machine at the other end

goes on, and on, and on, giving road directions, a film festival schedule, campsite regulations, and for some reason, the date of the next full moon. I make it short, sharp and sweet.

'This is Victoria Shepworth. I have a message for Jodie, Didi, Hilary, Paul and Roger. I am going back to Sydney. I have no clothes, so I am wearing a red velvet evening dress. I may be dead from pneumonia when you find me. Thankyou. Good morning.'

You have to laugh, I suppose, or you not only cry, you end up living in a bedsit at the age of sixty-five with two lovebirds in a cage feeding off your pantyhose.

Forty

I'm working on an idea for the Do salon at home when Hilary finally rings up from Byron Bay.

'What happened to you?'

Well, I can either give her the long story, or the very, very short story.

'Bill's a shithead.'

'Oh.'

'He was going to buy me a ticket to Paris.'

'Was he?'

'So he could reveal himself as Pierre Dubois. Then he changed his mind.'

'Why?'

'Because he thought I was after a husband. Because he thinks I'm a man-hater. Actually, he thinks we're all man-haters.'

'But why?'

'Because he sneaked around the flat listening to every bloody conversation we ever had, and took just about everything I wrote on the e-mails out of context, and if you ask me, because he's just a misogynist looking for a chance to wreck my life.'

I can hear Hilary breathing out now.

'Anyway, how's the film festival going?' I say.

'Oh, OK.'

'How's Roger?'

'He's turned gay. We think he's been rooting Boris, he's the black cat at the fish and chip shop.'

'Oh well, he'll fit in then, won't he.'

And we say our goodbyes, and I put the phone down.

I must admit, though, that until Hilary rang me just then, I haven't been feeling angry at all. Bill to me is just like Liam, or Dan. A learning experience. In a few years, when I do meet someone – and I will, I feel quite calm about that now – I'll look back on this and work out that it was meant to be. Part of a process, to get me to the man I'm supposed to be with, in the year 2002, or 2003, or whatever it happens to be. So far, I've managed to work this out. You get men like you get symptoms of illness – or even signs of wellbeing. They crop up because they say something about where you're up to, and what you're doing with your life. If you get men who produce nausea and fatigue, it's because something's going wrong inside you, and they're a reflection of that. If you get men who give you rosy cheeks, and a spring in your step, it's because something's going right inside you. And you're getting what you deserve there too.

Having Dan, Liam and Bill – three bad symptoms in a row – only serves to remind myself that it's something about *me*, first and foremost. So that's where I have to begin, now. Not with the divorced fortysomething male army. With me.

A few days after this, Hilary and Paul come back early, leaving Jodie and Didi to enjoy their newly won reputation as radical film-makers at the B. B. Women's Film Festival.

'Paul has to get ready for another trip,' Hilary says when she rings up again. 'They're all going to go white-water rafting in Tasmania.'

'What does he do again?' I ask.

'Public service. You can't beat it,' she replies. 'Anyway, what are you up to?'

'Not much. The health department wrote back about that job.'

'Oh, good.'

'Yeah, they're going to pay me a month's rent.'

'Wow.'

'I thought I'd move out of here, but I've changed my mind again,' I sigh. 'I just can't bring myself.'

'Well, it does smell. Her flat.'

'Poor woman.'

'Poor woman.'

And I mean it for her, not for me. I, Victoria Successfully Single Shepworth, am not going to end up like that.

'Shall I come round?' Hilary asks.

'Yeah.'

'Well, I kind of have to, because I've got Roger here.'

'Oh,' I reply, feeling guilty that it wasn't the first thing I asked about.

'Anyway. I'll see you soon.'

When they arrive, Roger and Hilary have matching expressions of smug, quiet satisfaction on their faces. I suppose his is the result of Boris, and hers is the result of Paul.

We sit down on the couch, which I refuse to think of as the haunted relationship couch any more, and talk about the film festival.

'I suppose they were all making a sacrifice to the goddess at the interval,' I say.

'Actually no.'

Hilary looks annoyed for a second.

'They were all normal people. Well, as normal as you or me.'

I think about this.

'You've got to get over this stereotyping thing, Vic.'

'Jodie and Didi.'

'Jodie and Didi are weirdos, OK. But that doesn't mean everyone else around them is a weirdo, too.'

'But all that stuff about giving the full moon on the answering machine. What kind of film festival does that?'

'You're weird, I'm weird, the whole world is. Even Paul is.'

'Even Paul?'

'He's going to be the first man in the history of the world to join the Women's Circle.'

I let this sink in.

'Why?'

'Because he's heard me talk about it so much and he thinks he'd like to try it.'

'And they're letting him?'

She sighs.

'Contrary to popular opinion, the Women's Circle is not the three witches in Macbeth dancing around a cauldron.'

'Sorry.'

I go off to make the tea, and she yells from the couch, 'You should come.'

I stick my head around the door.

'No thanks.'

'You should. You'd get a lot out of it.'

'It's not me. All right? It's you, and Natalie, and Jodie and Didi, but it's not me.'

I put in Natalie's name deliberately, and she knows it.

'What are you going to do otherwise?'

'Like, what?'

'Tuesday nights.'

I decide not to stir the sugar into her tea after all. 'Here you are,' I say, putting her mug carefully down on the floor. 'Well, Tuesday nights, let's see. I think that will be my meditation class.'

'You!'

'Yeah, and then on alternate Tuesday nights I plan to stay in, watch TV, switch off, relax and enjoy myself. A different kind of meditation. OK?'

'Well, then.'

She looks embarrassed. Good.

However, I can only keep this kind of thing up for so long.

'I lied,' I sigh. 'I have nothing to do on Tuesday nights. I haven't even planned to watch TV. OK? But it doesn't matter. It doesn't bother me.'

'This is not about me having a guy, and you not having a guy?'

'No it's not.'

'Well, come to Women's Circle then.'

'Oh . . .' I can feel myself giving in. I mean, what harm could it do? Paul's going. And maybe there'll be someone there who's done the anorexia thing. I have to get some quotes for the brochure, don't I? It's the sort of place you'd expect to be crawling with eating disorders, isn't it? Or am I stereotyping again?

'Can you pick me up?' I plead.

Forty-one

Two weeks later, after Paul is back from white-water rafting, and Jodie and Didi are back from Byron Bay, I prepare for my very first Women's Circle.

Before I leave the flat, I go over to the answering machine and do something I've always wanted to do.

I record a message telling the world I will be at The Women's Circle, Paddington tonight, and karate classes, Newtown on Wednesday night. Well, I will be, when I've paid them the money.

'Bring a blanket and wear something comfortable,' Hilary advises on the phone.

I groan.

'I knew it. We're all going to lie down and it's going to be touchy-feely. Some twenty-stone dyke is going to sit on me and crush me to death.'

'Stop it. We'll pick you up at seven. Didi's driving.'

It's too dark to see the combi van properly, but Jodie assures me they had to have it repainted after the accident. Being back inside it again reminds me of that awful weekend all over again, so I slide the window across as far as it will go, and stick my head out, eyes watering as the lights of Newtown whiz past me.

'Thanks for coming,' Paul yells across from his seat. I blink at him.

'I thought I'd be the only new boy,' he adds.

I smile back. He's one of us really, Paul. And, I suppose, in more ways than one if he's coming to Women's Circle.

When we get there, there are cars full of women unloading all over the place. I look suspiciously for another combi to match ours, with more Jodie and Didi lookalikes, but the car park looks full of the vehicles you'd expect to see at the supermarket. The women all look like supermarket people too. Normal. Talking their heads off to each other. And not a pair of nappy pants in sight.

We troop into the building, which is one of those old schools that's been turned into a community centre. As we pass one of the doors in the corridor, Paul gives it a friendly tap.

'That's the old white-water rafting room,' Hilary explains.

Our room is big, with one of those tragic orange and brown abstract carpets from the seventies. There's a whiteboard at the front, and someone's drawn a big circle on it in blue texta, with the legend WOMEN'S CIRCLE below. Because of the fluorescent strip lighting, everyone's face looks slightly yellow.

Everyone's arranged themselves into a loose circle, so we take our places beside them. Jodie next to Didi, Hilary next to Paul, and me next to a stunning-looking woman with a Linda Evangelista bob that actually looks as if it's worked.

Unlike mine, of course.

'I'm Georgia,' she smiles.

Then it's time to start. And much to my surprise, it's Georgia who turns out to be Our Leader.

'Every week someone takes a turn,' Hilary hisses to Paul, who looks at me to see if I've heard.

The first thing Georgia does is drag in a big green plastic rubbish bin from the corridor, and bring it to the front of the room, under the whiteboard. A teenager in dungarees with frizzy hair obligingly takes out the gum she's been chewing, gets up, walks over, and drops it in.

The room explodes with laughter.

I look at Paul. Paul looks at me. What?

'The bin,' Georgia explains, still having a bit of a giggle to herself, 'is certainly there for your gum or anything else you've brought with you. And I'd like to welcome some new people to the Women's Circle . . .' Paul beams, I look at the floor 'as well as all of us here tonight. However . . .' And she straightens her mouth up at this point, and looks serious, 'this bin is actually here as part of our workshop tonight.'

Oh no, I think, if you're bad, they're going to make you get in it.

'What I'd like to do tonight, as this Tuesday's leader, is get everyone to throw their rubbish out.'

Didi whoops.

'And what I mean by rubbish,' Georgia continues, acknowledging the whoop with a little smile, 'is anything that stops you from doing all the things in life you'd like to. Any *people* who are stopping you. Any attitudes that are stopping you. Any substances. Anything at all.'

It's getting cold in here. I'm glad Hilary forced me to bring my blanket, even if it is the old Roger blanket that I put over Bill as well.

Georgia starts handing out sheets of paper and pencils.

I take mine off the top, and pass it on to Paul. As

soon as he gets his, he starts scribbling. Smart arse. But I notice Hilary is peering over the top of his paper.

Soon, the room is full of women sucking thoughtfully on their pencils, writing down little notes, and scratching things out.

I look at my blank sheet of paper. It's like the Breakfast Grits Frisbee campaign all over again. Help.

Paul stops scribbling, and smiles.

'Can't think of anything?'

And I'm about to say that I can't, not in this room anyway, when I think of about fifty-eight things at once.

That thing my Dad said on the phone from LA that time – about 'Victoria, you can't be looking for perfection all the time. It doesn't exist. Just find a nice guy you can be happy with and bla bla bla.'

The thing my mother said about men being like buses, and if you hang around long enough, one of them is arriving over the hill.

Then I write just one thing in capitals: LADYBIRD BOOKS.

After that, I can't stop myself. Greg Daly and Anthony Anderson and Jamie Streeton. The funny woman in the smelly bedsit with the three toilet brushes. Dan. (I have to ask for more paper from the woman next to me for that one.)

Then finally, the one thing that hurts the most, the one thing I know I have the most to say about. Not just rubbish, but an entire tip, you might say.

I look up from my paper. Something's happened. Everyone's staring at me.

Georgia smiles.

'No, it's OK.'

She looks kindly at me.

'Some of us have quite a lot of rubbish to get rid of.'

Embarrassingly, Didi whoops.

Paul sticks his hand up.

'I was just wondering if we have a break at some stage—'

'Well, we can have a break now,' Georgia says. 'Anyone object?'

It's like feeding time at Taronga Park Zoo after that. Everyone scrambles to their feet and races out to find the urn, leaving me, by myself, still scribbling.

'I'll bring you back a coffee,' Hilary hisses.

When people start to wander back in again, I'm ready for them. I fold my sheets of paper neatly, put them on the orange and brown carpet in front of me, and put the pencil on top of the pile. There. Finished.

It's like being the last one out of an exam.

'OK,' Georgia says soothingly. 'Anybody want to share their rubbish before they chuck it in the bin?'

Jodie sticks her hand up.

'I think we should say that it's OK *not* to share your rubbish,' she says. 'Some people have the kind of rubbish that really stinks.'

God, I hope she doesn't mean me.

Then the teenager with the dungarees gets up, bites her lip, and reads out, 'Eczema,' and screws up her bit of paper and chucks it in the green bin – along with another piece of chewing gum.

She's followed by Georgia, who's also got a piece of paper. I didn't notice she'd been writing her rubbish down too.

'My belief that I am old and irrelevant,' she says very clearly, and drops her paper in the bin like a voting slip on election day.

I look at Paul, and he looks at me. The woman's

gorgeous. What on earth is she on about?

After that, there's no stopping people. Paul gets up and has a whole list of things. Things which mostly make sense to him, I guess. People's names, and even one address. Hilary squeezes his hand when he sits down again.

She throws hers straight into the bin and doesn't say anything.

Jodie goes on for ages about her fear of success.

Didi says just one name, and I recognize it as the school-teacher who molested her when she was fifteen years old. I thought she was over that. She doesn't screw up the paper, she shreds it into tiny pieces, and lets it all flutter in on top of the chewing gum and everyone else's rubbish.

My heart is clanging. I've got so much paper. Should I just throw it in?

There comes a moment in your life, though, when you know it's now or never. And I know I'm probably a victim of crowd behaviour here, and I know I'll regret this in the morning – after all, it's the behaviour of a drunk woman, even though I'm perfectly sober.

But I stand up and read it out anyway.

'This is my rubbish. Well, some of it.' Everyone listens, and waits patiently.

'Guilt. Guilt about wanting a white wedding before I'm forty. Well, I'm sorry, I do. It's not just a joke, I mean it. And I don't see why I have to feel wrong about that. I was brought up to want it. And I still do want it. And I'm *happy* being by myself. I can see how you can have a good life by yourself. It's just that . . .' And I read this bit carefully, because I think I've finally got it right, 'I reserve the right to be romantic. Without being manic about it, I reserve the right to be romantic.'

408

Then the door opens, and Bill walks in with his arm in a sling.

'I've just come 562 kilometres in a taxi from Dorrigo, because I'm in love with you, and I can't help it, and I got it wrong. Really, really wrong. I'm sorry.'

Pandemonium in the Women's Circle.

Forty-two

Because we can't go for a walk in Paddington – too noisy, too many cars, too many lights – we get on a bus and go down to Circular Quay. Then we make our way to the Botanic Gardens.

'It's closed but you can go around the outside of it,' I say.

Bill nods. So far we haven't said much at all. After we left the Women's Circle meeting (well, I had to take him out, I couldn't leave him there) I think we've managed to organize a bus fare together, and that's all.

'How much was your cab fare?' I ask.

'Five hundred dollars. He did me a deal,' he says.

He's walking more slowly than usual. His arm must be weighing him down. We make our way through the car park at the side of the Conservatorium of Music, past all the posters advertising the next Bach concert, and into a little, private park at the back.

'We could jump that fence,' says Bill, looking at it.

'I'm sure they've got security guards,' I say.

It's funny how things work out. A few months ago, I was on the other side of that fence, getting drunk with Liam and trying to sort out if I wanted a tryst with a relationship retard or not.

411

'How did you work out where I was?' I ask.

'You left it on your answering machine. I made the taxi go around Paddington until we saw the combi van in the car park.'

'You know I just spent about half an hour writing down everything I hated about you.'

He looks at me, and then looks down at his feet.

'You wouldn't be you if you didn't,' he says.

Finally, we find a patch of soft grass under a tree, and sit down, staring through the fence palings at the Botanic Gardens on the other side.

'You stole my sister's dress,' Bill ventures.

'I did more than that.'

A pause. I think I've actually managed to get him really worried here.

'I told the hypochondriac Pascalls that you'd insulted and humiliated me. Your name will be mud in Dorrigo.'

'Oh, that,' he smiles. 'Already is. Don't worry.'

We sit for a while.

'You're right,' I hear myself saying.

'About what?'

'It wasn't the right time. If you had given me that flight to Paris, it would have been a disaster.'

'And what does that mean?'

'Like, what?'

He smiles. 'You know I find it hard to express myself. I told you. What I mean is, did you mean, just then, that there *would* have been a right time?'

I think about it, and sigh.

'I don't know.'

He leans forward and kisses me, and I suppose I knew it was coming, but it's a surprise anyway. The kind of surprise that you fall into, face-first. Then I worry that I'm squashing his bad arm, and let go.

'What I actually came down to do . . .' he begins.

'What, not that?'

'I wanted to give you something,' he sighs.

I think I'm talking over the top of him again.

He reaches into his jacket, under his sling, finds a long white envelope, and gives it to me.

'Don't argue about this, just take it. I'm not going to be at the other end, don't worry, and you never have to see me again if you don't want to.'

I open it. It's a Qantas ticket to Paris.

'You can go whenever.'

I look at him.

'You know this was the thing that upset me the most, don't you?'

He nods.

'Because it was the first, the only time in my life, that a man ever got anywhere near doing something romantic and amazing for me.'

'And then I had to say all that stuff about you scaring me off with your wedding talk.'

'And slagging off men.'

'Well, you did slag off men.'

'But I had my reasons!'

I'm amazed at how pained I just sounded. What a night for rubbish-throwing this is turning out to be.

He pats my arm, and heaves himself up.

'What are you doing?'

'I'm going back to the hotel.'

'But you can't stay in a hotel!'

'Well, I'm not staying in the flat. The agent told me a couple of guys have just moved in.'

'Come and stay with me. I don't care. Don't be silly. You can stay on the couch.'

'No, honestly, it's OK.'

He waves me off.

'I had to come and apologize, and I have.'

'No.'

And this time it's me who kisses him, holding onto the back of his neck and balancing myself on the ground so I don't tip me, his arm and the rest of him over.

'Thanks,' he says at last.

'Is this really a ticket to Paris?'

'Yes, it's really a ticket to Paris.' He shrugs. 'You deserve it. Walking from the farm to Urunga in that dress. In the rain.'

'Putting up with your crap.'

'Yes.'

I put the ticket in my pocket.

'In the spirit of the thing, I take it. In fact, if I hadn't just stood up and told a whole bunch of strangers . . .'

'I heard. You reserve the right to remain romantic.'

'You heard!'

He laughs at himself, and shrugs again. 'I'm just an eavesdropper by nature. Can't help it.'

We sit for a bit longer. Then something occurs to me.

'Hang on.'

He looks at me.

'I'm sorry, but I have to ask this.'

'Yes?'

'I know I said I reserve the right to remain romantic, but I also reserve the right to have some common sense. For a change.'

'So?'

'You had two tickets to Paris. The one for you, that you bought to meet Rubber Beak, and then the one for me that you bought and—'

'And never gave you. Yeah. Well, I exchanged both of them.'

'Just for one?'

'Just for one.'

'So I'm definitely not going to turn up there and find you at the other end, then?'

'Victoria!' He makes a mock-shocked face. 'Why does the idea of it worry you so much?'

'Well, it doesn't.' He looks at me.

'I mean, now everything's changed – everything's still *changing* in fact – I'd like it. But, you know. Weird surprises. I'm kind of over them.'

He shakes his head.

'On my honour as a good Dorrigo boy, and a few other things, that ticket is for one person, you, and it's for one place, Paris, and if I hadn't done a swap, I would have lost about three grand, so do me a favour and *take* it.'

I mock-sigh. 'Whatever happened to my right to reserve romance?'

It's funny though, because as we walk down to George Street to find a cab together, and his hand finds mine again, I feel more romantic than I've ever felt in my life.

'I wish you'd just come back to my place and just sleep on the couch,' I find myself saying.

'No, really. I'm going back tomorrow.'

'Going back!'

For some reason my heart just dropped three floors from Electrical Appliances down to Menswear.

'And then I've got to find myself somewhere to live again.'

'In Sydney?'

'They kept my job open. But don't worry. My Newtown days are over.'

A cab with its light on zooms past, but we let it go.

'You get the next one,' he says.

'You will ring me?'

'Of course I'll ring you. Someone has to check that you're going to do this thing.'

'Will you mind Roger while I'm away?'

'Yes. If you do something for me.'

'What?'

'Get an e-mail account again. I want to write to you in Paris. I miss it, Victoria. Really miss it.'

One of us is going to knuckle a tear out of our eye, and it's not going to be me.

'Look. A cab.'

And I get in, and he stands there on the pavement watching me go, waving until the red traffic lights that were just behind us change into a cherry blur.

THE END